To
Rachael
"Thank you & I hope you enjoy.
You have a truly lovely Mother.
God bless

xx

Capella Alan Ryan

About the Author

Capella Van Ryan was born in Letterkenny, County Donegal, Ireland on October seventh 1984. Developing a passion for writing at a very young age after her mother died from breast cancer, finding it a means of therapy and escapism. Starting her career path as a paramedic instructor, moving onto become a personal trainer with her own company in the United States, going on to become an accountant. She travels extensively around the world in search for new material for her next novels.

Dedication

Without you, my Colin, this book would never have been written or created. This book only exists, I only exist because of your love, devotion, kindness, tenderness and constant inspiration and motivation. Thank you for always telling me that I can do anything I want to do. You have opened my eyes and shown me the world for what the world rightfully is. Because of all these special gifts you have enriched my life with, this book I give humbly to you. As on our wedding day I unveil my true self in these words I have wrote.

For a truly special mother, your loving and devoted daughter, Capella, I love you and think of you every day of my life. Through me and in me you live on. You are God's angel and my soul.

Capella Van Ryan

THE SNOWBOAT

A CIP catalogue record for this title is available from the British Library.

ISBN 9781785541568 (Paperback)
ISBN 9781785541575 (Hardback)

www.austinmacauley.com

First Published (2015)
Austin Macauley Publishers Ltd.
25 Canada Square
Canary Wharf
London
E14 5LQ

Printed and bound in Great Britain

Acknowledgments

If it was not for my husband Colin who works in the medical and security industry, putting himself in dangerous places such as Iraq and all over the world and who has spoiled me by showing me the world I would not have had first-hand knowledge or experience to write the *Snowboat*. Thank you for our trips to Switzerland.

Switzerland, because of your marvel and stunning glory, you are the initial birthing as to why this book has been created. The people are the loveliest I have ever known. It is a place where dreams are dreamt and sometimes come alive. It was the place where I was reborn.

The *Snowboat*, the place where this book was located, the ambience found within, the friendly and professional attitude of the employees and the owner. It is a great place to visit and situated in the most breath robbing location, the foot of the Matterhorn. Thank you for the wonderful experience and your charm.

PART ONE

The Kill

CHAPTER ONE

Burn to Execute

Home 1999

As he started to attack me he spoke words of filth, he had the most horrible voice I have ever heard. A creepiness danced in his sound; flutters rose in my blood like crows in a pack pursuing chase for winters food, and tremors in the night's stratosphere shook, creating an atmosphere of theoretical fear. A fear I have never before experienced or heard about and it made me physically sick. Poisoning the oxygen I inhale while polluting my blood. Revolted at what was to come; how tonight would end; what would happen before daylight breaks. What silhouettes shall hide. Who I would thus become because of the happenings of this night. The night when my life ended and a new type of existence began.

An existence where I belong to the coldness and the darkness. Never to belong to another. Moving behind the shadows alone. Shadows are my only company throughout time. While my youth slips me by. While my smooth taught skin becomes no more but that of an old used up witch with horror stories to reflect, becoming my only companion. Embittered. Lonely. Destroyed. Speaking his unlistenable, unfathomable words in a sick and injurious tone which made my stomach churn, proud of what he was about to conquer. A hollowness filled. Innocence stolen. A dark and echoing void raped. The soul need to vomit overpowered what I now considered my corpus. Acid burned from within. The acid of his disgusting words. Of his disgusting gift. The bubbling of vileness overwhelmed me and the mechanics of my body. Vomit soared up through my stomach into my trachea, lodging in the back of my nose and throat. For a moment choking. The warmth of his wounding hands warmed my wrists as he pressed down on me. Harder and harder in sequence with his thrusts. In sequence with his rejoice. His thrusts felt as though I were being punched repeatedly. The warmth from his hands felt like a hot poker being stabbed through my flesh, severing veins, muscles and tissue. Severing every part of what makes me who I am. Killing me slowly with each insufferable thrust only a lover should bestow.

Praying silently to die. To end my destruction. Dying this moment would be mercy granted. Only knowing nobody deserves to fall victim like I have this night. This very minute. In this very dark room. Also knowing I don't deserve mercy, and without delusional hope knowing wholeheartedly mercy won't be granted. It never is. Not in this world and not for people like me. Decent. Innocent… Trapped within fucked up circumstances. The people who deserve to walk in the light of day. Feel the warmth of the sun caress my ivory body. To live and exist with the very alive.

This world is the playground for the corrupt to win and thrive. And for losers to always remain losers. Never to succeed climbing out of a cesspit of lies, bullshit jealousy and hatred. Always drowning in the cruelness of people. And in the darkness of lost hope and spoiled stolen dreams. Laughter and tenderness escapes me.

My mind and eyes fixated on drowning out his face and voice. With all my might I tried, then harder and then harder than hard. Even the echoes of my screams. They echoed like death screams which have lost their hopelessness. They freighted me more. Knowing the inevitability without accepting it. When hope is gone there is nothing else left.

My goal is to pretend with all my heart what is happening, isn't. It's only one of those terrifying nightmares. The kind which terrorize

3

me when I'm most relaxed and in my safe haven, the kind I can't wake up from until it has its fun. My hands and legs bounded to the bed, spread apart, as though I were welcoming him into my sacred temple. As though this attack was voluntary. Sanctioned. But I know the truth. He knows the truth, yet he continues and goes on and on, disregarding reality and my faithful wishes. The handcuffs tightly cupped around my wrists and ankles so much so the true flesh colour skin typically has, could not be seen as it lies thickly under blood as they crack and bayonetted my flesh below. Gradually I could feel the contaminated air collide with my broken flesh. Blood escapes. Flesh dies. Infected with a nameless virus. A virus destroying everything in its way.

The smell of cologne and alcohol, a most detestable combination. Cheap and lowly. Lingering in the invisible air, the same air I have no choice but to breathe stinks of stale cigarettes and decomposing ash left too long to putrefy. Transforming into an unrecognizable element. The room he keeps me in against my will stinks of abuse, tears, hurt and cruelty. And if I breathe in deep enough and hold it for a moment longer than the rest, I can smell imploring. The strongest fragrance of all was the smell of his enjoyment and excitement. The thrill of it all. The thrill of being in control. Robbing my soul. Robbing my ability to say no and walk away, to be free again.

In this small and unimpressive prison, inside me he reigns his empire. Reaps his glory. A scent I will only ever relate to him now, when I am forced to remember by a lingering odour or when the cool dark nights won't let me be. Forever in badness's clutch. This will be a fight for the rest of my life to run away from, unable to escape my mind.

As he presses on me and hovers over me, the knowing that someday it is inevitable I will go out of my mind. I'm already starting to, I can feel reality losing its grip, I enjoy its dizziness and welcome it to consume me whole, and he hasn't yet concluded his attack. The attack he would categorise as play. In my mind I am not present. I find an escape in a place nobody can ever tarnish or find me in. It's a place no one knows exists because it only exists in my mind.

This night will continue to haunt me for the rest of my days on this earth. All I can hope for is that death will end the remembering and the shame. I am the ruining of a man's reprehensible game of glory seeking. I pay his price. A price which is altogether too high.

The persistent torture breaks me down. My mind weakens. My limbs tremble. His nauseating saliva sprinkles over my face entering my eyes and mouth. Now I am in every way invaded. Lesser than the woman I was a few moments previously before he forced me on my back. I want to scream, I need to cry out desperately in despair and pain but I don't dare. It will be his motivation to continue. To cause me merciless pain. The aphrodisiac he desires to heighten his enjoyment. To reach his climax.

Enjoyment is the only thing I am capable of taking away from him. The only thing… He grunts like a pig. Moans like a sick and sweaty pervert. Only blackness in an indescribable shape is all I can see. All I permit myself to see. Closing my eyes so tightly and hard that it hurts. And I enjoy the pain. It is my barrier between me and what is invading my body. The only thing… I don't want to see his features, his profile. That would be too personal. A stranger he must forever remain. A nameless entity of no significance. This way I won't be running from shadows of my abuser for the rest of my life. Seeing his face in a million other men. Imagining. Believing things which aren't there. I can't see him if I never see him. What else can I do? Nothing, this is the only thing. My only protection. The only way I can function in the aftermath. There will be life after this. He can't fully destroy me. No one can. I refuse to allow anyone that power.

He has no power over me I delude myself into believing. Flirting with the idea. Though he does things to me no stranger has the right to subject any victim to.

I couldn't hear his words, switching off my brain, hoping it would eliminate the pain he was about to inflict onto my body. Again. Yes for the second time tonight. For the last time I can only hope. Internally and externally I am made use of as though I do not own the body I am in. As though my body belongs to him and for his pleasure only despite my agony. Closing my eyes tighter now. The pain he inflicts breaks my body. Turning my head to the side to allow the vomit to flow freely out. Almost choking. Distracted to his torture. His body becomes ridged. His breathing alters. A moan. A gasp. A scream. I know what it represents, men are such predictable creatures. Sick and pathetic. One dimensional. Yes, I could feel him working his way up into a climax. He climbs higher and higher. The pain intensifies. I break further and further down. The grand finale. The conclusion of my pain for a short time at least is here.

The memories of rape I won't allow myself to remember. Yet his evilness rapes my mind. The bruises I will see when I look in the mirror in the morning light, I will pretend don't exist. I'm not tarnished. I'm not lesser than I was. I'm the same as I have always been. I won't allow him to destroy me. Break me down. Divide my being. Multiple the hell. Minus the soul I once owned. Or add to the agony. The remembering. I won't. I won't. I can't. I would sooner die.

Avoiding my image indefinitely if that is what it takes to forget. To pretend. At least to pretend to forget. Tonight the darkness is casted over, turbulence blows and wolves howl in the deepest mysterious forests, coldness felt, sun buried beneath, shivers up my spine creating paralyzes, it feels like a million years till morning. I wish I possessed the power of a wolf so I could sever my attackers head from his body with my jaws in only one impressive movement, leaving him to be supper for the rest of my starving pack.

I will suffer gravely tonight; but in a matter of hours the night will fade, saying goodbye to my attack. To him and to my sorrow and shame. The brain is a marvellous machine, selective memories is the equivalent to an archangel and prayers granted. Tonight, the thrusts I endure, the slaps he collides with my face will be a memory locked in a box inside my mind, with no key ever designed to unlock the badness I suffer in my life, the badness I have just suffered, tonight, it is bolted inside this box, deep inside my mind.

As I lay on a rape filled floor, smelling of sex and horror, still naked and exposed he looks over me. I feel no shame like I thought I would. I feel only one sentiment. Only one. I can't see him, I won't allow myself to see, not even now. I can feel his eyes burn into me like lasers. Like hells a blazing flames. My skin crawls as though millions and millions of maggots crawl over my body. My womanhood throbs with revenge. My heart races with determination.

6

My blood pumps hard with desire. My mind runs mad with design. And my hands burn to execute. My attack is over. The only thing I am sure of is there won't be any more repeated episodes, because as lay here I make up my mind, I made the decision to become a killer. Revenge those who have done me wrong. Revenge he who rapes me. An eye for an eye I truly believe in. A knife for a knife I believe in more. There is only one thing for me to do. Only one. His blood will run freely downstream. By my hands. By my very own innocent hands.

CHAPTER TWO

The Feel of Death

The feel of death is almost as joyous as the feel of a lover for the very first time. Excitement anticipated. Adrenaline sorrowing. Blushing expected. Silliness felt. Blood bouncing. Uncertainty experienced. Skin prickles. The splendid wonder of the unknown. Breathing becomes laboured. The climax worthwhile. The same rigidness to a body, but only one body experiences it. Wanting more, dying for my fix, then more is never enough.

Murder is like heroine: one taste you're hooked. No way of whinnying off. The only way to give it up is to die. Die or enjoy. Give in and go with it. Moving quickly like a panther in the night, beneath the midnight moon using his own knife to inflict righteousness, above all justice. Piercing his lung from behind, he gasps, he falls into my arms. He's vulnerable now like I was. He took advantage and so shall I. Dividing his neck into two from the side. Ripping his neck apart, I felt such power. Power and glory. Blood spills freely downstream. Showering him and showering me. I could feel his death enter my body through my mouth. Through my flesh. My very being is overshadowed. It was the greatest experience I have ever known. Complex yet stunning. Powerful and amazing. Collectively these words combined are not powerful enough to accurately describe the sensation of death. No word has ever been created yet to fully describe its beauty. As I hold his useless kicking body in my hands, I hear gushing water like that of a waterfall in the deepest forest on a spring day. I smell its cleanness. It lasts merely a moment. I feel the heat of the sun burn my skin. Looking down, it was the heat of his dying blood. Flinging his dead motionless body in a heap. Kneeling down over him like he once did me, I saw and saw until his head comes free. Till I am looking down his windpipe. Exactly how I imagined. Covered in my attacker's blood, dripping with revenge. It is only the weak who remains the victim. Beneath this midnight moon I become the wolf and the panther the revenger and all things strong. An existence where I belong to the coldness and the darkness.

PART TWO

Obsessions

SWITZERLAND
2001

CHAPTER THREE

Geneva

Wednesday 3 December 2001

It was a freezing December morning with misty skies and a hazed over morning moon. The air smelt light and clean. The usual in Geneva this time of year, when I awoke in my extra-large bed, in the most beautiful junior suite hotel room I have ever laid eyes on, at the Four Seasons Hotel George V, located in the centre square of the city. Making me feel as though I were a person of importance, when in actual fact I am nobody of any significance. A person lost to this world of billions of people, more important than I. More worthy than I. Why I was even born I do not know. But on a morning like this negativity was the furthest thing from my mind. There isn't anything with the capability of dragging me down today. Not this day. I could smell the goodness and exhilaration in the air. It smelt sweet, like summer roses on a warm June day. Today is going to be good. Very good. I can feel it in my bones. In my gut. Today belongs to me. The only clothing covering my petite body despite the freezing temperatures was a sheer black Gucci negligee, with lace trim and shining sequences. Perfect for strutting assets. Perfect for seducing. Not exactly suitable for the time of year with the freezing temperatures declining rapidly, as the new snow falls and the harsh winds blow. Regardless, looking sexy and looking my best was what I was about in those days. Attempting to be sexy in a conservative way. Only displaying the right amount of leg, accompanied by the right amount of breast. If neither were on exhibition, I would call upon a fitted dress to highlight my sexy curves which have always been highly sought after since turning seventeen. The joy of being a woman. It is always the unimportant things which take presidency when one is young and foolish, until one learns the lessons of life. When in later life we are all left with our memories to reflect. It is then the demons of our past which haunt us unremittingly until we join them in life after death. I was sure to be covered in goose pimples once I managed to roll out of bed. Usually when it is this cold I hated getting up; to be hidden beneath the covers of safety is heaven on earth. No one should have to escape the covers of safety before the sun cracks the night sky. Night-time makes way for a new day. Considering that I was in Geneva I couldn't possibly mind, there was no excuse pardonable to close my eyes on such beauty. Surrounded by this magnitude of beauty left me enthralled. As soon as the cold air collided with my skin, I not only felt awake but full of life and conquering. Ready to tackle the good and the bad. The exciting and the mysterious. I felt brave. Untouchable. No extreme too punitive. Not today. Loving winter time beyond compare; it is the time of year when I can be exactly who I am, feeling comfortable within my own skin. Designs can be executed. The darkness I hide behind. Forever fond of the long nights, the roaring fires, accompanied by a glass of hot brandy giving me a feeling of warmth before bed with each passing evening. Igniting a fire in the pit of my stomach. Helping to eliminate all knowledge from this world enabling me to have a restful sleep. Back in those days it took a great deal to achieve this. It was virtually impossible to erase my memories of this world for a brief seven to eight hours sleep. In my waking hours I live in hell and in my sleeping hours I relive hell. Forever trapped. Stuck on constant replay. Playing the same scene over and over again. Until I know it by heart. Until my mind can't stand it. Until I am reduced to begging. Begging to die. The stop button must be broken, or else my mind with no remedy to cure my aliment. Madness. Complete and unadulterated insanity, it's my only evil and my only sanctuary.

The snow on the mountain and treetops the most beautiful I have known, every morning managing to give me a feeling of tranquillity. Making it feel as though it was Christmas for longer than the usual day, it was never long enough for me. I was certainly a child at heart. Frequently reflecting on the innocent days all children are permitted for a brief time before being consumed by life and the selfish. The only aspect about me which did change was my heart. Hardening to life and life's challenges. With the time which passes, with each tick of the clock and each harsh wind which blows, pushing me further and further back, enforcing me to push that much harder forward the next time around. Life's pushing takes its toll, eventually. Hardening and becoming unsentimental is thus inevitable. The after effect to ceaseless bullshit.

Although the air becomes bitter thus making breathing laboured due to how thin the air is, I still manage to find a warmth and kindness within both the air and the people. Never being a cosmopolitan type of woman, but in Geneva and in its purity I felt at peace. The usual pushing and shoving, chaos of masses of people cities are famous for didn't happen here. It's a place where one can lose themselves, rebuilt something new only to find their true selves. Geneva became the place where I wanted to live all my life through, spending my eternity in Lausanne when my time would befall. When I was an old lady I hoped passing away in my sleep. For all I knew this particular day could be approaching faster than I had reckoned. The same wish us the innocent and gutless hope for. A lack of pain when being transported to the next life, wherever that maybe. No pain felt, but not thinking twice about causing pain to be felt by my own hands towards others. A selected and worthy few. I was guilty of being a selfish woman. Most women are. No place on earth compared to Switzerland; capturing my heart from the first moment my eyes fell upon it. An invaluable yet natural feeling of freedom and safety filled me. This was home. Never before feeling as at ease, longing for this to remain. Pressure not weighing me down. My breathing was undisturbed for the first time in years. Amazed yet grateful for the instant feeling of happiness. For the first time I felt safe. This feeling made me greedy to experience it more frequently. The need became part of who I am. Finding it strange as to how a feeling, any feeling, can make one addicted for it. Needing my fix for the day in order to get by. In order to see the beauty surrounding me. To smell the purity of goodness blowing in the air. Diluting the stench of rape, torture and murder. The humiliation. The giving up. To accept the truth. Becoming that of an addict, I'm no good without the thing I crave the most. It is in the consuming which makes me great and able to function. It gives me purpose. Ability. Tenacity. Clearing my head from the nonsense and bullshit which lingers outside my mind. How harsh my life had become at such a tender age. Switzerland had become my first obsession.

PART THREE

The Return with a Definite Purpose

CHAPTER FOUR

Coppett

Summer 2007

Sailing on the bluish greenish water of Lake Genève, on a seven-hour trip exquisiteness didn't lack, everywhere my eyes scanned it was there to be treasured in its magnitudes with no exceptions made, from Lausanne all the way down through Evian. The boat was painted white and blue, in the region of fifty metres in length by thirty metres wide; with a flat hull, white panelled roofing and stairs of solid mahogany, the outer edge of the steps were gold trimmed, signs overhead, taking one from second class on the lower deck to first class on the upper. A small but modest café was in the centre of the upper floor, in the region of twenty wicker and steal seats with grips bolted down preventing sliding as the boat journeyed on stationed on either side. The smell of coffee was conciliatory. Sea and sun lodgers were plentiful to the bow and aft of the boat. To the sides of the boat hung Zodiac inflatable rescue craft. Handmade wooden panelling with ropes of pink tided around them. Red circular air vents above the doorway where I firstly sat when I boarded. The water was so subterranean that the boat had a heavy feel as it glided through, with pressure pushing my body down and backwards. Moving around periodically when the greater sights dictated. The Nikon camera which I carried around my neck was in high demand, with over two thousand photographs captured during that period of seven hours. Capturing him. The one I'm after. He who is my prey. Finding myself sitting too close to the microphone, my ears paying for the mistake when the horn was blown, jumping out of my skin with ringing ears. The shock caused flashbacks to enter my mind, seeing my attacks before my very eyes as though I were watching porn on YouTube. Flashing from black and white images to full elaborate colour. Suspecting it was the adrenaline which caused my hands to tingle and a cold sweat to break, my pores hurt from the density. Never to be left in peace. My eardrums throbbed intensely. Observantly on top of the trees encircling the Alps in contrast against the dark mountains and pale blue sky, powdered clouds floating by. Clouds topping the mountains like a white heavenly halo. Every once in a while the silence and my thought process was deserted from the sound of aircraft, as I sat dreaming up story plots for my books, once I got around to starting them, when airplanes flew by overhead, bringing in new holidaymakers and businessmen from all around the world. Before executing my designs it is important for me to always take a day out to enjoy life, the kind things in the world and the truth underlining the rest of the story plot. Research is paramount. In case it all goes wrong, blowing up in my face. In case I end up dead. In case my plan isn't perfect. I must enjoy one last day all to myself, breath in life, happiness and splendour, taste what could have been, wherever I maybe. A day in the life is nothing in comparison. Tall green trees, the healthiest green ever seen. Alpine mountains, clouds of low and mist kissing everything it obscures as delicately as a new born baby's skin. Flowers hanging from buildings and growing up through the soil in every town and dock, idyllically decorated by colourful petals, with stone of old erecting virtually every building. Classic stateliness.

On approach of Coppett the blue vibrant skies above, sitting back in my seat I studied intently, by now not a single cloud in sight, perhaps they faded across into France. Like I will soon when it's all been taken care of. Through my binoculars spotting mountains, castles, stately homes, steep vines, medieval châteaus, chapels and fields afar. Houses seemed to float on the surface of the water. The wonder of technology, my two hundred and fifty Euro Nikon binoculars made sights miles afar appear as though I was up close and personal. Literally standing in the centre of a field or room. A marvellous aid in my current employment.

Crew members courteous and polished, wearing their uniform of navy shirts and caps with darker navy trousers with pride. Elegant ducks and swans with their long delicate necks pecking at the water, begging food from the passengers on the boat. Two were fully grown with a string of goslings lagging behind in pursuit. A sweet sight to cherish. Boats in their abundance lined up on every dock, some out in the distance casually sailing and appreciating the marvels. Time stood motionless. There was no shortage of amazing yachts disembarked below millionaires and billionaires homes at the end of their gardens. Further down the lake we cruised into the centre of a yachting race. Everyone filled with exhilaration screaming encouraging inspirations. With hundreds of yachts of all sizes, in the colours of pink, green, yellow blue and white, competing against one another, in what appeared to be a friendly and nonchalant contest. Not a vengeful competition instead a fulfilled endeavour on a sleepy warm day. Speedboats on the outer perimeter and swimmers triggered my mind back to a movie I watched years earlier with Cary Grant and Grace Kelly, *To Catch a Thief*, greatly insulted by being called old by a young French girl while swimming in the Mediterranean to Cary Grant's dismay. An impeccable day for a race. The sky, water and my blood sat still. Such calm glorious days. There has never been a more passive diurnal. Happy families, lovers adoring time spent together. Financial conglomerates exploits and responsibilities frozen for a day. Today called for fun and relaxation with a bottle or two of wine. The people genteel. Sailing pass the towns and villages, people sunbathing, swimming, smiling, waving and calling after the boat with friendly asides and kindness, with excitement in both their faraway faces and voices. Happiness prevails and exudes through the people and their ways of being. The day was clear, peaceful, water calm with a cool breeze now present equipoising the roasting sun. The silence of the peaceful day briefly subsided as the boat docked by Coppett, the sudden and unexpected noise catching my immediate attention. It was out of place. Moving to the other side of the boat for a better view, there were masses of people queued up and waiting to board. There he stood with a woman as beautiful as the Mediterranean. Some remained for only a short journey to the next town of Nyon. But not him. He was doing his research too, as I was researching him. Each town was as endearing and enchanting as the one before and the next to come. On approach of each town millions of bright vibrant flowers of every kind and colour decorated the docks and the edge of the towns. There fragrance perfumed the air miles before arrival. Clouds may abate and showers subside but beauty throughout Switzerland only proliferates.

Sweat building on my face, trickling down my forehead, streaking my makeup, after spending two hours priming myself before my departure. My sleeveless peach-coloured dress starting to spoil beneath my arm pits, becoming conscious. On occasion wiping my carefully applied makeup to remain refined. Tempted to slouch down on my seat instead I hold my pose, straight backed, head up high. Vacuous face. My hair hot to the touch. My forehead nose and arms burnt. My persona was that of a professional woman who isn't a pushover. Strong-minded and strong-willed.

To my right-hand side a Turkish man for the past several hours absorbed by my every movement, coming into my viewpoint he winks at me. Blushing and insulted I turn away, hoping my sunburnt face would cover up my flushness. To my left-hand side a man of African descent licks his lips seductively, then flashes an overly done smile. Feeling as though I were under a magnifying glass being examined and analysed for a cure for some sort for a life-threatening disease. Becoming flustered by thee unwanted attention, abandoning my seat to enter the café, an escape from the flagrant eyes. Purchasing my tenth bottle of chilled Evian water of the day and ordering an ice cream *(coupe Denmark)*, desperately necessitating a break from the overly large outside oven comprising of no off switch. With a passionate love of coffee, the continental style of course, had to be sacrificed temporarily, as the temperatures had risen higher than hell manages to reach. Quickly becoming dehydrated, pleased when lunch was served. Stepping down the fourteen steep stairs, directly in front of me was the opulent dining room. The restaurant reminded me of the grandeur found inside the Titanic with the golden wooden panelling walls, with pictures of flowers etched into each board adding a striking appendage from plain and simple. The tables were covered in spotless white cloths. Pine chairs with blood red seat coverings. The material was of a high quality. Thick. Triple stitched. Nothing went disregarded conveying opulence in every part of the boat. Everything was done to the highest degree. A red rose was nicely placed in the centre of the table, held in a clear glass vase half filled with water, floating with ease. Blue water tumblers were already sitting and waiting in their fastidious position. Greeted by a courteous waitress approximately five feet tall, with short blonde hair and heavily applied makeup, but pretty nonetheless. Her age was somewhere between thirty-six onwards. Upon the badge was printed Lily Rose.

"Hello, Madame, here is your menu. What would you like to drink?"

"Water please."

"Still or sparkling?"

"Still."

"Very well."

Removing my Max Factor compact in the shade of porcelain from my Prada handbag I touch up my sweat ridden face.

On return I am greeted by a warm and friendly smile.

"May I take your order, Madame?"

"Please."

As an appetizer I was presented blended watermelon, ideal for hydrating my desiccated body again; accompanied by traditional bread rolls with sweet succulent currents entwined. For my main meal a decadent veal with raspberry sauce. Dessert was spectacular indulging in a most refreshing multiple paradise, firstly raspberries drizzled in a white chocolate sauce, with cream on the side then salacious cranberries showered in a raspberry sauce. Each dish was presented to me on a white porcelain plate. In effect it was an artist's canvas as each feast was attractively and skilfully vaunted, reducing me to feeling guilty for obliterating such tempting pictures. A crime to destroy. A pleasure to consume. To finish with one merkur kaffee, the first and only of the day. I couldn't resist while being obscured inside, shaded by the heat, with pleasurable overhead fans cooling my body. False illusions. Starving when I entered, more than satisfied by the time I returned to the upper level. It was fine dining of the utmost, small portions but voluminous overall. In retrospect the day was more like food in other ways. It was worth every penny I paid, all one hundred and fifty francs. A day to remember. An experience to relish and recall for years to come, perhaps reminiscing on my deathbed. That day was the closest I will ever get to heaven;

for the things I have done. The things I was forced to do. The person I was forced into becoming.

Stopping off in Lausanne, near the dock, people were selling memorabilia of all varieties. From handbags, hats, to wine glasses and T-shirts. My head had suffered enough, giving in and splashing out on a new summer hat, costing me only twenty-five francs. A price so little was a bargain in Switzerland. It was sandy coloured wicker, with a pinky peach scarf tied around the centre, matching my dress ideally. It was meant to be. Instantly relating it was my kind of hat, reminding me of Miss. Marple from the British villages on a bike with a wicker basket. Traditional. And very much me. Searching for the more innocent days in time which no longer exist. Strolling through the streets, at the front nearer the dock the paths were relatively flat, further back the smallish town was overdone with hills. The heat exhausting me, draining my body, it was a struggle to take a breath. My legs shook. Passing one souvenir shop typical sweet Swiss style, like something from the eighteenth century and seen on traditional Christmas cards or chocolate box. Situated on a street where I could envisage soldiers lined up in the middle of the road going off to war, during World War One and Two, with bands playing music and family and friends on either side of the street for moral support. Their final Farewell. Yes, I could visualize that street booming with cheers, tears sorrow and fear of the drastic possibility. And the very sure inevitability. Today, however, was serene. From the outside, the window was crammed with everything imaginable: from dolls to kuku clocks, watches to magnets, choo- choo trains and mugs, all in traditional Swiss style. Inside wasn't any different, walls and tables displaying a magnitude of stock for sale, it was overbearing and a challenge to really see what was on offer. With only a narrow lane to walk down to the other end of the shop. Getting jammed in the middle, trapped by an obese American woman who must have misjudged the size of the lane or her waist, she was terribly rude. There's always one. The shop was filled with Americans and Germans. Buying myself a blue ceramic wrist watch with gold trim and dial, with customary flowers of edelweiss printed upon. Disappointed yet glad as I returned closer the dock, walking around the corner of a café a gust of wind hit me harder than I expected, blowing my hat from my head. Slightly embarrassed as I had to run across a road to attain it. Finding that the people weren't as polite in Lausanne as everywhere else I visited; out of the entire town only meeting one elderly man who was lovely, as I sat beneath a shaded encircled garden of tall and full trees, with a few monuments staggered around symbolizing famous and noble locals through the years, of what courageous and charitable work they endeavoured in, on an endearing rot iron bench overlooking the water. He sat abreast of me furnishing me many kind and warm smiles, we communicated in French. He was handsome and chic. Would have been a heartthrob when he was younger. Well dressed; wearing a highly expensive yellow short sleeved cotton shirt, accompanied by a pair of designer stone-coloured trousers. Wicker style tan shoes with a wicker tan hat which had sprinkles of black throughout. He spoke and held himself with dignity. There was no doubt he came from money and was now retired. He possessed that relaxed and eased expression, with time to kill or time to enjoy. Nowhere to be and nothing significant to pursue. Distracted by skaters who were performing for money, participating in many impressive stunts. From there I sat watching the Alps with peaks of ragged and the ever still water, as I waited for the boat to return. Looking at my new watch I had fifteen more minutes to wait.

Water and the Alps sharing the same shade of blue, merging into each other, impossible to distinguish where one begins and the other ends. The only other shade of colour breaking all the blues up was the white buildings made of stone around the mountains. The Alps with glaciers and patches of snow and waterfalls of white bluish water just behind the building. The contrast of the lake as the evening wore on, was the Alps no more reflected in the calm water which was no longer a turquoise blue, instead a sky blue. The flotilla of sail boats which were hulled in the morning's race were now just small white patches in the distance. The heat made them appear as though they were melting before my very eyes. The heat caresses my skin similar to a desirable lover, delicate and never harsh, yet passionate enough to swirl a thrill of badness within. Stirring the beast and goddess all at once. Igniting love to be wanted and will be conquered. The heat, the breeze a combination at once unbeatable an attribute only the Swiss sun can give. Overheated by the orange circle above as I am when being rocked back and forth by a lover, but the breeze upon my body making my nipples stand, with shivers expelling up and down my spine making me feel I do not want to die.

Indeed a foreign deeming for me to narrate. Catching myself a moment, too late once I reopened my eyes. The gentleman next to me gazed down in my direction with both admiration and confusion shining through his kind and safe green eyes. Perhaps he thought I had gone a little mad, it's very much a possibility. Yet, I know he enjoyed the free entertainment, assuming I had brought him back to his younger days when he was a Romeo. The sexual expression on my face was more than what any stranger should see. Realising I had been fondling and stroking the inside of my thighs, too high up for public and legal acceptance, rubbing my legs together in desperation of sex and much of it. Unsure if I moaned aloud. I do hope not. As I stood to my feet I could feel that my thin and fragile thong was soaked in the sex I longed for. If I breathed in deep enough I could smell the naughtiness lingering in the hot summer air for everyone in the garden to experience.

As the voyage continued I could feel the consequence of such long hours on the boat and beneath the sun, it began to sap my strength longing to find a nice cool place to hide away, lie down and close my eyes for a few moments. Refusing myself to live out my persuading inclination I had to stay sharp and quick-witted for the task at hand. Coming too far and planning too long to let sleep interfere with what is on my agenda. Keeping my distance from him allowing him and his beautiful companion to enjoy their day. Pretending all is at peace and no sharks reel beneath. On return at Genève dock I was awe inspired. Everything good I wanted to delve into. Being here reiterated that I am more than what I was led to believe, with the execution of my plans thus proving this fact. Although I have forever since been a winter lover, today I had found a new strength within to take on anything and anyone. The summer sun of Switzerland had a way of making me feel secure and relaxed within that security. Relaxation is something I find difficult. Always with a plot in mind, I forever have a battle to fight and win. As the trip drew to an end, I sat on the boat going over details, time and time again. The how, the when; the who, had already long been confirmed. Ensuring that every minute was thought out precisely, each minute was occupied with an intention until the plan was no more in use, continuing like a never-ending circle. A wedding band with a promise of forever. Meticulous in each detail when constructing an end. The end is the most important part and everything must come to an end, it determines who is left standing, who leaves with everything.

CHAPTER FIVE

A Wild Horse Is a Woman

Ever since a small girl I loved to breathe in fresh air as I walked the countryside, consequently making me feel bursting with life. Fresh air was all I needed to recharge my battery. It gave me the opportunity to have some alone time, to get lost within my thoughts, pain and dreams. It is important to have dreams. The cold chills upon my skin allowing me to feel the pain within. When I felt pain, I knew I was alive, at times I feared I had died trapped in a no man's land. No entry or exit. Lost to nothingness. My youth taught me to live in the grace of pain. It is then you know you are alive. When one feels nothing at all the fear of the unknown gives rise. Walking became my escape as a child, when I needed to get away from my home from the beatings I was exposed to, the hell which was imposed on me. Destroying my delicate years. Becoming embittered never forsaking. Even if it was wandering out into the deep country, being surrounded by animals at least it was some type of living communication, opposed to being entirely alone. Regardless of the animals unable to speak to me, at least not in a language I could comprehend or respond to. Sometimes when humans abandon us any type of interaction will do, in this world where we are held prisoner. Such love can be felt by being close to animals. It is as though the goodness within them evaporates from their pure bodies entering the one who loves them the most. I felt more loved by wild horses than I did my own family. Humans are too involved in hating. I suppose that must be why they claim that "a dog is a man's best friend." For a woman who does not own diamonds, wild horses can be a woman's best friend.

In many ways a wild horse is like a woman. The freedom desperately craved to feel exhilarated, in order to feel alive. A heart full of love unsure whom to love or to whom to bless with giving it to. Enriching a life. The biggest obstacle for a woman who is like a wild horse, is to know when to love.

The flowing hair when running mad dispersed in the air, a most captivating sight to behold. There is such a breathtaking beauty about a wild horse, something unspoiled, untouchable. This is very true about a lost woman, unable to find her way, unable to find help. It is a lost woman's innocence which is her killer.

With the passing of time the struggles of life hardens us, it is then we have survived our innocence and when murder is much easier to commit. It is then demons will not haunt because no soul remains.

Innocent eyes shielded. Innocence nurtured.

Innocence destroyed. Innocence forever gone.

Many times as an abused child I found derelict barns deep in the country, lying upon the wooden floor crying my eyes into nothingness, needing to feel a release from my grief.

I have no doubt there will be one day I will no more want to survive. Giving up will be my success.

When all my tears were cried and had fallen, then was my time to pray. Still it is the one thing I knew which would ease my burden, a chance to focus on becoming positive when the encumbrance of life had dragged me down. Struggling to keep my head above water. Struggling to remain that survivor I worked solemnly hard to be. Not wishing to allow the wrong doers to have the glory and win.

Before I gave up, I have a hell of a lot of life to live, and take, a waterfall of tears to fall, and fight after fight to win. The only way to win is to kill. To kill and kill and kill. I must kill my way through life. And when I do fall I will fall my way.

"The evil can never win, never!"

26

CHAPTER SIX

Genève

Genève was dissimilar to Zermatt in many ways, still each were equally as wonderful as the other, merely offering different things. The streets were heavily congested later in the evenings. Cars, motorbikes, people coming from every direction and out of every corner of the city, finding it breathe robbing. The perfect place for murder to be performed. No eye witnesses, no listening ears. Restaurants and bistros jammed-packed after working hours. The city very rarely quietens down. Strolling the street and there were many streets to wander, everyone with the exception of the American tourists were dressed with the highest of pride. Not seeing one person not dressed in designer clothing. All wearing expensive and impressive watches. In other parts of the world modern day is slowly losing the interest of watches, mobile phones overriding their convenience. This would one day prove significant for me. But Switzerland isn't like dwelling in modern day, for the most part it is a step back in a bygone era. I blended in well with my pearls, emeralds and refinement, my ladylike dress sense, unearthing that everyone I met was as reserved as I was to my relish. Old men were most respectful. On a daily bases I seen the city as a competition of the best dressed. Wandering down by the far end of the lake, from a distance I could see people diving and swimming, along the long path people were sitting beneath trees and on benches. The heat tiring everyone. As I sat below a thick branched tree for shade, a coward of the sun, I was most entertained. The police in their cars came speeding down the footway designed for pedestrians, catching up with three men. All three looked to be from Romania, they were similar looking to those who hang about the train stations and airports, scanning for potential victims. There is always a criminal on the prowl. They I do not mirror, they are small time criminals. Watching them remove several small bags from their trousers and shirt pockets, throwing them into the water. Two police officers grab and push them up against the small wall barricading off the lake. Finding more small bags and propelling all three into the back of their car only to drive away promptly. Astonished to see such crime in a paradise on earth. To a certain degree elated that I was not the only criminal in the country, and proud that I am not a lowly thug.

CHAPTER SEVEN

'The Evil Can Never Win, Never!'

There was always a multitude of people, mainly tourists I believed, due to the little groups gathered around the small cobbled streets; taking photographs, holding maps given to visitors by hotels, asking questions about grand buildings and their history. The beautiful St. Pierre Cathedral, and the Chillon Castle in Montreux. The one major giveaway – asking for directions. Regardless of the masses of people around, this did not deter me how it would have done in the past. I felt secure within their ambiance. No longer intimidated by large crowds, no longer a coward. My appreciation for this feeling of security was beyond measure. It took many years to acquire. And from the multitudes of tourists I sat back, I listened and I learnt. From these strangers I have learnt many useful things. Developing an immense interest in the thirty various museums the city had to offer, from the ultra-modern Museum of Modern and Contemporary Art (MAMCO), to ancient Maison Travel the confusing style of art. The art found within was out there, but in a beautiful and intriguing sense. Opening my eyes to modern life. Constructing new curiosity. After spending two hours within the MAMCO I became inspired. Not to create art, but to become more of a modern woman. To recreate me. Stop playing it safe. When looking deeper into it that is an art in itself. Complex, intense, daring and thrilling all at once. But so divine. Not hiding away from technology and colour. It was time to ditch the black clothing, the classic attire. I felt like going a little outrageous like the canvases I stood before and took interpretation from. Trying new things. Experiencing a new way. Dare to wear yellow and bright red, maybe a little green. Colour is said to improve the mood. Colour has the ability to make one feel the way they long to feel. The fuel to spark off innovation. The country showed me I was not indeed living, merely existing, I wasn't doing that very well either. That my life has been one of seclusion. There is a diverse world out there, I've found it. I'm among it. It is in my reach, I won't ever let it go. Enthralled with how Geneva captured the full spectrum of its cities history, from medieval times till modern day complimenting one other perfectly. Stealing my heart away making me feel my future is here. Something profound came over me, the reason I did not know. I only knew I could not leave. My heart had been stolen by Switzerland and my love for it flourished.

The beauty of St. Pierre Cathedral which has been standing since the eleventh century, with its stain glassed windows, views of the city from the north tower made it impossible for me to walk away. I felt like I was in a musical and the world was my oyster. Happiness, fortune and all good things were coming my way. Here I seemed to find myself. The sweet story behind the Palace of Nations, now used as the headquarters of the United Nations, the building was gifted graciously to the city by a wealthy family, under the condition that the land will indefinitely contain freely roaming peacocks. Becoming lost in the architectural treasures to be found with everything that is to be learnt. There is much history throughout this country which is said to go back as far as seven hundred years. The most profound fact I discovered was the most heartbreaking. The entirety of people who have died over the years on the Alpine mountains. Their lives being taken from them by both climbing the Matterhorn and falling from it. Becoming stranded on the mountains only to freeze to death, climbing much too high their futures doomed. Skiing accidents caused when strong avalanches, gusts of winds and heavy snow obscure the innocent souls eye sight. The outcome thus enviable. As a result of weather suddenly turning hazardous many lives have been claimed. Giving rise to my plans. Death in beauty. Death creates beauty. Strolling around the well-groomed graveyards saddened me, reducing me to tears, despite not knowing any of the unfortunate souls buried there. Yet there was a strong feeling of empathy lingering within the air, moving me. With breathing in the saddened air I was immediately affected. Affecting me in a way I never knew before. The emotion was such a strong one that I could not help but feel the pain, their pain. The beautiful yet unassuming headstones made in commemoration of the lost souls which the snowy mountains claimed just did not seem to be enough. What affected me the greatest were those graves where nobody knew the names of the perished individuals who occupy them. Thinking how nothing could be more heart retching than being lost forever. That could be me, I thought. No one to know, no one to care. Lost for all time. OH yes, they may have found the person's body, but no family to mourn them where they lay, say goodbye to, pick out the coffin they were to be buried in. Their home to spend eternity. No one to come year after year to put flowers upon the burial plot in remembrance of that person and when they once lived. Never to be remembered. It would be like I never existed. The emotional thoughts which entered my brain, the sadness which filled my heart, much too harsh. Too much to control as I stood at the foot of graves, tears welled and drop by drop trickled down my cheeks. I had enough baggage of my own to deal with to be able to overly feel for others. Even so, it was this aspect which made me able to understand others hurt. I am humble and human enough to understand. And wise enough to accept the inevitability, this will be precisely how I will end up. Alone. No one to know I have gone. No one to care or remember me. Never to be mourned. I live alone and I shall die alone. The good always die first.

As I roamed around observing the stunning hotels and restaurants, like a dehydrated plant crying out for water, scorched from the unremitting blaring sun, I was taking everything in. There were such glorious long-established time-honoured buildings with sheer opulence and grandeur. I have never known such success. The charming but more so exquisite botanical gardens, I became lost within the wonderful flowers, trees and plants on exhibition. It was a peaceful place to be. It is a place to catch ones breath from the demanding life which lurks outside. I felt safe there. In wonderment as to how so many striking specimens could be taken care off as perfectly as they were, to survive, the landscape thus flawless and unspoiled. Their perfection inducing me to think, *my flowers never turn out as healthy-looking, as bright or full of life. Does everything I touch turn to darkness then death?* As I became spellbound by their splendour. Appreciating how much love care and devotion it had taken a great deal of people to present such a high standard of quality. Quality is something which is easily perceived throughout

31

Switzerland; patience's mastered, due to their small vineyards and steep hillside, locations complicating and limiting production of fine wines. Never lacking. Gladly waiting until perfection has been born. From their philosophy I have learnt significant lessons, primarily patience. And these have aided me greatly in all my illegal designs.

The place I felt most at home was the little chapels. Mainly a little quaint chapel named Maccabees located on the hills of Zermatt. From the outside the church was traditional and sweet. The interior wasn't any different. It was far from large, with a powerful ambiance nonetheless, in the region of ten pews on each side. For such a small chapel it was certainly grand and oozed gold from every stain glass window to the statue of Jesus Christ. The altar was the most opulent I have ever seen, appearing as though gold was overflowing caressing everything within. Creating a golden carpet for the righteous to walk upon. From the pews to the pillars to the window panes figurines and cherubs were carved into dark wood. The pipes for the organ which were standing above and up against the wall behind the altar appeared to be dripping gold down onto the altar. Everywhere my eyes scanned was sumptuous and extravagant in excess. It had a glorious feel to it. Never knowing the reason why this exact chapel overwhelmed me as compellingly as it did. A shimmering longing for to visit it regularly consumed me. There wasn't any doubt there was something perhaps from within which drew me there. This feeling of over emotion was a surprise. Not able to ascertain why this little traditional church elicits these strong sentiments. Could it have been to ask for forgiveness for my despicable sins, those I hadn't yet committed? Can sins truly be considered despicable when one is forced to defend oneself? Or did a force greater than I know ahead of time what was going to befall me? Was it a warning which I was responsible for overlooking? I had become a tortured soul, over time I was what I dreaded. When there is too much beauty or too much of anything, is that a sign indicating something is not as perfect as it firstly appears. Is that a warning to get out, get away beware?

During 2001 I could not have conceived the idea that anyone evil lived in this country. While I was a tortured soul everyone else seemed to be at peace within their lives, within themselves, enjoying every moment they were spending surrounded by the borders of this astounding realm. Revelling in life and grander. I was in awe. The Swiss are people who are fond of life and living it. Who are rich and love it. Where I was fond of taking it away. I felt more than happiness here. There way of being does something to one. It affects one's life, inspiring one to improve, to want more. Giving their life everything. Inspiration is what this country personifies. Making me feel as though nothing was out of reach. Making me believe I didn't have to commit murder anymore, I didn't have to be the victim any longer. Today is a new day and tomorrow will be great. It is okay to dream because dreams can come true. Mine did.

Unable to stop myself from dreaming how differently my life would have unravelled if I had been born here. How much happier I would be. The opportunities which would have presented themselves. The family who would have loved me. The education I would have obtained. How smart I would have been in my youth. I would not have had to learn from trial and error. The harder and harsher ways. Pain and heartache. Slaps and insults. Rape and abuse. The morals I would have learnt. Not to highlight the joy which I would have been filled with, hence giving me warm memories to reminisce if I had children of my own. Thus this would afford me the chance to tell them about my life before they were born. The truth is, my past I do not want to confess to a soul, my secrets are that dark. No one could respect me. Love me or trust me. How could I tell such darkness to ingenuous children? A force came over me, the realisation that I could rewrite the past. I can design the future. Why should the evil beings take away from me? Why should the evil tarnish my life, my past and my death? Evil can never win, ever! Life is what we make it. We do not have to be held down by the selected few who were encouraged to succeed or the masses who set out to destruct. My life is what I am going to make it. For the first time in my life feeling envy for more reasons than not having a good family! I am swamped with envy because the Swiss people are perfect, overlooking my perfection. This was a lesson I would learn. They opened my eyes. In the beginning I could not see that I was just like them. Striving to become what I already was. I could not see myself as anything good or worthwhile. Switzerland saved me. It offered me everything and more. Switzerland offers honesty, truth and inspiration. The best of the best. The greatest of everything.

CHAPTER EIGHT

Star of the World

Each day after experiencing something new, I would stop at a new café or a bar; accidently stumbling upon a charming little brasserie of which I was most grateful. Flavoured coffee pervades the air, imbues my smell senses, at once my body becomes limb and relaxed. Customers were bounteous. I never knew exactly what it was which attracted me there, yet I loved it. It was the pleasantest place I had ever known. What captivated me most was how polite and respectful people were here. Feeling greatly at ease. Feeling like I did exist among the living, I was no more hiding behind the shadows of the shadows. A coward to the daylight existing only in the darkness. Switzerland was the only place where I felt comfortable regardless of not knowing a soul. Becoming my escape. It shines above everything else in this world. It is the star of the world. Concluding, not knowing a soul was best for me. It was what I needed to make a new start. Escape the world, the past and all things shameful. Be not what I necessarily was, become who I wanted to be once and for all. Become what I could, who I was predestined to be. Refusing with passion in my soul not to be held back by the obstacles which emerge. People. Jealous ridden and venomous. Hateful people. Mounts of them. Grateful how the feelings of safety and happiness kept coming to me! Freedom. I was utterly free and untouched. It made me want to scream with glee.

CHAPTER NINE

007

Instantly falling in love with the uniformed décor in approximately ninety percent of hotels restaurants bars and cafés, with the all wooden walls and ceilings, giving one the feeling of their tradition. Its sophistication reminded me of the Orient Express, when Charles and I were on honeymoon with its opulent grandeur. Café Warwick located on the square by the train station in particular, reminded me of a nineteen-sixties James Bond movie with the décor, waiting for either Roger Moore or Sean Connery to appear at any given moment. With their voguish suits and deadly well-disguised yet very appealing guns. Sleek and sexy. Them and their enticing ways both mouth-watering and tantalizing. Fascinated by the flamboyant avant-garde designer styles; for a strongly traditional maintained country the people are unprejudiced. Everything was luxurious. Finding it easy to get lost within the luxury of this country, it was everywhere to be found.

Going back in time it surely felt. Old school respect and pride. Traditional recipes and techniques mastered and never falter. The exquisite pictures of the towns and cities, mountains, waterfalls and valleys were on show in virtually every establishments. Pride of their origins was everywhere to be sampled.

CHAPTER TEN

A Country Made of Money

A country filled with money, splitting at the seams, rich in excess. Dedicated to wine making, mouth-watering cheese and epicurean chocolate. All their superb creations excel beyond anything capable of comparing it to. The Swiss Alps thus included, they are much more supple and soft refined like the people, as for the French sector by far harsher and hostile, jagged like a deadly knife or perhaps the Parisians. Stopping in at a small bar, my kind of place, Vertigo on the lake front. Wooden panelling on the walls in keeping with the traditional style, however the lighting and furniture was more modern and colourful, with yellow lounge chairs, purple lighting and blue and red dinning seats and bar stools. Out there but inviting. The bar man who I suspected to also be the owner for two entirely disparate motives. The male who was approximately five feet six and aged fifty-five, was gracious in his manner. Holding onto a little extra weight, but would have been handsome when he was younger. He still was to some degree. Serving me a cosmopolitan with complimentary breadsticks with a bowl of mixed nuts. His manner was too courteous and his way too professional. He cared more than a usual employee. In addition to the fact most establishments were run or managed by the owners, participating in a large part of the day to day running of their businesses. Flicking through the menu deciding to treat myself to something naughty, despite having millions, but being a millionaire was still new to me, still not fully accustomed, the prices making my eyes bounce. The price for one glass was the equivalent to one bottle in Britain. The lobby held approximately twenty people who exited the elevator from the above floors where the hotel rooms are situated. A party entered the small bar adjacent, they were celebrating a business promotion. A business man now in charge of fifty Matrix banks across the globe, meaning bigger salaries and taller drinks. Inviting me to join their celebrations we drank and danced the Genève sun down to the horizon.

CHAPTER ELEVEN

Glacier Express

Friday 11 December 2001

Living in a Chateau once owned and occupied by my husband Nicolas before his sudden departure from this earth a year ago. Enthusiastically anticipating the daylight hours to awaken me, enabling me to embark upon another glorious day. Loving life greatly hence refusing to squander it carelessly. Those were the days when I felt young, loved and surging with life. Never knowing when it would either end or merely be taken away by society, the law or a mafia. I wanted to live each day as though it were my final figuratively and literally. This was my philosophy in my youth and forever standing by it. Never wanting to look back over my life as an old wrinkled woman, only to think to myself what if? What if I had worked harder for that, what if I had done that differently?

What if, what if, what if?

This prospect scared the life out of me. This was not how I wanted to remember my life, when I was an old lady on my death-bed awaiting death to claim my useless body. I was going to make the most of my life, particularly after wasting many of my younger years in vain. Now was my time to subsist and shine. It was now my opportunity to prove what I was capable of doing. Categorically refusing to allow others to waste my life for me any further. Life was given to me to live, otherwise I would not have been given it. Life had been hard on me, or shall I state people in my life had been excessive. I deserved to be happy once and for all. I was determined before the day which comes for me to leave this world forever and hello dear Lord, that I would make something good of my life before entering the next, whatever it may bring, wherever it may be. Whatever the next life holds for me I hope and pray it is not more pain. Otherwise what is the point in living? I agree we all must endure both good and bad, it teaches us how to be, how to accept and how to survive. Above all I have learnt it teaches one to appreciate the good when the good times are present. When the bad times shows it horrid face, revel in those good memories until the good days once more arrive. Understandably no person can be happy constantly, too much of anything is unhealthy and most unwise. What would I have done to deserve more pain after all I have already gone through? I must make myself happy, it does not just come my way. We are the masters of our own destiny. We are all here for some reason, let that reason be known. With the new winter morning came chilly air, goose pimples awaking me. Stimulating the life which flowed beneath. With the bedazzling sun shining above the mountains, blaring into the kitchen as I was savouring my breakfast. A very expensive breakfast of champagne and ousters. Fit for the lady of the manner. I recollect thinking, that winter sun is harsh, as it so easily cut through the morning fog, still managing to blind me. Feeling like a laser destroying my delicate corneas. Burning through the lenses of my eyes, hitting my optic nerves, it felt as though it was being pierced by a hot needle. Literally feeling my optic nerve twinge. No toast, no orange juice, not even the exclusive Italian Lavanzza coffee for this lady. Only the best and nothing less. I've earned everything I own and the hard way, I am damn well going to enjoy it while it lasts. As I stood drinking my very chilled champagne from my overly priced crystal champagne flute, costing me five hundred Swiss Francs which had also been chilled, I looked out over the gardens where part of them now remain, thinking how lucky I was. How wonderfully lucky!

Innocence survived.

Wanting to look and feel my best when seeing Claude later that day, deciding to take a refreshing milk bath with lavender and honey. Granted I ran the risk of smelling like an old grandmother. Lavender has forever had a way of calming me. If I was caught for my crimes, certain it would be the lavender which would help me keep my cool under the strain of any integration. Then it was time for my usual two- hour beauty rituals of face masks and face creams, working my way through to the anti-wrinkle serums. Always feeling energetic after my mashed banana facemask, as the effects made my skin tingle. It gave my skin the sensation of receiving small nips. It was a weird sensation. Not one I particularly liked but the effects were beneficial. Beauty is worth all discomfort. My eyes never failed to shrink from being puffy and red to somewhat normal, after my chilled cucumber slices which woke me up, refreshing me. Almost capturing my teenage days once more, I could hope. Eggs mixed with olive oil for to make my hair glossy. A true Italian I did look. During this process I looked more like something to bake and eat for dessert, opposed to ending up looking even more beautiful than men had already told me I was. I was merely taking care of my assets. There is not anything wrong with nurturing what one has in this day and age. In fact it is of great importance to care for ones assets, when they are gone they are gone. All advantages are required to get by, how hard this world has become, for women. The entire world has become one overly large America. A lonely place to be. No one is a friend. A wild west of fighting back or losing. Life or death. Blood and guts. When one loses they die. There is no such thing as truce. Love hate with nothing else in between. One can only depend on themselves to get by. No one cares, no one wants to know. The only thing to do is to keep the head low. It has always been the case of life being strenuous, we simply were not here to experience it in the past? Now it is our time. A different time, a different era. I live in the real world not a bubble in my own mind. Pleasing nobody but me. No one will do it for me. Understanding the harsh realities. Those whom feel the need to judge me for accepting the things I am incapable of changing, they are the fools, not I, not I. When reality hits them they will be the ones to sigh in despair. Since my hell commenced I took my appearance seriously. Very seriously. I was almost deprived of my beauty. Almost losing everything. A fortune lost in a blink of an eye, when gained over almost two decades. I must nurture it back to health like a mother with her new born baby held close to the breast.

The hell had taken its toll on me, now advertised over my face, my body of which clothing hides, thankfully. Never to be the same again. Unfortunately everybody notices one's face, it is paramount I cared for it as best I can. I was neither prepared nor willing to age before my time. When my time had come, I was still not prepared or willing to take it lying down. I was a fighter and a fighter with gravity even time I would be prepared to take on, beating the crap clean out of it. Over time I seemed to have turned into a soldier. Trained to kill in a war zone, given the license to kill without repercussions. But if I was found out for my underhandedness I would have my freedom to lose. The only way to survive in my new life is to think like a soldier, to murder like a coldhearted Muslim extremist after Britain and America and anyone who sympathies with their cause.

After dressing to the nines in my excessively expensive black Prada suit, single-breasted of course (but well worth every penny I paid), with a silk Gucci ivory frilled blouse, my Jimmy Choo heels, Prada (handbag), accompanied by my classy Gucci sunglasses. The extra large, extra dark pair which make a sophisticated statement, (I am successful and not to be taken on), wearing my favourite Channel five perfume smelling successful. The ultimate walking exhibition for designer clothing. People principally assuming I was victorious in some kind of multi-business adventure. To me being alive and being allowed to live is more than enough success. Strangers would never understand this. Presuming I was living above my means, flaunting airs which were not my birth right to do so, thinking me a fraud if they knew the truth, my truth. I was guilty of being greedy – perhaps that's the woman in me, but never that greedy. In the same position as Kate Middleton having to learn to be a certain way, learning everything from scratch to blend in, be accepted by the highest of society. Conform.

Deciding to take the glacier express to spend the weekend in my favourite little old town and world famous Zermatt, deep down in the valley to visit my new very handsome boyfriend and to spend some quality time with. Lovemaking is on the cards. Quite simply the most perfect man on earth. Better looking than Brad Pit, Johnny Depp and Liam Neeson rolled into one. A rare beauty he was, never before seeing such construction of facial features. With the greatest dick any man has been blessed to be born with. No matter how perfect Claude was, in my heart of hearts no man compared to Charles. No man ever would. Charles was long gone yet he still held the key to my heart. He left without returning it, now he never would. When Claude had finished work that evening, there was not anything which could keep him safe from my body which was ticking like a clock, needing his hot and steamy sex. I was the kitty cat who required his cream. Starving for a lick or two. I was a sexual bomb about to go off at any moment until I was consumed. Needing his body inside mine, opening me up and filling me up with all of Claude, both girth and semen, like the blossoming flower I became each May. In fact everything he had to give me I wanted. I needed. I required. Each time he would touch me he made me feel like a flower, with petals spreading out after a peaceful sleep in the shade. A flower starting as nothing more than a bud. The moment his hands touch my body, blossoming into a beautifully wanted sexy woman. If I were to be a flower I am not sure what kind I would be, there are so many stunning different kinds to choose from, but red is the colour I would surely be. The minute my petals would open, my sex would become out of this world. Like the wild horses I once watched running feral in the fields as a lonely child, I became every bit as untamed. With Claude I was in my natural habitat. There was no doubt about it he gave the best sex of all.

Riding the Glacier Express to Zermatt was an attempt to silence the haunting memories which persist within. So I could be somewhat normal before I reached Claude, otherwise I would be a nervous wreck. Shaking and behaving weird, possibly guilty. I can't let him down. I can't let myself down. Having to conduct myself appropriately. As it was a four-hour train ride from Geneva to Zermatt I brought a book which I had written three months earlier and had published to keep my mind engaged. Absorbed and searching my work to see if anyone could detect the truth in the words I had written. Recently, I tended to read out of it rather than into it, regardless of the book. Scanning the words without absorbing their meaning. My mind was preoccupied. I was disinterested. With every opportunity it was presented it would wonder and refuse to let me forget. I believe it is that little thing called a conscience, which really is not that little. It is the full size of one's body. If I can figure out a way to sever it from me and my mind, I would gladly and without regret. People claim that the conscience is what keeps the human race real. Keeping one in touch between right and wrong. The little clock which ticks like a bomb awaiting to explode informing me I am about to commit a wrong. A sin. A crime. It was not the book which bored me, it was the truth insisting on coming through which displeased me, more so irritating me. I loved to read back in those days. It was reading which gave me life in the days when I was low and feeling too much like giving up on living. At that time I thought it must have been one of those traits acquired from my pristine occupation as a novel writer. As I thought deeper, how much was fiction and how much was nonfiction? Was I really formatting a diary, hiding behind characters I invented to tell my story for me, because I did not have the guts to tell it myself? Ashamed of myself. Now I am addicted to reading and writing. It has been good therapy. For which I changed my name to become much more professional, more paramount not to be uncovered for what I really was, nor who I really am. A murderess. This was something which merely occurred. It was not my lifelong ambition pertaining to both my new career and disreputable history. I have experienced a great deal, I have a great deal to tell. Confess more like. It was my calling for many reasons. Moreover, figuring if my story was to be revealed after becoming a time-honoured novelist, unquestionably it would enhance my career. To me it was not worth going to prison or being sentenced to death for. Time-honoured novelist, what a waste it would have been if I was exposed. Equalling to a long hard fight for nothing in the end. The multitude of hours thus invested, research, discarding of ideas and possibilities. The writing and rewrites. The half a million rewrites of the rewrites. A skyscraper of notes building up. The frantic searching for the one perfect word. Eyes crossing unable to stand the sight of words even letters. Fingers incapable of typing any longer. Going blank, mind shutting off. Forcing my mind to work a little harder. Give me something more. Something better. The mind refusing to work. Sleep deprivation. Hunger. My brain refusing to do what I want it to do; which is write another word. The need for another glass of wine. Now that I have achieved something great from all the mountains of shit I've managed to climb and come out clean in the end. Not pristine but not as black as the earth. I could not permit the law to deprive my fans of my creations. Nor me from roaming the world, for new and fresh ideas. New and fresh characters. I will not let down my loving and supporting fans, who have given me all I have, and in so doing giving me a new lease of life. Now able to see that there are good people in this world. People with sentimental hearts and know how to use them the way they were designed. For goodness. It is I who has decided to take the cards into my own hands. My choice to tell the truth, my truth. I have lived in silence for long enough. Nonetheless, I will do it and do it my way. The time has come to confess.

Already sentenced to prison twice in my life. In my very short life. Going back was not an option. I have already served two life sentences, a third I did not have the ability to bare. I have served my time. I refuse to serve two further life sentences for the same crimes, death would certainly be better of this fact I am certain. I would surly then be Cleopatra killing myself by my own hand when danger draws near. At least then I would have peace of mind soul and body. All my sorrow should at least amount to something, something good! Not to have been in vain because that would mean they have won. *Evil can never win, never!* Figuring I could write about my pain, my trials and tribulations helping to confront my demons? An attempt to be therapeutic cleanses my soul for what I was made to do in my life, my past, enabling me to have a type of therapy without needing to confess my sins to another soul. Risking the chance of capture by detection. I could advice others. I could let people who are suffering and in heartache within their own miserable lives, realise they are not alone. There is a way out hopefully for everyone! The answer is not always found by dying from one's own hand. But either way one must fight. Find the strength which can only be found from deep within and fight to the death if one must. Fighting is life and to live life one must fight. Let the weak fall and the strong triumphal.

Forever revenged.

CHAPTER TWELVE

Zermatt

2007

On the train like every trip, I would capture the attractiveness of the scenery surrounding me, meanwhile men would capture my attractiveness. Men admired while women had daggers in their eyes. With illegal intentions in their hearts. Never becoming bored by the trees, mountains or lakes. Lake Geneva was ultimately the most splendid I had ever seen with the Alps encircling. The equivalent to royal icing on the cake. On taking a bite, one enters a delectable heaven. A new obsession craved for. Thus reminding me how lucky I was to have the opportunity to live in such a picturesque country. A country I had come to love. Without hesitation the most envied nation on the globe. Yes, Switzerland in size was relatively small with approximately seven million people. However, it has more to offer than the United States and Russia put together. The two largest countries, the two greatest super powers in the world, or so it is thought by the fools who do not know any better, considering how one establishment had the United States flag hung inverted. Zermatt is located in the best possible location, as it borders Italy of which is possible to ski over the margins of the mountains in Italy, France and Austria.

Today was different since the physical torment ended and the mental hell commenced making every day difficult. Although today was much more intense. For the past year I have hated spending weekends alone at home in Geneva. It did not feel like a home; still after time passed reminding me of a prison and of them. It is a shame how such beauty can be tarnished by venom. That house was situated in one of the finest plots in all of Geneva, especially as it overlooked their monumental pride and joy, their lake and adjacent forest. The weekdays were demoralising. However went even faster since I forced them to. I insisted on keeping myself occupied preventing their resurrections. Forbidding their resurrections to prevail, becoming the hunted once more. I was wishing my life away merely to arrive at the weekends, it was then I felt exhilarated. I could relax. Feel at peace. Fuck. Self-satisfy. Fantasise. On occasion romanticise about Claude and me, together, committing almost illegal activities. Both of our sexual organs in constant engagement. Why weekends had this affect over me I did not relate. It was an instant feeling or else going out of my mind was inevitable. Unquestionably this would be the next chapter of my life. Asylums and doctors, restraints and possibly more abuse by doctors who take privileges with their patients. Enforcing hobbies to consume me, its purpose was to drown their images out, and every now and then their voices. Wanting to work more than anything, develop a structure to my endless days. As a result of all my agony by their hands I had become socially awkward. I was no doctor but I knew I was suffering from something which was not normal, an ailment very definitely a consequence of what I had undergone. The feeling in the pit of my stomach. The physically feeling sick when faced with being sociable, the shakes, cold sweats, the panic and racing of my heart, panic attacks otherwise known as, I could not stand it. I was sure my heart would burst. Desiring to live without physical or verbal communication. Be left alone for the rest of my days and live in peace. I could not stand to have anyone near me. The loneliness becoming too much. In fact people's eyes on me was more than I could bare. A rock and a hard place. After researching for hours on the net, reading many articles and definitions about mental disorders pertaining to the symptoms I was suffering. From what I ascertain, I had developed a mental disorder where anxiety and avoidance behaviour predominated my functioning. Unable to trust being around people or engaging in conversation, it was too gruelling a challenge. Every part of my self-confidence had been taken from me. People's voices even their laughs, I felt I was drowning in sinister sneers. The distress gradually though frantically increased. I felt I would die. I had become a wreck of panic and nerves. Even loud noises which would appear out of nowhere had the ability of scaring me out of my mind, enforcing my heart to skip a beat with unreserved alarm. Sweat would run from every unblocked pore. Result, becoming completely soaked in fear. Frequently destroying many blouses and dresses. Until I had mastered how to control my panic not alone nervous, my plan was to write about my suffering. A potential cure for me, hopefully helping others at the same time. Wasn't this a great deed, as selfless deed? Was I on my way to making amends? Regrettably, this was me, my life and my plans never went according to plan. Ever! There was always that unseen obstacle which presented itself to either impede my victory, or hold me back permanently. That one person who would do anything to ensure I failed. Fortunately after everything I had gone through, from episode to episode, being equipped above all organised for any and all slip ups. Time would not be wasted and triumph would be mine. I must find a cure for myself that much I knew. I could not trust a doctor, the possibility of being captured was not a risk I was prepared to take. Therefore taking the advice of the articles I read online, that was the best I could do. Google and medical websites are a godsend. Writing therapy. Deciding not to be imprudent at this stage. I was not about to write a diary intentionally, a self-confessed confession signed and dated for the police to find one day. When I had become self-satisfied danger was behind me only to be incriminated by my own hand. No. I could not make it that easy. If the police want to catch me they can do their own job, get off their fat, aggressive, paranoid asses and investigate me. Deciding I would write and make a living from my therapy. Going on to be complimented by my ability of imagination and skill. And my fucked up characters. In reality my role would be the mysterious lady, with the alluring aura people will wonder have I lived such a dark life, or am I just an amazing author. Blowing my readers away. Never letting my tails be told. Entertainment for my fans, therapy for me. Guilt veiled.

I was done being subjugated in all episodes of my life, being the conqueror was now what I was. I found the will, endurance and the strength. Defeated I will not be. Between working like a dog with a bone unable to drag myself, my tired body and drained mind away

47

from my desk. In some aspects this was the freest I had been blessed to feel for many years. Write as much as I can concoct, feeling amazed how great it was to get things off my chest. As a consequence I felt light. Cleansed. Guilt evaporated. Forever to be with the clouds on a stormy day. Having to turn one of the reception rooms into a new study, unable to stomach that old study on an hourly or daily bases. I could feel their evil spirits consuming my mind, wanting me to lose all grasp of reality. If I had remained, it would have worked. I knew they hated me for writing the truth. Showing them up for what they were. I hated being in there at night, it reminded me too much of the last night they occupied those four walls. Feeling a chill overcome me each time I'm in there. I feared how it made me feel. Many times within the past year, I contemplated having a Persist to not only bless the house, more significantly that old study. Although they still haunted the house, the study was the worst of all, that was where they seemed to still live, be alive in some way, in some dimension. Ceaselessly spying on me. I could feel their reptile eyes burning into my flesh. Or is this called going out of my mind? Was I sicker than I realised. That was where I felt the most vulnerable. Having a priest bless the forest and the garden may be a stretch too far. The irony would be a most definite mockery. Forgiveness or peace cannot be found there. Only evil spirits which lurk. What remains in that adjacent forest is lost for all eternity. Leave the things which cannot be changed, forget about them if I can. Ideas ran through my brain as idiotic as, could the wind have blown their spirits into the study. After all, the garden runs in line all the way to the top of the house directly into that room. How gullible I was when I was in my twenties. Astounded how quickly a novel can be created when it is indeed based on fact. The words flow. Conversations once spoken. Emotions do not need to be found. They have once be felt. Details easily given. Insight to the terror. That scene was played before. Becoming consumed by hobbies was the mere start, I had my gardening. The sick irony which it represents. I had without hesitation turned into an old lady before my time. Wearing that Miss. Marple hat. Had I become Doris Day, isolating myself, no friends and no lover? With just a pillow in silence. No phone ringing driving me out of my mind. Like any murderer I was categorically determined not to get caught for my crimes, therefore unable to leave the garden alone. Every morning I awake the garden is my first thought. I had turned into its mother. Ensuring that there were no tell-tale signs giving me away. I would dig, plant beds, make herb gardens, plant seeds and transplant grown flowers. Objection, guaranteeing there was much activity of standard gardening for suspicion not to be generated. Gardening started out as my new hobby, instead quite literally it became my baby. In the middle of the night getting up from my warm and comfortable bed to check on the flowers, feet away from the house, in order to rub olive oil upon their leaves, watering the soil in the dead of night, preventing them from being scorched after a day spent beneath the blaring sun like a mother nurturing her small infant child, from danger of being small and defenceless to safety and strength. Olive oil as in the milk from my breast. The sun and the warmth tender touch from my hand, as in the bonding with baby as it suckles. A relationship built and strengthened. Unbreakable bond. Soil, seeds, compost, grass, watering cans all became distractedly important to me during the aftermath. The aftermath of everything had changed my life. It was everything I needed to create life and give life. Become God. In the Old Testament where life as we know it all commenced, God said to have needed the rib from Adam to create Eve. I Nicolette Beaumont need a packet of seeds along with a bag of compost, hey presto life I gave. Somewhere in my illogical unconsciousness believing this would make amends. If I gave enough life it would be my penance, regardless of what form it came in. It all sounds absurd looking back. Believing that life was life, what did it matter if it was human or botany? Isn't all life form important? Each inhale oxygen, feed and require water. Each flourishes when healthy, yet dies when ill. Plants do not cause harm to a living soul, surely I get extra points for that and for riding the world of scum. The dangerous, the disastrous. I think that was why I loved Zermatt so dearly. It has a special place in my heart. Representing life. Health. Hope. I carry the remembrance of that Christmas card village with me every day. Bright beautiful plants everywhere to be found, with faint aromas of floral moving in the air, as fluently as a Latino dancer. When the warm rain falls the stronger the scent becomes being blown in the air. Being in Zermatt was like walking back in time. No cars permitted in the village, silence in every corner to be found and no polluted air. Grateful that Nicolas did not destroy my memories of Zermatt. He didn't go that far. He and his family spoiled the beauty of Geneva for me, thankfully Zermatt surpasses all the beauty to be found in the city, for me that is a small mercy.

Not wanting another husband at that time. Nor did I need the bull which came along with a pretty shinny diamond ring. A ring no matter how lovely isn't worth the hell attached with it. A woman who longs desperately for a husband has not previously been married. A lover I was dying to have consume my body. A whore I was? Err…. Perhaps. It's a woman's prerogative. A man who I found to be physically attractive not caring about his personality. No complications. No strings attached. My body had been left alone much too long, it needed desperately to be touched, to feel the warmth of a man whoever he maybe. Showing me I am still a woman. My body did not need any more abuse just tender love. The physical kind. Not in the same capacity Nicolas once treated me. Craving a wet tongue to lick my nipples, making them stand in the cold night air, gently sucking them. Fuck it! Being honest with myself, I wanted my breasts to be devoured. My legs longed to be spread to sanction a man's manhood to penetrate my pussy. Yes a lover I wanted. A lover I did not take, not then. Going out of my mind from sex not had. It was sometime after I took Claude. The garden I seemed to have become obsessed with diluting my sexual cravings, thus my second obsession. In my twenties and since moving to Switzerland, I had developed many fascinations. This country had a powerful effect over my being. In Switzerland, but not because of Switzerland I lost my mind.

Finally I had my photography. After buying a three thousand euro Nikon DS800 camera, I became obsessed with taking black and white photographs, hence my third mania. This was a diversion which never interested me before, until I needed to engross myself in anything that was not memories of them. It most certainly appealed to me in my new life. In retrospection of the events which transpired, it was clear that the types of photographs I was then capturing to any well-versed psychologist or murder detective was the confessions of my crimes, or another guilty party like me, my photographs had now become my opened and much published diary; the dairy of my more recent sins of defence. I had confessed without realising. It is just a matter of time before I am probed about the events which took place during 2006. I was vigilant with regards my writing, as for my photography I was reckless, complacent. Creativity was how I filled my time, my mind. Taking me an extended period to appreciate these three interests, they were a form of cleansing. Unaware it could give me away faster than a sworn affidavit. The awful days I lived through. The days which had become nights, I would answer to. To my new love, he put the deep dark eerie photographs down to my understated hard upbringing I once endured. Due to Claude's privileged upbringing he had a soft spot for me knowing my story, most of it. Making him the only man I have ever confessed to, almost fully. In all reality perhaps it was a bit of the two. A combination of both hells, a toxic cocktail to be discovered, and consumed. Needing desperately to tell my sins and ask for absolution, scared of the penalty, needing to keep my mouth shut. I was going mad, mad within my own mind. I was a tortured soul once more. Instead of drowning in water I was drowning in memories. That was all I ever seemed to be doing. There was no alternative. Only thankful I did not personally know any psychologists or detectives, at least in that capacity some good luck was prevailing. Over the passing years I have often wished I could have sold that old house. It has been my punishment, never loosening its grip from around my throat nor setting me free to gasp for oxygen. It was once my home for a brief five months when I first went to live there as a young bride. In the days succeeding the days transformed into protracted nights.

In the beginning I fell in love with the location, the surrounding scenery plus that stunning Italian handmade solid wood stairwell which was imported from Rome, said to be over three hundred years old. I felt blessed to be able to enjoy the beauty of two amazingly stunning countries at the same time. Lake Geneva and Mont Blanc from my own bedroom window. I was lucky. I was his legal wife, yet he never added my name to the house deed, binding my hands unable to sell. Concluding my dear sweet loving husband number two, must have known in advance his plans for me, anticipating I would not need to sell the house. He would outlive me. Despite his age, my youth and good health. Of course if he had died legitimately and a body was presented to the law, I could have had the paperwork altered. An autopsy I would have no need to fear. I could then have sold. Nevertheless, how could I have explained three bodies? No this was something I had to endure, perhaps a further punishment, something to keep me grounded. Having no choice but to hold tight to the property. Ordinarily I would not have minded. Complacency was one sure way of making idiotic mistakes, resulting in getting myself caught unnecessarily. I was not going to take that chance. The risk was quite simply not worth it. I did not want to lease the house, taking the gamble of something pertaining to them, their victims and what evilness took place there being discovered. Something belonging to them, something they were guilty of. It was in my lap. I could not take the risk of me being blamed as the perpetrator. Accused for their murders of the victims they chose. Unable to get rid of it. Burning the damn thing was out of the question. The insurance would go only to Nicolas, for that they would need him alive, a signature, a meeting, some kind of communication in person. If they could not find Nicolas Beaumont then a guaranteed investigation would take place. Although everything would go to me if there was no will and testament made, I would never have seen the light of day again. The entire process could take years. I could not enjoy the beauty of the property or grounds from a jail cell. In that case everything would be lost. It would have been in vain. I would have no home in Switzerland. With the high prices of property I was not going to tolerate a gem as exquisite to get away from me. It was the only thing good which came out of this entire mess. It was not a perfect situation but it was good. Far from the worst. I had an elaborate and impressive home. Monetary it was free. A home for life. An even more impressive bank balance. As a foreigner regardless of being a European citizen, I would require permission to buy land and property given the small size of the country, hence why property and land is expensive throughout. Gold dust. It's a free home for as long as I can manage to keep everything related to Nicolas and his murderous family concealed. Knowing my luck, I would be blamed for their murders. Perhaps one day when I had the chance to search every square inch of the house, made alterations to ensure no secret rooms would be found, no secret panelling in the wooden walls or secret cameras, I could lease it making me a profit, a steady income. Not that I need the money. That would be one day in the far future as I had more pressing matters to attend to, like keeping myself out of prison. Swiss homes are excessively expensive, this furnishing me with the excuse of refusing to sell it if I could have found a way, for the time being. A positive spin on a bad situation is paramount. For these reasons, once I figured out a way to access Nicolas' bank accounts and spend his money for living expenses I'm sorted.

My backup plan was to find a dodgy estate agent, who I could manipulate and blackmail into altering paperwork permitting me to sell when the time was ideal. Prepared to create a scandal if the situation required it. Nothing was beyond me when I set my sights on a goal. When I was young and calculating. If I needed to perform some out there crazed sex shows, video recording or take photographs, using it as leverage to get what I needed. I learnt not to get fucked over. Fuck first and get out of the door before reprisals occur and a dirtier situation I am landed in. I was more than a pretty face. More than tits and ass. And a pussy between my sculpted legs. If I needed to, I would not have thought twice about solely fucking him or killing him. Whichever needed to be done would be done, for survival I had no scruples. Instinctual behaviour, fight for survival. Humans and animals do it. It is the way the world is. Obviously, it had to be a male in case the situation called for me to fuck him senseless to keep him sweet, but more pointedly blackmail was the key. Women are more difficult to manipulate. Stubborn. Plausibly because the female sex have brains and use them according, most of the time. The male sex only thinking with their dick and use it inexcusably. I would have done anything to survive including fucking a lesbian. If I knew how! My role had to be the damsel in distress. The alluring mysterious lady. Men always fall for that scenario. The lady he wants to fuck but would not dare try too soon. The risk of repulsing me would not be worth losing the chance of screwing a cunt as pleasurable as mine. Dripping honey between my legs. They aren't found often.

The money I made from my books was more than enough to take care of me, enabling me to get the permission I required to buy property, eventually. After years. Purchasing a chalet in Zermatt eight months preceding worth twenty-two million. Containing twelve bedrooms, three levels of living space, an indoor heated swimming pool and five balconies. The village I wanted to live in the most. Zermatt, that picturesque town made me feel free. No husband to interfere or ask permission from. No criminal record to discredit me. I was now surviving and doing it on my own. The only issue which bothered me, I was then overcompensating for my past. In my present I was trying too hard to be hard. Pokerfaced. Zermatt was a place to hide. Few people, no danger, no watching over my shoulder or concern of who maybe behind me. Everyone knew everyone. Watching out for each other. Not yet aware I could not run from myself, my mind, the past, what I have done! What I was forced to do. Not even what I had been subjected to. There is no getting away from something when it is in the mind continuously and branded upon the heart. With every blood flow from each heartbeat, the memories pumped giving me flashbacks. Is it possible to run away from what is unmistakably a living hell, when every fibre of one's body is smouldering in unadulterated endless torture? What has been done cannot be altered. I must find a way to come to terms with my actions, without consideration for the reasons my actions transpired even theirs, which is the most unjust of all. Find peace, I must find peace within. This is much easier said than done. No matter how difficult this may prove to be, this is something I must conquer.

As I drifted in and out of memories of what has occurred to me during my adult life. My heart began to thump in my chest, feeling as though I were taking a heart attack, besides feeling dizzy, clammy and in distress. Things had not changed in all the years since which have passed. Closing my eyes, an attempt to shift the dreadful thoughts from my mind, instead closing my eyes encourages the memories to flow more profoundly, reducing me to feeling nauseas. After realising this struggling to keep my eyes opened, then seeing Nicolas's face all around. Men and women become Nicolas. The blowing leaves turning into Nicolas's face. The shape of the tree trunks reminding me of Philippine's unattractiveness. The mountain peaks sharp and ragged, evokes the knife I once used to cut my very own wrist to end the incessant relentless torture. The knife which caused my wrist to bleed in six different places, each was a long skinny line, the width of my wrist. The scars still remain and flaunt. Another poisoned reminder that they once existed. The rubbish bins at each train station takes me back to the poisoned coffee Philippine once bestowed to me in the best china they owned. A sweet touch thus the bitter gesture, an attempted means to an end. Lampposts at each train station jogged my memory back to the polls they beat me with. The poll I then used in retaliation on Philippine, picturing my wicket family with each blow I inflicted. I should not have stopped. I should have beat her brains in, splattering them all around my bedroom walls, until it resembled nothing more than discoloured

54

vomit. Covering my face, my body with death and life, all at the same time. That was my chance for salvation. I turned my back away for two purposes. The first, the most idiotic, I was a better person with a stronger sense of right than them. It is being the righteous person which causes trouble. The second, I did not want to murder. I was in a false sense of disbelieve. Relating that I would never be set free, but hoped that I would be proven wrong someday. Fictitious hope. Such a small word with such a profound meaning associated. Everything reminded me of them. There was no winning. Realising that there was no escape awake or asleep. I cannot discontinue. My hours of sleep were less agreeable than my waking hours. The only thing keeping me half sane, is the fact I Nicolette Beaumont know to be the god's honest truth, I was a victim, their prey. I did not really have what it took to be a cold-blooded murderer, despite having killed a few people in my lifetime, but not once profligately or in cold blood. Well not exactly… Well maybe once. I have all my life been a firm believer in a taste of one's medicine. I am more of an old testament than the new. Treat others how you wish to be treated. If one treats you foul then do the exact same deed to them, then ask how they like it. If they do not, then rightfully they ought to ask for forgiveness. If they do like it, they are sick bastards. This is what makes the definitive difference between a survivor and a monster. A survivor will do only enough, a monster his extremes limitless. They were the monsters. I was the survivor. I was a fighter. I will always be these things. No monster will ever strip me of my life.

Life is mine.

Power is mine.

CHAPTER THIRTEEN

Wish

We can all wish for something good or bad.
We can all wish for something kind or cruel.
But how often does something good or kind actually arise?

When happiness is needed it rarely comes.
When misery could be obsolete it always shows.

We can all wish for love,
We can all wish to be loved.
But how often does love find us?
How often are we ever truly loved?

When kindness we would love to be shown,
When contentment we would settle for,
When the giving of love we would be happy with,
When does any of this ever show?

We can all wish for something good.
We can all wish for love.
We can all wish for anything,
Dreams and wishes are limitless.
But whatever we receive we can always wish.

CHAPTER FOURTEEN

The Man Who Loved Me

Recollections of my dreadful past which haunts me day and night.

2001

It was a freezing December afternoon in 2001, when I first arrived in Zermatt. At this junction in my life I was isolated, I felt desperately lonesome after my first husband Charles suddenly died. The shock of unexpected deaths more abstruse to accept. I was missing him like I had never missed anyone before. Before this time I never really knew loneliness to this scale. Certain that the world in one swallow would gobble me up. I was out of my depths. His lose truly was a heartache, the toughest ordeal I was forced to face in every area of my life. I was never destined to get over his death. True love is a struggle. True love conquers all. Wishing I understood this aspect to marriage before the path was unchangeable. Youth hands us harsh lessons. Lessons learnt. Smarter minds develop, mistakes no longer made. But what about the mistakes already made, how does a wiser mind deal with that torment when it plagues?

Going back to school the year formerly, approximately three months after Charles's death. An arduous strain. Main objective; to keep my mind engaged. This was an effort to continue on with my life, in spite of not wanting to. I wanted to die, lay alongside my husband the man who truly loved me. A part of me did not want him to be lonely in that six feet cold damp earth known as a grave. In death loneliness is felt. In a grave loneliness is felt more so. The one and only fuel which possesses the power to keep a corpse warm is love felt, experienced tasted and enjoyed in life. A mausoleum is the loneliest place on earth. Wanting to keep Charles warm, warm with my love, be there with him until forever. Move on if I was able to, was what Charles wanted, it was far from what I wanted. We understood one another impeccably and with the greatest of ease. Almost always knowing what the other was thinking. Perfectly in tune. Walking the same path. Dreaming the same dream. Somehow from somewhere I found a little strength each day to push myself out of bed, to know that I was not failing him. I believe by my doing this I was making him proud, as he knows, yes, I am sure he knows how challenging it is for me to live without him. Regardless of everything being my fault. Often wondering if he could ever forgive me, or would that be a task too hard? Asking myself, could I forgive someone who killed me? I alone am fully responsible. What I am guilty of doing is of the utmost betrayal. We would still be married, have a family and be idyllically happy. I changed what was intended for us that preordained path for the future. One morning it may have been the empty space next to me in bed when I awoke, the space that was not warm, nor had been slept in. Still taught and wrinkle free. The coldness of that empty place rang home much truth to me. It will never be slept in again, not by Charles. My insides had been consumed by emptiness. A hole, a crater. Landed, exploded. His love, his warmth and tender touch has gone. All I am left with is the memory. A used up sentiment to recall. Another day and another memory which would be responsible for triggering a heartrending remembrance, would be when I was dressing, this would have been the time when compliments would have been given. He always had a magical way of making me feel good about myself. For him and only him, I was good enough. Not many men have that ability. He was not like other men. He was special, with a compassionate heart the size of the world ten times around. Or hanging ironed clothes and there his things hung. Not recently worn. His manly scent fading with time. I did not have the heart to move them. They belonged hung up, it was his home. It was a reminder to me that I did not dream such happiness, it was in fact real. I had been granted a special gift. My life had been great. No more feeling sorry for myself. A sad and impending feeling of doom filled my crushed heart. I could not endure the pain any longer. The pain was crippling, I felt I would die. I hoped that I would die. I wanted to die!

Feeling I needed good hard exigent work. Something! Anything which would have taken my mind of Charles and our past, a distraction from my recollections of our life together and how his death transpired. Guilt has a profound way of haunting ones conscience. We were barely married nine months proceeding to the accident responsible for claiming his life. During the winter break from school, five months later I was aged twenty; deciding to take a holiday for two weeks to Geneva and Zermatt, Switzerland. Hearing a great deal about the country I had never before set foot in, having an intense longing to visit the land of sophistication and movie stars looking for a quiet life. People who mind their own business who don't spy on thy neighbour is there such a place? Inner peace was what I was searching for. Struggling to keep occupied when the holidays approached. I had done as much gardening as one could stand, during the spring and early summer, although it had not been of interest to me before Charles's lose. Gardening was forever the one thing I resorted to after taking a life. A psychological state of mind instinctual; such as bathing after an argument, trying to find absolution to bury the guilt. An attempt to try and feel blameless. Clean. It was essential for me to have diversions. The thrill of seeing my flowers and tomatoes blooming had died away. My home; yes singular my home, when it once was our home, did not need any more decorating and another opera would have killed me. I could not take any more of those snobs acting more superior than their worth; because they have excessive funds with fancy names to parade around functions and galas, automatically believing they are Gods. They sickened me. Very often finding myself lowering my head, frowning heavily and throwing massacring looks. Looks which could kill, I wish would kill. Killing me would not have exactly been a bad thing. The answers to all my prayers. They were killing me; killing me slowly in absolute torture. Blaring screams for this pain to cease. The rich are a disease. A spreading pandemic. If another opera had stopped my heart beating, my blood flowing, I would have kept him company. I was not then scared of death, I am not frightened of death now hence why I am laying my cards on the table. Showing the weak hand I hold. The first time I have shown what I clutch. The time has come for the truth to be told. The moment of truth always comes. Secrets can only be kept temporarily. There is no such thing as forever. Honesty always insists on showing its face. Sometime does come! Spending my entire life concealing my hand, holding my cards close to the chest. I did it well. I knew better than to publicise my game. The lack of fear is the reason I am telling my story today. Death is coming for me; I will meet it head on with open arms, above all grace. We all are destined to die, I am not going to the next life a coward. Every night over the passing years I have prayed wholeheartedly for death to rescue me. I live through the grace of pain. Deciding when I left Charles and my then home located by Lake Garda, the most beautiful villa I had ever laid eyes on. With twelve bedrooms, three receptions rooms, with twelve inch ceilings, a porch, a sauna and a swimming pool, but the most wonderful aspect of all, was the twenty thousand acres which belonged to the grounds. Peace and solitude was easy to find. Hiding away from the world was even easier to do. My idea of heaven on earth. The same property which once belonged to the Italian Royalty. Charles's family was lucky to buy during the First World War, after remaining dormant for many years. The building had been subjected to multiple bombings and searches by the Nazis over a period of seven years. At one point the Nazis has taken over the building. It was their location for planning bombings on politicians and the Polish. Jews and traitors. Torture had taken place on the lower floors. Hanging was done out in the acres of land attached. It was the ideal place to kill and not be found. No one around for miles and miles to hear a scream, a moan of pain. The pleading for mercy to be granted, to spare a life. Anything! At that time the sellers were giving it away, understandably. It was Charles's pride and joy. What he was most proud of owning. I could not blame him, it is magnificent. A rare find, a rare gem. Nothing bad seemed to haunt it or linger within like Nicolas' home in Geneva. Love and peace were both very much apparent.

For Switzerland I designed a stratagem; no matter who I would meet in Switzerland, I would refuse to declare my personal business, or past to anyone who may inquire, particularly if they were a potential lover or husband with substantial assets. The best action of self-defence is not to wiggle the tongue too much, just a woman's shapely rare. There and then I made up an entirely different past, a new story, a new life. It was not altogether a lie; it was a dream of what I hoped could have been.

My Strategy

"Which kind of life have I always desired to live," was the question I asked myself when designing my plot. The answer was an easy one to find. It was a life which consisted of happiness, love and success."

This would be the easiest way to remember, ensuring I get away with my story. No slip-ups! Both smart but primarily cunning I was quiet and observant, I listened, I watched. I learnt. Never brash. Letting others make fools of themselves by talking too much and making a spectacle. Thinking down to the fine details, polishing off the rough edges until they shined with perfection. The names of uncles and aunts, siblings and so forth; naming them the names I liked for my children; if I was ever to have any. That would be my ultimate dream. Once I have made my way through all life's bullshit. Mountains and highlands of bullshit and oceans wide and deep. Being a good mother or not I do not know. How good of a mother can a murderess be? But having my own child, my flesh and blood in my arms and seeing resemblances of me in them, must be a most magical experience. I think then this hell I could get through. I would have someone to live for. Until that day, I have myself a good man to find. Not necessarily a rich man, but it wouldn't hurt. My dream would be to find a man who truly loves me, in the thinnest of times stand by me, right by my side and protect me. If I fell ill to a life-threatening disease, he would feed me, wipe my ass, wash me, and still love me no matter what. Dignity would not be lost. That is real love. That is true love. Will I be lucky enough to find this in my lifetime? I highly doubt it. I did have that with Charles. I couldn't see it until it was gone. Perhaps we can only find this once in a lifetime. I would do all this and more for the man I loved. But what would he do for me?

Checking myself; I was too human. I longed for things only normal people did. They are not designed for me. I must have been conceived or born during a full moon, or when stars were not in alignment. If I were to have a child of my very own, I probably would fuck up its life, like my family fucked up mine. If I were lucky enough to find a love, I would probably end up killing him too. My life only ever takes me to darkness.

Check List

✓   Change of name
✓   Apply for paperwork
✓   Have paperwork signed by lawyer
✓   Have all ID changed with new name affixed
✓   Apply for new passport
✓   Open new bank account
✓   Alter deed to house with new legal but illegal name upon ownership
✓   Change appearance
✓   Skinny to curvy
✓   Short hair to long
✓   Change hair colour
✓   Change coloured contact lenses
✓   Have a mole or two removed
✓   Draw on a mole or two
✓   Have a scar or two thinned out to not be as noticeable
✓   Cosmetic surgery

After being lucky enough to be with Charles, I came to know I was a very beautiful woman at the age of twenty. The answer to all my prayers. No matter where I would roam there were at all times a countless number of admirers. So much so, it was not foreign when it came to the stage persistently when this unsettled me, more so my husband. It could either be a headache or an advantage; it solely depended on the day. At other times when I was not being inconvenienced by admiration, I would become submerged within it. It made me feel as though I were laying on a beach, upon a golden blanket of sand with waves of saltwater splashing of my body. Teasing me, encouraging the dreams to surge. Not because I was immersed within myself, simply because I never thought of myself as attractive when I was younger. I was always the object of ridicule at school, for not being the prettiest, instead I was the smartest! Going home to be made a mockery of by my family, as I was not the cutest daughter one could have produced. If they were as handsome as they proclaimed, surely this was their fault. Beauty is said to be in the genes, their genes are in me undoubtedly I would have inherited? This illogicalness all came from a father and brother who thought themselves as Casanova, unsuitably I might add. Never believing I would turn out as appealing as I have done. I was proud that I did turn out as well groomed, refusing to use it to cause detriment to any soul nor flaunting it in other people's faces, particularly other women, unless I had to, if she was asking for it. Personally, I thought I would remain ugly all my life, when I looked at my father and brother, the pigs they were I did not think there was hope. Learning there is always hope. Impossible to be unlike them. To me I was the exact definition of the ugly duckling turned swan beautiful. I remained auburn with no interest to become a blonde. The old stigma I did not want to be attached to me, seeking male attention, being dense and so forth. People perceive us from the second their eyes scan and their brain interprets their findings. First impressions is paramount often ultimate. I continuously tried to become more of a lady, being a woman of brains not merely beauty. There is more to being a lady than clothes, good manners and pose. I read, I studied desiring to become intelligent. I did not simply want to be skilled; I wanted to know a lot about a lot. I wanted to be more than what most women could offer. I was a reserved type of woman, with high morals and higher standards. I am only guilty of doing what I had to do. I was certainly traditional moreover observant. I noticed that women were no longer the way they used to be. They lacked a great deal in many departments. Craving to appeal to whatever man I decided I wanted. Wanting to possess the essential assets I required to land the man of my choosing, or a bank balance of my dreams. I could not have settled. In my youth I believed all women should have been like my mother: able to cook, sow, attend to everything and more that a house not alone a man demand. Men even homes demand a hell of a lot of complicated wishes and services. I did not want to be just seen and never heard. When it came to my husband, the man I choose, I wanted more than anything to be able to hold an intellectual conversation. Wanting to be with an educated man who could teach me much. A man who respects me for my inclination to learn. Needing him to respect and admire me, keep him interested in me, in us. This was in the days before I understood men. All my hopes were not to be, finding they were childhood fantasies. Reality is much more complex. I did not want for him to lose pursuit of me, or the attraction he once seen when looking in my direction and loved. I had to keep the flame ablaze. The steam in the bedroom, the wanting to come home early from work to fuck me, the anticipating until I was in his sight to be able to have me, make me his for another time. Stimulating my body; make me crave his, his cock deep up inside me. I craved to feel the heat of his Lyons inside mine. Make me scream with sexual pleasure. Have me begging for more, never granting mercy. Never stopping when I plead with him to cease, the pleasure too intense but amazing nonetheless. Constantly having me drenched in sex and immoral thoughts. I want to purr like a cat when I am looking to be shagged. I would purr and he would know my sign, the sign of come on jump on board, fuck me! I would be the wife who would listen, sympathise and give advice no matter how impractical, all to let him know I did not misunderstand him. For these reasons I do not deserve to be cheated on, because I loved him with all my heart, more than my own life. I wanted to amount to something and be able to be proud of myself and our marriage. When my pussy wants to be stroked; I only have to purr to draw the attention to my call for admiration.

Whatever husband I truly loved with all my heart and beyond doubt wanted to spend the rest of my life with, I wanted him to be proud of who I am and what I have to offer. I yearned to see admiration for my accomplishments in his eyes. My husband's pride for how I look, because he still finds me beautiful after twenty years of marriage. Is that possible? That starry look which glistens within the eyes, indicating he loves me for what I have done. More so for who I am. This was essential to me. Not wanting to get mixed up in the wrong relationship, to a man I faithfully loved mistakenly; having him let me down in more ways than one. Having him beat me, demoralise me, stripping me from my well-deserved and earned independence. My personality, my unique characteristics. I was not going to be a doormat for any red-blooded male. I refused to allow any male to bring shame onto me. What makes a male the superior force? Just because their physically stronger than most women, that reason is not good enough for me. I was well on my way to being the woman I wanted to be. By this stage of my life not solely men, but women noticed my careful mannerisms and decorum. Manners, decorum and ladylike perception were what I was notorious for in Italy. I was sure males could smell my lust, the wetness between my legs, more than my beauty, perhaps this was what attracted them in their great numbers yearning a piece of my hide.

After Charles's death there were many rich accomplished men on my tail. Wishing to stroke my pussy, the feline I was. Staying true to me, my morals and standards the person I faithfully am, I did not disgrace myself by disrobing my ethics to attain wealth. I had millions. With Charles's death came along my wealth. No more requiring permission for anything. I no longer required a man, no more the damsel in distress. Playacting. I only longed to be wanted. What I did need was a friend, someone to spend time with. Talk to. Learn from. Not once confessing. I had been lonely much too long. I only killed when I had to, that was no reason to become a whore. Primarily due to the fact I did love Charles he gave me plenteously, more than any one woman could want. My life would not be as comfortable as it is today if it was not for dear sweet Charles. My Charles. He will always be my Charles. On the day I die he will be my last thought, I will see his beautiful face and walk towards him, to be with him, I will whisper *"I love you,"* just before drawing my last breath. My eyes closing never to reopen. I genuinely was grieving for his lose. Not wanting to go through anything as arduous again. It was through grieve for him I spiralled out of control. I was struggling to find who I was, after the nine months of mixed feelings and emotions. I hated myself everyday still till this day for being so fucking stupid, impetuous and selfish. I was a selfish cunt. I had to take responsibility for my deplorable actions. It was this recognition which crippled me. I hated who I had transformed into. I was no victim, in all reality I was a fucking murderer. A cold-blooded and heartless murderess. In that instant I became the monster, not a survivor. Taking a life happens so quickly. For what I did to Charles I deserve to go to prison. I killed the only man I ever loved, the only man who ever truly loved me. I robbed him. He gave me money, kindness, joy – above all life. I took his life because I was angry. Just because I was fucking angry! I was so far up my own ass I overlooked what I had transformed into. I turned into a monster because for the first time I had been spoiled. I then acted like the wives of the pillars of society, those whom disgust me, thinking myself more than my own worth. Superior. Becoming carried away by having everything. I was given everything, earning none of it. The truth be told even if I had earned the millions in capital in that Zurich bank account, that was still no reason to think myself superior to everyone else. The rich would kill me slowly. Draining the life out of me until my death gasp.

My traditional beliefs were one aspect of what attracted Charles to me initially. What he came to love. Never failing to impress or to act like a lady at all times, that is, of course, while I was in the public domain. In the bedroom I was his bought and paid for whore. His legal whore. Knowing we legally belonged to one another made the hot steamy crazed sex that much more tantalising. Breathless. Gasping. It is only marriage which makes it this sensational. I loved being Charles's whore. For that man I would do anything. He was the only man who I would ever allowed to ass fuck me. That was Charles's duty. That shit hurts too much to allow just anyone to take the ride. Men are sick. They inflict pain while going out of their minds on pleasure. Pleasure junkies. Sex junkies. At any expense. I only wanted to make him happy. His beautiful smile I longed to see each day. My transmutation was one of extremes. To society I was virtuous, the next best thing to being a nun. The only men who got to know what kind of woman I turned into were my lovers; the selected few who I fucked senseless. Sometimes beating them with leather whips, wooden sticks other times mental poles. It depended on how angry I was on any given day, and how much steam I needed to blow off. Making them bleed, scream and cry; heightening my sexual bliss. If they can give it and enjoy it, then they can take it while I enjoy their agony. Their open cuts I would force my fingers, nails into making them scream for mercy. I created art. It was an art. To see the trickles of blood flowing down the arms and backs of the men

66

I levied pain onto. Waterfalls of blood. Rivers splashing of red waters. The men I secretly hated, I loved to make grown men cry. I long to reduce them to the lowest degree of humanity, then further down into the soil of worms and death. I was taking out on them what they (man race) had done onto me. An eye for an eye. While I was shagging their thick succulent cocks with so much cream inside, I made them cry out for their mothers. This giving me the ultimate climax to organism. My tits stimulated, nipples soaring, chills up and down my spine making my tits stand all the more. My satisfaction came through their pain. My crown of glory. They themselves did not pleasure me a way a man ought to. Incapable. Inside my gut I had an extreme elation. These men disrespected their mothers for me. My uterus filled with man, the pumping made my uterus throb arousing my body to want more. I was his wife. A whore was what I was supposed to be. Sexual desire, whichever positions a husband prefers is what a wife is taking on along with the taking of her vows. No matter how deplorable. I loved to be used, abused and stretched by his thick sensational cock. Each time his dick entered my body he was informing my cunt that was his home, no other man had grounds to be inside me. Almost every night of our married life Charles fucked the life out of me. Ripping my cunt apart. Making me lay on the bed or the floor, legs spread apart, my own come trickling down the inside of my thighs, my cunt thirsting for more sex, more roller coaster fucking. Voice cracking, unable to scream. Crumbling until there was no audio left. I loved his fucks. The best part about Charles's rides was that they were free, higher than all the rest. The aspect I adored the most was he could give me so many different types of sex. In my younger years my favourite kind of sex was rough, hard deep and plentiful. No emotion. No warmth. Pull my hair while he fucked my pussy. Shove all that manhood all the way in and then some. Make me beg for him to stop, once he yielded the trusting, making the sex that mind-blowing I beg for more punishment. Legs refusing to close, wanting more than anything to be filled up with cock. Greedy for dick and impure pleasure. There isn't anything richer than a husband's cock, knowing it belongs to me and only me. A powerful compel of admiration and sexual stimulant.

In my older years desiring passionate sex. The playing and the games were then concluded. Understandably all games must end. A winner and a loser. I needed to feel a man's tongue run over my entire body, licking wine from my flesh, pouring it down the insides of my thighs waiting till it seeped down to my ankles. From my ankles to my vagina licking the wine, once he had reached my naked pussy rubbing his tongue around my clit. Going onto devour my entire pussy, licking my arsehole neglecting none of me. I needed a man to fuck me with his tongue. There isn't anything quite as good as oral sex. The taste of sex. In my youth my philosophy was, if it fits try it. I wanted to experience all kinds of long, thick, hard items entering my yearning body. My goal was to determine if anything felt better than the genuine. I wanted my man to become drunk on me. An alcoholic for my body. Eye contact intensifies. From many trial and errors finding, there is not anything which feels better than a husband's dick. Nothing comes close. Husbands have more zest in their stick of love. With the real Mc Coy a woman can actually feel the pulsating of veins ravelled around a dick. The feeling of stiffness as a man blows his heavy loads of cream into a woman's kitty-cat is unbeatable. Bonding. Passionate affection. Special connection.

Making my husband happy and proud – this was important to Charles as he was a much older man with a successful life, hence being highly important to me. There isn't anything I would not do for him, and him alone. Charles appreciated my efforts to ensure his pleasure in every way. I treated him well, he treated me better. We owned something special. In my anger I did not merely rob him, I stole from myself. I took the only love I knew, the tenderness he brought into my life and a thrill I had never before experienced. Support I never before had; from anyone. A love that was real. What is making my husband happy and proud when I have murdered him? When he is no longer here to see me, be with me, and love me, no longer here to be seduced. It was all for nothing when he is not here. On a daily bases Charles thought how lucky he was to have me. How great his young wife was, how great his wife looked. He maintained I looked my best on the end of his dick. Sweat flowing down my body as we fucked; I couldn't disagree with that. Licking my trickling sweat he claimed it tasted of honey. Also maintaining I looked sexy in a pair of jeans and a T-shirt, with no makeup upon my face, my hair pulled back in a bun or pigtails when I would be gardening, with my little flowery gardening gloves and when I was trying to tantalise him by playing schoolgirl, which was the role which always scored.

Men always like schoolgirls, the power they have over fragile minds, powerless to decline. Most of all he loved when I would wear a tight white T-shirt, with no bra on beneath. When a chill would blow from Lake Garda stimulating my skin, giving rise to goose pimples over my body, of course he loved how my ripe plumed breasts stood up. Twenty-year-old breasts. They only get better with age. My dark brown nipples poking through the cloth, while a shadow of nipple could just be detected, this thrilled him every time. To him I was the sexiest woman alive. His motto was, *"give this lady a black bin bag, she still stole the show."* How sweet. This is what true love is. Acceptance! Acceptance for what a person is without attempting to chance them, then everything else follows. A natural harmony thus created. When beauty is genuine not merely drawn on upon the face with cosmetics, or stitched into position by the means of surgery. True beauty is not simply every strand of hair being in place at all times, no makeup mistakes and perfectly straightened teeth. Beauty shines through thus projected in one's eyes and nature. It is responsible for indicating to another if this person is good or bad, if this person looking at you is heavenly or hellish. Purity shines through, honesty shines through, all this and more is beauty. It all shines through the eyes. The eyes are the key to everything. Beauty is in the eye of the beholder, while evil is within the soul.

CHAPTER FIFTEEN

Waterfalls of Blood

Waking up breathless and in a panic, soaked in a cold sweat, my limbs tingled from distress. The smell of blood, that coppery metal smell was overwhelming. Robbing the air I breathe. Nauseating. The only noise in the night was the sound of the ku ku clock in my bedroom sitting in its rightful place above the mantel piece with pride, giving me a weary sense with shivers juddering up and down my spine. Hairs standing on the backs of my arms and my neck. Eyes on me I could emphatically feel. No breath or movement heard, but eyes are undeniably on me, watching and savouring my fear. Smelling and tasting it as it drifts in the air as though I were being freshly cooked in a scolding hot pan. My dream consisted of two components. Firstly, I could hear and see waterfalls of blood running down from a jagged Cliffside. The second, blood and death was profoundly tarnishing the scent of untainted river water.

CHAPTER SIXTEEN

Death in Beauty

I was not high maintenance due to the poorer lifestyle I was accustomed to in my earlier years, evidently I came to enjoy the richer lifestyle I was given immediately. It was easy to adapt. I was not a New Yorker or Californian, hence unfamiliar with having massages daily with servants at my beck and call, of which Charles appreciated. Charles loved that there was more depth to my character. That I was not destroyed by being spoilt. I knew how to appreciate. Yearning to be pampered undergoing manicures and pedicures, this bored me. Pampering once in a while after earning the right absolutely, enjoyable, rather than compulsory. Unless, of course, I was making an effort for an important event, then a bit of pampering would be called upon, ensuring my husband would be proud to be seen with me, this was expected by his fake rich friends. They were rich, but nice absolutely not. Only for Charles I desired to look my best. I did not care about anyone else. My goal was to seduce him once we made it back home, this was when my debt would be paid for his appreciation of me. Gratefully those important events died out with Charles. Our so-called friends were too ostentatious for my likening. Proudly to denote I was the party who detached me from them. Charles always insisted I could not tell them what I truly thought; he needed them. Needing them to spend their obscene amounts of money in his businesses keeping him wealthy, in a life he had come to love. Luxury. Leisure. Ease. Safety. Let the money keep rolling on in. Many times he had begged me to keep my silence. Aristocrats do not publicise the truth. Poker face.

Expressionless, is the key to becoming successful in the world of the supercilious upper class. Smiling when it is expected, nodding in reinforcement with the crowd. Telling people what they think they want to hear, opposed to the truth, only to sneer behind their backs. The truth affronts such people. They have learnt this trait well from the politicians they rub shoulders with at society events, merely to fit in. When the rich wives who have not worked a day in their lives, conduct themselves as though they have accomplished more than merely marrying hardworking men, who provide them with everything they own. Wives of the rich, the pillars of society would deliberately belittle me in public purely for their own amusement, glorification and satisfaction. Feeling I was too beautiful and young for my own good, chiefly to their dismay. They would reduce themselves to dirt for five seconds of glory. With utter envy and contempt they yearned to disparage me. To give themselves that tingle of worthiness inside and childish giggle. The rich are the same as lowlife bullies, forever making people feel worthless. Juvenile behaviour of course all the same a compliment. Not a great compliment from the money grabbers, even so, I seen through what they were attempting to achieve, failing every time. They are no better than prostitutes. Marrying rich and successful men to fuel their ego, living in a life of luxury far beyond their own means and ability to earn. With no love in their hearts, no compassion for their husbands, for the men who gave them everything. Working themselves into early graves while these wives sit at home or in beauty salons; there faithfully is no difference between the two. I did not take these types of compliments to heart, or reflect on them in any significant fashion. They were simply the unexposed type of admiring compliment. Knowing this, therefore I laughed at them while they were seeking to hurt me. Hurt me they never did. Taking more to affront me than what these selfish whores can achieve. It would take an educated person to understand. Perhaps someone who has experienced what I have experienced. My beauty spoke for itself.

Wanting my life to be more interesting. Not wanting to be read like a book. Mysterious was what I wanted to exemplify. When men tried to predetermine who I was without knowing the first thing about me. Preconceiving, I was a clone of a million other useless women. How wrong they were. The way women have treated men over the years, gives rise to men in these modern times to judge every woman harshly. Most of the time protecting them from a paroxysm crater of shit. The men I came into contact with astounded by what I had to offer. When women thought they knew me because they knew themselves. I was not them. Gladly! Thankfully! Plausibly this annoyed me, when both men and women would declare they thought I was high maintenance not knowing how to do anything. Being pretty was all I knew, hair, makeup, clothes they claimed these were the things I cared about most. Untrue, unfair, unjustifiable! Attempts to be degrading. How narrow-minded. They who know nothing should remain silent. They did not know me to analyse, in order to scrutinise the picture of perfection they seen when I stood before them. My perfection intimidated both sexes. When men realised how wrong their opinion was, they had the balls to apologise for their misconception of who I am. As for the women, typical women, too gutless to admit when there are wrong. A weakness of character. A person not to be trusted.

Hard work is what I know best, regardless of how people described me, wanting to overlook my factualness, unprepared to see the truth in my qualities. I would not have gotten this far if it was not for sheer dedication and time invested. This was why I and those types of women could never see eye to eye. I did not need to. I did not need them. When I would open my mouth to speak, those bitchy women with the evil tongues and beady eyes, the glory I took in their ignorance of life and education. I was the one who reaped the fulfilment of their humiliation, not once having to stoop to their level of being a nonentity. They were too smart for their own good, by not being smart enough. They showed themselves up for what they were all by themselves. In silence I sneered. It was my perfection which caused me to be hated all my life long. It was my flawlessness which made me women's worst nightmare by being their biggest competitor. Their probe for my imperfections willingly was an inequitable assumption, merely tarnishing me with their brush, since this was what they were. Ashamed of what they are. Wanting me to be alike. Knowing I was not. Wanting to be me. Not wanting others to see their guilt. Like the guilty who typically tell their stories first, causing them to think they will be believed. Brewing a war to explode. Life is a very tough world for the beautiful. To be beautiful and to be perfect is the making for a lonely life. A bloody game. My innocence quickly slipping away, simply to get by in the game of life. It is my beauty and my perfection which will be my killer.

Initially when people would meet me when I was young and impressionable, people mistook me for being sweet and kind. This I was to a degree. In the beginning only. Not altogether. Although when people we do not know see this quality within one, they have the tendency to underestimate one and ones abilities, ultimately overlooking ones intelligence. To their disadvantage. They are then under the assumption one is ingenuous. Treating me like the fool I am not, attempting to make me look like an idiot in order to discredit me. Jealously is the cause of too many wars. Admittedly, this was not always a drawback. It was this very aspect which let me get away with a great deal, accompanied by the look of innocence. This being another great compliment which they try not to highlight, hoping I could not see through the idol gossip and insults, the blackening of a good name. The wickedness they exude, they think they disguise. All these great compliments I did not take on board. They mask their bitterness by sugarcoating with smiles. With acid emphasises still detected. These lowlifes I would not reduce myself to filth in order to accept compliments. If one is as insignificant as they proclaim, certainly they would not waste their precious time discussing someone as low as they attempt to make their target out to be. Sweet and kind yes I was, when people allowed me to be. Naïve yes, dumb never, not since my teens. The person who is underestimating me is the fool. It was transparent like a window. It was transparent because I am a worldly woman, with a mature mind. It is a universal quality the jealous have. It does not die out from generation to generation. If anything it inflames. The leaving of a young and stunning corpse left to decay. In the end death is in beauty.

Beauty hated
Beauty ruined

PART FOUR

Family/Enemy

CHAPTER SEVENTEEN

An Insufferable Family

My hard and bothersome family made life insufferable causing me to be depressed often as a teenager. Being a teenage girl is difficult enough, without being subjected to mockeries made by idiots who think themselves better than their actual worth. Holding themselves superior to others within their small town. Yet they spread spiteful gossip about their neighbours behind their backs, while hypercritically being pleasant to their faces. At all times declaring they could beat up anyone of their choosing. This I detested, refusing to degrade myself to their level I raised above them by conducting myself with respect and grace. The greeting of a stranger with a smile. I lived life refusing to declare a bad word about anyone, unless it was absolutely necessary. Determined to amount to more than all my family which would not be difficult as they did not amount to one molecule of a decent human being. Not once receiving encouragement to neither excel in life, nor achieve great things. Until I met Charles all I was given was put-downs. Charles was the only man who ever seen me for who I really was. Indubitably he was not the greatest man in the world. However, he was the first and only person to tell me the truth about myself. He was my saviour. Charles was the first person to show me who I am, what I am and the woman I would turn into. He was the only man who did not want me only for my body, loving me for being exactly who I am; with no desire to mould me into something he wanted me to be, until the end. Causing the end to occur as early on as it did. We were two completely different and separate individuals. Yet, we complimented one another to perfection. Both of us had our own minds, with ease to verbalise our opinions without fear. If he believed I was wrong he never bullied me into submission, or beat me black-and-blue. He would simply explain why he believed what it was indeed he believed, asking me my invaluable opinion if I had one. He respected our differences in opinion. Claiming I often reminded him of himself when he was in his early twenties. Believing with both passion and conviction he was right, failing to recognise five years, ten years down the line, he would believe something entirely different. Looking back merely to laugh at himself and his immaturity. He always maintained *"changes are the best things which comes with life."* Charles was too much of a wise man, a gentleman to be the negative sort. My Charles did not get to where he was in both wealth and education by giving up easily or by being a defeatist. At the start of our life together he was everything I wasn't, but learnt to be in time. He could never have gotten along with my family. I had no doubt my family would have sicken him in the pit of his stomach if he was ever unfortunate enough to meet them. This realness to Charles was what I not only loved, but admired with my entire mind and everything that was in me, about my precious husband. I lived each day in admiration of him. In his shadow. Learning from the greatest mind. He understood we all make mistakes in life, therefore stood by and let me make mine, knowing I had to learn. Identifying being the oppressor; trying to prevent me from making those mistakes; in turn I would recent him, to the extent of hating him. Consequently, our marriage, our love would die. Based on my savage upbringing, Charles was exactly what I needed. He understood, was compassionate and encouraged. Forever claiming he was my saviour of that I have no doubt. The day we met I was planning on killing myself that same night. Only wanting to see the sunset one last time. I was on the end of a cliff. All it would have taken was a deep breath, saying *"thank god this is the end"* and one step forward. Unable to take anymore abuse and debasing insults from my family. Unable to change my mind and go back. Dragging me so deeply down I could taste and smell the earth, the soil which leads to hell. From the dampness of the upper earth, all the way down to the dryness of the lower earth. From the coldness to the warmth feeling like a blanket covering me. On the day Charles walked into my life, I was sure I could feel the heat from the blazing flames in hell. Instead Charles came to me, took me and gave me life more so reasons to live. He wrapped me up in a blanket of love. And showed me heaven.

Opposed to being encouraged by my family to have confidence, build a positive mind and demeanour, the regular things parents are supposed to teach children, within my family it is forever a constant competition. Being told on a daily bases:

"You will never amount to anything." "You're stupid" ... "... fat. " "Ugly." "You will never do well in life." "You're selfish." "Nobody will ever marry you, why would they you, you're a fat cunt?" "Nobody likes you." "You're nowhere near as good-looking as I was, when I was younger and you never will be." "I've forgotten more than you will ever learn." "I'm more intelligent than you could ever dream of being." "You're a waste of space and life." "You're a dreamer."

Indisputably, I was subjected to much verbal abuse as a small child, in addition to all the beatings with iron bars and bamboo sticks. The punching, kicking, the murderous threats, all so very unforgivable, on the positive side has moulded me into the woman I am today. Without those brutal experiences I would have been like the common place little girls, who would cry with an abrasion upon the kneecap, or a bump to the head. Of course I envied those children when I was growing up. In retrospection due to what my life brought it was an aid, a silent and advantageous aid. But to have an entire life filled with abuse is to nurture self-destruction. For many years I have been under the illusion that both a parents and the families duty is to inspire and reassure their children and siblings into achieving, becoming educated and doing well in life, in general and to be happy. When one is told with conviction projecting through their venomous voices, dirty smirks upon their repulsive faces, in attempts to belittle one further, to grandiose themselves, telling me that I will always be stupid, when I was not stupid to begin with. I would never amount to anything, regardless, of my ambitions and determination. My hard work and efforts. Deliberately holding me back when opportunities arose, because they did not have the opportunities I was presented with. How can one help but be dragged down by life,

78

people, position or lack of it, and not adopt to a negative outlook, how can they not hate these people? I know I do. I know I will for the rest of my life, more so when it comes to the end. Comprehending it was their inferiority which make them the negative underachievers they are. Talking big and talking bad. Achieving zero. Knowing I was apt, that I had the hunger required, fearful I would achieve, therefore putting their ore in before I showed them I could and I would. What I am made of. How pathetic? People with egotistical issues should never be allowed to reproduce, only to fuck up their children's life. Fucking up their own life isn't enough for them.

There could not be a more perfect woman in every capacity, excluding psychologically. I am not modest when calling myself perfect. I was perfect, I made myself perfect. I worked hard at it each day. Achieving this was my mission. Watching old black and white movie, after black and white movie; from Virginia Mayo, Elizabeth Taylor, Sophia Loren, Grace Kelly to Audrey Hepburn. I watched, practiced and leant. Through this dedication I became the perfect woman. I became me. Due to the fact I had practiced till I was nothing less than perfect, I became the envied. The envy of all women! Who could be mentally healthy after everything I was exposed to? This could be asking too much from any soul. All the evilness in my childhood had unquestionably dissolved in my adulthood, making me a stronger person including a go-getter even if it was only to prove them wrong, and I right, in my own mind and their eyes. I had every right to degrade myself to becoming a piece of scum, a criminal. Those delinquents who presume that they are entitled to get away with their unscrupulousness, for that matter corruption. When standing before the judge being accused most criminals who are caught proclaim, *"it wasn't my fault, my family didn't want me,"* *"they didn't love me,"* in order to get away with their crimes. Being slothful an utter waste of humanity, going as far as to being an oxygen thief. Many would forgive me for wishing my family wickedness in return, praying for them to die or for bad luck to fall upon them. In addition many would not hold it against me to want them to feel pain, like the pain I once felt by their hands. Literally pain, tears and blood were shed by their doing. A taste of their own medicine I would love them to feel! Instead there was a certain purity, an innocence within me, which was known to even I that they were unable to touch, incapable of tarnishing, making me shine with beauty, with kindness. This was what people seen and hated. This was what gave me strength. It was this which made me beautiful. I knew they were suffering in their own wasteful lives, I did not need to sell my soul to the devil by wishing them pain. They were the cause of their own destruction. Never wanting to harm any soul, only wanting to live without pain in my life, but pain was constantly being inflicted onto me. To be left alone is not exactly too much to ask. When I was young and beautiful, this I was gullible enough to believe. Solitude does not sound like it is something which should be unattainable. Solitude is something which should not be prayed for under healthier circumstances. Now I am older and wiser I have learnt, the more beautiful one is the less peace one will receive, the more people will want to take away from you. The more pain they will want me to feel. If I want peace I will have to make my own peace.

Filth will never be proven right. My father and brother were not men, positively no gentlemen, when they bullied a small child, a little innocent girl. Weak. Incapable. Frightened. Frequently telling me I should never have been born. It is always the same type of person, never picking on someone their own size or age, afraid of being made a laughingstock. Afraid their weaknesses will prevail. Picking on what they know will not be able to fight back. This is no man or an oppressor. This is indeed a coward. A sick minded and useless coward.

All my ladylike performing brought me along way; it got me away from the living hell I was trapped in for almost two decades. That is, of course, until Charles began to affront me. After a short marriage, after a brief encounter with love, love abruptly ended. For a short time I had a family, a unit I could trust. Charles gave me everything; I have no right to hate him. It seemed almost overnight. All of a sudden Charles had changed. There were no signs, no differences to lead up to the new Charles. I owed the hundreds of thousands he bequeathed to me, not including the millions in property and real-estate. I was selling everything that was in his name until 2002 to attain the capital. I did not wish to be inconvenienced by the daily running of Charles's business ventures.

A million phone calls in the early hours from estate agents wanting to know if this property could to be sold, or should be held onto until the property prices escalate. Gold dust. The answers to their prayers. Or being harassed by lawyers wanting to know if I would be interested in selling this plot of land for farming, or if this building would be considered under offer, as a foreign investor will be prepared to pay whatever it takes to attain the ideal business enterprise. As a rule I had come to realise, that those foreign investors who were prepared to pay ANYTHING were typically from dangerous countries in which we did not want in our christen countries. More than enough of them were already in circulation. It was not their nationality I did not like, I was no racist. Indeed it was the religion which could bring terror and death onto a blameless country, as eccentric over the top believers wants to dilute the disbelievers. It was merely as matter of keeping the dangerous and deadly out for as long as possible. Nullifying the possibility of another war. I was no Politian capitalist nor socialist, I was not about to sell a prime piece of real estate to anybody who is attempting to be the next Saddam Hussein, wanting to overtake the world, killing anybody who crosses their path; regardless of how much I did not want the headache. Their charming sweet talk to persuade me to go their way all too uninteresting I found, giving me many migraines. I did not want anything more than to wash my hands of the business dealings entirely. Understanding that I still needed to be smart, consider what was potentially best for my country including my future. When it came down to it, I just did not care about business. There was more than enough bequeathed to me, ensuring I would never have to work a day in my life, caring for me for the rest of my days. Even if I blew one hundred thousand Swiss francs a day, I would still be set up for life. It was not the capital, it was not the expensive diamond jewellery − no − it was not any of this I was the most grateful for. It was simply the self-confidence I once lacked immensely. It was the showing of me I never knew existed. It was the inner beauty Charles pointed out to me which I possessed. This is what family is meant to do, show their children the good.

After a few months of marriage Charles could not take the attention I his young wife received daily. Once being engrossed within the attention I was given, that very same love and enthusiasm turned very quickly and bitterly into hatred. Charles was nineteen years older than I, with grey hair on the hairs he still owned and had not abandoned him. He was five feet eleven with broad shoulders, but by no means holding onto extra weight. He was neither the bodybuilder type or slender. He did have strong shoulders. Strong hands. The kind of hands which are formed over time from excessive hard work. Heavy lifting, heavy pulling. As a rule he ate healthy, never the slightest treat. Not even at Christmas. Taking vitamins each morning with his breakfast out in the garden. He loved his fresh air first thing in the morning. Charles maintained that fresh air was his stimulant, a tonic which cleansed his stomach, revitalising his blood, purifying his skin and the key to giving him longevity. His meal times always on the hour every three hours. Certain this was what gave him a high metabolism. Standing in our garden at Lake Garda each morning breathing in deeply, profusing his lungs with clean crisp oxygen. This he claimed give rise to his constant motivation and business success and for his business mindedness. Maintaining humanity was nothing without clean fresh air and we were only as good as the air we breathed. The ability to think straight. Make precise and methodical discussions. The very same reason why he did not drink much. Just casually. No foreign body consumed to cast over a haze of confusion, end result losing his entire fortune.

Charles was charmed that such a beautiful woman could not see her beauty when everybody else around her could. He was fascinated by the fact everywhere we went for dinner or a show, both men and women would stare at me in awe. As time passed it seemed to Charles the younger men were getting younger, and prettier inflaming his love for me to utter contempt. Overlooking reality, I did not want those men even if I were a free woman. One thing I detest is the pretty boys who think themselves something they are not, like Cristiano Ronaldo. I have twenty-twenty vision, I still don't see what he sees. Each to their own. I like men, real men, grown men. Men with years behind them who know what life is about, who are real to themselves and genuine with everyone. Younger men or mere boys who play too many games to intrigue me, I am not about to mother any male. I live in the world of the living, not in a game ruled by points or sex. Attracted to only men who take control. Poor Charles was reduced to feeling convinced I would leave him for a younger model. Not permitted to have friends or socialise. I could not speak my mind nor grow into the woman I was born to become. I quiet simply and sadly could not be myself anymore. I went from having freedom given to me merely to be snatched away. The things that I deeply loved and respected about Charles were gone. Quite simply he was no longer the man I married. Charles became a different person; a stranger. A man I came to resent for tarnishing my happiness. The happiness I longed for all my life. He had destroyed my escape. It was at this stage I came to believe nothing good lasts forever, I still know this to be the truth. My life was not designed to be happy. Within my mind at that time, it translated that Charles had destroyed my life, our marriage, making everything seem like a brief dream. One of those dreams I dreamt each night as a child, of how my life would be when I was old enough to escape my present hell. My heart shattered. At the same time he could not understand why my own family discredited me the way in which they did, for this he cultivated a silent hatred towards them. I loved him for that. Nobody had ever had my back before. A hatred he only spoke of once to me, but it was very much present. It showed through his loving eyes.

On our wedding day he vowed to take care of me, make me happy and to love me everlastingly. On our wedding night he underwent further private and tailored vows. These vows he was not true to, consequently he was untrue to me and our marriage. I did not want attention from men once I was his devoted wife. To Charles I was truly devoted. I was sincere to him and our vows. I would never have found interest in another man during our married life. That wasn't the woman I was. I felt after everything he had given me, all the happiness he granted, I owed him more than I could ever hope to repay. In so doing, I figured what is giving him what he wants? It makes him happy, making him love me all the more. My husband deserved to be happy. When I achieved this it did not make me feel as worthless. I would have done anything to make him happy without question, trepidation, or self-consideration. If it came down to it, I would have lied to the police, robbed a bank, gone as far as to murder for my man with no apology. No road was too far, no sea too deep and no extreme too intense. No torture too unbearable. That is love. With the love I felt for him my love knew no boundaries. But the time came within our marriage when I was living the life I had fled. It was happening all over again. Flashbacks. Nightmares. Cold sweats. Insane moments. The constantly feeling nauseas from fear. Too frightened to sleep. Too tired to remain awake. Losing grip.

Losing the battle. The name calling, the belittling, the tears and the misery principally the beatings commenced. The beatings started and my nightmare inaugurated once more. With the threat to hit for the first time, came along the smack on my left cheek. On the second occasion, he threw a crystal champagne flute smashing over my skull like diamond snow. It was in that instant what flamed up within me, what was boiling within my skin, muscles and tissue was scaring the hell out of me. Terrified of what I may have to end up doing. Did I have the guts or was it mere imaging. The wanting to do it, but incapable. Unable to go through it again rendered me to a pile of bones; factually I refused to eat for months. I cried every minute of every day. Eyes bloodshot, raw. Face scorched. It was then what I was capable of, what he took out of me was very much a surprise, rendering me speechless. After nine months of marriage and recouping my life, Charles's life was over. Our marriage had officially ended.

It was on an autumn evening October seventh I recall, we had returned from a long two-hour walk in the countryside. Down past the flowing rivers, over the hills and down by the valleys. We both loved to walk, that was one of our main interests in common. As we walked we noticed cows in the fields, wild horses running with such a freedom about them. It was a rather lovely and calming walk, the paradox was staggering. We enjoyed walking during the cooler nights. Loving how the cold made our cheeks tight, with the falling golden leaves descending around us. Trees arched over small roads, giving a strong feeling of romance and tranquillity. It was a delightful feeling. Wasted. Once we returned the goose pimples had gone as soon as the warmth caressed my skin. I jugged a glass of cold chardonnay which came from a vine in Lausanne, which I had removed from the fridge in the study down my throat, hard. Then another glass much harder. I was building up false courage. I went upstairs to greet my Charles, who had gone up to change into lounge clothing, to give my husband for about the next ten seconds a glass of his customary brandy. Meeting him at the top of our grand stairway, I walked slowly up the thirty-six steps. Feeling like a queen as I approached. I reached out to hand him the glass, leaning over to bestow a kiss on his lips, with a twinkle in my eyes which indicated goodbye. Charles understood at once there was meaning in the twinkle I flashed; before he had the opportunity to respond, with a scream and a shout, then a sigh, the fiercest bang to one's head I ever witnessed, Charles's life had ended. As I rewind this day, I still cannot believe how quickly a life can be gone. At that time I was filled with anger for what I felt he had taken away from me. Not instantly feeling grieve, in that moment making me the most evil person alive. Wanting to forget entirely about Charles, he was a mere regret, for the longest time wishing he was only a mere memory. A memory I could control, if I wanted to recollect him or not, opposed to him dropping by uninvited particularly at the most inconvenient times. Learning along the way during the journey of my life, evil people within my life, the people I have had to eradicate for me to try and survive, it all being in self-defence have the most annoying way of resurrecting themselves in my mind. As a rule I was guilty of believing that once flesh and blood was dead, they were dead for all time. Dead and gone. Never to see again. Since growing up now realising that is not necessarily correct. Eradicating ruthless people was never going to be that easy.

When I married I did not inform my family, thereby I did not need to worry about them discussing the man who broke my heart or dragging up my painful past. This they would have laughed at. Bathing in joyousness at my misery. They did not need to know anything about me. Not that I remained in contact with them. As soon as I ran away from home, Charles saved me, I never looked back. Not for a moment. I was grateful not to have the need to reminisce. I tried as hard as I possibly could not to think of them. Hardships one suffers during their lifetime, has a harsh way of recalling itself when it is not wanted. A time, a date, a place or a resemblance a stranger has to a person from the past with no trouble evoked. There have been many years in between communications. No Christmas or birthday cards. When I come to think of it, I do not know if they are alive, not that I could claim I care. That would be a blatant lie. We are strangers to one another. They never cared about me, why the hell should I care about them. They are not my family. I have no family. I was more than happy to have the distance remain. They are not worth the trouble they constantly caused. By no means do I need them. For being as independent and capable as I am this I am grateful. Although my kind ways made me wish often that my family had been close. We got along with one another, we remained in contact. Having large Christmas dinners together, year after year, making memories. Giving one another lots of gifts, filling the large gap beneath the six foot Christmas tree which stood in the handsomely decorated living room. The laughs the jokes exchanged, the happy memories to recall, the photo albums to look over during the passing of years. The smell of Christmas throughout the house, the feeling of love so tender and warm, none of this came from my family. Wishing I had someone to lean on when I needed advise. A call away for support. Wanting so badly for someone to give me hard love when I was on that floor and giving up. The support I desperately yearned for. None of this would happen regardless of how much time passes. It was not in the cards for me. I had to become accustomed to doing things solo. In turn this made me a strong-willed woman. The only thing I was ever jealous about in my adult life was families. Happy families and close families. Families who got on with each other, who hugged and kissed, helped and advised, who were there without end. To a family there is no such thing as an inconvenience. Devotion I guess it is called. This I envied with all my heart. I was not too shy to admit. At times within my life all I needed was a hug. Somebody who cared enough about me who would tell me, *"everything is going to be fine."* But like everything in my life, it was all only ever going to be a dream.

Discarding the thoughts about Charles and my wicked family as that was a myriad of years ago. Thinking there is no point, no reason for me to think about them any longer. That part of my life has been dead for an incredibly long period of time. I have no family, only I thereby it is nonsensical to dream. One can always wish, but how often does those wishes and dreams come true? With that the logic of desire is unsubstantiated to the point of being unfounded. There is neither sense nor need to look backwards. Keep looking ahead. That is all one can do, just look to the future, *my happiness lies within the upcoming days.* Forever being the person to ridicule myself, being condemned was all I knew, often to the point of being too hard on myself. Put-downs were all I could relate to. I was finally comfortable within my own body, my own skin. After many years of wishing I could trade my sexy body in for a woman I considered to be sexier. Not being able to predetermine that I would become the ultimate in that definition of my own wishes. This was the greatest gift for me, more so than the strength my family's brutality bequeathed.

When I accepted the hardships I would be subjected to due to my beauty, I found peace. I was able to deal with anything. My beauty was beyond compare, this brought me comfort in times of disappear. My strength found within, from everybody else's hatred ensured I would not die when they demanded me to, but when I was willing. Finally accepting myself for what I was and who I was. Just like Charles did. This was a very powerful thing for me to develop, when I had developed this ability it brought me great happiness. What else can one do when they are entirely alone in the world? The one soothing fact which brought me much comfort during times of melancholy was my attractiveness above all success would have scorned my family deeply. What I was guilty of believing was the healthiest thing I could have believed. Be successful, be happy it is the greatest revenge of all, it does not destroy your soul and it does not belittle you. In turn, making the wretched filled with resent destroying their souls further, because their sinfulness had no grounds yet it is boundless. In their own failure more spitefulness is born. They were unsuccessful within their vice. Failure for their iniquity is the best gift of all. Who needs family and who needs friends? All we need is to find peace within, happiness and strength then follows. This leaving one out of the reach of the ill doers, sequentially, hatred builds stronger and stronger within the pit of their soul. They destroy themselves. Sit back and enjoy the ride as they slowly kill themselves.

PART FIVE

The Unexpected and the Hated

CHAPTER EIGHTEEN

Swan Beautiful

After years of ridicule and mockery nobody could deny that I had grown into what was without doubt a striking woman. With curves in all the right places, beauty so strong nobody would attempt to discredit me, knowing it would be detected that they were jealous of my fortune. By the age of twenty-five, when my beauty was almost lost, I commenced a beauty routine to which I had never strayed. Dead Sea face masks, cucumbers on the eyes, ice baths, in later years skin peels, Botox, laser hair removal, I was too young for anything more drastic such as acid peels and face lifts. I would never live to see the day when I would need to resort to that kind of help. When I was twenty-one I understood that I would die young. I was guilty of thinking that eyebrow plucking was painful enough, but those laser peels were something from another world. Even the thought of it was too gruesome to contemplate. Yes, they worked and yes they were a girl's best friend, when it came to rolling back the years, but painful they also were. So much so each session brought tears to my eyes. That was brutality. Between hair colour and conditioning every two weeks, manicures and pedicures once a week, extra moisturising bubble bath once maybe twice a day, with a drop of milk like Cleopatra was renowned for in hers and lavender, to ensure my eight hours or more beauty sleep. Preserving my newfound beauty, was not an understatement. I was not about to let it slip away nor treat it shabbily. I was going to nurture it like I would my very own child. Beauty was something I had longed for all my life, to make it a little easier. Finding it most ridiculous how people can be fickle. Beauty possessed, you are on the receiving end of popularity and respect. Without it, one is the laughingstock of many. Forever to be rejected. It is never about the kindness in one's heart, the happiness their project through into other people's lives. It is never about the real things. Yet if one is beautiful and an utter contemptible bitch, one is liked more than those good precious souls who do good during their lifetime. For me, however, this was pure luck and I refused to disrespect it. By which time I had been on the receiving end of ugliness and beauty. I knew without hesitation which side I preferred. This was the chief reason when my good fortune was born, I did not go out of my way to harm another human being, mainly women. I never rubbed it in other women's faces to make them feel less than me, unlike the women who once did it to me. This is one difference between people who are pretty in their early years, they take it for granted, treat it badly as though it will last forever. Drinking heavily, that evil Russian vodka, after shots, and whatever else sets a person's insides on fire. With a gulp igniting the ruining of one's internal organs, over time destroying the outside too. Taut skin makes way for leather affect and dried out prunes. In the end women who smoke like a choo-choo train, gradually but eventually destroy what they were lucky to have been given from the start. I was not so lucky, thus I was not going to abuse my fortune. I have since referred to my looks as my fortune – simply because in the beginning when it all started for me, it gave me my fortune in many ways. Every so often I found myself wondering if the pretty girls I went to school with were still as pretty as they were, or had their early luck dissolved with time, was this simply poetic justice. No, I was no longer the ugly duckling. But are they now what I once was? Do they feel now what they once made me feel?

What I did not realise when I was a young girl, I was blossoming into a striking and charming flower? My school friends would never have guessed I would turn out the way I have. If they see me now, oh how they would hate me and how I would love their hatred; revealing in it. Dancing in it. Proud to announce it would feel like I were bathing in money. Something else I did not apprehend at that time, were the best things in life come to those who wait. In the years since my painful and haunting past has taught me a great deal of patience. Patients of a saint, though I was far from being a saint. I waited, eventually achieving the result many have begrudged me. I

90

was without doubt a desirable woman. With a more desirable mind. At first I questioned it. By the age of twenty-one I came to know this without my own reservations. These assets I used to excel in life. I used them in a justly honourable and sincere way however, many men have harmed me and many women have hated me. Guilty of being a pain in the ass this being a compliment nonetheless, some of the greatest compliments are found in the insults the jealous voice. Mankind harmed me as my beauty was beyond compare; they wanted a piece of me, not metaphorically speaking regrettably. Men still to this day feeling they own the world and everything in it. Those powerful men with status and control would be the guiltiest of this philosophy. Women are their possessions to play with discarding at their mercy. Women hated me for stealing attention away from them. I was everything they wanted to be, but being honest with themselves even if it was only in silence, knew they did not have what it took to match me. I was that beautiful. They could forget all notions of surpassing my flawlessness, in every aspect. Engaging hatred within these women, including many hateful thoughts and wishes of badness to fall onto me, between voodoo dolls and chants of sacrifice, who knows if their curses worked and this is what brought me immense pain over the many passing years, or if it was written in the stars. Due to the fact I refused to degrade myself, falling neither to the wayside nor to their level of being wretched, this inspiring many further detestable wishes. *"Hell has no fury like a woman's scorn."* When it is multitudes of women, their venom can be multiplied by at least ten million, making them unforgivable in their nature.

PART SIX

Rewind

CHAPTER NINETEEN

Memories

Followed by more persevering unconstructive memories, hence drifting in and out of thoughts about my second husband Nicolas, who never knew I was married to Charles. I did not exactly not tell Nicolas about my first marriage, because I did not wish him to know. It was not the fear of him finding out what happened. Nobody found out the truth. I saw to that. There are no leads to follow. I am the only soul alive who knows; that tail goes to my grave with me unspoken. It was the pain which came with talking about the past. Instead of facing my hurt I have forever covered it up, fixating a brave face for the world to see, pretending the past did not exist. Pretending that I'm alright. The crippling ache which formed deep down within, like a barb wire fencing wrapped around my heart and every internal organ. Expurgating me from the inside out. Bit by bit my blood had no choice but to drip, as did my tears. It was only when I thought of Charles my entire body felt warm with love and tenderness. This had been the only time I was loved and had truly loved in return, despite Charles not being my ideal, but no man is perfect. No woman either for that matter. With guilt dragging me down while tears of regret were shed. As soon as I let my emotions down and became sentimental about Charles, Emilio and his malicious family go straight for the attack. Right where it hurts. Paralysing me. This is what haunts me indefatigably; Nicolas, Philippine and Emilio. During my hell I had more than enough time to reminisce. They haunt me unremittingly, with no mercy ever granted; I am never free from their grasp. Unsure as to how I can become free of them.

Certain I am lost for all time. Unable to be one hundred percent honest with myself at that time, for the first time, as the scars were too much for me to analyse, as a result I cannot say goodbye and put my misery to rest. A limbo if ever there was one. Oh yes they may be dead now, but they are not gone. Their physical bodies no longer linger around their impressive grand home, but they remain though it is on a different level, even if they cannot be seen, they are still with me of that I have no doubt. I can feel them. Their eyes are never off me. Not for a moment. Every day and every night they never leave me alone. Their ghosts float about not solely in my mind, but around this house. Not in the same sense as in the movies, where white figures fly about rooms and mess with one's mind, doing everything possible to ensure I go out of my mind. I mean their evilness was such a strong force when they were alive, that it still lingers, never to perish with them. Never to cease, only to remain, perhaps until the day I die, or the day I get rid of this house. They are too evil to enter heaven, perhaps they're competition for Lucifer. Nobody wants them. Perhaps even they are lost.

But how does one get rid of people that are dead? Their ghosts!!! The memories The hell?

Corpses are easy to dispose of but has anyone figured out a way to discontinue the memories of their previous actions, their torture when they once lived? Or do they actually win in the end. Torture for the rest of my life.

It is not as though one can call upon the Catholic Church to request the Pope to orchestrate an exorcism, and expel the poignant memories to where they rightfully belong. Hell! That would be too easy. Confessing to a priest was also out of the question, considering the new laws assigned granting them to breath those secrets, if it is such a harsh one for them to keep. The height of hypocrisy when one considers the secrets they keep for themselves: the sexual abuse on young defenceless children, the lies, the threats, the bullying. Their glory. Their reprehensible actions. They would stab their congregation in the back, perchance, quite literally if it meant their names were not dragged through the mud, yet again, in order to keep their depraved and vile secrets. Their ungodly sexual compulsions. Getting nuns pregnant and the taking away from innocent children, who they should protect. The plotting and the discretization of others ensuring they get away with their illegal and corrupt activities. Listening to confessions from the distraught, dictating to the rightful path of absolution. One hundred *"Hail Mary's"* and ten *"Our Fathers"*. This will buy ones way into heaven. Who are sinful creatures to ordain a righteous remedy? A cure for the evil. The very reason why I changed my religion with Charles when we married. Shame and humiliation was all I found from being a Catholic. I cannot trust anyone. This is what life has taught me. Without any doubt it was best I kept my secret to myself, always recalling:

"You cannot trust anyone but yourself and even then be sceptical."

With the evilness which possessed Nicolas's family they could not have let me get away that easily to start afresh. To be a happy young woman I justly deserved. The Beaumont family could not be that forbearing. Being evil was all they knew, the very reason why they sought after the young and the impressionable. The Catholic Persists, their MO is searching for the most vulnerable children, the families who trust them the most, manipulating them into silence, in order to harm the innocent. This is something which cannot be denied, not even by Pope Benedict, after concealing the names of the guilty parties in order to save them their punishment, he would become even more hated than he is today, regardless of remaining pope or not. Expecting their congregation to pay ten percent of their income to them in tithing, is he not responsible for ensuring our children's safety when they represent the church? It is only because of those who pay their tithing they live in grandeur. While they claim to live humbly such as Moses and the rest of the disciples, chiefly Jesus Christ himself. The small children whose lives are destroyed by their abuse, not doing anything to deserve to have the rest of their life ruined. The memories of their abuse exposed to. More than anything they deserve justice. I did not do anything to my abusers. Underestimating my strength, I was not cut off to life or pain. It was due to this which had kept me alive as long as this.

"I have lived this life before, I am no longer a stranger, my new family reminding me too much of my old. From those I have ran away from in order to escape the clutch of misery."

95

This was a chilling thought which I was unable to shake. At this time I was even more of a lonely woman, after my second husband Nicolas died after four and a half years of marriage. Being lonely was something I knew too well. I was a scholar of loneliness and doing everything alone, as being alone most of my life I was. I was too young back then to know such loneliness. We are not always given the things we need or deserve. This is something the young should never feel.

When I first met Nicolas I was a young woman of twenty. Whereas, my now departed husband was twenty-eight years older than I. Nicolas was a rich Swiss business man who was very successful within his conglomerates, his wine vineyards throughout Switzerland, France, Greece and Italy. As well as many other endeavours, even those shady ones I never knew the details of, nor did I wish to know. Ignorance is bliss when one only wishes to be happy. I did not mind a little overlooking here and there, so long as I was loved. To know too much is when happiness is sure to be tarnished. Accountants do it all the time. Skim a little here and skim a little there. A perk of the industry. Unsuspecting to reality at the beginning. My obliviousness was going to prove to be my killer. Nicolas seemed like a great man at the start, all men do, some women too. Turning out to be anything but what he had portrayed himself to be. The only truth he perhaps indeed spoke, was the fact he was a rich man, not through his own efforts however and that his name was Nicolas. Having no impeachable proof to dispute this, regardless of my reliable gut feelings of disbelief. Those little flutters which indicated I was correct, when shady issues would ring the bell on my door. Charles was not a perfect man but a better man than Nicolas he certainly was. Between them there was no comparisons. I mourned Charles death to the point I was going out of my mind with sorrow. Unable to shake Charles's memory, living a dream, running after the past. With Nicolas I was not lonely because I missed him and mourned him like a wife ought to, I was lonely because I had been kept a prisoner inside a house which was never my home. Not even now. All it is, is a roof and walls keeping out the cold and the rain. Shelter from the harshness outside. It may sound foolish, yes I hated them, all three of them, Nicolas, Philippine and Emilio, yet they were the only company and interaction I had and came to know in almost five years. It does not take long to feel isolated when being held against one's will. My life for the duration of time I was married to Nicolas I was not living life, I was simply existing; sometimes when I think back, I was not even doing that. I was only there, only inhaling and exhaling. Sleeping, and when I was awake I was day-dreaming. My days wasted. Nothing of any importance. All men turn out to be nothing at all how they were in the days when things were new. This is their disguise merely to lure and to seduce. Behind the sweet and kind smiles, the corny jokes, the gentlemanly attentiveness, those long intimate and highly suggestive stares there is an opaque reason. With men it is never too long before the truth prevails. Yet the truth is nearly always known and nearly always the same. They can keep the act up until they attain their desires, if they have the patients. To keep it up long-term is impossible for the male sex, due to their impetuous and immature ways. They are overgrown children. Tantrums surface. Regardless of the Ivy League education a man may have been lucky enough to have father pay for, men are all the same. Whether he is thirty or ninety, he is still momma's little boy of five his whole life through, suckling on her milk tit. Therefore their cards, vice and dices shows within a relatively short space of time and the male sex shows his face. This is an advantage for the female prey that happens to be in his sights. Affirming this is one thing I am lucky to understand about men.

Nicolas Beaumont was married previously, but his first wife died many years prior to meeting me. Nicolas never mentioned his previous wife; it was almost as though he forgot about her, or he was never married. After Nicolas's death I could barely recall his wife's name, it had been that long since he mentioned her. The first night we met in Zermatt in 2001, was the only time he breathed her name in fact. Finding it rather strange that Nicolas was as vague about his marriage with Gabriella as he was about most things. There were many times throughout our marriage I recollect; he appeared to be detached to his late wife, including the event leading up to her death. Finding it even more peculiar how he never visited a grave, or had an urn on the mantelpiece. Never remembering a date to mourn her, a birthday, not even their wedding anniversary. There were no photographs about the house, no photo albums with her inside. A strange atmosphere thus created during our five-year marriage, anytime I have tried to ask him questions regarding Gabriella, changing the subject quickly. His tone becoming assertive, hostile enough to stop me in my tracks, this was his aim and he triumphed.

That scowl of his face made the hairs on the back of my neck and my arms stand up from pure fear. Shivers up and down my spine. My heart shaking. Often imaging his hands around my throat when he would explode. Becoming unsettled to the point he would sweat like a pig in Africa. A grey complexion would cover his face. A look of sheer culpability kidnapped his expression, with fear transpiring through his cool blues. To be more accurate, he presented himself as a guilty man, struggling to control his demeanour to conceal that guilt, failing gravely. Opposed to veiling he publicised. Frequently reminding me of those serial killers seen on death row, who agree to record documentaries, with that distant look in their eyes from life and people, their guilt obvious to see. Shark like eyes. The eyes every member of my family have. Incapable of hiding the truth. At no point during our life together did he demonstrate having had any self-reproach, remorse, or shame. Not risking upsetting him, I refrained asking questions. It was better for me that way. I wasn't being selfish, I knew it was too late for Gabriella. I could not help her. She was before my time. I had no doubt that someone was before her. Often referring to my sixth sense as my sick sense, it indicated she was dead and long gone, without a christen burial. Going as far as to firmly believing her remains were still in this house, somewhere, or at least the garden. Somewhere out there in that vast forest. Beneath a weeping willow tree, in the pond. Perhaps bricked into a wall in the attic or the cellar. Thinking deeper, it may not be the most obvious place. Nicolas was like a hurricane when he got started. There wasn't anything powerful enough to yield him. As Nicolas showed only after being married a brief period of time, he had a violent way about him. To be entirely honest even to myself, the thought about it all give me an eerie feeling, from head to toe accompanied with a chill up and down my spine. This man frightened me like I had never been frightened before. The only nice thing I heard him say was in Zermatt in 2001, was she was beautiful, and until me he thought Gabriella was the most beautiful woman he had ever laid eyes on. Then he seen me and I won that trophy in his heart. Finding his approach and technique overdone; but he was older, how much harm could he cause?

Going onto assume mainly for my own comfort, although my gut conveyed I was indeed wrong, that he loved Gabriella so much, it was too painful for Nicolas to discuss. Perhaps too uncomfortable for him to remember their life together, if he indeed loved her as much as he portrayed. This would be an acceptable answer. People do deal with death and grieve in many different and strange ways. Ways which cannot be translated to others easily. People's lives are private domains, the things they do cannot be easily explained to others, thereby society does not have the right to judge or ask questions. Those who judge shall be judged. Everybody has the right to live and have their secrets. The party grieving may not be aware of their improper behaviour. Therefore, unfortunately due to one's ignorance onlookers categorise others as being guilty, strange or weird, this being most unfair. What people do not comprehend they are frightened of. No myth undoubtedly a fact. Therefore one should not judge, and if so (as it is human nature and they shall judge regardless), not too harshly. As a consequence out of fear advising myself:

"Perhaps he was ashamed of the way he treated her and the guilt is eating him up alive, as he may have been physically even sexually abusive with her like he is with me. Maybe. Maybe not."

Every so often my imagination would get carried away, imagining all sorts of deep dark dangerous even depraved transactions which may have went on between them.

"Was it the same kind of immoral incidents he has exposed me to?"

It was a sensitive topic to be addressed. In those days I had no idea how sinister the truth was. Figuring my imaginings were just that, nothing more than crazed notions. One thing which came with knowing myself as well as I did, which horrified me greatly, was recognising the fact my gut feelings were never wrong. Longing all these years to be incorrect even once, or at the very least half wrong. But I was always right, exactly right! During the noxious times how I hated those intuitions. Opposed to being helpful and coming to my aid, I often felt those warnings were more of a disability, as my life with Nicolas had become one of fear and blackness. A life filled with secrets and suspicion. Then again what marriage does not have their fair share of secrets and suspicion, lies and deception that is indeed what the spine of a marriage is? It may not be this way in the beginning, or else it might; it purely depends on the individuals in question and what they are seeking from being married, but either way, somewhere along the path of marital living, lies and secrets will display. There are always lies and something to hide when a couple has taken their vows. May it be a secret from the past, or secrets within the marriage? A life I had come to wish I did not have to lead, but I was not willing to capitulate to their requests for my death. At least not the easy way.

When Nicolas and I first met in Zermatt while I was on holiday, I was young bright-eyed and optimistic about my life. I had much in me to give and to accomplish. Plans were what I had, big plans and the drive. I had never been on a proper holiday until that time, so before going back to school after the winter holidays ended, I felt I needed a change of scene. A break to get me back on track once I returned home. I was currently studying for my Bachelor's degree in Medicine; I was a very intelligent and dedicated woman, with an incredibly mature mind. Possessing exactly what it took to get far. It had seen me through the toughest times in my life, subsequently making me grateful I was not wrapped up in cotton wool as a little girl, as the past events have given me balls. So much so, many people had mistaken me for older than my years, proclaiming I was filled with wisdom for such a young woman. My mind was indeed older than my body. This was a kind and very much earned crown. It pleased me that people observed that way about me. I had a great deal to prove to myself. Always being told I cannot and will not amount to anything. I had to prove to myself that the people saying those negative things were the fools and not I. Therefore I went on holiday alone to get away from my tragic demanding life. Take a pause to forget all about the problems which had presented themselves recently and from having to prove something all the time. Hunger to achieve, hunger for anything can sometimes drive one insane, it was starting to happen to me. For the first time in my life I was doing something for myself. At first it felt weird. I felt selfish, I figured I was wasting money and I ought to be prudent, but when life gets on top of you, you have to do what you must to relax and let go of the pressure. We all deserve to be spoilt sometime. It may have been only a holiday and not exactly something to do with rocket science, nor was it mentally challenging, but for me it was the craving to forget about my catastrophic life which awaited me over the border in Italy, which had haunted my every breathing moment since beginning. If there is such a thing as being born with bad luck, then I Nicolette was the poor unfortunate child who was. Every aspect of my life was one of misery and abuse. From childhood to womanhood the abuse never ceasing, merely changing in the form of the attacker. If any soul deserves good luck it was certainly me, even if I say so myself.

CHAPTER TWENTY

Perfection

Immediately falling in love with the picturesque scenery which surrounded me and how surprisingly safe this charming country was. I had no doubt badness and danger would not find me. No such things as drugs, prostitution or Mafias existed in heaven on earth. The government would not permit such scum to subsist here, of which I was most grateful. Giving birth to a higher admiration. With the only concern of being attacked by a stray mountain goat! Providing I was terribly unlucky. I was that unlucky, but I had much more demanding situations and people to be concerned about, in contrast to a stray mountain goat. On the other hand it could have been fun. I suppose the only thing I could have done would be to grab its horns and laugh. A lease of life and adrenaline. A much needed laugh. On my flight to Geneva enthusiasm filled me before having landed. All I could see were the glorious Alps, water and dark green alpine trees never witnessing anything as breathtaking. My heart was captured from the sky. The minute I landed at Geneva airport I caught the train to Zermatt; the train station is conveniently located beneath the airport, an advantage for any stranger. A genius idea. When I first arrived many years ago I became captivated by the beauty of the countryside. There was a great deal of countryside to be seen. Truly grateful for the four-hour train ride it took to reach *The Grand Hotel*, presenting me the most wonderful chance to catch sight of the country's most remarkable settings, from a first class viewpoint. With the train's large windows on each side of the cabin, surrounding each panorama like an elaborate picture frame, parading a Raffel chef-d'oeuvre, affording me the perfect opportunity to observe the scenery. The lakes and mountains, streams, waterfalls and parks, vineyards, thousands of old buildings, it appeared to be never ending, bringing me thrill after thrill, hour after hour. Becoming greatly disappointed at first when the train reached the station at Zermatt, when I was forced to exit at the square and wishing I did not have to leave to check into the hotel. This disappointment was short-lived lived. Although I was exhausted after my flights, struggling to keep my eyes open and to remain awake. The long winding train ride I was fascinated beyond compare with all the surroundings and with each surprise I was presented with not wanting to give into tiredness as views such as these I was not blessed with seeing on a daily basis. Although Lake Garda being beautiful and charming but in a very different way. Something new came over me, not knowing what it was called, only knowing I wanted the feeling of this new and exciting emotion to remain. My brain acting as a camera, attempting with great difficulty to capture the beauty which surrounded me, fortunate to have seen a great deal, deflated I could not have seen everything on offer by the passing train. When I exited the train station and was greeted by a driver from the hotel, with a charming black horse and a blue carriage. The horse was not like the horses I witnessed in the Dominican Republic, those who sat outside the hotels waiting for guests to be taken sightseeing. The beautiful sight which met me on the square was healthy and was the proud owner of a shiny coat. Pleased to see that there were no bones on show. My face hurt from so much smiling and polite greeting. Astounded by how much splendour was in one place, as I was being transported through the small village.

When I first went sightseeing in Geneva, Bern, Zurich, Visip and Lausanne, I felt such a feeling of amazement as to how exquisite everything around me was. No one part lacked. Like a child in a toy shop behaving like a magpie, everything shiny I was enthralled by and wanted. Wishing that Santa did exist. My eyes could not match the speed of the train or the speed at which my brain was processing the surroundings. Usually finding that when I became interested in something, after a while the thrill of it all would vanish, as a consequent everything would become stale. In the past five years which I had lived and remained within the Swiss borders, I have never lost the pleasure of being surrounded by the Swiss' splendour.

Never before known a country of such elegance from everyone residing there, nor people with such respect for others. Swiss citizens are the crème de la crème. They are in a league of their own, with no other country as a contender. Having read and understood what the definition of dignity was, but on no account known anybody to live it, work it not alone breathe it. To my relish this was not at act of attempting to be superior. It was natural for them. They are superior. It was in their blood to be at all times dignified and regal. To be simply just what they are. What they are is indeed a far cry from being plain or simple. I finally found a place I fitted in. No more did I have to feel uneasy. Every person my eyes seen and studied reminded me of an extension of the royal family. Perfect. Not anything like the over-the-top people of California or Florida. Wishing people throughout the world would take a page out of the Swiss' book that would be a perfect world. Idealistic, romantic but highly improbable. Despite the Swiss' perfection looking effortless, it was sincere to them, it was inborn. To anybody else from outside their country, attempting to be alike would pose a struggle. With contenders merely in their own minds, the Americans who claim and believe they are perfect, with the most wonderful nation in the world. They are simply delusional. The self-possession, in addition to stateliness was purely inherent from generation to generation. Never looking as though they struggle to be poised at all times, since it was in their blood. When a way of being is meant to be, then it never looks exaggerated. When one attempts to be more than what they actually are then and only then can the cracks of ill skill be discerned. They are not acting; their quite simply are living it. It is what Switzerland is legendary for. This country reaped opulence without being tacky or in excess. The people I found to be at all times casual but composed. Sloths are not the Swiss people, it is the Americans. America certainly does not parallel in any respect and could do with learning from the best.

The one thing I would always think of when I would be dining at restaurants was less is more. The very reason Switzerland could never be classed as being tasteless. For me it was the closest to heaven one could get on earth. This was how I wanted to live, where I wanted to live and where I wished to die, spending all of eternity. I knew if I were to spend every day and every night on Swiss soil whether it is in a six-foot deep whole or on land, I would be the happiest woman alive, or dead. Knowing if I was buried any other place I would turn over in my grave and never be at peace. A tortured soul I would surely become. This was the first place I had ever been, yet felt like I was at home, I belonged. All of my life I wanted to belong but never did. Not until now! Above all I loved the fact that these people have drive. More than anything I admire people with ambition. My philosophy about people without this ability quite bluntly has been, I find them to be intolerable that was the bottom line. The Swiss people work hard and are passionate about whatever they do. This was indisputably the most elite country on the map.

PART SEVEN

The Move

CHAPTER TWENTY-ONE

My First Move

The Swiss' splendour induced me to think about transferring colleges, from my station in Italy to the St. Gallen's College of medicine, after seeing how magnificent it was during my first visit. Invoking me to believe, that it would be much more soothing to live there permanently. It was my cure. For the first time I was genuinely elated. Switzerland became the therapy I needed to leave the past in the past. Where it rightfully belongs. This country to my own surprise instantaneously brought me peace. Peace in my heart, soul and mind. I could forget everything bad which had happened to me, in my life and precarious past. My family and my Charles could finally be put to rest and I could finally move on and live. LIVE, LIVE!!! For the first time.

I felt Switzerland was a virtuous and pure country, in turn, could only make my life richer. Despite the fact I was not originally from there I automatically felt devotion, becoming patriotic. When the Eurovision Song Contest is televised I rooted for Switzerland all the way. It's a pity I was too young to remember Celine Dion win for them. Including the Euro football matches, or Roger Federer at Wimbledon, it was Switzerland I supported. Not to forget the Winter Olympics. Finding how expensive Switzerland could be to reside, forced me to prepare my plans about relocating there flawlessly! I legitimately appreciated that I was not in the position to have to wait until I had earned my degree before moving. Thankful that my

Charles's savings and life insurance were more than enough to care for me for an indefinite period. Considering I was wise with the inheritance. Due to the large price tags associated on all land and properties. Intimidating me, regardless of having more than enough funding. I was amazed by the remarkable potential found within the country to progress in life, education furthermore health and wealth, due to the fact of the atypical prospects in my country of origin. From being highly educated people with high standards, they were on the top of the game when it came to finance, technology and medicine. If I was going to be sick, this was the country I wanted to be in to get better.

Delighted the Swiss people treated me as well as they have done, making me feel I was special. They liked me and accepted me. The Swiss liked me, me Nicolette, when people only hated me once they set eyes on me. But the Swiss, the country of respect, high class and everything special. I could not believe it, they actually liked me. In turn it made me proud. Proud that people of their class can and do accept me, but the lowlife's from my hometown treated me as though I were no better than an animal. A contagious disease. When it was only scum who always sought out to hurt me. When I didn't hurt anyone. After years of being segregated, it finally dawned on me that I was not the reject. I was not the person the problem lay with. They were the people who felt inferior to me. Not because I made them feel this way, they made themselves feel this way, due to how classy I am. I stood up tall, straight back, with pride, and respectability. I was educated, hence why they tried each chance they grasped at to discredit me, not wanting me to do well in life. When I have done. Not wanting for people who did not know me to realise the truth, how good of a person I am. This my enemies resented. Back in those days gone by, I thought I was the leopard, in actual fact I was the superior force and they knew it, therefore exiling me. They realised and acknowledged this over a decade before I did. When the inferior want to be more than they are, understanding they are inferior, they hunt for a means to harm the greater. Having to reduce themselves to being vicious and attempting to destroy everything good which came my way, wanting to take it away from me and everything substantial I've achieved. Neglecting how hard I have worked to accomplish all I have undertaken. They looked at my accomplishments as though I were handed everything on a sliver plate. Overlooking the sweat tears and heartache I underwent. The fighting I had to do. They were filled with loathing. Filth does not care about how hard people work. This was why I fitted in perfectly in Switzerland. I was high class and everything which was good. I was like them, they seen this, for this reason they accepted me. They considered me as one of their own. Through seeing their beauty and acceptance of me, this was the first time I was able to see my qualities, because of the gift they gave me. I was finally home. Why must it always be the good and righteous who suffer at the hands of the debauched? When will the game of life be fair? Is this what life is, a game for the corrupt to win, targeting the innocent, enforcing them to lose, to feed their egoistical cravings? What is the end objective? Is life meant to be this complicated? Or is it just the people in it who make it this way? Life is a devilish game, a game of pain. Some have the winning hand, while others must hold the losing. With the losing hand one must fall. Fall for all time, unable to ever stand again.

CHAPTER TWENTY-TWO

MY DEATH

When I die it will be either from a disease to which has overpowered my body and healthy blood cells by formidable microorganisms claiming my life, or by my own hand. Yes, my own hand. When I say I want to die, when I am ready and how I decide. Not when they are ready to end my life for me. Never that! Who are they to dictate? Many times feeling demoralised, I wondered why my life had to be one of abuse and being the victim. What about me was it that people wanted to take advantage of? What was it people hated about me so much from the onset? Was it because many have claimed I was the envy of everybody? But could so many people hold it against me for being as damn perfect as I am? Was my life designed to always play the role of being the injured, but at all times honestly being the victim? I had a face of an angel, the soul of a saint. Powerless to be the saint who was within. Could it have been my angelic appearance, my virtuous way of being which offended people? Why are those who are perfect, who are not rich and famous, hated more than those who are? While those who are rich and famous, are admired for their perfection and goodness. Why is it impossible for people to take a page out of the perfect person's life, make an effort to become alike, in contrast to becoming that much more imperfect? Why hate someone for being the way they desire to be? The logical perspective ought to be, figure out what you want to be, try and try again, until one reaches their goal. Not envying someone until hatred is seeded within to permit hatred to grow, spiralling out of control only to commit more offensive sins.

CHAPTER TWENTY-THREE

IF

'

If you believe,
Truly believe,
Then nobody can harm you,
They will be set free.

When someone tries to hurt you,
They hurt themselves.
When someone tries to belittle you,
They belittle themselves.

When someone tries to be the winner
By someone else's lost.
They are not the winner
And you have surely not lost.

CHAPTER TWENTY-FOUR

The Gamble

December 3, 2001

Deciding to stop in at a bar and restaurant I had fortuitously stumbled upon while mountain climbing, coming down from the Matterhorn. Fancying a drink before going back to my hotel to rest for an hour, maybe even taking a swim prior to dinner. The exterior caught my eye as I strolled through the idyllic village. I was freezing cold, shivering. Necessitating something to warm me. Something stronger, something which the effects would last me longer than a cup of cappuccino! It was a small and intimate place, not exactly huge by any means but very relaxing indeed. Not too ultra-modern. Not too ancient. Just the right balance of each. The ambiance was tranquil. It was the first place my mind felt as peace to think. Adoring the fact it was essentially built in the shape of a boat. I could not stand when establishments were symbolically named after certain things, without any correlation and parallel link from one thing to another. I still can't; age has not altered me in that regard. Simply naming a business after an emblematic article or person failed to impress me. Failing to understand why people must do such a thing, thinking it was simply a means to impress. A means to be grander than one actually was. This place was wonderful and unspoiled. Something which drew me there. Was it destiny? It took me years before I realised what it was. On reflection I found the answer. When I finally put my finger on the reason I found happiness again. Ordering a shot of bourbon to hit the spot quickly, warmth immediately felt, then having a glass of white wine, my customary drink while out in public, in a bar named the "Snowboat" located at the bottom of the glacier river in Zermatt. Forever hiding the fact I truly enjoyed a much stronger alcoholic drink while at home away from prying eyes unable to be held witness against me. It would not be considered respectable. There are standards and rules set in stone and must be adhered to. At home anything goes. Rape. Murder. Alcoholism. Crazed sexual predators.

The train ride back to Geneva would take a lengthy four hours. Knowing I could take my time as the trains departed every twenty-four minutes. A feature I appreciated. Affording me more time to enjoy the places I became mesmerised by. The days went in fast. They always do when I found myself feeling content. As I was training to be a doctor back in Italy, figuring it was instinctual to be accurate, punctual at all times. Everything had to be exact. If it wasn't, it could potentially mean the difference between life and death. I adapted this mind track in everything I did. In turn this was what made me perfect. Even when it came to a hobby, like gardening, everything was done exactly like it said on the back of the packet. Guilty of being an authoritarian when it came to things being done just right. Not because I was a control freak. I simply cannot stand having to redo things. It takes too much time. It is a waste of life. Most times we only have one shot, one moment. Then it's gone never again to be recaptured. Living life and do everything in that life as though it was the last minute no second chances are to be guaranteed.

The bar was open plan, Nicolas could see through into the entire building located at the front, as he was walking by on his way to climb the Matterhorn Mountain, shortly after I stopped in. I caught his eye. Instinctively he instantly changing his mind, modifying his plans, deciding to come into the bar. His goal, to break the ice with this fiery beauty before his impious eyes. Nicolas knew in both his mind and heart, what he was doing was wrong but my beauty was too breathtaking he could not resist. He found me too enticing. The stranger before him was his exact type of woman. The kind of woman he has been looking for his entire life. He could not walk away from that. What man could? It has been globally known for decades, men mature much later than women. If they ever do! Not even Gabriella, Nicolas's first wife, was perfect to this degree. And she was a rare beauty. A precious find. One he never should have let escape his grasp.

When Nicolas first met Gabriella he was besotted by her, thinking no other women could compare to her greatness. She was a Goddess. Like everything in Nicolas's life things were short lived. When it came to me he thought differently. I possessed all the breeding he favoured in a woman. After twenty-eight years of searching for the right woman, it is not possible to walk away so easily when he has seen her. Instantaneously capable after all his searching to interpret what I was about by a single glance. So he proclaimed. Nicolas was rather proud of that ability, considering it took many years to acquire. All of his twenties and thirties. Bragging about his special skill often. Using it as a weapon. A netting to trap prey. A gun to shoot dead. His only hope was that I was as intelligent as I appeared. Many attractive enticing women had fooled him (and the rest of the male race) in the past, by looking and acting the part but failing when it came down to the test. Paying for it with their life for fooling him. The very reason for my dedication and years of practice. It always comes back to bite one in the ass when a job is sloppily done.

Standing at five foot two inches tall, I was considered a small woman, particularly in Switzerland. I have had a countless number of men tell me over the years small women are the best. Tall women were unattractive and unfeminine, in the Swiss, French, Italian and Austrians men's minds. However, tall and blonde women were more often than not what they were present with. Therefore, appreciating a change, something new, something special and unique was how they perceived it. With a very small frame, long auburn wavy hair, large green eyes, ivory skin, petite features, tiny ears and the cutest nose he told me he had ever seen. He thought my eyes were outstanding. Big eyes he adored, especially when they were magical like mine.

Nicolas told me, "Your eyes are like stars in the night. They brighten up the darkest corner."

With conviction I believe that eyes are the key to a person's true self and to their soul. The real truth lies within the eyes. It is the path to righteousness. Eyes tell a person's life story better than wrinkles unable to hide a single thing. The pain, the joy and the indifference are found within a person's eyes, whether the person who owns them know it or not. It cannot be controlled. Not like a fake smile. They tell the story of life accurately. Exposing the evilness or kindness within one. Eyes are like wrinkles upon a face, but better, they tell a unique tailored story, the journey of one's life. Unlike creases, in the sense they can be erased, eyes never hiding the truth. Everything revealed. Not even evil is able to get away with being uncovered. More than a dog which is said to be a man's best friend and diamonds are proclaimed to be a woman's, these are inconsequential when it comes to the imperative matters in life. Eyes are everybody's best friend if one knows how to read them. They can save a life. They have saved mine once or twice.

Nicolas entered the Snowboat staring at me with each step he took, not realising I was watching him with my peripherals. Unable to drag his eyes from me as he moved towards the bar where I was sitting. On approach, he claimed at a later date when confessing, he could smell the sweetest smell; it was my perfume. "Obsession," he was certain of it. As he wanted to avoid my construing his question, of what perfume I was wearing, by being sleazy, in contrast to being innocently inquisitive (despite knowing the answer). He refrained from asking despite it would have broken the ice. Breaking the ice is always the most difficult part; it is either the make or break. It is the most difficult, in so doing, the most important part. One chance. One moment. Never to be recaptured. With a lady such of this auburn, he could not risk the chance of destroying this fine opportunity. If he had scuttled this wonderful opportunity, he may not be alive in another twenty-eight years to find the next one. If he was lucky enough to be alive and kicking, who is to say a woman as young as I was at that time would want Nicolas then? Sometimes things are once in a lifetime. No matter what the circumstances, if the feeling is right and blood pumps like a wave and is strong enough, indicating someone is right for you, do not waste the chance for eternal happiness. Infinitive love, it is the most difficult crux to find. Not everyone is lucky enough to find it.

Sitting down at the bar, a couple of bar stools away from me. My heart fluttered. He was struggling to breath, his heart was beginning to thump within his chest. Finding me intoxicating. Nicolas ordered his customary brandy. With the look in his eye, I could have sworn he had enough to drink. Without one drop of alcohol in his system. A rich and cultured drink for a very rich and cultured man. I must admit that Nicolas was a well-travelled man, who oozed sophistication. He was a genuine scholar not one of those who acted the act, yet incapable of walking the walk. He earned a degree in law, in addition a degree in psychology at a university in Zurich, as well as at Saint Gallen, located in Geneva. Nicolas took great pleasure in possessing the ability to read people. To know ahead of time if they were sane as much as could be expected, or if one was dangerous. He was very able in reading people's body language, this he found beneficial throughout his life. Thus knowing, or at least having an idea as to what impressed certain types of people. Women in particular. It was always about women with Nicolas. This ability was what made him all the more cunning, unfortunately into the bargain all the more appealing. He knew how to allure. He knew how to charm and flatter ones ego. It was his tool. Sex appeal was also his most effective tool. The instrument for stealing a life. More so how to sweet-talk a woman's clothes from her body and to water her blossoming buds. He knew this best because he had an egotistical way to his character. He needed to be told how great he was. He needed to believe it. More crucially he needed others to not solely believe it, but know it. Not feeling great to Nicolas was a weakness. The ultimate insult. The one thing which would drive him to commit cold-blooded murder. Without regret, remorse of any kind. He would sooner die than feel unimportant. Yet understanding and appreciating that each candidate was different. He was skilled, able to know how to approach each individual to get what he was in quest of. After twenty-five years of luring he was masterful. His obsessive nature was what drove him; making sure his schemes were faultless. Nicolas could not deal with failure, it scared him senseless. Being used by a woman would have destroyed his entire being, unable to live with it, thus becoming cold and calculating. The only reason capable of driving him to commit suicide. His philosophy was to attain his desires, competitively even sexually, treat women badly, his purpose was to discard of them. It was the discarding of them which made him feel boundless. Pleasuring him more than sex. It was his orgasm. Just wanting to prove to a woman he could do it. Making her feel loved, treating her tenderly, proving how much he thinks of her, in order to achieve the end result. The climax to his game, this was better than any orgasm any woman could make him reach. Regardless of her beauty or tight pussy. The taking away of love. The insults given. After the façade and the relentless fucking, treating his women as though she were a bought and paid for corner girl, with a skirt stinking of many men's semen up and around her rear. Making them feel substandard. Never the other way about! If a woman had ever been cunning enough to fool him, knowing himself as well as he did, even if it was not well enough at certain times, it would literally have meant the end of his life. Killing himself through the sheer shame and loss of control. He was a sick man, sick in his mind, destroying his existence. Nicolas's mind was poisoned on glory. Self-attained glory. At that time I had no idea just how mentally ill or how severe his infirmity was. If I did, I would have without indecision not have fallen for his charismata. The most dangerous men have the most profound captivations. I had a hard and insufferable life; I had more baggage than Heathrow flings through its airport, perhaps on a yearly bases. I would love to be able to declare that I would have helped him, attempted to at least, but I was mentally dysfunctional in those days, I needed help myself. I could not have helped him even though I would have loved to, if I was able. But out of all honesty, who am I to attempt to help the mentally unstable? I would probably have fucked him up even more, good intentions or not.

Remembering how he explained to me what interested him in studying people and minds. His obsession started when he read an article about a Russian serial killer. Never wanting to get caught up in anything as deplorable. He wanted to know how one could read people's mannerisms, if they had traits of being a monster, or if they were ingenuous. He considered this knowledge to be of the utter most imperative, during his travels around the globe. Unprepared to remain safe by chance. Refusing to abstain from his lifelong plans to travel and become educated in other cultures. He yearned to learn as much as possible about people, their actions and traditions. He was a supreme diplomat in those days. He was smart enough to acknowledge the fact anyone can become a victim. Anyone can become a killer. And the same victim can become the killer. But not everyone has what it takes to be a serial killer, not even a cold-blooded murderer. He was also smart enough to realise that not everyone looks like a killer, therefore the people who could be mistaken as a predator, usually are not the guilty party the police are searching for. It can be the handsome-looking male, with his sweet talking lies and sexy smiles. Those gentle words he uses. And the best kisses a woman has ever been given. The sexy twinkle in the eyes making her soaking wet within a blink of an eye. The one a young female detective would sooner screw before sending him to life in prison for taking a life wanting her share of the delectable body.

Often like the Irish policing service ignoring the guilty party, impulsively jumping at the obvious. Never digging deeper. Doing their job. That takes time and is too much work. Without evidence they hunt the innocent party down, conducting themselves like tyrants, demanding that the innocent are the guilty. Without evidence of any kind, never mind impeachable prove, insisting that one is guilty of something they just are not. Hating and refusing to admit when they are wrong. It is in many public domains advertised their policing skills lack, therefore permitting dangerous people to walk the streets, free and without consequence for their prohibited actions, while they try to prosecute the most innocent. Unfortunately the innocent are condemned and convicted for being weirdos, known to be accused unfairly for other socially accepted members of society's crimes. As it is mostly the person nobody expects. The stereotype, sweaty, greasy, fidgety socially awkward, porn addict everybody is nervous of. The sinister baleful character kids around the neighbourhood egging his windows, playing mean childish pranks on and deplorable name-calling. Just out of being misunderstood even different. For the small-minded people, being different is no different to being a terrorist. The children who believe he has an old grandma or two buried in behind the walls of his house. Opposed to the clean-cut politician or prosecutor in their designer suits, fancy expensive cars, wining and dining in the most elite restaurants around town. Not forgetting the buying of charities and other wholesome undertakings to obscure his ruthlessness. A pillar of society tends to be less clean-living than they endeavour to publicise, the very reason for their reputable persona. One smear the good will not be remembered. Perchance, why so many serial killers get away undetected for as long as they do, to afford them the time to keep killing. The good acting and the correct poise, knowing not to fidget or look to the left-hand side repetitively, practicing looking people in the eyes at all times, and never crossing the arms. Using the best anti-perspirant ensuring their own body is not what gives away their guilt. Practicing their lines over and over, until it becomes second nature, not having to think what the next line will be. This becomes more believable. When a person is being questioned, hesitation of any kind is considered lying. Rightfully or wrongly. The faster a response, the more likely one is too be believed. Therefore practice is paramount. Continually practicing their lines and facial expressions in the mirror, safeguarding they make the right face at the proper time, making sure they give the appropriate façade. Not ever to give half a performance. Rehearsing what types of questions would be asked of them, if they were to be questioned and which tones to use, or perhaps not to use. Yet at all times remembering how important it is never to overact. Not overly portraying anything, especially when attempting to illustrate they were the victim. If the European police are anything like the Irish police, then they will be useless at detecting the guilty. It is too often a common occurrence. The most useless and unprofessional *muppets* in a uniform one will ever encounter. This is a good thing for somebody who is actually guilty, hence the very reason why their streets have increased in violence rapes and deaths, there are sure to get away with their crimes. Still, if they are caught it is no shock that murderers and paedophiles walk around the streets without little or no prison time served. Does this really sound like a legal system or more of a paradise for wrongdoers and egotistical assholes to fuel their self-worth?

CHAPTER TWENTY-FIVE

Charismatic Act

As a young man Nicolas learnt plausibly his most vital lesson when it comes to landing a woman. As little as it may appear at first glance, ultimately being the fundamental winner, a classy woman as a rule refrains being intrigued by a man who orders beer or rum. For this reason, he knew by ordering a brandy would more than likely catch my eye, as it did most women. Stylish women. Women of a higher class. This was a test for me without me realising it; but I did realise what he was doing, however, I did not enlighten Nicolas. Defeating the purpose. I held my cards close to my chest. Not once prematurely flashing my hand. He wished to play games, I did not mind playing to win. As long as one knows they are in play or being played one has every chance of winning. A dance with the devil. A twirl to the end. I did not mind letting Nicolas win, more accurately, letting him think he won. He was too dangerous of a competitor to lose. Men are easy to tease, merely stroking their ego is all it takes in most circumstances. It's so easy to toy with men. Too easy – sometimes it's sickening. Unless a man has been used abused and thrown away like a used up pieced of cheap beef before, not worth sinking one's teeth into. In that case, he is a professional and won't let it happen again. A skeptic to all women, even the best of the best. Lessons learnt. Eyes opened. Bitterness seeded. I was holding the winning hand in this contest; I will laugh longest and last. It will be a long and tiresome game, a game of many different chances in advantages.

When a man, any man is seeking a woman's affections, a smart woman will ignore him. Not dancing his tango. Taking her step. When a man gets his way too often, complacency seeps in, a woman's worst nightmare commences. But when a woman gets her way too often she is like a dragon engulfed in a raging fire. I did not flash him my hand by reacting. Poker face was I. Thus, from this time Nicolas was impressed and starting to fall under my spell. Mesmerised by my charm. I was aware of his game. He was unaware of mine. He was starting to eat out of my hand like a little lost starving puppy. In essence, he was curious as to what impressed this flaming beauty before his lustful eyes. He knew I was a hard woman to win. This made him that much more interested, thus determined to succeed. Wondering how far he would have to go, how hard he would have to try. By this time fully aware that captivating this particular woman would enunciate something of a problem. I enjoyed making matters problematic for men. They should never be given anything easily. They respect a woman better when they are not treated as well. Treat a man like a king when he is not, enjoying the perquisites yet the woman is still beaten down like a tramp this is inevitable. Believing I was worth every square inch he would have to invest to earn, before complying with my requests and having me all to himself, to toy with or simply do anything he wanted with. Typically dissolute as he was a degenerate. When it came to other women, Nicolas was not willing to neither capitalise nor devote as much time as he was with winning me over. Enthralling me. I was the woman who boiled his blood and started an inferno in his loins. To Nicolas it was the chase which gave him the most pleasure. Pursuit gave his immense ecstasy. Like most men wanting to prove their ability, thus becoming bored consequently, acting like mama's spoilt little baby, who wants his dummy. Mama's tit. His reason for becoming bored with his first wife Gabriella and dismissing the way too easy and very much a sex addict Sophie. The type of woman men use abuse and fuck off. No time for during the daylight hours or would want to be seen with in public. Sophie the woman with no self-respect, respect for any other human being opposed to Nicolas; a woman without a conscience. The cutthroat sex beast who would stab anybody in the back as soon as look at them, doing so with a smile embracing her face and delight projected through her reptile eyes. To her own disadvantage. The one thing she did not grasp was she tried too hard. I learnt the hard way not to trust anyone who tried too hard. It is they who have a hidden agenda. They who aim to pleasure for a particular purpose. It is they who have a motive, a secret, a goal and they who are out for themselves, in so doing will do whatever it takes to achieve their desires. Even if it means taking a life. The type of person I describe has no morals, principles or sense of right from wrong. The people I describe are those who lured me only to destroy my life.

That very first day Nicolas was aware and everyone else who was captivated by me, I was not like other women. More importantly, I was aware of this. I owned quiet assurance and quiet confidence. Oozing sex appeal but not in a brash fashion. Never in anyone's face. It is only whores who make spectacles of themselves. I came to know this not because I had a high unsuitable opinion about myself, nor was it within my blood to be pompous. It was because I practiced. I wanted to be alluring, I wanted to captivate. I took note of men as they watched other women. The reason I came to know this so well was because I observed men! What men liked, desired, most importantly what repelled them. In the beginning I sat in the background unnoticed, blending in. Not a stitch of makeup upon my face. Hair curly and undone. Dressed like the lesser of society. Part of the furniture, simply acting as though I was a nonentity. The best way to learn and learn much is to become a shadow. Much is to be seen when one is invisible. Mouth shut, head down, eyes scanning quickly. No small talk, absolutely no conversation. Certainly no laughing. People remember. I would sit for hours watching the most sophisticated women, the most mysterious men. I sat in bars and restaurants, parks and museums. Even sitting on street benches watching the world go by. I learnt my mannerisms adapting to my womanhood. In doing so I learnt how to be a woman. It was something I already had in me, I just did not know how to let it out, how to use it. I was never shown. I practiced never-endingly until I perfected my mannerisms, my charm, my ability to be captivating, doing it like no other woman could. I perfected my abilities. I perfected me as a woman, as a person who had to survive in this unrelenting cesspit of a world.

I was not blessed like other women. I did not have a family to support me, to turn to, to love me. I have never had any of these things. I was very much a lone. Too alone. To be too alone makes a person unhealthy. I had to depend of me. This gave me hunger, the yearning and the burning fire in my gut to push myself to be somebody who was wanted. The only thing I wanted in my early days was to be loved. That was all. That was all, but too much. I detected what it was men found sexy about these women, adapting their intriguing ways, yet bettering them when I had finalised my skills. They were simply doing enough. I was going to do my best. I was going to be unique. I give my all or I do not give at all. I may not have been the prettiest girl back then, but I was going to have a winning way about me, a mesmerising way. And I did. Capable of stopping men in their tracks. Distracting them from their important business, being important to the magnitude that they put me first, before all business and work, before money. This was my ambition. I knew I would be someday significant to somebody. When a woman can become more important to a businessman than money and work then she is a winner. Special. Above the rest. She possesses something magnificent and rare. There are many beautiful women who walk this world, but not many women have such a disarming aura to their character. I do not know if this can be learnt or if it is something which comes naturally. Or is it pure luck? I never do anything without giving it all I have. When I dare endeavour onto something I gave every fibre, every drop of salty sweat, I give my blood, my tears, my energy, my heart. Above all, I gave my time.

Investing my time to sitting in front of my bedroom mirror performing my role as a woman, training myself to be a lady. Almost as though I were a serial killer, perfecting my alluring techniques. Dressing up, dressing down. Blending in like a bodyguard. Reading magazines to study the fashions, posses, makeup, and elegance. Spending hours which ran into days, the days emerged into weeks and those long and tiresome weeks transformed themselves into two long years. Intense years of training. The amount of makeup I went through practicing was worth a small fortune. To help keep my figure I spent my money on cosmetics, hair colour and clothes instead of food and treats. The only treat I did allow myself was purely for professional purposes. Wine, I needed to practice my dinning etiquette. I needed to be certain how much alcohol my body was capable of withstanding, in order to prevent an embarrassing situation from developing leaving myself vulnerable. Adapting to a rich man's mind-set humiliation could never be pardoned. Ever! Sitting on the toilet seat before the largest mirror in the house rehearsing my sitting, my etiquette for every occasion. Pretending to be at expensive restaurants, and opulent galas accompanied by sophisticated men who thought enough of me to wine and dine this nobody. They wished to spend time with me, their goal, to put a smile on my sad innocent-looking face. Make the winter stars shine and dance in my eyes. In time they put me on a pedestal. This pedestal made me feel as though I were living in a palace living like a queen. For the first time I had my own podium, people looked up to me, admired me and wanted me. Above all this they listened to what I had to say about anything. They wanted to hear what I Nicolette had to say, yearning to learn from me. Me Nicolette! Walking up and down in a straight line the entire length of my bedroom for hours, rehearsing my walk, my famine sexy walk, which would not be overdone but eye-catching nonetheless. Hips swinging, feet placed down before me not too heavy or hard, but with great care. Demonstrating grace. I applied my posture and looked like a queen on my thrown. I held my head high and bared my expressionless face. My mask. Not giving away my emotions. Giving away one's reactions, emotions of any kind could become ones death. Their weakness. Opening one up for attack. Suppressing them is undoubtedly a lifesaver. This I learnt from the Scandinavians. I gave it my all. I gave me my all. Otherwise there is no point? I am not a woman who is about half measures. It is those same half measures which could leave me gravely wounded or have me killed.

I was hard on myself. Being hard on myself was the only thing I understood, my family treated me abominably growing up. Nothing I did was ever good enough. So I became a perfectionist. I did not stop practicing nor going out and testing my charms on men, when I was good enough. I learnt from other women's weaknesses; this was when I decided what I was going to do with my life. Rich men would become my career. I had the right amount of drive and ambition, these two attributes are needed to get anywhere in life. It seems to me that the more one lives life, with each passing day the harder life becomes, with no clemency granted. This world is not designed to give mercy. That is what heaven is for. One could be pardoned for thinking that the longer one lives, with anything the better one becomes at doing it. The more experience one has one becomes accustomed to, the easier it will come to pass. Any wise man of a hundred and ten, can confirm it gets more complicated with each year that passes by. More baggage is accumulated. The very reason why older people become shut off. Ignoring most things of unimportance. Not taking things to heart because they have developed an iron skin. An armour which protects them from the things which do not matter, the things which would have broken their hearts during their youth.

Once I knew I was perfect and capable, I sought after what I wanted, at all times attaining my desires. Never failing. I could never have allowed that. (I was the perfect competitor to compete against Nicolas Beaumont). For the first time in my life I was grateful that my malevolent family was as hard on me as they were, it gave me colossal strength and innovativeness. Vitality to prove them wrong, when they would put me down, claiming I would never amount to anything. Anything that was good. My abilities scorned them greatly. Refusing to settle for less than I deserve. I amounted to great things, things which would never have been thought I could. We only live once, live to our fullest potential.

Ordering another white wine. Nicolas noticing I ordered a small glass. Thinking this was a good sign. I could see in his eyes what he was thinking, experience gives one those abilities. Firstly, he was happy I drank a little, it was socially accepted even expected by women of my stature. Secondly, grateful I was not a raging alcoholic with issues, nor possessing a foul attitude which tends to go hand in hand with an alcoholic. Obnoxious. Provocative. This was imperative to Nicolas. He already had enough baggage in his life, mostly from his own doing. For this reason not needing additional complications. He was oblivious to my baggage. I was perfect, this was all he could see and was concerned with. Like the Northern Irish people, only ever seeing the surface, never delving further finding the truth. I knew how to play the game. The game of life. And to allure. Many years of build-up came down to this. I could make a smart man forget all his smart rules. The rules he built up, a code of conduct he lived by for his own safety. A sword he created. I could make them forget about everything I needed them to, in order to achieve what I wanted. Yes, I was that good. I was that desirable. It did not happen overnight. It took many years to acquire this ability. In time I was able to play all games. Nicolas's games, men's games all with a charismatic act.

Nicolas was studying me almost critically. Establishing I was a stable woman as far as women can be scaled. This he determined because I was able to suppress my emotions. If he only knew! At the time when Nicolas came into my life I was unsound of mind. Fucked-up to say the least. That winter trip was to distract me, helping to make me sound of mind once more. This was to enable I would have a wonderful New Year. A fresh start, a new life. A bright-eyed young woman. Allowing me to put the pieces of my life together again, as though I were a jigsaw puzzle. Just slightly scratched and torn. Not too many pieces missing or damaged. Not that I was ever truly normal. It was mostly the edges which were dilapidated. I could not have been not with the unstable, illogical and ailing family I was born into. No, I was never truly normal. Unfortunately I was not given the chance or the environment to flourish and thrive. I was murdered from the day I was born. The moment my mother pushed me through her uterus, I breathed oxygen and carbon dioxide independently for the first time, my life ended. Why did I have to be the strongest swimmer? It was not the impurities, the microorganisms that float about and are present in the air which killed me, it was my family. The only member of my family who was good and worth anything was my mother Rose. I have come to believe, uncompromising and categorically believe, are there any women who are normal? We all tend to be somewhat unapproachable, emotionally up and down, screwed up, unpredictable or too predictable whichever the case may be, more so self-absorbed. Nicolas was unaware how good I was at hiding my fears, pain and problems. Another advantage of growing up in a dysfunctional family. When in pain I would smile, laugh even, hiding everything I did not want to be publicised. I hide things well. In turn, making me numb to life, love and people. Not knowing how to function.

When I was happy I would still smile or laugh. When things were grinding me down and rendering me to suffer, craving for death to come and take me, save me, I would still mask my feelings, smile and laugh. Figuring it was a weak person who advertised their hurt. I was never hugged or shown affection when pain would find me, after my mother died. My father and brothers did not believe in that. Taught that demonstrations of affection were weaknesses. In turn making a person useless. I had no shoulder to cry on. Mentally I was messed up until I met Charles, he was starting to make me better. He was showing me what life was meant to be like. He was the medicine I needed to cure my disease, he became my sole support. Nicolas showed me how people are supposed to express themselves. Thus not giving the enemy leverage, enabling the nemesis to know how to hurt and where to strike. Give people zero influence over you then they can never hurt you. Becoming powerless. Knowledge is power. My hard, demanding life groomed me into a professional when avoiding being emotionally hurt. Physically hurt was an entirely different card game. A game I had not then mastered. That was the next lesson I was forced to learn. Lesson after lesson, there is forever a bloody lesson to be learnt.

I was not an attention seeker in the same sense as most girls, or renowned for making a laughingstock of myself by being loud and flirtatious. I never ran after men. I never flirted back. When I was a child the only attention I received was when I was being beaten. If I had died nobody but my mother would have cared. Nicolas could read despair in my eyes, disconsolate and a hint of depression. He did not have to study me for long, he already knew too much. More than I cared for people to know. Damn eyes. They can be a person's best friend and their adversary. He could not figure out what would be hurting such a beautiful specimen. He thought of me as a delicate flower who needed to be cherished. Becoming flustered because I knew he knew more than I was comfortable with, I remained dignified, though it was a strain. Admiring this about me. Ashamed with myself as my breathing was starting to elude control. Too heavy, too conspicuous. When I knew that somebody admired me for something it made me that little bit stronger. As we both sat at the mahogany bar men were passing by acknowledging my desirability. Even women passing comment with absolute jealousy. I was so striking, in fact, that Nicolas was not the only man I stopped in his tracks that day, which Nicolas recognised. Not taking any notice despite knowing it was happening, not that I advertised. I silently recorded it in my mind. I did not need to speak in order to make a statement. Silence is golden. Indicting more than words could. Being graceful within one's silence can get a lady far in this cutthroat world. It is bimbos who need to give a show for free. Out of all the men that day I believe that Nicolas could read me better than anyone. At that time I did not know just how foolish I was. Learning just how wrong I was. Wrong beyond compare.

I carried on reading my novel, Nicolas could see how submerged I was within the book, which I held in my tiny hands. Being submerged was what I wanted him to believe. My scripts, my facial expressions I had mastered. Influencing ones interpretation. If I had the opportunity to become an actress, I would have been the best Hollywood had ever known. I could act happy and elated when I was a complete wreck. It was in this ability my strengths were strong. Nicolas sat there watching me for hours fascinated. The clock ticked away minutes into hours. Drops of wine sipped and brandy downed. A billion stares. One could possibly declare he was entranced, appreciative for each second that past, feeling blessed that I came into his life. Nicolas sat perplexed by what could be making this woman disheartened, throwing ideas around in his brain and coming up with literally nothing. He was unable to shift these profound thoughts. Seeing with his own two eyes, I could have any man I desired there could not possibly be anything or anyone who could demoralise this precious being. Not understanding that anyone who is not beautiful could possibly comprehend the loneliness a beautiful spirit feels. Beauty brings along a great deal of heartache. Heartache inflicted by those who hate and envy the other for what they own. Nicolas was romantic enough to believe that I was one of those rare beings, who deserved happiness every waking and sleeping moment. My forehead was more special that anyone else, it does not deserve to frown. My eyes are the most stunning they do not merit to be made misty and cry a single tear. Although he did not know what was affecting me, this aspect disturbed him greatly. This made him for a brief time almost fatherly. Then I respected him. He desired more than anything else to guarantee I would on no account feel sadness again, for as long as I lived. Love at first sight. As this notion was genuine, yes at that time it was sincere, I found this demonstration and him both endearing. This act won me over. Won my heart before my head, foolish I letting my heart take presidency. This will never happen again. Coldness is the only winning way. It was this imprudent lacking of judgment which got me into all this trouble. Taking too many years out of my young life to clean up. Compelling his thoughts back as to what or who was injuring me, or what had happened to make me feel dejected. Nicolas went as far as to feel insulted by my pain. Thinking whoever it was who has harmed me must be insane, blind, filled with spite or quite unmistakably a complete and utter bastard. This person deserves to die. Slowly having the life squeezed out of them. No bullets. That would be too fast, the lack of pain would not be justice enough. Nicolas's perspective on justice was to let the culprit know they are going to die, why they were dying dragging it out as long as possible. Sufficiently. Without placing himself in any danger of being caught. Reminding me of a heinous aunt I knew as a child, who I wished would die. If only she would die and give me peace, I was sure she was either Satan himself, or his wife. She was that nefarious. She was one of those beings who hated me passionately and with immense venom for perfecting myself into the lady I now am.

My eyes I hated most, despite owning beautiful bright, kind, full of life eyes like a deer, they told too much of my story. Loathing people knowing me. I could perform my act like non-other, but my eyes told some of my life's story. Not that I wanted to completely disguise who I was, what I am. I only wanted to be me. I wanted to veil the shameful people in my past, which I had the misfortune to be related to. They were an embarrassment. They disgust me. There were a multitude of things which perplexed Nicolas, one thing he was certain of he had found his new wife. Yes, he knew he would marry me before the week could conclude and I would never feel sadness again. He would not permit me to be sad. He promised himself this as he sat there watching me, he later announced. Knowing he would get me and make me his, providing he got to me first. Nicolas was not the type of man not to get what he wanted. Similar to Elizabeth Taylor wanting everything she could have, looking for gifts from everyone around her, whether they were rich or not. The pleasure was in the conquering. If people were willing to give, she was willing to take. The receiving excels the giving. Not that this was necessarily a negative. That first day Nicolas was so sincere he swore he would kill for me.

Nicolas was guilty of being impetuous. Age did not dissolve nor dilute this aspect to his character. He was still as much the little boy at heart as well as in mind, as he was at the tender age of five. Throwing tantrums when he wanted something he could not have. Becoming unpleasant to the point of violent to his adopted mother when she would refuse him. The only aspect to his character which has changed since those days was his body grew older and grey hair had protruded to his dismay. No vain man could accept age creeping up. This gave rise to his weekly hair colouring. Nicolas like me did not do anything by half measures. His beauty routine was as intense as mine is now. His vanity reminded me of an overly pampered movie star, unaware of what the real world consists of. Neglecting to accept that life is more than hair colour, face masks, cosmetics and cosmetic surgery. There are too many shallow people in this world and Nicolas was one of those divas.

Unfortunately when Nicolas becomes obsessed by something or someone, he could generally get away with the unpleasant twisting of things, making them sound romantic. Just like a person being insulting but doing it with a smile to soften the blow. If one were to delve into matters further it would be evident he was an utter nut. A complete fucker. Due to Nicolas's education in psychology he was a first-class twister, making people feel foolish to get his way. He was able to twist every little detail around, painting himself the saint, the most innocent party when indeed he was the instigator.

"I will break this spell she is under. I will make it my mission in life to ensure at all times a smile is on her delicate face and happiness is projected through those wonderful eyes. She will never frown, cry or feel sadness again. I will love her and take care of her for the rest of my life. I shall treat her like a queen; I will make her my queen, and give her everything I have, which is a fortune."

Nicolas was in possession of a dangerous drawback, like a child when Christmas was on the way, wanting that little white Labrador. Throwing more tantrums than most children. Yelling till his voice would become horse, dry only to break into muteness and crying his eyes out, because he maintained that was what he wanted more than anything else in the world. Torturing his poor adopted mother into submission. Kicking and biting her. Puncturing scars into her flesh. Promising, swearing he would take care of the mutt and love him dearly. After Boxing Day, the poor mutt was left out in the cold, wet and snow to fend for itself, when it still needed a mother's teat for survival. Before New Year's Day approached Nicolas's little white Labrador pup died. Like most things in his life it was mainly a phase, one he becomes bored with much too quickly for his own good. Unfortunately others are hurt along the way. That is, of course, if they live to tell the tale. But Nicolas's life has forever consisted of death, like mine, but in two completely different ways.

Whilst Nicolas sat on the bar stool, watching every move I made, he was planning our wedding in his mind. All these plans arranged before even speaking to me for the first time and without knowing my name. Crazy. An impulsive man. At that moment it was probable to conclude that Nicolas was overconfident, like he was in most situations. Seeing woman as enterprise ventures. The style of wedding dress I would wear, the wedding present he would bestow to me on our wedding night, the hotel we would avail of, where we would honeymoon and how long for. Part of him maintaining this would be considered a romantic gesture. Knowing most men only wish to turn up to get hitched, reluctantly, with one arm up behind their back! After father pulling out that double-barrelled shotgun he had not registered owning, ensuring no trace would lead back to dear old daddy murdering the unwilling son-in-law? Going to extremes in order to teach the young man morals and how to treat a lady accordingly. Not in the same fashion Pistorius is said to have treated his girlfriend. The true part of Nicolas's mind knowing it was purely the dominate streak in him. The control freak he always was. Knowing to word his plans sweetly, in caring passionate tones of voice, seductively suggesting; certain he would pull it off. Simply because he would not settle for not getting his way. The leviathan in him sure to come to the surface. This one entity along with his obsession to control has injured his life. Unwilling to change! Only to hinder my life. This is not merely unfortunate for him but for the people he encounters. Some have claimed he is as controlling as Tom Cruise is said to be, but is he really as extreme as they declare? We all have the right to believe in something. I trust that Nicolas was much worse and more radical. Nicolas's attitude was too similar to those eccentric Albanians, no negotiating, no maybes. Issues are absolute and in their favour. Nicolas understood what he was, but not to its entire degree. Not that he would have cared. Not seeing anything wrong with how he was. Acceptance of reality he did not do. King Henry the eighth and Nicolas Beaumont would not have gotten along, they had too much in common. Dictatorship. They would have been too much competition for one another. Measuring the length and girth of each other's dicks. Whoever had the largest would be sentenced to death. Living within his little dangerous world of threats, sugar-coated lies, abuse and dominance. Not dissimilar to the Albanian Mafia forcing their will onto others. Cold and ruthlessness attaining anything they wish. The only difference between them and Nicolas, Nicolas lived in luxury. They live like pigs. Treating the entire human race like animals. To them everyone is expendable. Unprepared to try to change his ways, trying to cover up his flaws by perfuming his actions. Instead of the true smell of shit and death, lilies was the fragrance drifting in the air. Covering up veracity. Together with fancy and charming words to divert the attention as to what he truly is. A monster. For years he spent making these actions out to be an act of kindness and romance, when in reality he is an obsessive compulsive. A man with bad blood and an evil soul. If he has a soul. He lived to bend people's individual and independent wills, making him feel like a god. A god, a king who rules his own monarch in Switzerland. A god to have such control over another human being. When one man was conquered, one was no longer enough.

Men were intently watching every movement I made; it was as though I was a cancer study, or a study for a momentously important cure which would aid the world. Finger flirting, as I ran my long thin feline fingers around the circular shape of my wine glass. Licking my finger from the sweet fruity juice of the contents. Flicking my finger through my hair, throwing my head back, still with a vacant expression upon my face. Not displaying interest in the others around me. Every so often uncrossing my legs, only to cross them again, throwing an exaggerated kick out as I maneuverer them into position. Much like Angelina Jolie drawing eyes to my legs. My sculpted pins. My pride and joy. The legs I have worked out six days a week since I was sixteen, when I knew that my womanhood was starting to flourish. This was to Nicolas's delight more so displeasure. Unsure which emotion he should indeed feel. These rich men were intoxicated by not solely my beauty, but refinement. I could see in their eyes they were drunk on me. By how placid and composed I conducted myself. Not becoming agitated or losing interest after a matter of hours, as I sat quietly and peacefully reading my book sipping my white wine which was vined in Geneva. These were true gentlemen, a true gentleman never gives up quickly and never becoming anxious. It is a man of high values and respectability who relates it is a hard job to find a true lady. It is not a job which should be rushed. A lady is such a job like a fine wine, sipped, gently tasted and savoured. It is enjoyed better and lasts longer. Its true taste can then be appreciated for its glory. Although I remained much longer than I originally intended, I was being a shrewd operator. Every man who was analysing this rare find, who sat before them in order to scrutinise me, in turn to make it much easier to walk away, as I qualified to be a respectful wife in every capacity. This they found to be invigorating but terrifying. Disbelieving such a speciesism existed. Rich, successful businessmen are trained to scrutinise perfection, ensuring a good deal is found for the cheapest price possible. More profit is to come. A businessman always wants more than everyone else. This happened to be a mixture which made for a very complicated and deadly cocktail. A cocktail should be as easy as a 007 martini. Vodka, Vermouth shaken, stirred perhaps an olive, the possibilities are endless. Except this was no movie. All these men who were considering me as their next spouse, they knew I would be admired everywhere we went. Every dinner party, theatre, opera, tennis competition, horse race, I would be the envy of the town. Women would hate me and men would want to fuck me. Hoping I would be a lady in public, never bringing shame onto him and his family name. Shame could not be accepted, justified nor defended, with their distinction in society. It would never be forgiven. Rich men must worry about that kind of affair. If I had brought shame onto him, I would have been left out in the cold faster than I entered his warm and sex filled bed. He would not solely worry about whether I would love him in return, but that I will be modest whilst in the public's view. Only while I was in the public's eye. Yet silently hoping I would be a whore in the bedroom, making all his wildest, dirtiest, immoral even depraved desires come true. He would have made sure I did. At that moment planning how filthy they would treat me when, or if they got their hands on my fine body. All the while knowing how proud he would be to have such a trophy upon his arm. An accolade to his already collected awards. With conviction bringing upon him further honour and praise. A glorification onto himself and to the way he would be perceived in society. Successful in business, family and in love. This man would be seen to have everything, translated to being an indeed intelligent man. A man to aspire to. These men were yearning to take me put me down on a floor having their vile way with me. Defiling my innocences was their hunger. My innocent appearance was deceptive more than they could resist. Surely I could not be as innocent as I looked. Sequentially, it made me look as though I did not know anything about sex or anything at all for that matter. Thus, making the craving to make me their piece of play gruelling to cope with, going home alone was more than they could abide. These preconceived ideas affording me to get away with a great deal. Reminding me of that cheeky faced boy at school who had the craziest crush on me when we were five, thus annoying me constantly and refusing to take "no" as an answer. Allowing him to get away with a hell of a lot, if he told me he fancied me like mad. But I did qualify to every respectable man who happened to be wife shopping that day, including those who weren't. It was evident that I was the most suitable suitor throughout the towns and cities, valleys and mountains, which they had stumbled upon. Thus giving cause for their immeasurable attention. Any man in his right mind could not, nor would turn their back on this matchless discovery. Although they were able to appreciate my rarity, that same rarity intimidated them. Not wanting to repel me by bombarding me all at once, it became a waiting game. They were waiting to approach, or for the want of a better word attack. They were waiting for the first opponent to approach and be unsuccessful. Learning what not to do by the guy before him who fucked up. Kissing me goodbye, without his lips every being placed upon my hot flesh. Choosing the perfect moment. It was intimidating for even me with the numerous eyes watching me at one time, while I watched everyone else to see who had the guts to confront me first. That was a special day. Hoping that the other men studying me would not approach me prior to their opportunity arising. This was the ultimate distinction between men and gentlemen, or a man and a mouse. Gentlemen respect an appropriate time and distance to prevent from scaring of their prey. Not standing too close invading one's personal space. Knowing not to flash a lady those bedroom eyes, the flirty eyes which danced about and all over their heads, making a woman sick in the pit of her stomach. Men simply attack! With no thoughtfulness for anybody else or appropriate body space, but for their own loins, desire and sexual erg, men are selfish fuckers who intend to only fuck. Gentlemen have much more depth to their manliness and their character. They make love or passionate wild love or a combination of the two. It is these very qualities which make it more difficult to find a gentleman in these modern days.

What I was ignorant to or so it was believed, as this was what I wanted them to believe. In reality women who possessed my intensity of beauty, would sit at bars throughout Switzerland were looking to be picked up by millionaires and billionaires. None of these women read books, nor got lost in what they were reading; their only thoughts were about money, this they certainly dreamt of getting lost in. Swimming in the most stunning beaches of blue saltwater did not compare to swimming in coloured paper which smells so sweet. More tantalising than the most exclusive wines. This was a quality they found charismatic within me and about me. I was unassuming. I did not advertise that I was trying to attract, or that I wanted their millions as much as the next woman. Rich men learn from a young age how to read women, guaranteeing they are not solely after their capital and assets. This is something that their coldhearted, dominate mothers teaches them. Beware of gold diggers; or in the inopportune position where a man finds a beautiful woman who is searching for an easy ride, but is willing to be subservient to his needs, requirements, demands, he would be prepared to take her on, of course providing that a prenuptial decree has been put in place. Protecting everything except his life. Not fixated about the fact she may never love him, providing she is not a public humiliation. The more I travelled and the more men I have come to know, it is natural to hesitate with all the uncertainty, giving rise for a man to become suspicious. Women don't give them much choice. Attributable to why men in their later years tend to be hardened as they have gone through their mistakes with falling in love with women, the wrong women, who were only in love with their bank balance, not them. Never to be in love with them. To a socialite it is one thing to be purely after a man for their wealth, or woman for that matter; this is accepted, even expected under certain circumstances. Nonetheless if a woman will make a spectacle of herself bringing embarrassment onto him, this could not be stood for under any circumstances. So a loveless marriage would work, providing dignity is demonstrated at all times, or at all the right times, when in the public's scope of view. My quiet manners and interest in reading made me stand out; in turn, interesting to onlookers, regardless of the many authors who live in the country.

When Nicolas had seen how many men were watching his impending wife, he became intimidated. Jealously. Fury intensifying through his blood. His temples pulsating, a deep frown creasing between his eyes. Adding twenty years to his current age. Squinting with contemptible anger, resembling a Chinese warrior who was about to snap the neck of a Vietnamese's enemy. A feeling he never felt before. Instead, of being confused as to why he felt this way, when he had not as of yet broken breathe to this captivating stranger. He was delighted that someone in his fifty plus years had this colossal affect over him. From first sight I was his property. This being the most noteworthy compliment he could ever have given me or any female. It wasn't a selfless interest.

Nicolas knew he needed to break the ice soon, considering there was only a matter of days to organise our wedding, more importantly before someone else gained the backbone to present himself to me. The clock above the bar, and the watch on their wrists ticked on. This he confessed on our wedding night. How insane I thought it was, not at all romantic, more lunatic. Letting another man come near me this he could not permit, nor take the chance of losing me. The risk was too great. Certain that if another man approached me first, he would bounce over the bar to break his neck. Shaking it in front of the rest of the bar as a warning. Beware, stay away. She's mine. Though there were a sufficient amount of adequate and younger millionaires, who were wanting to make me their hunt, to take their prey (dead prey) home with them. There were none as perspicacious as he. Nicolas was rich, intently attractive; a man who had a lot to offer a good woman, the right woman. In spite of this he was the most conniving perilous man who one would ever have the unfortunate bad luck to meet. There was no darker character to be met. Dangerous perhaps, darker definitely not. He was the serial killer without the characteristics to make him known to the world, moreover the police, to his gratefulness. This to the victim's misfortune. I loved the initial thrill of taking Nicolas on, dancing around his mind, above all playing spinning games with his mind. I took on too much with the Beaumont family. My youth made me too ambitious. Too hungry. Too much of anything is deadly. Even too much love. Sex and lust. On the other hand, too little of love is more potent.

The clock read 19:03. Nicolas got up from his bar stool he commenced walking over to me, countless envious eyes which were watching him in recent. He entered the bar four hours and fifteen minutes earlier. The tension grew. Without looking around me I could feel it. I could taste it in the air. The air becoming dense. As though thunder was in the atmosphere. Forcing my shoulders to stay in place, as the tension was pushing them down. I could not show I was being affected by these small men searching for guts. Not now. This was the climax I sat there for hours waiting for. Pleased that his new wife had this affect over men. He loved to own things that other people did not, especially when what he owned was indisputably better than anybody else's possessions, they always were. He was a spoilt man. These reasons making Nicolas feel essential, significantly fuelling his egotistical ambitions and high esteem about himself. Most of the things he owned within his home granted were rare objects. Things one would not widely find in regular family homes. Nicolas's chateau was not a family home, therefore many expensive belongings were on exhibition. Children could not be stood for in a house of great. His collectables held more value in monetary terms and human affection to Nicolas. Objects which were much too expensive and lavish for most to be able to afford, he knew this and loved this. This gave him a sense of purpose. Nicolas was not a conventional man not by any means. Being illogical was his logic. It was like a new language, a language of which nobody had ever heard, or spoken. With nowhere to learn this new vernacular, making Nicolas himself distinctive, but more significantly dangerous, as he was often misunderstood. They were things he collected on his travels in his earlier years from around the world. He loved atypical objects but loved exceptional finds when it came to champagne, brandy and food. Much greater when it came to women. Since his early twenties he collected Swiss army knives and women. When it came to women he collected them, used them, and ditched them. When he had concluded his play, covering up all traces of their existence. Not allowing anyone to have them. His collection of knives and guns displayed honourably with pride upon his library wall. On the wooden panelled walls over the fireplace, exhibit thirty-six different types of army knives. The most expensive, also the most dangerous. This to his glory; almost loving them as though they were his very own children, his flesh and blood. But actual children who drool, cry, need love and attention, substantially time, this man could not have dealt with. He was too much of a child to care for another. He was too much the attention seeker to allow a small helpless being to take over that role. Knowing a real child of flesh and blood he would hate. Somewhere along the line he would have killed it.

Understanding I was considered to be an atypical find, he believed I was a difficult and arduous task above them all. It was this I took my praise from. Due to his past encounters with women although they were all very beautiful, he was spoilt with beauty his entire life. What one man may have considered breathtaking, Nicolas would have categorised mediocre. This even Nicolas had to admit, purely if his reaction was the only thing to go by, I was classed as rare. This was what he loved the most, even more than me. Being more in love with an aspect of someone opposed to the actual person. Being in love with what glory the other person could bring, what glory he felt it should bring him. In turn, this has brought Nicolas many unhappy days and nights, unable to learn from his mistakes, flaws and constantly remaking those mistakes with each passing year. His shortcomings were always everybody else's fault. Besides applying these flaws to each passing wife. Learning it is one thing to make a mistake, especially when one is young. There is no wisdom in youth. The key principle is to learn, equipping one with the knowledge to avoid making the same mistake again, eluding the heartache brought by it. One truly is asking for trouble when they continue to make the same mistakes, neglecting to adopt common sense. This person then deserves whatever badness follows them, when it is indeed self-induced. Nicolas was a little boy who never mentally grew up as much as he should have. Being spoilt is indubitably an evil within itself. Sometimes when one has everything it is essential to be stripped down to the bare essentials, evoking how lucky one is to have more than they need in order to appreciate their

138

luck and fortune. The selfish are some of the wickedest people of them all. It is universally known that selfish, wicked people are unhappy on occasion mentally unhealthy. Are we therefore to believe that being selfish and wicked, makes one mentally unhealthy? Or is it the mentally unhealthy people who as a consequence become selfish and wicked. Or are they merely too complicated to comprehend. If a sergeant were to dissect the ill inflected person's brain, retrospectively locating the area in which is ill, can answers then be found? Or is the illness unrecognisable? Incurable.

PART EIGHT

The Beginning

CHAPTER TWENTY-SIX

The Snowboat

Beneath the ambient lighting at the bar from behind me I could hear a strong French accent in a sexy upper class voice.

"Bonjour, Madame, Ca va?"

Appearing to my right-hand side. The first to take the bait. The man with the most guts and the largest balls regardless of the size of his dick.

"Ca va bien, mercy. Ca va?" "Tres bien"

"Je m'appelle Nicolas. Et toi?"

"Je m'appelle Nicolette."

Nicolas properly introduced himself like a true gentleman does, I in return by means of being courteous. Offering to buy me another wine, noticing I had two more mouthfuls left till the crystal glass I held in my hand until it was empty. Being the lady I am refusing his kind submit. Never owe a man anything. Pay my own way. This encouraged Nicolas to go for the hunt. I was not repealing him instead antagonising him to carry on. Knowing it would. Men like Nicolas never give up that easily. It's too much of an insult to their ego. I was the fragile rabbit and he the robust fox. Knowing he would need to be frugal with his questions, avoiding becoming intrusive or else prohibiting his progression. Trying to talk with me; at first I was simply polite not drawn into conversation. I knew his game. I played it many times in the past, it was how I practiced. Winning each time I played, men are universally predictable, yet every time it was the man who led. Men are too sneaky and to win.

"Tu viens d'ou, Nicolette?" (Where do you come from, Nicolette?)

"Je viens de* France, Paris. Tu viens d'ou, Nicolas?" (I come from France, Paris. Where do you come from, Nicolas?)

"Je viens de* Switzerland, Visip."

(Are you enjoying our exquisite country?)

"Beaucoup." (Very much.)

"What do you do for a living?"

(Am I being interviewed for a job?)

An offended haze misted over Nicolas's eyes. Squinting. His complexion turning grey. His cool blues quickly transformed to a coal black. Barely giving me the opportunity to answer his questions never mind asking any in return, becoming quickly incensed.

"No, no, I do apologise. I suppose I was asking you questions very quickly. I do sincerely apologise, Madame. Please forgive me. It is none of my business. Just polite conversation."

The typical questions strangers ask one another if they met on a train. His enthusiasm was too intense, too interested too curious too soon for my liking. Setting off alarm bells in my head. Suspicious conduct. When someone asks more questions than they are prepared to answer asking myself the question why? The innocent sounding questions to lure me into a false sense of security, waiting for the perfect time to pounce on the disabled deer when hit by headlights. Men's questions no matter how innocuous they appear are perilous. They always want something, they always tell lies. There wasn't anything intrusive. To a smart man they never are until they think they have their grip over a woman. To be a smart woman is to refuse to let a man have his clutch, she remains in control. Being discreet was something Nicolas could do well. To his own hindrance he could not keep up the act long. As a result his impulsive behaviour often leading him to inadequacy in everything he seeks out to do, rendering him to great frustration and disappointment. Blaming others for his shortcomings. Leading to a temperamental state, becoming his most dangerous. Causing fear to upsurge within the parties who have been present to witness his bad temper and ghastly threats.

My aim directed to be chivalrous. I gave brief answers to his questions without giving details. Not telling him anything he did not need to know. In spite of this fact I swore to play it cool, keeping people at arm's length. Staying true to myself, the promises I made. My answers were straight forward, candid, but in a civil tone of voice, "yes" and "no" "please" and "thank you." I refrained from asking any in return. Not wanting to be seen as intently interested. My attempt was to draw him in. Make him want more, make him want me. That is, of course, until I knew for certain if I wanted him or not. If he ended up wanting me, and I didn't want him I could walk away. Spending a little longer with him to maintain was he worth my time? Was he worth the investment? Like any shrewd businesswoman I did my homework and related the less time invested in a job the better, this equals more time spent on a new stronger endeavour. It was then I learnt I held the winning cards. I was way ahead. Caution was key. At this game and this stage I have no reservations that I would win. It was his second game which I did not know we were playing, until he took all my aces, royals and anything decent preventing me to win. By the time I was in the know we were playing a new game, he already won.

Identifying I was playing it cool, this he respected but wanted to neglect and rip the clothing from my petite body there and then. Put me on the bar and have his dissolute way with me, whether he made me come or not he did not care, he just wanted to occupy my body. Showing me he is in control. To an extent this was a compliment. He would not have been phased if the people around would have watched him be a beast before their very eyes. Shocked eyes. When it came to his urges he didn't care about anybody, merely himself and accommodating his desires and emptying his bulging sacks. No matter what they were or where he was he conquered the moment. Nicolas wasn't an exhibitionist and didn't want people to see the private act of fucking, but occasions have arisen when he did not care what strangers could or could not see, or hear. Spontaneity was the recipe to a spicy relationship. Nicolas acquired too much spice

143

smothering the objective of his interest and for the time being affections. There were times when he would love to show off but even to Nicolas fucking was more a private deed, performance and accomplishment. Perhaps he felt his performance would not stack up against other much younger attractive men or his dick wasn't as long or thick as it ought to be. Maybe age was creeping up and his machinery didn't work as well as it once did. Rusty and stiff but not in the right way. Jamming while in motion. Deducing a woman as beautiful as he found me should be aware that they would be fancied and should expect to be taken and fucked senseless at any time. Whenever a man would decide it was the right time. Whether she approved or not. Nicolas lived in the Victorian ages. The downside to being beautiful. Men automatically believe a beautiful woman is a whore because she was given a beautiful face and a fine body. Whereas an ugly woman just had to be a virgin, because nobody would go near her, unless nothing better presented itself and balls urgently required to be emptied. An ugly dormant pussy was better than no pussy and a self-inflicted hand job. With men there is no in between. Except for in between the legs, but he would treat me accordingly to his regret merely for the time being. That clock was slowly ticking away. I would not be safe indefinitely. He did associate there would be plenty of time for that type of conduct once he had won me over (or so I lead him to believe), having no doubt he would as he has always been successful in that department.

At certain intervals gently touching his hand for only a split second, not to indicate I was being flirtatious more comforting. I was making him work incredibly hard for my time and attention. Appreciating his efforts. Demonstrating to Nicolas it was not in vain. An act of encouragement like rubbing a puppy's stomach, a sign to reassure him that he was achieving but I would not be giving anything away and not that quickly, so he need not ask. Picking up on my silent signals. This being the foremost reason for his self-satisfied attitude, he was nothing more than a smug little boy. He knew there would be many sufficient acts once we were married. The main reason for the prompt marriage. Not rushed because he felt it was romantic or because he didn't want to risk losing me, the truth was he couldn't resist my body terribly long. It was all a game to him. Not wanting to scuttle this opportunity and seize this potential prospect by a quick disappointing fuck. Disappointing for him or me,

I still had not determined. He was smart enough to know to conquer a woman like I, he would need to be less impulsive and more prudent. Being fake was a technique he had performed down to a T. Practicing it for close to four decades. His birth mother was a tremendous help in teaching him how to become counterfeit. I did not much care if he was being fake, my main objective was to make him work for it, work for me. The one piece of instrumental advice I held onto is men are always counterfeit. Lies they breathe, lies they live for. Lies they announce. Not incapable but unwilling to enunciate truth. This way I knew how much I could push for, what my worth with him was, whether or not I would need to keep on searching for a new man of wealth, a man who would appreciate me and who deserved my time.

Complementing me many times an effort to impress. Gravely failing. To my distain. Emphasising his wealth certainly was unproductive, lacking to excite, moreover irritating me. Immediately after announcing his wealth, my tone and attitude altered. Nicolas observed my eyes, detecting in my more aloof manner he had lost every square inch of interest he may have established. I stopped focusing on him and making encouraging eye contact. My time was not devoted to him any longer. My eyes scanned the room, there were a mountain of people who were watching and listening to our conversation. Many heads turned abruptly once they realised they were caught. Not expecting me survey the bar. A few men nearer us realised Nicolas was on a losing game, self-satisfied sniggers crossed their faces. Making it obvious to Nicolas he had failed. Not giving him any definite answers or come-ons, I was allowing him to question his ability and remain on shaky ground. I wanted to know how pathetic he was. Knowing he must start over again or lose me forever. Thus understanding I was more than worth starting over from scratch for, despite it being tiresome and tedious work. Feeling a silent giggle free itself. Laughing at him. Sniggering at him. Not behind his back like a coward but to his face like a brave warrior. It sickens me how men feel they should automatically have their every wish, desire and command adhered to, merely for the fact they are the male sex. The superior sex. With a machine between their legs. To catch a woman the process is similar to that of a turbulent tornado. Rough and coarse, caution cannot be thrown to the wind. Younger men are smug and arrogant having the brass neck to tell a woman they do not have to earn anything, because they inevitably feel they have the right to demand from a woman. Thinking women were only placed on this earth for two things. One, men's pleasure. Two, a fuck feast. Modern men refuse to accept that there is a significant difference between being a woman and being a lady. Their ignorance of woman and the world gives me a blinding migraine. These little boys with bum fluff on their maxilla and mandarin have far to go and much to learn. They will have women leave them. The more they insult and displease, the more bitter they will become. A vicious circle for the immature male who have a hell of a lot to learn but never will. Their heads are already too large for their necks to hold up. People who think they know everything cannot possible learn anything. These are the people who create misery for themselves, blaming everybody else for their inadequacy. Taking great joy in tiring men out. Refusing to give them anything for free. Nothing with me was made easy. If they wanted me they could damn well work for the right. The more a man is prepared to work the superior the man is. The more the man is. The better and greater his intentions. That's the man to marry. The man who deserves to be treated like a king.

Nicolas was incapable of reading from my lack of expression that I was silently pleased knowing he was a wealthy man. Reminding myself men who brag about their wealth often lack in funds they emphasise having. Bragging about what they do not own is purely a means to create interest, understanding what they have or rather do not have, will far from impress the object of their attraction. The lure to trap them in an unbreakable net. Then there are the men who brag, who do own what they claim their intentions are not honourable. On the other hand entirely, there are those egotistical men who must announce their worth, not solely to women they are reeling in but anyone who will listen; anyone will do, so long as they attain the attention they crave. They are the men to stay away from. Being rich can also be a lonely life to lead. Disbelieving those who brag. Finding it is those who are inferior who must talk to build themselves up in other people's eyes, as they lack the skills or the education to fulfil their actuality. Wealthy people for their own protection, unless they are prima donnas do not boast. Nicolas was a very proud man, this oozed throughout his character and presence. I gambled on the second bet, I felt I could spare an evening at least to try him out. Like a wild horse never before rode, I was breaking him in. Luring him in.

I hate to waste my time on unproductive matters. A moment wasted is a million lost. While he was casually yet quickly walking into my netting, he was failing to get me into his. Walking with eyes wide shut. But knowing Swiss men as well as I do in a relatively short space of time, observing them as they intently observed me they do not need to brag. Unlike like the Texas cowboys who attempt to mislead, mistreat and use innocent woman. Luring them into a false sense of security, merely to discard of them like last week's rotten trash. They are the kind who think too highly of themselves for their worth. Overly valued in their own heads. It's true what my grandmother told me as a child when a John Wane movie was on television, during my summer holidays from school, the year was 1996, *"Cowboys are known as cowboys because that is what they are, stupid, uneducated, cocky, rough and ready, lying trash. Pulling a trigger doesn't take much of anything. Certainly zero brains. That's something no cowboy has, brains."*

There must be some truth in it, if only considering the high rate of divorced embitter Americans, opposed to the longer, happier marriages and fewer divorces throughout Europe. With the amount of cowboys who accidently shoot themselves. Swiss men have principles. They are refined, candid and everything a real man ought to be. Abandoning that strain of thought immediately. Money isn't everything. If I had only known at the start how those words would follow me. Reminding me of my mistakes. Rubbing coarse sea salt into my open bleeding wounds. If a genuine lady wants to be loved and respected but above all happy, then a man's wealth or lack of it should not deter her, as Swiss men are the perfect creation. They are the men women want to marry. The princes charming little girls dream about after mother reads them their bedtime story. It was simply a cautious thought. After hours of engaging me in conversation we were on an encouraging level of conversation.

No swimming before dinner. No dinner consumed. Closing time approached, everybody left grudgingly. Not wanting to leave to go home solo. They had no alternative but to go home, as they were being thrown out for the night and without me on their arm, with the exception of Nicolas.

Why didn't I make the first move? I waited long enough and now I have wasted the opportunity to buy myself a new trophy.

All eyes were watching Nicolas escorting his slightly caught prey out of the premises with lingering concerns. No leg or neck was currently broken. Nonetheless my leg and neck were caught tightly and firmly in his trap. A slight fracture was soon to form.

Closer to the exact truth Nicolas waited to leave at the same time I did. A prospect he was egger to accomplish if he was indeed permitted to walk me home. Nicolas illiterate to the fact I remained at the Snowboat because of him, wanting to fascinate this man who was captivated by me, not wanting to leave precipitately before becoming successful. Being impulsive was Nicolas's forte not mine!

"May I walk you back to your hotel, Nicolette?"

To his dismay I initially refused. Preconceiving I would. Going onto encourage me to change my mind, he could not deal with losing anything, not alone a woman he became obsessed with which took no longer than a blink of an eye. Debasing his character by acting sweet and kind almost fatherly to entice me. Ensuring he got his way. An insult to the true Nicolas Beaumont. Perhaps it was his last card to play with.

"I wouldn't want anything to happen to you, I would feel more comfortable if I knew you returned home safely."

Laughing aloud, a rather girly and childlike laugh somewhat overdone on my behalf. I was a rather girly kind of woman, in a woman's body.

Thinking how these were the most obtuse words I have ever heard. In that dim-witted sentence, I knew he was eager. I related just how desperate he was. He may have possessed a sick mind but he was a high-class man, he was a swish kind of Swiss man. He had too much to offer to debase himself to running after any woman. He never would have demeaned himself to that. She had to be special. She had to be perfect. Today it had to be me.

Abandoning my strain of thought to remain polite answering his dim-witted question.

"I do not know what plane you intended to catch but we are in Switzerland. You do know we are in Switzerland? So I will be perfectly safe but thank you for being as considerate as you have been, you are terribly kind."

Nicolas laughing at the top of his voice. Finding my comment awfully amusing, laughing to extremes. Tears flowing down his face. I suppose it was funny how I said it. Then I thought he was trying to make a fool out of me. I definitely did not think it was that funny after hurting my ear with his screaming like laugh. I was never as insulted.

"I know, Nicolette, but I am from here, as do I live here. I did not catch a plane but I understand what you mean. I do not want this night to end I would love to spend more time with you."

Immediately becoming embarrassed wishing I had shut my dumb mouth. By trying to make a fool out of him, I made a fool out of myself. In view of that I became nervous not knowing how to respond. I hated being caught on aware. Usually I wouldn't mind, as having a quick mind was of an advantage, nevertheless, being embarrassed was something foreign to me. Decelerating my response time. I was not accustomed to having the disadvantage. I have worked too hard to observe taking note of everything around, developing my mind to think and react like the speed of light to have the disadvantage. Priding myself on my awareness. Delays were never my style. I was too stylish for such foolish conduct. Becoming aggravated with myself out of annoyance, mumbling under my breath;

"You stupid, stupid girl. Your family were right – you are docile."

Tears welled up. The whites of my eyes transformed from their natural colour to transparent. Briefly feeling ashamed of myself, hating that I proved my family right even if it was for a brief moment. Struggling not to permit my tears to flow colliding with my cheeks, advertising to him I was humiliated and that I was the guilty party who did it to myself. Child's play. I did it to myself by trying to be too smart. Never try to be, just be. I have no excuse. If tears fell from my eyes soaking my skin that would have been embarrassing and unforgivable. I would have died in front of him. Thinking if I cried, would I melt his heart and wrap him around my little finger? Could this be possible? Discarding that thought as it was too soon to start playing that game. At least wait until we were officially together. Using that card only when I have to. That would be the time to start reeling him in. If I use that card too soon men tire with it. Leverage weakens.

My original plans were firstly to take the train back to Geneva that evening, going onto taking a swim, enjoying some dinner, maybe taking a long walk around the city. There isn't anything like a city at night, bright lights, the feeling of being untouchable. Quieter. A new viewpoint. A beauty of its own. A beauty in darkness. Followed by relaxing in my oversized, cosy bed. A luxurious bed with lots of cushions and comfortable pillows after a long eventful day. What a blissful notion. I found mountain climbing to be exasperating work. I had never climbed before this trip. I was far from accustomed. Eager to get back to the hotel to rest my tiresome feet. Hopefully to restore them back to health, after being beaten black-and-blue in my weighty ski boots for several hours on top of the Matterhorn. With entering the Snowboat I noticed that many men, just like they were on the Matterhorn admiring me. Thinking this could potentially lead to marrying another rich man with excessive funds. No pain, no gain. Deciding to put my feet through a little extra torture. More importantly a man who would treat me well not merely by buying me expensive possessions, he would give me the important things in life. It could lead to a happy marriage with no more problems. I would make him the happiest man in the world. He would have everything I want to make me happy and someday I might even love him with all my heart. Who can foresee the future? Perhaps he would give me children, I would love nothing more. The typical fairy tale but not a typical love story! Unless one was alive scores of years ago and one's rich family were forcing their daughter to marry a partner with excessive funds, or for an upstanding family name. Power then born. Attempting to combat shame due to the fact the once notorious wealthy family were now bankrupt; or families with some status who were greedy for more forcing their children to marry for a higher standing. For many years there has been various types of marriages. Some marriages which are happy, abusive, trapped, dysfunctional, what's more almost every person who takes their vows have a less than acceptable reason to marry, unless they are poor. One of the only lucky things about being underprivileged, is being able to choose with one's own discretion who they wish to spend the rest of their life with.

That sloppy stuff has never interested me. Deciding to seize the moment which was liberally presented to me, wanting the time to figure out where this appreciation for my beauty would lead. I was smart enough to comprehend that love is not solely enough to be happy in life, not anymore. Not in these crazy times. Society has made marriage a more complicated affair than what it needs to be. Now people analyse, read psychology books and attempt to predetermine people from the onset, before one word annunciate. Opposed to simply feeling what it is they feel and going with it. Don't force it, don't second-guess it that is what love is a simple emotion, a sensation in the body, in the bones. Love is something that is felt. It is not something which can be analysed. At least it shouldn't be. Feel it and spend the rest of one's life happy looking at the same person and being grateful they have stood by you through thick and thin, mainly being appreciative they stood by you through the worst of times, supporting you and will be there right by your side until the day one of you die. In the aftermath they will spend the rest of their life in perpetual mourning for you and your love. One needs a home, children and food. It is all the little things and more which come into play and count along the way. The honeymoon phase maybe exciting and fun for a short time, hence why it is called the honeymoon phase. When life kicks in. When reality hits home, living on cloud nine and living in your own little world, as nice as it may be is not enough by any means to get you through.

Thinking very silently as not to give anything away and advising myself:

I gave up my evening to remain at the Snowboat, don't be stupid and pass up this potential prospect, just because you don't find him your ideal. He obviously wants you. He's exceedingly handsome. Let's take this ride as far as it can go, even if it is only for tonight. I smiled then blushed, making me look angelic and even more virtuous than I already did. Grateful that my skin was pale and snow white so he could see me blush, advertising my purity. Older men adore that quality when I can blush with bashfulness. Constantly thinking from every angle, never missing a trick.

"Thank you, Nicolas, that is the sweetest thing anyone has ever said to me I truly appreciate such a kind comment and you freely wanting to spend more time with me. Nobody has ever wanted to spend time with me, it is very refreshing to know you do. How about we take a long walk? This night air is amazingly passive. I don't want to go home just yet either. I love looking at these beautiful chalets, with all the bright flowers overflowing the balconies making everything appear to be fresh clean and pure. They have the sweetest scent in this night air. I love the wood they are made out of and the shapes that are carved into the wood, so interesting. Don't you think?"

"'I couldn't agree more, Nicolette. Of course we can. We can walk around all night if you wish, or at least until you are ready to drop, or your feet refuse to let you walk anymore, whichever comes first."

Laughing aloud and with a cheeky smile almost smirk upon his face.

"Not to worry, in any case I would gladly carry you home if you were to tell me where that is. If your feet get sore from walking I would happily rub them to restore them back to life. I didn't tell you before as I didn't want you to think I was on the make, which I absolutely am not, Nicolette. I'm much too old for that these days but I think you are an exquisite woman and indeed very lovely. Any man who is lucky to be in your constant company is the luckiest man who walks this world."

Staring deep into my big green contacts of which he believed to be my true coloured eyes, with a look of honesty. Instead of being pleased by this intent gaze of pursuit and attraction, moreover this look unsettled me. Accordingly my gut stirred up a feeling of nervousness. A feeling I did not care for, nor desiring to know its meaning.

Again I smiled and blushed struggling to keep my composure, not wanting to be misconstrued as being indecorous.

"Please don't think me rude by asking you this but I am not used to anybody being kind to me, never mind as kind as you are being. But why must you tell me such kind things, what is behind it? Please do not take any offense to my asking, but I have learnt a long time ago, that people are rarely nice just for the hell of it, there is usually some kind of motive."

In astonishment and feeling slightly offended, but not indicating this, and not taking my comment to heart as he knew I did not mean to be odious. A creature like me (who I was portraying to be) does not possess a bad bone in my five foot two inch tiny little body, so looked me in the eyes again to say;

"Let me assure you honestly there is not anything behind it my dear, Nicolette. I sincerely think these things. I relish in telling you as I see such pain in your eyes. I see such purity. A purity I have never before seen in a woman. I like to have that pain subsided, even if it is only for a moment by telling you the truth, of which you do not realise to be the truth. You understate your ability as a person, your competence in general and personally. You need to have more faith in yourself. People will always let you down; you are the only person who can come through one hundred percent of the time. You are the only person who will never let you down. I do not tell you sweet, kind things to flatter you, I am telling you what it is I faithfully see. I understand you have never been loved or shown love and this saddens me. A beauty like you deserves so much love, more than most people I dare to state. You are the most wonderful woman I have ever seen. Trust me when I tell you this night, that wonderful women and purity are two rare finds and never come within the one entity, like you."

Letting out an unmerciful laugh from shock. I was flattered, this I desperately wanted to conceal. Always having the unseemly ability to laugh at the wrong times when becoming both nervous and embarrassed, thus embarrassing myself further. While embarrassment was written over my entire face, I knew this as I could feel the blood rush from my tiny toes all the way up to my head, knowing I was now beaming like a clown's nose. Perhaps if Rudolf isn't well this Christmas, Santa will take me to guide his sleigh. Embarrassment was too visible for me to try and hide. But I was glad I could hide my initial thoughts;

What a liar attempting to get me into bed only to fuck me, then fuck me off. If he carries on I'll be fucking him off, understating me, what a laugh. This man isn't sensible enough to be sensible. How dare he. He of all people, this old grey-haired loon telling me I have never been loved. His charms will not work on me. How dare he disrespect my Charles's love for me? Charles was the man who loved me more than anybody ever has. Nicolas couldn't dream of being like Charles. No man could. No greater man walks this earth.

My natural instinct kicked in to automatically disbelieve men, defending myself! Only a foolish woman would believe a word that was spoken from a man's mouth. Men's lips manoeuvre such foul lies; their lips should be cut off, preventing them from seeking to harm women. Men are the worst creation on the face of this earth. Their abominable! All they are fit for is being used and abused, treated objectionably for all their life. Not dissimilar to the way they treat womankind. No respectable woman who is demure needs any man. Not even to play with, if she was honourable and modest. A real woman does not have need of any man.

Of my own accord, even to my surprise, an attempt to hide my disbelief, I took Nicolas's arm and began to lead, walking up a hill into the small town square. As I glanced at him, his eyes before my very eyes transformed into diamonds. Sparkling beneath the darkness of night. Not many people were about. There rarely were at night in Zermatt. As we walked past the expensive chic shops, Rolex and Omega, we didn't once window-shop. Both of us deeply involved within our conversation, about Nicolas's past, about his deceased wife Gabriella. We did not need 22 carat gold watches smothered in diamonds to keep us entertained. Not this night. I was sincerely empathising for Nicolas to have lost his dear wife, a woman he was trying to impress me he loved more than his own life and was completely dedicated to. I knew how he felt after losing my dear sweet Charles and my loving mother. The greatest mother any child could be blessed to have. That was why he didn't successfully mislead me. Instead of hot-blooded love, he was frozen. This man never felt real steamy love. Not in all his fifty plus years. All this declared in my ignorance of the truth. Nicolas neglected the fact that one day, be it in five years' time down the line or not, I would finally

154

find out the truth. I was willing to be impressed by a man as charming and alluring as Nicolas was. I was hiding my truth, I was already besotted by him besides the fact I was now charmed by his kind ways, despite annoying me by his insult of my Charles's love for me. His soft tones were fooling me into feeling secure. Feeling that his arms would be the safest place for me, imaging I could remain in his secure trustworthy arms for the rest of my life or his. Playing around with romantic notions, how crazy! Figuring I'm hiding my tales, perhaps he's the best thing which could ever have happened to me. Perchance I should take a taste of what he has to offer. I must not be too judge mental. We all have a past, a secret to hide. Some embarrassing, some foolish and some catastrophic.

Guilty of thinking I am not conceivably thinking this surely?

Guilty of absorbing every story, every lie he voiced. Was it the night sky, the sentimental falling snow, which made me want to believe him? I was wanting for Nicolas to be the right man, the perfect man. The man to come save me. Surprised as to how immediate I renounced my own methodical strategies, my preconceived idealistic ambitions. Taking into account all the rules and objectives I set myself to live by. My way of being, the switched off intangible attributes I wanted to adapt to excel in life. Of all people to capitulate and relinquish playing around with unrealistic prospects. I knew better. What I did not know was what came over me to neglect my knowledge.

I don't know what this was, only I entered a dangerous, romantic state. Anything which involves romance always leads to trouble.

Yes, I became besotted too quickly; this was always my problem, attempting to deny it even to myself as I was trying to shake him off. He is no good for me. Knowing that this was not a good idea. It wasn't smart to trust a man that quickly, it always turned out badly for me, and only me. I reduced myself to putting my newfound craziness down to being the night air, the vibrant colours of the flowers, the romantic and ambient lighting from chalets afar. The delicate aroma present in the air like wine affecting my senses. Not alone the mountains and glacier river making such a peaceable noise as it rushed down stream and through the town. The freshest cleanest air I had ever been blessed to breathe, on the whole had an effect over me. That part is true. Not exactly minding this, providing it only lasted the night and I composed myself appropriately next morning. It would then be only a little bit of harmless fun. No harm done. Everyone is entitled to go a little crazy sometime. A fantasy, a wish of what nothing more than what I wish could happen, knowing I'm not a lucky person, these happy loving things don't come to me. It's always for someone else, never me. I'm Nicolette the unlucky one.

We walked in a circle bringing us back to the Snowboat.

"May we please walk around again, I'd sincerely enjoy it, Nicolas, or are you too tired?"

Permitting my request, thrilled I was now volunteering, thus initiating interest and not wanting to go home. Feeling he had now won me over. I could feel his breathing on my arm relax. It was more casual. His demeanour less strained.

Nicolas couldn't help but continue studying me as he was still in awe of my childlike innocent appearance. He knew academically I was intelligent. He also knew that I had been exposed to harsh realities in my life for this reason they have scared me, hence, as a result making me both a guarded and hard person. No matter how hard I tried to veil this truth, there was frequently something which would broadcast my bitterness. This was probably the only negative aspect about me, one which I would never be able to change or conceal, as I felt it too strongly. It burnt my blood. I was too badly damaged. This was the one part of truth and realness which would for all my life advertise some kind of pain even hell I had undergone. This could be what would catch up with me before I was an old lady in that death bed! The way I walked, talked, presented myself, told anybody with a light on upstairs, I was well-turned-out. That was another thing Nicolas admired, my style. I was elegant and dressed respectful, in a mid-length deep blood red dress, not revealing a great deal but enough to conceal everything, which makes a man's mind envisage and every part of a woman a man can conceive of. It was blood red yes, strong enough to attract and catch the eye, but it was the dress doing the work, not me, in an indirect way of course. I made the dress, it didn't make me. I was wearing a long black cardigan, and a black lace scarf, with a long black coat with fur trim on the collar and wrists. For some reason it was unbuttoned, despite the snow and the freezing temperatures. I appeared to be so content that I did not feel the cold. As the wind gently blew upon my soft skin, blowing my dress softly and tenderly between my legs, he was dying to consume me body and soul. His heart pounding again in his chest, loud enough he was sure I could hear it. Nicolas desperately wanted to caress my lips, and every inch of my body. His breathing increased. His body language intensified, becoming uncomfortable within his own skin and clothing. A stronger wind blew, within seconds I was wrapped in goose pimples. At that very moment, he wanted to wrap his body around me, making me sweat and my heart race inside of my body, much faster than his heart rate currently was. Instead of doing what he wanted, deciding to do the gentlemanly thing. For the moment anyhow. Thinking damn life's hard.

"Could I offer you my coat, Nicolette?"

"Thank you but I have one and I'm not cold."

"Aren't you?"

"No, Nicolas, what would make you think that I am cold?"
"Apart from the fact you are covered in goose pimples and you're shivering, I suspect not much else would indicate that you are cold."

Both of us laughing, feeling somewhat embarrassed again and stupid.

"Oh, I am aren't I?"

Not answering, Nicolas merely smiling and gestured a nod.

"I didn't feel cold, I still don't but I guess I must be."

"Well one would think, my darling."

Smiling yet again, appreciating the view of my firm breasts while my nipples were stimulated and standing from the cold. Taking a quick glance of how they stood in the night air. I could read in his eyes what he was thinking. I wasn't guilty of being that innocent not anymore. Men are so easy to read.

I could certainly stimulate her with my hard thick dick. I could fill her up with my girth and make her scream her head off. I swear, the first chance I get, I'm invading her wet pussy I am going to give it to her hard, deep and plentiful. I will start of slow and gentle, gain her trust, then bend her over a table and shag the pussy off her. Pull her apart. Spank her ass!

Noticing a faraway look in his eyes encouraging me to ask:

"Are you alright, Nicolas?"

As he came back to reality, to earth, not daring to confess his impure thoughts he simply smiled with his eyes this time and answered. He did not realise I had an idea as to what he was thinking. I was aware his thoughts were dirty and smutty, but how smutty I was not quite sure.

"Oh yes, darling, I'm fine, just getting tired now."

"Would you like to go home yet?"

Being the typical man with an impure mind misunderstanding my invitation, when it was more of an implication. Becoming more aroused with a sexual stirred up look upon his face, with a mystified look in his eyes, now broadcasted clearly and with little or no room for misinterpretation.

"Oh yes please, I'd love nothing more than that right now."

Replying with a little schoolboy squeaky voice, the kind of reply children have when they've been good children and are going to get a treat. As I was such an innocent child not realising what was on his mind or what I had asked had been misconstrued.

"Are you staying in a hotel or do you have a home here, Nicolas?"

"I have a chalet just a few moments out of town. It is only a few moments literally. I've owned it for over twenty years. I love this little village."

Answering with excitement to his voice, barely waiting to get undressed and completely oh so naked.

"Oh how lovely. My feet are painful now after walking in these heels, they aren't the fitting footwear for walking round and round. I changed after coming from climbing the Matterhorn and my walking shoes would have been better suited right now, they would have been much warmer."

Another manly misinterpretation believing it was a ladylike candid excuse to get home faster, for a twenty minute shag before passing out.

"Your feet are sore?"

A cheeky I can't believe my luck grin appeared on his face and a sweet look of appreciation came through in his eyes. I issued a gentle innocent laugh as I was not certain exactly what was going through his mind. Thinking, perhaps I am being a little paranoid.

"Where is your hotel?"

Feeling silly, hesitating as long as would be appropriate as my face expressed my reaction ever so lucidly. My face was as red as the dress I was wearing. If anymore blood flowed to my face through sheer embarrassment, it would be plausible to suggest that I may have disappeared. My effort to answer him without shakiness to my voice prevailing, which I knew would embarrass me further. I smiled a nervous smile, hating he asked me the question I was avoiding the entire night. Taking a deep breath to console myself and give encouragement to my efforts. A gulp of saliva to support my bid to give the truth, knowing in three seconds I would collapse out of shame. Hoping desperately he would find my longing to spend more time with him in return adorable and not indeed insane.

"My hotel is in Geneva."

"GENEVA!!!"

Nicolas yelled out with the utmost disbelief, astonished at what he believed his ears to have heard. Unfit to grasp what I had told him for a brief moment.

"Why did you stay here until this time if your hotel is in Geneva?"

"It's a safe journey back I wasn't tired so why not? I did not come on holiday to go to bed early missing out on what's on offer."

159

"Why yes, I do understand that aspect, but that is a very long journey back at this time of night, or shall I correct myself and state morning. I am glad you think like that. I am pleased to have spent these hours with you. But wow what can I say?"

After looking at his Omega watch which caught my immediate attention.

"It is almost one in the morning."

"I know, so I must catch the next train back. I'm very tired now. It seems to have caught up with me almost all of a sudden. Isn't it strange when that happens?"

"Yes, it is. I know how you feel, my sweet. Would you like to stay at my chalet tonight? It has five bedrooms. I feel awful for you taking such a long journey back at this time of the morning, particularly when you look so sleepy?"

"No, thank you. I appreciate greatly your offer; it is extremely generous of you I must affirm. With all due respect I don't know you. I couldn't, no matter how sleepy I was. It would not be decorous of me to consent. With no disrespect to you."

"I do understand, I hope I have neither insulted nor upset you by offering. I was trying to be considerate, especially as you are a young woman. Feeling it was the gentlemanly thing to do. I truly would not want anything to happen to you, whether this is a safe country or not. I hope you see that, my dear sweet girl?"

"Oh yes, Nicolas, I do. Like I said, I truly appreciate your bid, I sincerely thank you, I do but I ought not. It would not be a ladylike act for me to accept that invitation, at least not tonight undeniably. By my demur I hope I have not upset you in any way, as that honestly is the last thing I would desire to do. I must be dignified at all times, or else how could I possibly expect or wish for a man to marry me one day? I do hope you don't find my morals laughable. I truly believe it is vitally important for us all to have standards to live by."

"I do understand and respect your wishes. I recognise where you are coming from. I am not offended, honestly. In fact I am elated that you have not accepted my bid, as you so very gracefully put it, not that I would not love to make you welcome within my home, you are by all means welcome. Even so, I have such respect for your values.

That is a very attractive endearing quality, which is too often rare during these modern days."

"Thank you for being a dear gentleman. That is such a rarity, in this day and age I must disclose. I suppose we are both one of a kind. In such a large world it could be said that it is atypical for us to have even met, wouldn't you agree?"

"I most certainly would, you are a very in tuned young woman and that is another attribute I must admit I respect about you. I will be forever grateful to have met you. Don't you find it peculiar that we would have names somewhat similar, although yours is much more beautiful than mine?"

"I thought the exact same thing when you introduced yourself. I wonder why we did meet. I have no doubt that there is a very definite purpose."

"I believe we all meet for a reason and that every person we come across in our lives are there for a purpose. I find it most interesting when two people meet and come to a junction in life ending up on the same path. To be on the same path there is very much a reason. May it be to make one happy, to teach us something important, even if we meet someone who wrongs and hurts us; I think that is to make us a stronger person. That is the very same reason I do not hate anyone who has done me wrong over the years. Not that I respect them for harming me, or that I forgive them, but I am grateful as they have helped me be a better and more of a vigilant man. It is when we have seen the harsh reality of what this world offers, we cherish the good and the special.

May I walk you to the train?"

"Of course you may. That is, of course, if you are not too tired and your chalet is not too far from the train station."

"My chalet is in the same direction as the train station, just a little past the station in fact. So it is on my way home."

"Isn't that perfect? Another coincidence. Thank you very much indeed, Nicolas. It almost feels as though the stars, the moon and the Gods are on our side tonight, everything is so at ease, unproblematic even tranquil and everything in conjunction with us and moving in the same direction. We have the same mentality, the same interests and outlooks, yet it is all coincidence."

"I couldn't agree more, my days usually are problem some and pose a great deal of effort but since I have met you, it is almost as though we are comparable, parallel within life. It is odd to feel this strongly about anything or anyone for that matter, in such a short space of time. But I must state for the record I like it. I am intrigued by you and all you stand for. I personally don't believe in coincidences, we have met for a reason. You have a power over me. Trust me when I say nobody before has ever affected me the way you take my breath away."

Nicolas beginning to laugh from mortification.

"Oh dear I must apologise that was definitely very deep, particularly for this time of night."

Hesitating to answer as I seen the train station drawing near. A heavy feeling of gloom rose within me, I was saddened. On arrival at the station I stopped to thank Nicolas but the chance was gone before I was able to do so. Nicolas disappeared for a moment in a quick and frantic burst, to the information desk.

Immediately becoming curious as to why he was at the desk. With astonishment beheld over my facial expression. Too curious to hold back. When Nicolas returned, somewhat flustered, informing me, he had bought a ticket to escort me back to Geneva safely. I immediately felt stunned by his cordial act. Yet I undeniably was happy that he was making the effort to show his appreciation to spend time with me. He was doing everything I could possibly expect any man to do, ensuring he extended our time together. I found this to be special deed. Instantly feeling guilty with him being an older man and it would be at least 05.24am before we arrive at Geneva. Then for him to return to Zermatt it would be well past 09:00. The night gone on my behalf, no sleep, no rest. I felt bad, I did feel guilt along with that I felt important. He was making me important. Making me feel significant. I could feel admiration for his kindness filling me for his considerate gestures. Initially he was a dear gentleman, filled with too much alluring charisma. To own too much charisma allows one to get away with too much.

"Thank you, Nicolas, that is very kind of you. Now I feel just awful."

"Not at all. It is my pleasure. I couldn't have the sweetest and kindest woman I have ever encountered traveling halfway across a country, in the middle of the night unaccompanied. What kind of man would that make me? Why on earth would you feel awful, my dear? If you enjoy my company as much as I enjoy yours that makes me delighted."

"I feel just awful you are going to be awake for the rest of the night on my behalf, just because I was being selfish because I wanted to get to know you better."

"I don't mind missing sleep to ensure you are back where you belong. Safe and sound. I will have plenty of sleep when I am dead. Right now, I shall enjoy life by enjoying wonderful company from a faithful lady."

Too tired to speak I threw Nicolas the biggest smile which had ever until now occupied my face. In that instant, Nicolas truly believing he was the luckiest man alive to be in my company.

Overflowing with butterflies and bliss, he struggled to stay awake. We sat abreast on the train both requiring sleep, so much so, neglecting to be in awe of the amazing scenery, we would usually value during any other circumstances. As I was nodding off to flimsy and light sleep, Nicolas was hoping I would not awaken until his erection, which was stubborn and refused to go back down, was sub passed. Thankfully I had not awakened to see his cock ignited and full of volcanic ash, to save Nicolas from humiliation considering the fact that he is desperately conveying himself to be someone he is not.

Four hours passed finally arriving at Geneva train station we exited the train. Starting to walk up another hill and within moments, I was back safe and sound where I belonged, like Nicolas desired. As Nicolas walked me home, all the time with awaiting and unbearable anticipation, wanting and needing desperately to consume me whole. Both saddened that the day was now ended. A wonderful day filled with long lasting warm memories.

"Thank you so very much, Nicolas. This is so far from your chalet and I feel like the most selfish woman in the world, truly I do. It was both sympathetic and compassionate for you to do this. I do not know how I can thank you. Just saying thank you does not feel enough. Nobody has ever thought enough of me to be this kind, I am very flattered. My heart is overflowing with appreciation."

"My sweet child I appreciate that you permitted me to take you home, regardless of the duration of time in which it took to get you here. I was being selfish if I were to be totally honest with you. I hope you can forgive me for that trait?"

"Selfish. What do you mean by selfish? You are the most selfless human being I have had the fortune to meet."

Nicolas laughed aloud.

"I didn't want this night to end. I didn't want for the moon to fade and the sun to take its place. I wished and prayed all night as we were walking for this night to be the longest night in history. I do not want to leave you here all by yourself. I want to be around you all day and every day. I wish you were my everything. Even the reason I awake each morning, the reason I live. I want to tell you this and so much more but I don't want to alarm you. You are a special person. I know I will never meet anyone like you for the rest of my life. The reason I know this is because, it has taken me all these years to meet you and no other woman has compared to your perfection this night. I do not want for you to not be in my life. To turn and never see that glorious face again."

"Why must you talk this way, Nicolas?"

"I am sorry. I don't want to frighten you. That's the last thing I want to do. I want to always be truthful with you and tell you how wonderful you are. The truth be told, I'm mesmerised by your serenity. I have never seen anymore as magical as you. I kept silent about how I felt all night. Now I'm afraid, I will never see you after tonight, after I leave in a moment's time. It saddens me."

"If you feel that way about me and want to see me you may. I am here for a further three days. If you want to see me, you are more than welcome. There is nowhere more lovely than to be in a place where nobody knows you. I have never met anyone particularly a man who possesses such a pure heart. This time it would be my pleasure. Any time you desire to see me you only need to ask. I am incapable of thinking of any other soul on earth I would much rather spend time with. When I return home if you would like to stay in touch I can give you my email address and telephone number. We can be friends."

"Thank you, my darling. You have no way of understanding how much that means to me. I don't want you to misconstrue that I am a lonely old man, who has past my expiration date. I can assure you I am not that …"

With a giggle and a cheeky twinkle in his eyes. He looked innocent and harmless, a man with a dearly tender heart.

"… I am relatively content within my life. Ultimately I am spell bound by you and your kind heart, which shines through your eyes, like diamonds glistening upon freshly fallen snow. Your tenderness, your warmth will help make me a better man. Your prolific way will last more than a few days for me. Your kind-heartedness will last for the rest of my life. I sincerely wish you did not have to return home. I will miss you deeply if I could not see your face."

"You are so sweet, too sweet. You have left me breathless by your magnanimous analysis of me. Your generosity with the evocative words you use to describe me, they are inspiring me to become those things, you either think I am, or hope for me to be. I am the person who is frightened now. I am frightened of failing you by falling short of those expectations. I may offend you. I couldn't have that; it would hurt me, if I knew I had disappointed you. You are too special to be hurt."

"Nobody is perfect. We both know that. The world certainly is not. All one can do is to try. Try to aspire to something and earn it. We may not succeed right away, does that mean we automatically and ultimately gave up, because we are under the illusion we will not achieve success, in any case? Or do we strive for what we want? Be that a person for love and companionship, a career, money anything. As long as we try, giving all of what we have to give. If we fall short at first, we should become more willing to try harder the next time and every time, until we finally reap the awards of success. Some of the most successful people in this world had a long hard climb. Knowing that and how much effort one invest we can then bow down at the end of our life and be proud not ashamed for not attempting first of all, formerly surrendering. It is very late or early whichever way you wish to look at it. May we go for breakfast, say nine?"

"Oh, yes please. I would love to. I take such pleasure in your company. You are indeed well-informed about life with an independent mind. I like that. Nine o'clock, it is. Where, Nicolas?"

"I shall pick you up here nine o'clock sharp, that way I will know between now and then you are safe. I would like you to know that I am here for you like no one else. At least, if you wish as a mere friend, a person to talk, a person to exchange thoughts, wishes, whatever you like. Good night and thank you for an amazing day having become historic in my life from this day forth. That may sound dramatic to you but nonetheless it is a fact."

Nicolas smiled a wide smile the kind which indicate sincere happiness. Tears welled in his eyes. Kissing my hand and parting for a short time, prior our confirmed next engagement. As Nicolas turned to walk away, leaving me to catch up on sleep I desperately required. I felt the need to say one last thing, almost bellowing after him as he had turned on his heels excitement and delight took over my being.

"Nicolas, thank you. You have already given me so much. Shown me a great deal by your positive manner towards life and myself. I have never not once seen the beauty you see in me. You understand me already. Nobody has ever understood me, not even when they have tried, and that was uncommon. You have interest in me as a person, as a woman. You see me for what I am, not what I should be. You see me; you see even what I overlook within myself. For that I have tremendous gratitude. Oh, Nicolas, will you make it back in time for nine o'clock, if you take the train back now?"

"Did I not mention I have a chateau in Geneva as well, I will stay there tonight, it is only five minutes away. I will get plenty of sleep before meeting you later. Thank you for your sincere concern and your sweet, sweet words."

Briskly turning on my heels I ran into the hotel. Tears also welling in my eyes, still managing to glow with gratification. I was touched because of my prize winning performance. The prize being me, I will be the trophy on the arm of a filthy rich man who thinks me pure at heart and kind. If he only knew, poor Nicolas if you only knew.

On that night I was genuinely gullible enough to believe I was taking him for a ride. I was winning this game I honestly thought. Not realising that he was ahead, Nicolas Beaumont was winning all the games he was playing. Innocence is death. A murderous intent. He was the master of all games. It was not until the very end, until I took the upper hand and I won. After years of trials and errors, and many punishments I finally won. For the time being I was in ignorant bliss, after all, that is what love is.

CHAPTER TWENTY-SEVEN

Black Beauty

Beauty is his, beauty is hers.
Beauty captured like the night hills.
Beauty can be a blessing or a murderous intent.
Either way it helps to possess it.

Beauty will take you far in this world.
Sometimes it can give you utter bliss,
Or be the taking of your life.
Either way it helps to possess it.

Beauty and the beast.
Black beauty.
Falling in love with beauty, is beauty captured.

The memories held within your mind.
The dreams one has when in another land.
Beauty surrounds us whether we possess it or not.
Either way it helps to possess it.
Beauty is his, beauty is hers.
Beauty and the beast.
Black beauty.

CHAPTER TWENTY-EIGHT

Beauty Captured

Thursday 4 December 2001

Unable to sleep that morning, butterflies throughout my body the exciting sensation that began. That splendid feeling of being in the honeymoon stage, that feeling never lasts too long. I thought intently that first night, how long the honeymoon phase would last for us. Would it mean anything a week from now? Would we have a life together or will I be home in a few days. Am I to forget him? Should I make certain I do not fall in love spearing myself a broken heart. Don't become attached. I lay in bed thinking about today and what would follow. My sleep briefly subsided. What would we do, where would we go and exactly what kind of man Nicolas was? Really was. Beneath all that fine talking and good manners, the educated persona. Who was Nicolas Beaumont? Now I was too interested. Wanting to know too much. Unsure what my motives were as of yet. Supposedly, one cannot know unerringly what way another human being is from one day spent together. Not even after twenty years. Only a rough estimate can be deduced. Men in particular play their stupid games, making a woman fall making it impossible to resist their mesmeric charms. All this to ensure when they tell a woman for the first time he loves her, having her eating every lie right out from his hand. Chocolate covered lies. Potent with fatal repercussions. Sweeter and juicier than fresh ripened strawberries. Tossing. Unable to get conformable. Kicking my legs out in fury. Too much useless information and unimportant thoughts rocketed through my overactive mind. No matter how many times I puffed up my pillow I was uncomfortable. I have forever been disappointed in my life, I was not expecting miracles this time around, after all, he is a man and men almost always let women down. I had not being blessed meeting men who told me the truth. To say the least I was a sceptic. Wanting to believe more than anything but unable to. The past remnants lingers in present time.

Nicolas unable to go to bed taking a stroll around his bedroom, thinking about that beautiful face belonging to his newfound love, his wife to be. That evening's conversation each move I made, how I smiled played and replayed over and over in his mind. Like real time. Like a movie videoed. Not one solitary move or word missed. A photographic memory. That irrefutable cockiness which was indicative within him, the attribute of I always get what I want when I want, in no way deserted him in actual fact augmented too greatly. My face so small and fragile, he just wanted to hold it tenderly and kiss it. Staring at it for hours. Undisturbedly. In awe of my formation; how each bone was knitted together. No camera could have captured my beauty more absorbedly than reality. Both of us knowing a nap was simply wishful thinking. Both thrilled and in ignorant bliss, with designs of our own for one another. We were to have breakfast together, the first of many over a lifetime. That was my plan. Concluding this man was worth my time thus invested. Each of us knowing how we wanted things to turn out, each of us wanting similar yet very different things. We were both complicated people. We wanted each other nonetheless.

Nicolas collected me at nine sharp that morning in his black Bentley. I was up from six twenty-four getting myself put together, with maybe a twenty minute power nap. Aware I would look awful from literally no sleep. Hoping I would have him by my side for the entire day. Extra concealer and foundation was required. The twenty-four hour extra thick, more expensive product party girls like Kate Moss is renowned for using. Having his chauffeur opening the car door for me, an attempt to flatter. Sweeping me off my feet with opulent grandeur. He had succeeded. Not confirming this. I was certainly charmed, thus not advertising my pleasure never confirming my delight but always projecting my distain. I was keeping him on his toes like a woman ought to. Not that I was the kind of woman to treat them mean to keep them keen. Detesting women who possess that mentality. Not simply because it does not work, it is simply inelegant. My game was simply play hard to get. Never give men anything for free. Who are men after all? They are not what they think, that is one certainty in life and life demonstrates very few of those. I do not believe in proving them right. They do not control me. I control me and my own destiny. Like all smart women should. Nicolas intended to cajole me into longing for a sumptuous life style, wanting me to say yes once he proposed. Overlooking that I already possessed the capital to give myself these things. I chose not to live this way. Certain that a woman of my statue would unquestionably want the life style in which he could and was willing to offer me. Able to distinguish that there was something behind it. Knowing it was not merely companionship, he could have or buy any woman he wished, many women go for that set up, especially those Russian and Ukraine brides for sale online. Of course, there are masses of Chinese tourists whom travel to Switzerland during the year; they are as famous for marrying under similar circumstances. Give them an easy life with no work, stashes of money in the bank and a wardrobe of expensive clothing accompanied by a jewellery box and volt filled with highly sought after gems. No, Nicolas was too upmarket a man for that type of affair, he wasn't desperate; he was anything but. That was what made me wonder from the start. I did not have to wonder why me, why did he pick me of all people, when there are countless numbers of women around. I knew why he picked me. I was what I wanted to turn into, this was why I was picked. But why so quickly, this to me was the question which owned an interesting answer. A mysteriously dark answer. If I had asked him this question, I had no doubt he would have made his response sound romantic melting my heart and making my knees weak, from sweet, sweet chocolate coated lies. The cheap kind of chocolate with excessive sugar quantities. Over compensating for the bitterness beneath. After teeth crack the outer coating to allow the truth the seep through.

Being an in tuned women, due to how I lead my life in the past, made me smart enough to interpret that Nicolas would take me to a café for breakfast fit for a queen. Thus, knowing to dress to kill, my aim, to show I knew how to perform. I knew the role which would be expected from me in an upper class milieu. I had to demonstrate my etiquette, pertaining to dress sense, respectability, fine dining, and how I am capable of conducting myself in public. Informing him I was a force to impress. Today is a test. Dressing almost to the extent as one would when on the red carpet, elegant and chic. I was impressing without being ostentatious. Men translated my mannerisms by being poised and dignified a woman who possessed a great deal of self-respect. I dressed well, all the time even in bed, even when alone. Apart from the times I have been guilty of walking around the house naked on hot days. It gets rather hot in Italy during the summer. A feline must do whatever it takes to cool down. I had great posture, oozing confidence and grace. At times people considered I had attended a school intended solely with an objective, of turning out well polished and gracious women. I was not blessed to have attended such a school. People not knowing this nor did I highlight the truth. I earned my classiness, I invested wisely. Why should they know the truth, it is none of their business. Learning from their mishaps never to presume, only dealing in facts. To deal in facts very rarely is known to bite one in the ass. Everything I signify was self-taught. My demeanour was one which would indicate that I was from a nineteen-fifties move. Ladylike, couth and bashful, knowing my place, opposed to the modern day woman behaving more manly than a man. What I was most proud of was never becoming complacent. There is no room for cockiness when one must survive. Complacency makes way for mistakes. Mistakes makes ways for capture. Teaching myself isn't as easy as it sounds. It takes a great deal of time, effort, discipline and motivation to do more so to do it well. It is not something which can be taught and learnt in one week, three months or a year. It is something one must live, breath and work at. Practice day and night and every waking moment. Implementing it into everything one does. Each sentence one speaks. Each move one takes. With this in time, it allowed me to have a quick mind. Perseverance is key. In time I was then able to make up my roles as I went along. In the beginning I had to predetermine what men may say to me, how I must respond, verbally, tones used, actions and so forth. Extended pausing to get my action correct. Now that I possess a quick mind I am ready for anything. I could take the lead. No, society does not have to know my truth merely to judge in order to ridicule. What would be the point in them discrediting me when I taught myself everything I

172

know and acquired? Incompetence to their wealthy parents paying obscene amounts of money to have their children educated at a school which taught them how to sit, when to drink, how to handshake and what to say at the appropriate time. Upper class manners. How to use complicated words to impress and mislead. No, I am proud that I was able to do this for myself. Indicating I have a more dynamic mind than most. Nobody has done anything for me. I gave this to me. I did this and I did it well.

On a multitude of occasions strangers assumed I was royalty with my refined elegance. Being asked frequently where my bodyguards were to my amusement. Of course I did not show my hand. Due to my underprivileged and destitute upbringing making me embarrassed and ashamed to declare my roots. Making up a story of fiction to support my unfounded and disreputable stories about my family, feeling secure that this story could not be disproved. For this I will never apologise with a family as horrid as mine. Predecessors rarely if ever think about the shame they will bring unto their offspring. The murders they commit. The rapes the molesting. It is unfair that high society tarnish us all with being the same as our dead relatives and anything they may have done. It is wrong. I was not going down. I worked too hard to be respected. Seen for who I am. I was not going to be degraded by my dead family members, or the living for that matter. As far as I am concerned I am not related to any of them. They are all bloody dead and gone. How could I be related to monsters, the bogeyman? They did not think about how their actions would affect me, so why should I think about them now? This nobody bar a husband could take offense to. My life was one of hardships and pain. My childhood resulted in me making drastic mistakes in adult life, only to become further ashamed. I have learnt over time that if somebody loves me enough they will overlook the mistakes I have made, especially when considering the upbringing which contributed to my reprehensible actions. I wished I was a luckier woman who had a nicer story to tell. I envied but never begrudged other families who had a great relationship over and above closeness. More than anything I wanted to be close to a family, but not my family. Not that I was overly biased towards them initially. There were many times throughout the years I attempted to become close with them, always in vain. They did not deserve the respect or the forgiveness I once gave, so I stopped. Never willing to try again. My family should have stopped reproducing. Why they wanted to have children I cannot understand. I want to get married – be close to a family who see me for me. Just me for who I am and what I represent. Desiring to marry a man to become his everything, marrying into a perfect family who love me as though I was theirs. Call me "daughter," tell me they love me. Offering me advice on how to keep my marriage healthy. Giving me a hug anytime I needed it. A shoulder to cry on. People who care enough to demonstrate a little human compassion and affection towards me, just a little human contact, so I know that I am real. Being more in love with being in love, in contrast to the actual person I would marry, lead to an assortment of problems. In effect I suffered from depression in my earlier adulthood, again, which still leaks through from time to time. My despair had led to me becoming self-destructive. Praying to the god above to claim my body. The body and soul which has brought me only despondency, which I am incapable of carrying upon my enervated shoulders any longer. It has worn me down. I have nothing left to give. I've been robbed from the things I deserve most. When I was faced with a bridge I was forced to burn, only the year prior to meeting Nicolas I decided to run away. At that stage I did not comprehend that running away was not an option, finding this out too late.

For breakfast Nicolas brought me to an expensive and exclusive café, The Remor. The Remor over the years has welcomed beautiful and important people such as Princess Grace and her husband Prince Reiner, Audrey Hepburn and Ingrid Bergman. These two actresses were who I respected the most. As my mother died when I was five, I had no other women to neither look up to nor teach me all the things a young girl needs to know. Turning to amiable actresses as these two to my advantage. If it were not for their elegance, modesty and alluring demeanour and soft vocal tones I would not be the lady I am today. Instead of paying large sums of money to have decrepit old women being rude to me, claiming to be teaching me etiquette, instead I watched both these actresses's movies over and over, studying their photographs, the poses. They were taught by the best, I learnt from them. Studying magazines for makeup tips, learning to do many different hairstyles. I then learnt how to hold myself. The end result, everything and more I needed to be to excel.

Everybody at Remor was most certainly a millionaire if not billionaire, considering the prices on the gentlemen's menu alone, as well as the grand menu with the gourmet they served. I, found the café over-elaborate; personally, I preferred charming and relaxing. The very reason The Snowboat stuck in my mind. My opinion of people who wined and dined at these places were only out to be seen and greatly narcissistic. It certainly wasn't the quantity of food. Rich and elite restaurants equals excessively priced and skimpy portions. I did not mind being there, I was not be paying the bill. A change of scene was nice. For breakfast we drank champagne and ate fancy courses, of which I had grave difficulty pronouncing and knowing what I was actually consuming. To start I had coffee, bread and jam, while I was waiting for my champagne with Rosti to be served. Rosti is a traditional breakfast and potato dish but in most establishments have been replaced by the famous birchermuesli. Their jam was the real kind of jam. Quality. Not laced in sugar. Juicy fruits, crisp on the outer, and melting on the inner. Mouth-watering. Nicolas watched every move I made as I was eating and drinking, instead of observing he was studying me. Pondering over in his mind am I good enough, am I who he thinks I am. As I sat there eating and posing, I wondered how these rich people could drink champagne on regular bases for breakfast. I found some of the food a little too rich for my taste. I could get used to this lifestyle like anything if one eats it frequently enough, one will with the passage of time acquire a taste for it. Just like rich men and their brandy. Like most things new, it merely takes time to adjust, when one has altered themselves, preferably for the better, they would not have things any other way.

Everywhere I went in Switzerland I noticed the deco was similar, with wooden panelling on all the walls with built in seating. As we sat in Remor, Nicolas was as close as he could get, without being bad-mannered to the public's eyes and to have us thrown out, but enough to make me uncomfortable. My heart skipping and stomach fluttered. Finding it difficult to cut my food, no elbow space, he was right on top of me, literally. I refrained with difficultly to tell him to move out of my personal space, avoiding being seen as rude I declined. We sat in a supposed romantic corner of the restaurant, with dim lighting and professional waiters who honestly loved their job. We sat in an out of the way corner. I remember thinking it was as though we were hiding from the police or the mafia, not wanting to become conspicuous. We sat around a very heavy mahogany dining table with a white table cloth. It was a high-class establishment, there were no stains or off white colours on the cloth. A crystal vase in the middle of the table with a flower centrepiece, white carnations. Genuine sliver cutlery and coffee pot, which was as heavy as a gold block and fine light china crockery. High class indeed. Feeling out of my depths. I left rich people behind in Italy after Charles's death. I enjoyed the life style but I wasn't in my natural habitat. I don't mind trying anything once. Acting just as well as the rest of the people, I did myself justice. Purely by the way people were looking at me, I knew they had no idea I was not rich born. I was simply acting the act. This was how I understood most of them were also acting. Anyone who attended places such as the Remor despite how beautiful it was, they are all acting in one way or another, particularly with those airs and graces. I was not raised in a wealthy domicile, making ones attitude narrower when they are unacquainted with something but this was to change in the near future. In time I came to love these places. Becoming my regular hidey-hole. What I once thought when under the uninformed frame of mind, I came to laugh at myself for being so dumb. Never take seriously what you believe when you are young – one's perspective changes with age.

Walking for hours around public parks and crematories and down along Lake Geneva. The sun shined above it was deceiving. It was freezing cold. A chill present in the air, it blew in land from the water. Refreshing. Birds flocked in the cold winter sky, chirping. Attracting my attention. As I looked up, birds flews in sequence. Dancing almost. A pretty sight. It was then I realised today I had found a new love. After a few hours of pleasant yet interesting conversation and plenty of clean crisp fresh air, deciding to board Nicolas's Bentley to visit Lausanne for the rest of the day. Lausanne located in the French sector of Switzerland, only a short drive from Geneva exuded all the charm I could have hoped for. It was an old town and reaped the character of a period long gone. A class towns just do not have these days. Lausanne had a great deal to offer when it came to beautiful buildings, it was indeed the definition of adornment. I felt like I was in a movie, a setting from Van Helsing. Reminding me of San Francisco with steep hills the further into the town one goes. Souvenir shops along the streets with pretty clocks, dolls and ornaments displayed in their windows. Eye-catching. Adorable. Following a day spent dedicated and appointed to visiting museums and parks and attaining a fine collection of souvenirs, a day of culture I was wore out. Nicolas bought me a medium-sized trinket box with a carving of the Matterhorn upon its door. Beautifully handmade, stunning to look at. I have treasured that little box all these decades later. I still have it. It still sits in its appointed place upon my dressing table. There is not a day which goes by which I do not think about the day I was given it. The happiness and shyness I then felt. Long gone. I enjoyed my experiences and visiting Lausanne's gothic styled cathedral. The dressing up in medieval clothing was thrilling, giving us a lot to laugh about. I was mesmerised to learn that Cathedral Notre dame was completed in the twelve and thirteenth centuries. What's more I was fascinated by the fountain of Justice overlooking a basin, which was said to have been created as far back as fifteenfifty-seven. It was a special day. A memorable day. Nicolas still full of energy and zest. He did not look his years. In those earlier days of our relationship he did not act his age.

Prior to meeting me, Nicolas's favourite pastime used to be reading, anything and everything. He had such a curiosity to learn. Now that he had encountered me, I had become his leisure pursuit. Enjoying every moment together hoping that today (every day he was with me) would never end. And it would carry on to be a long endless holiday of laughs and making memories. Photograph after photograph taken to look over with the passing of years of how happy we were and lucky. When he was old, a moment of nostalgia and picking out the memory which brings him great comfort. A smile governs his face. With many sexual experiences together to recall. Reminding him how amazing it was to be young. The energy which went into having the time of one's life. The days long missed. The old regular things he loved to do was to be buried along with his dark secrets and evil past. In its place was going to be me. Spending his days and nights with Nicolette. From that moment on it was all about me.

Nicolas was still searching for the appropriate time to propose, all the time thinking, would it be uncivilised to propose to such a flaming beauty without an engagement ring the size of Mars? Or would she be flattered I did, knowing I befell to her magnetism. Powerless to control myself. Resist. The feeling which swept me off my feet to my knees in humble appreciation. Begging for her hand. Her life. She has to know that I am in her enthral mesmerised by everything she is and even to become.

PART NINE

Promise of Forever

CHAPTER TWENTY-NINE

Illicit Proposal

Friday 5 December 2001

"I should take you back to your hotel. You have had a long day yesterday and again today. You need to catch up on your sleep, you look so sleepy, my dear. I shall call my car and have us taken there immediately; after all, it is one in the morning, again." Leaving the distinguished restaurant Zodiac located in the heart of Geneva. The lake could be seen from my seat. My heart was calm. My heart is never calm. But it was tonight. With its intimate lighting romantic music, candid tasteful décor and milieu with thoughtful flowers as a centre piece, along with a delicate candle upon the dinner table enhancing the romantic mood. Blood red table cloths to match the deep red walls with gold outlining; gold door frames, and painted ceilings which resembled the Sistine Chapel in Rome. Giving one the feeling there in a 1950s movie starring either Elizabeth Taylor or Audrey Hepburn, being wooed by Cary Grant or the ultimate sex symbol Dean Martin. Who had the right amount of sex appeal, the right amount of lust to his voice and the right amount of thirst in those alluring eyes? He was seduction. Without a word just a look in those dark, dark eyes. Above all, only what Deano could pull off, was an overabundance of charismatic eminence. For some an overabundance just as the word indicates, would be too much but not for Deano. They don't make men like that anymore, aside of Liam

Neeson that tall Irish beast, with the pronounced nose, sexy accent and sexy body. The right amount of hard man, with the ideal amount of gooey filling. Now that is a man, and three halfs. Long, tall and full of sexual steam. My kind of man! The Restaurant was surrounded by many prestige hotels, boutiques, salons and architectural heavens. Delectable envy.

Nicolas still working out how, when and where to propose. As we came to the street in front of the restaurant walking through yet another square to enter Nicolas discerning Bentley. It seemed as though France, Italy, Belgium and Switzerland all had squares in common. As I took a deep breath and in doing so a gleam of stars shining portrayed through my eyes. Knowing that would happen, making me look more alive at that particular moment in time, than I had in the past year in spite of desperately requiring sleep. I softly stopped in my tracks before reaching the car gently turning to Nicolas.

"Nicolas, would you walk me to the hotel instead?"

"Of course I shall. Anything that makes you happy."

"Even though my feet are sore and tired, I desire to walk the night away. Walking seems to be our thing. I have felt so alive today that is down to you. I must thank you for all your kindness and making me feel alive. People are forever calling me young, for such a prolonged period of time now I have felt awfully old. Ever since last night it feels as though you have brought my youth back, just when I was sure it was lost forever."

"It has been my pleasure, Nicolette, more than perhaps yours I dare say my dear. I would love to spend all my time with you. Each day doing something special and exciting, bringing life back into my old and almost useless veins. It is amusing how we have both made one another feel young, especially considering when one is young and the other is old." Smiling in reply. Throwing that innocent, kind smile, indicating how foolish he was. The smile in which I decided to throw him was one to flatter his ego. After walking the squares and small back allies around distinctive hotels and restaurants, bumping into famous people and becoming embarrassed. There were so many to be seen. It was the land of the famous. Unused to this style of living made me blush like a schoolgirl. Sophia Loren and Michael

Caine were both seen coming out of Kaspinski on the lake front. Walking around the beautifully cared for graveyards, which were unlike any I had ever seen before, they weren't creepy they weren't overdone, with half a mile tall headstones, no statues making it appear to look more like an altar of sacrifice opposed to a burial site. They were simply taken care of and modest. Little candles lit nightly, a *touching sentiment.*

It was five in the morning when he finally returned me back to the Grand hotel, after a long and comforting day and night together. Both feeling like children again. We both felt we had something to live for once more. Each other. I could already feel the influence of love ingraining. Guilty of feeling both scared along with an immensely strong emotion and rush of exhilaration. It sounded like waves gushing within. Ashamed of my primary motives. Honest to God I wanted this to be a man to become mine. No games, no bullshit. Nothing but the truth and real sentiment. Forgetting myself, what my plans were. Not permitting myself to feel love, it always ended badly. Badly for me and only me! The broken heart, the tears, the pain, everything I didn't want to go through again.

"Would you care to come up for a drink? There is a bottle of champagne in the minibar, they also have Jack Daniels, Vodka and Gin if you like. Something to relax you perhaps before sleeping?"

"I am going home to my house here in Geneva right after, would you like to go there now instead of going into your hotel. It has eight bedrooms. I hate knowing you will be alone in a hotel. We could have a nightcap there if you wish. I know the hotel has been paid for, but at least you could wake up in a nice house surrounded by beautiful views. We could have breakfast together on the terraced if you like. Would it not be better than having breakfast in a large room with a lot of strange faces staring at you through sleepy eyes? I know what hotels are like." He said laughing.

"I would love to but I must be honest, Nicolas."

Forcing a blush making me appear to look saintly and shy.

"I think I am falling in love with you…." A long pause from shame and embarrassment and of the unknown.

"I'm pretty sure that it's not the wine talking, my mind isn't on the cloud of romance. I never let myself get that fussy. If I were to go to your chateau it would not be fitting, I would not be able to control myself. I will have womanly urges. I would desire to make love to you, I must not. After all, we hardly know one another. Because I want to, does not make it right. It is only lust. A man like you could never love a woman like me. I must not delude myself." Said with deliberate trepidation.

Once I concluded my flattering statement, my enticing charms, instantly feeling I was doing a great job luring him into my deceptive trap, while all the time remaining innocent-looking both in appearances as well as in deed. I was such a great actress – always masking my true feelings and intent, never sure when the appropriate time was to express my sincere feelings. Thereby hiding them I felt safer and more comfortable of not making a fool of myself. Therefore, even still I refuse to let anyone know me and what I am truly thinking. What I think is not always a negative, but it could be used to harm me at a later date, so keeping my lips closed ninety-nine percent of the time and the remaining percent is spent flattering. Ensuring I do not dig a grave for myself. In my twenties I ended up not knowing what I felt or what I was meant to feel. I had played in a great deal of games, I didn't know what genuine emotion truly felt like. Most men in Geneva are rich boys with money and toys. Geneva is a playground for the rich. It is where dices are thrown, games are lost and won.

"My sweet child, I understand what you mean…" A kind smile easing my nerves.

"Just because you come to my home does not mean you are obliged to have sex with me or obligated to do anything for that matter. Do not forget I am old enough to be your father. I respect you. I adore you. You must never doubt that. You are rare, not solely in beauty but also in the sense of possessing the quality of honesty and directness, these qualities are loveable. You have no idea how difficult it is to find a woman who speaks her mind, who tells is as it is. I can confirm you are the woman I have been spending my life searching for. These attributes in a woman I have been searching for, for many years."

Moving towards me with his hands stretched out. Placing his left hand on my right arm. Reassuring me; I have not made a fool of myself by opening up. This was what he wanted.

"A woman who is refined and graceful along with telling it like it is, until you, of course, is something I have never been privileged to see, know or experience before. Collectively all this intrigues me, this captivates my entire attention. I admire you. You can always speak candidly to me. I flatter myself in believing we have an atypical relationship. Always frank and open. Never to hide or sugar coat."

"So if I went to see your home that would be it? A nice conversation and a drink as usual, perhaps a grand tour around your fine home or we could leave that till morning after we're refreshed after two nights of zero sleep."

Now certain I was doing a first-class job of deceiving.

"Absolutely! ..." he said with enthusiasm. (Now thinking back after experiencing what I have, I now understand it was said with too much enthusiasm.) "... Unless you sought after more than that, but you do not need to if you do not wish. I do not expect anything. You most certainly do not need to feel forced. Or anything less than safe and at ease in my presence. My one promise to you is that you will always be safe with me. Always. I am not going to lie to you, my dear, I find you to be exceedingly attractive. In fact attractive would be a sombre understatement to what I truly think to be completely honest. I cannot think of a word strong enough to describe you, I don't think a word has been created yet strong enough to use. I am having a difficult time keeping my hands off you and remaining a gentleman. It is arduous to refrain, if I am to be brutally honest. Please don't disrespect me for my honesty. But a gentleman I am and have been all my life. I will not neglect being that now, although it is a task which is causing me a great deal of anguish. I hope you can respect my truthfulness."

"If you would like my company, then I would be more than pleased to escort you back to your home. It would be the least I could do after you brought me back here safely last night and again tonight. It is my turn to escort you home safely. Plus I trust you, Nicolas. I do trust you. It is my turn to keep you safe. I know without doubt I am safe with you and I wish to thank you for that from the bottom of my heart. There aren't many if any men like you or at least they are hard to come across. I'm never that lucky. I know that trust between us is of the highest importance, I adore you for that. It would be an honour to wake up and have breakfast with you first thing in the morning. We're almost there."

"Where does the time go to when we are together?"

I sincerely believed the words I spoke that night. Later to swallow them all. What an idiot I was. Feeling as though I were a helpless woman who married a dirty cop. The one cop with the good looks, the hard as nails body and the violent temper probably caused by the excessive steroids. Cops stick together. No one would help. No one would believe my story. Because it is only a story. Men of their degree don't do such things. It is only for the lower class who are no better than animals. The scum class.

Laughing aloud with incredulity. How helpless this older man was. My conscience starting to kick in.

"There is harm in most people but not you, Nicolas. You are the most perfect person I have met."

"I wouldn't say that, Nicolette, there is destruction in everyone who walks this earth."

"Everyone but you, Nicolas."

Uninformed and unable to read through Nicolas's fine manners and decorous ways of conducting himself, from years of experience in deceiving people made me the fool. I was the prey, unable to see my neck was being placed around a noose. I was getting further and further out to sea and deeper and deeper in treacherous water. I wasn't stupid I simply had youth against me. Unable to recognise that I was now in danger. In my own little bubble I thought I had met my prince charming. I overlooked his flaws as I was out for myself; I had my own goals to obtain and a future to secure. Impetuousness got me caught. Although I had learnt a great deal in a rather impressive short period of time, youth was not my friend.

Driving up to a very large gated chateau with two security guards at the front gates, in disbelief. Gasping at a breath. I knew that Swiss people were richer than most and live a higher quality of life. But this was a dream, making me feel like a starving orphan going to the castle to look for work. Feeling giddy and silly like I was drunk, as the car entered through the eight foot or more gates. Giddy was not a reaction I was accustomed to.

"This is your chateau, Nicolas?"

"This is my home and you are most welcome. I am very pleased to receive you here. This house has everything a home could offer. You have everything a woman should be, and that is the most remarkable combination. Not every home is lucky enough to have both. A woman like you is the only thing this house is missing. The only thing I am missing. Tonight this house has you and I have your company. Tonight! I hope not only for tonight."

Feeling embarrassed, not quite sure how to respond to such a highly regarded compliment but managing just about to say ...

"Thank you. Those are such fond words you speak. You embarrass me."

"Do not be embarrassed, my dear, you have absolutely nothing to be embarrassed about. If anyone is to be ashamed it is I. I am an old man and you are a sweet child. So young and so wide-eyed with innocence."

Feeling uncomfortable I needed to change the topic briskly, to stop myself blushing more. Genuinely!

"Come in, my dear."

Entering an elaborate front hall which was the size of ten small houses, I approximated. The kind I grew up in. Daylight was cracking the sky, shadows lurks in the corner of the hall, giving it a Dracula feel. All walls and ceilings decorated in the traditional wooden panelling with designs upon in dark wood. Red carpet was laid throughout the hall and all the way up the stairs with chucky wooden banisters on each side. The type of stairs I've loved since a small child but always believed that a girl needed to be a princess or queen to own. In the middle of the hall there was the biggest chandelier which I had ever seen hanging over an Italian handmade table, with a crystal bowl in the centre. Nicolas leading into an even larger and grander reception room. Do the rich called those living rooms I wondered? This room was wooden panelled also; the only difference was marble flooring. French doors which seemed to open onto a patio or garden. The night sky was too dark to determine which as the heavy drapery was fully closed and the light in the room was as black as night. Six feet tall windows and doors, with blood red velvet floor length curtains with gold embroidery. Nicolas indicating for me to be seated as he severed me a brandy with ginger beer. I sat down on a rather masculine leather sofa. Thinking it was rather out of place with the rest of his furnishings. Too modern. As soon as my body touched the sofa I instantly understood why. It was extremely comfortable. There was a rather large fireplace with wooden logs in the fire, unlit. A stags head above the fireplace and a tiger skin head and rug on the floor in front of the open fire. A beautiful animal. I was hoping he did not have the poor thing killed especially for his decorations.

"A double, Nicolette, is that alright, I thought it might warm you up and help you sleep?"

Expressing a shocked expression.

"Well, that's a lot of brandy for me, as brandy is not really my drink but it will be fine. I will drink what I can. Thank you."

"I'm glad to be having breakfast with you again in a matter of hours. It starts my day of well. You always make me smile setting my day up perfectly. I hope you aren't too busy tomorrow and I'm not holding you back from business or anything."

"Even if I were busy, my darling, I would rearrange my agenda for you anytime. Thank you for placing joyous excitement within my heart and this pathetic old body again. I believed without doubt that the best days of my life had passed me up and was eternally lost, merely a memory to once in a while recall, relive. You have shown me one is never too old and it is never too late to be loved and happy, in any case not until one is dead. No business affairs comes before you. I didn't get to my age without learning a thing or two about priorities. And the right woman comes before anything and everything. Most men fuckup their lives by fucking up their marriages. Amazing women left distraught. Shattered. The men they love more than life itself don't love them in the same way. Loving and holding higher regard for that old devil, money. No me. Not me, Nicolette. Love and a lovely woman is more important to me than any amount of money. Why do you think some people wouldn't change their struggling life for mine? Because they have richness of a higher degree. I would gladly and without a second thought give up my riches for true love."

"Please do not say such unpleasant untruths about yourself, they are simply not true. You are very hard on yourself. You are not old by any means; you are in your prime. I do not permit you to say untruths such as that when you speak so highly about me. Understood, my dear Nicolas?"

Nicolas laughing, feeling very boyish and nodding in response as though I was his mother chastising him for a reckless stunt. Nicolas was always the bad boy who played to role of the angel, something he never was, however, his professional acting won him roles like no other. Deceiving people was his entertainment. The Dr. Jekyll and Mr. Hide. The transformation between two entirely different personalities. The ability to flip between the two at any moment in time thrilled him.

"Understood, Nicolette!"

Saluting me.

"Do you care for anything else before bed?"

"No thank you. After two forced gulps and the burning inside my throat and chest. Nicolas, you were right it has warmed me up. That stuff is hot and strong."

"I'll light the fire so we won't freeze while we are asleep, the servants are asleep at this time and will be up in a short while, no need to wake them up for this. There is nothing worse than a bad night's sleep because of a cold room, the new day never starts off well."

Nicolas feeling overly confident that I was in his grasp. I was feeling proud I had achieved so much square footage as I had in such a short space of time. Both unaware this relationship was one of a double-edged sword. Each having secrets, each out for ourselves, each wanting different things but each just as dangerous as each other. As we sat upon that tiger rug on the living room floor, before Nicolas's ablaze opened fire sitting quietly, listening to the wood crackling, watching the flames rising. Changing from blue to yellow, to orange then red. A feeling of warmth grew. The stronger the flames raised, the higher they engulfed. Romance was in the air. Both of us perfectly calm and wrapped within each other's company. Both were exceedingly sleepy but unable to drag ourselves away.

As we sat there the more captivated I became by the flames, I found myself thinking that at first this was a cold-blooded allure, to bid him into asking for my hand in marriage. It has now turned into warm-hearted companionship and legitimate affection. To my dismay.

This is not what I am about. He is not my type of man. Oh yes, he may have the heart I have always tried to find in a man but strongly doubting that any man has a good heart. They are all conceited. None could be trusted and none would treat a woman well, beyond the first few weeks. But right now I am not looking to get lost within charismatic enticement. I don't mind taking comfort from him to get what I am seeking, he really believes I am falling in love with him. My God he believed me when I said that. He is such a pitiful man. An utter fool. Feeling guilt-ridden and rueful, only a minute amount. Tangled up in should I or shouldn't I? Should I leave without hurting this poor old man? Or should I get what I can from him? He is clearly an easy touch, the easiest target I have ever stumbled upon. More to the point – he sought me out. Thinking further is this too easy. Perhaps? With that thought a heavy feeling enveloped my gut provoking me to think manifestly. My gut I felt without hesitation was trustworthy over the years, it has gotten me through life better than not possessing that sixth sense. I was grateful I had such a decisive sixth sense. I had no vacillation that without it I would be rendered disabled. Recalling that I had read articles over the years when nice innocent little old ladies and harmless old men have lured children into a false sense of security, only to murder them profligately. Blatantly disregarding such ridiculous notions, Nicolas is a sweet older man looking for companionship. Nothing bad happens in Switzerland. I am safe here, I am safe with him. He is a lonely man and that is the entire story. We are both lonely; we can be each other's confidants. This could be the perfect scenario for me. Better than what I could have hoped for. I could marry him, make him feel loved and anything else he is pathetically craving. I could do with some smiles. I could be the sole beneficiary of all his substantial funds, businesses and property. It couldn't work out better. Perfect may not be the word to describe this setting. If I had a younger model, I would have substantially more to prove, signifying more work which would become more complex. This would be an effortless and undemanding job. I smile, agree receptively, tell him what he wants to hear and sweet-talk myself to even more millions than what I have right now. This is the setup for the rest of my life. One last job. One last thrill. It is not like I am a black widow or anything as malicious. I plan to stay married to him until he is to die of natural causes and God calls him home. Freeing me to live my life exactly how I want to. He's getting on and we may only have a few years of marriage. I am not about to kill him with anti-freeze tonight or tomorrow. I don't know my luck. It is a blessing that Nicolas claims not to have any close family members or children. There isn't anyone to stand in my way to pose a hindrance to my plans.

"Would you please walk me to my bedroom, there are so many rooms in this big house, I would surely get lost. I am already dreadfully sleepy; I don't want to get tied up in a maze? I just want to crawl into bed and get warm."

"Of course I will. I know this is a sizable house. It takes a day or two to get use to the rooms' locations. I must pass your room to reach mine anyway. To be totally forthright I was hoping we could have fallen asleep on the rug, by the open fire. We would have been very warm until mid-morning. I would have loved to watch you sleep."

I smiled as though to say, how can everything be so perfect all of the time when it comes to this man?

"What are you smiling at so beautifully, darling?"

"Remember last night?"

"How could I forget? I shall never forget that night for the rest of my life. It was the most breathtaking night. A night to remember. What about it, baby?

As we walked up the grandiose staircase fit for royalty to the regal hallway, Nicolas ever so softly placing his hand on the lower of my back, as to catch a quick feel and walking as close to me as a person could get to another human being without actually having sex.

"Everything was perfect last night. Neither of us wanted to go home and when the time came to leave, your chalet was in the same direction as the train station. Everything is so perfect for us all the time. We seem to be walking in the same path of life, does that make sense or does that sound stupid?"

"I completely agree, my love. I have thought the exact same thing as what you have just now expressed. It's been on my mind the entire day. It is almost as through it was meant to be. We were meant to meet, there is no uncertainly about that. I know that now with conviction. I won't call it fate or destiny, that is too overstated by fools who think they are in love ruining it for the rest of us. But it was meant to be. You have come into my life because you were meant to play some kind of role within it."

As we walked down the hallway Nicolas began to walk in a strange manner. As not to embarrass him or myself dismissing my observation without question. Unaware he was aroused intensely. Finally arriving at my bedroom for the night. The embarrassment of Nicolas's indiscretion made the long walk seem longer. It seemed more like the walk of death. Once we reached the bedroom door, Nicolas squeezed my hand extra tight. Under the influence this was an adorable act of affection as he was sad to say goodnight as was I. Not recognising that Nicolas was roleplaying in his mind, how he was going to do me firstly. How on earth he was going to make it to his bedroom three doors down when such a large size of meat was occupying his trousers, making his trousers feel tighter than they were a few moments previously. He could swear it had a mind of its own, there was nothing he could do to control it. Unfit to walk, struggling not to rip my clothes off from my body upon the stairway or push me onto the bed where I would spend the night. Before giving me the chance to say goodnight and perhaps giving him an innocent kiss on the cheek, he's already down my throat, with his hands in my thong. My pussy was wet I must confess, I had been fighting the urge. The quick thought enters his mind, before forcing his broad and bulky dick into me and filling me up with all of Nicolas Beaumont. He was pleased that he did arouse me no matter how much I was disclosing this. I was screaming in terror. I had never before been taken in such a forceful manner. I wasn't expecting our sex rampage to have commenced like this. With Nicolas's tenderness I assumed it would have been more love making than this craziness. Going onto run his tongue around my stimulated and standing brown nipples, running his teeth around them and flicking them in-between sucks. The bedroom had no lights yet switched on, therefore it was too dark for Nicolas to see that I his now piece of play was not enjoying his fucking. I didn't want this. Not in this way. Nicolas under the assumption I was enjoying every thrust, every moment as much as he was, if not more so by my screams getting louder and louder. As he enjoys occupying my compact and tiny pussy I was in agony and wanting nothing more than for him to stop, never to see him again. He had me shoved up against the bedroom wall, my legs spread and around his waist. With every thrust he drove into my pussy, I was having my head bounced against the bedroom wall. I was going to end up with a raw cunt and a concussion. To this Nicolas was unconcerned and unaware. As I pushed him on his shoulders, an effort to push him away from me, from my body and off me, he jumps to the conclusion I was pushing him in the direction of the four-poster bed. Grabbing me roughly not in attempts to hurt me, but to ensure he did not drop me before reaching the bed. Throwing me on the bed but before giving me a brief moment to explain I was not consenting to this act of sex, Nicolas had grabbed me by the ankles and flung me over onto my stomach, grabbing at my hips pulling my ass into his crotch he quickly and aggressively exhorts his weeping thick ignited cock into my cunt.

"Are you enjoying it you beautiful thing? Does it feel good? Do you like being filled with thick juicy dick? God how I love your small wet cunt, it feels amazing. I've desired your body all day and now I'm in you, you feel fucking wonderful. I'm struggling not to come. I can usually go on for hours. That's what you do to me, you bad, bad girl. I need to explode like a bomb."

He could feel my heart racing, I felt my blood rushing. Tears streaming down my face; Nicolas thinking its sweat from being fucked like I had never been fucked before. It was a great fuck. I just didn't want it. I'm thinking, he's not wearing a condom and I am not on birth control. I've had no need for it. I'm unprotected oh God. The thrusting becoming harder and harder. I'm ashamed as I was starting to enjoy this madness knowing I was now sullied. He's whispering filth into my ear to arouse me, his aim to make me feel incredible, wanting to blow my mind with how much he could give, and how he can award me for my beauty. Wondering when it would end. Praying it would end now. But it did not, it went on and on. Two hours, maybe three. I think. How long for precisely I have no idea, it felt like an eternity. A never-ending subjection to a bumpy ride in hell.

"Nicolette, oh, Nicolette, you feel… Fuck that's it, that's it, baby, harder give it to me harder. I love you. You're my whore. My one and only cheap whore."

He pulls himself out of me, I thought it had concluded and he came! But I didn't feel his stiffness. I didn't hear his moan of sweet relive. Grateful that it's ended but shamefully wanting more as he does have a large dick. It filled every empty gap of my cunt. I had never been this full with a man before. I was so full I could feel him in my throat. Pressure in my toes, tingles everywhere else, in between with flutters in my stomach. Only to find out he hasn't come YET! I start to feel warm sensations. Surprisingly finding myself coming to his hammering. Moving with it. Dancing with his thrusts. The sensations I was feeling I loved. I wanted this more often. Throwing me over in many positions, managing to get on top of him and give it to him cowgirl style. "Yee ha. Getty up boy." I scream.

Nicolas struggling more and more to not come just yet, he wanted more of me, much more. Instead of starting off slow and building up the momentum to fucking him senseless, I became like a bull in a china shop, almost breaking his dick at the roots I gave it such a servicing; now eager to empty his pipes. Getting back on top, Nicolas roughly throws me over and grabs me by the front of my hips, directing my ass upwards to give me it doggy style again, as in this position I screamed my head off more. Being dominate got his off. After a moment I start to scream mercifully and unremittingly.

"Nicolas, oh fuck me. Fuck me good. Harder, harder. You're a fucking animal. I love it. Fuck me like a panther was about to consume me. This is fucking wicked. Screw me like a horse with a five foot dick would fuck a woman. That's it keep going. God don't you stop you dirty bastard. Don't you dare stop."

"Oh you're fucking good you wild bitch."

Taking offense to his whore comment, deciding to punish him. Unable to get back on top at that stage, deciding to scratch his back, to the point of drawing blood. Sticking my fingernails into the open flesh. Making him scream for his mother. I came, then came again. In between my legs were drenched in sex tasted.

"You feral bitch, that's wonderful! You are a feisty whore aren't you?"

"You haven't seen anything yet, you cock sucker."

"There's more room for you to get in deeper, oh Nicolas, fill me up to the brim. I can feel you in the back of my throat. Come on, make me come again. Make me orgasm. Screw that fourteen-year-old cunt. Come on, what are you waiting for, you dirty fuck? Has your cock stopped working? Has your machine stopped working, old man? You wanted to shag between my legs all day, give it to me if you're going to give it to me. Or climb off and I'll find somebody who can give me all I want."

Nicolas shocked by the minx which came out of this lady. No lady was I tonight. The bedroom is the one room in the house, any house where a woman can be a woman. Fuck good manners and dinning etiquette. Wondering to himself as he was trying to satisfy me what have I unleashed? Good manners decreases the soaring sensation of heightened hormones hindering a most sensational climax.

Is there any such thing as a genuine lady when it comes to sex?

I shamefully became highly aroused for Nicolas. Directing him as to what he should do to get me off. Grabbing his hand putting it between my legs from the front, getting him to rub my clit I was soaked in my own come. Again. Flooded. So much so it was running down the insides of my thighs and onto the bed. The bed was drenched. I was moist more than enough to have plenty of sex. Squeezing my tits from behind, pulling on them as he drove himself in and out of my body. Reaching and holding onto my shoulders, becoming more ferocious with his drives. He wanted to get even more erotic, flipping me around in many different positions, he would coarsely and violently force his erected dick up inside me. Whispering into my ear while having my ass in his groin, with his, unmerciful cock up me.

"How many times have you come?"

Unable to answer as I was completely limp, words couldn't come, ramming more cock into me. I felt worn out. I couldn't take anymore. My pussy yearning for more my body incapable of catching up.

"How many times have you come, my dirty whore?"

"I don't know, I can't say. I've come so many times, I just don't know."

"Okay, baby, I'm going to fill you up good and proper, get ready here I come.

"Oh god. Oh. Yes, yes. AWE."

"That was amazing, Nicolette, I've near felt such heights before, god your fucking good, I can't believe how much of me you took. Where did you learnt to take dick like that?"

"Where did you learnt to give it like that?"

"Good answer."

For a brief few moments resting his head on my shoulder. After catching his breath he carried me down to the living floor to spend the night as the room was warm, I was too exhausted to get up. The bed I was to sleep in drenched in our semen and sexual sweat and everything impure. Dirty. Delicious. The covers now stank of sex. And so did we. We smelt good, bad and filthy. Laying on the living room floor both depleted. Breathing hard as though we had only just completed an intense hour long Jillian Michael's workouts. Nicolas unaware that I was in too much pain to walk, even move. We lay there in silence until daylight cracked the sky. I lay with my legs apart. In too much pain to close them, certain I would be covered in bruises when morning came. It will be sometime before I can enjoy dick again.

Nicolas awoke a few hours later, becoming cold as the fire had by then gone out as I lay on the floor asleep. Nicolas had been pondering in his mind a thought which came to him many hours earlier. Deciding to ask me the question he wanted to ask all day. Rolling over onto his side to feel my skin near to him. Unconcerned that I was still asleep but unable to keep his question in any longer, he was dying inside. He shook me whispering softly and tenderly into my elf-like ear.

"Nicolette, will you marry me?"

Laying upon the living room floor lifeless and still receiving electrical sparks up and down my spine as my pussy was feeling very used, very abused, stretched and not so new.

"Nicolette, will you marry me?"

"Wake up sleepyhead."

Stirring. Opening on my eyes. Nicolas's face right over me. Staring intently at me and deep into my eyes.

"What time is it?"

"Haven't you heard anything I just said?"

"Awe, I don't think so. What did you say?"

"Nicolette, will you marry me?"

Long pause of awkward silence.

"Are you serious you're asking me to marry you?"

"Yes, Nicolette. Last night that was amazing, I never fucked that way before; I want more of you. I want you anytime I get the urge for your tight pussy, I want to personally and legally own it and you, devour you whole and fill you up when I am feeling erotic. I can be dirtier than that you know. I will get you any ring you wish, but marry me before the week is over please I need more of you? I can't lose you, not now. Without doubt you are the woman I have spent all my life searching for."

"Ask me tomorrow after you fuck me like that again."

"It is tomorrow."

"Can I please sleep for another few hours, these past two days have worn me out and you certainly have. I have nothing left in me."

"It's a deal."

Nicolas said lovingly with a sparkle in his eyes. For an instant I could see a sparkler flashing.

"Come on I'm chilly. It's very cold down here now that the fire has gone out, let's go up to bed."

"Nicolas, you go up. I can't walk right now, I'm too sore after that ruthless fuck you bestowed my pussy with."

"I'm not leaving you down here to freeze I'll carry you up to bed."

Smiling a self-satisfied and conquered smile down at me:

"That was a good shag though wasn't it?"

He knew I was his, that he would own me entirely like he wished to. Too tired and in too much pain instead of telling Nicolas how thoughtful he was to carry me up to bed, I thought it in its place. That night or morning I was unable to sleep as we lay in his bed with clean unused sheets, feeling shame by Nicolas's wild and undignified attack. I lay in bed feeling cold. My mind was racing with thoughts of that evening. Quietly laughing, because I thought, a dramatic idea and how ridiculous it was for one moment that his attack was to some extent notorious. I now felt tarnished and humiliated. Searching through my mind as to what encouraged him to almost molest me. I was such an untouched young woman and wholesome, I was unable to imagine I would be forced to endure anything like this. Knowing that the next morning I would be mortified, consequently wanting him out of my life forever. Pondering doubts and questions around in my brain as I was unable to sleep. I couldn't then leave. I couldn't then move.

What encouraged me to invite him to take me tomorrow morning? I know I was scared when he expected me to speak after he had me, could it have been that? I really don't know. He is acting as though I initially wanted him, that everything which happened here tonight is acceptable, when it is not. I must get up before him tomorrow and put everything straight. He will never have me again I did not want any of this. With regards the case of marrying me, he isn't serious. He couldn't be. He will have forgotten all about it tomorrow. If I were to mention it he'd act as though I was dreaming it. Making out I was trying to trap him or something as pathetic as that. He won't fuck me again tomorrow either he will have forgotten about everything by the time daylight reaches; with hope in my heart. The morning I will dread. My body terrified. Wishing I would be right, knowing I was wrong and possibly having to endure his cock making my pussy his home for another episode of depraved sexual behaviour. After morning arrives and I am able to walk, I will tell him what he did, how he frightened me, then tell him goodbye. I will leave his home and never see him or think of him for as long as I live. I will not permit my mind to think about him or what has happened here tonight.

CHAPTER THIRTY

Proposal

Will you marry me you ask?
Will you be mine and make me happy?
Love me and cuddle me.
Will I do this and will I do that?

You tell me you love,
You tell me you want me,
But what will you do for me?

Will you be mine and make me happy?
Love me and cuddle me,
Will you do this and will you do that?
I haven't even told you I love you, so why would you ask?

CHAPTER THIRTY-ONE

A Wedding Fit for a Queen

Monday 8 December 2001

Next morning while Nicolas was enthusiastic, I was humiliated. Soon immobilising those emotions once Nicolas did exactly what was agreed the night before. Damn alcohol. Damn fear. I did not want it as much today as I thought I did last night. It was simply the wine, the brandy, the romantic effects of the midnight fire and the moonlit sky talking, causing me to get carried away. I am guilty of getting caught up in the heat, the spur of the moment. Nicolas was significantly forceful, I was a little too frightened to inform him I did not want his sex. It was too late for that right now. He was not a man to refuse. I lay there without any choice, at least that was how I felt, allowing him to have me and lick my cream directly from my saucer. In my life I have never been reduced to feeling this ashamed. The entire time he was occupying my body I wanted to cry. I wanted to scream. I wanted to beg for mercy and forgiveness. From God, the man, the entity I never believed in before. All the time thinking, I would never see this man again once he had finished his playing and I had left. He will never have me again. After he finished blowing his load I lay on the bed drenched in his semen, his sweat. His filth. My legs to east and west. Nicolas talking about our wedding day, how he was going to buy me an engagement ring. I did not hear a word which seeped through his mouth; I wanted him out of my life.

FOREVER! He was talking, I was in a different world. I could hear noise but details of words and sentences, no. It was all terribly abstract.

"You look like a traditional lady, how about an antique style engagement ring, would you like that? What kind of stone and setting would you like?"

Laying in a daze upon the bed. Nicolas left his chateau to go into Genève city centre to one of the exclusive boutiques for an explosive engagement ring. At first I was fooled into believing that he was a man of honour, a man who kept his word. A man I could trust. Forgetting his name isn't Charles. Unconcerned that I did not answer him; he was in his own world, one of control. This was something Nicolas frequently was guilty of, entirely aloof to reality. Overly caught up in his plans to notice that something was not quite right with his wife to be. It was plain to see if he had taken the time to notice I was in pain and disarray. In my defence, I was in some sort of mental purgatory. As for Nicolas he remained like a child his entire life through, in mind at least, taking fancies, coming up with rash even reckless ideas only to abandon them. Behaving like a child who did not know what he wanted. Clueless! Getting fantasies into his head, adamant that was how things would be. No if, ands or buts. He was a man who became bored quickly, much too easily for his own good, not to mention other people's life's he entered, or forced himself into.

Spending the day apprehensive with anxiousness in my bones. Everything was vague. No colour, no sound. Trying to figure out how I would let him down. Worrying the entire day long to the point I made myself physically sick, vomiting every turn around. My limbs shaking from nerves and fear, my heart feeling as though if it continued to beat I would pass out and it would burst. Trying to figure out how I would explain that at first he attacked me, now it is all a terrible mistake. How was I going to explain I felt remorse for the way it transpired? Not meaning it to happen. It shouldn't have happened. Not the way it did. Knowing I cannot tell him it was forced, that wording would have to be revised, despite it being the unadulterated truth, he is sure to think I'm playing games. Knowing from the start Nicolas was not a man to listen to the truth. I was unaware then he was the player. I was being played, toyed with and teased. Treating me like a muppet on a string. Telling me to dance. I danced. Demanding I pissed, so I pissed. Insisting I fuck. So I spread my legs and I shag, not until my body can't take anymore, but until he tells me he can't take anymore. Nothing was about me. Nonetheless, a man as prevailing as he who is as eloquent can much too easily twist the situation around to benefit him. With his articulate wording to persuade me I am indeed the wrong party, when in actual fact I am in the right. Able to make a strong-minded person doubt themselves. A dangerous power to possess.

Resorting to a preposterous idea, I shall lock my hotel room door refusing to let him in once he arrived, if he arrived back at all. I will leave word at the desk to not allow anyone to disturb me. Going to extremes, planning to pack my belongings right now, this very moment. I only had one bag of clothes; take the next train to Zermatt, or Zurich maybe Bern. Cancelling out the Zermatt idea, immediately after thinking it, he knew I had been there, he could come after me. Zermatt is much too small of a village to hide from a man like Nicolas Beaumont. He could and would buy information from anyone. Every cent will help in a country as expensive as Switzerland. What I need now is distance. I shall be gone within an hour. He will never lay eyes on me again. He doesn't think enough of me to hunt me down. Why the hell would he want to marry me this soon? He doesn't know me; the lingering thought persisted. Love is not what he feels, it's lust for his loins. After a day or two if I was lucky my face would be a distance memory. My name he shan't recall. Our meeting never existed. This would all be over and done with; it would be a lucky escape for him.

Looking in the bathroom mirror, catching a glimpse of myself, talking to myself as though I had lost my mind;

What a dim-witted suggestion. You have got to think sensibly this is serious. You are dealing with a tyrant wannabe, a person's feelings, I must be considerate he doesn't deserve this. I'm more of an adult than to run away. Be sensitive to his feelings. Tell him to his face. Be honest. Respect him. He will respect me and appreciate my honesty in return. He may get angry, he has that right, he is going to purchase a ring. As long as he doesn't harm me. But I have the right to be angry too, he attacked me. Instead of letting me say goodnight he attacked me. Not perplexed in the slightest, it is uncomplicated.

Easy to decipher. It takes no effort to understand that reality. Altogether facts which make up the truth, yet he is a man. Men twist making matters into something they are not, never have been or ever will be. He will find a way of turning the tables around making it my fault somehow. This is what men are skilled at – man are incapable of taking responsibility. They do something unforgivable to a woman, they play the realisation down. A woman does something to a man, nowhere near as unforgivable, she is the worst human being alive. Amplifying the situation. It is always somebody else's fault; it is always the woman's fault. Damn men.

Several hours passed I still had not thought up a plausible excuse, no matter what I told him, Nicolas was the type of man to think up some kind of justification greatly impressive it would convince me. Trying to convince myself that he wasn't coming back. I couldn't imagine it taking hours to pick out and purchase the perfect ring. Especially if he was to have it sent away for to be resized, it still would not take this long. He lied to me. I am here freaking out, he won't be returning. I'm driving myself insane for no reason. Stopping in my tracks, my heart skipping a beat as I heard a knock at my hotel room door. The knock turned into a bang. The bang increased. More assertive. Trying to convince myself a false reality. He did come back. *Fuck! What now? Now what do I say, what do I do?*

I just won't open the door, certain that would work. Part of me for some unexplainable incomprehensible reason felt relieved. I was pleased he came back. My heart had wanted him to all along. I was simply fighting the truth. What the hell is wrong with me? I did not want the urge, I was trying to conceal it. If he had not returned, it was at that very moment the truth hit home, I was falling in love with him. I'm just behaving like a typical indecisive woman. Not knowing what I want. Proving I can have something which possesses a problem of having. A fight to get. Nicolas and I were similar in certain respects.

The moment I heard the knock at the door, glee filled my face my eyes, falling in love flutters filled my stomach. It was the falling in love flutters which made me realise.

"Darling!"

I could hear his voice.

"It's, Nicolas. Are you there? Can you hear me?"

He came back with an expensive engagement ring. A man like Nicolas would not have bought a cheap ring. It would be beneath him. No doubt the ring will be out of this world. To throw it back at him now would be too disrespectful, too discourteous. Personally Nicolas is nice, too nice to be treated this foul. He has been good to me. I am not that kind of woman. I do not use people. I do not for the hell of it mistreat anybody. We are all people. We deserve to be treated with respect. I must respect him now. Deciding to dig myself out of this later.

My heart pounded quickly, I felt faint.

"Yes, darling, I'm here," I shouted in a squeaky, high-pitched nervous voice which almost broke on me like a teenage boy's, feeling nauseous. My knees went weak. Buckling. Thinking I should have cleared my throat before speaking. Or better yet I should have stuck with my earlier plan, avoiding this uncomfortable situation entirely. I don't want to fall in love with him. It's not love, it's only the thrill of having someone want to be with me. It's the attention I require.

"What are you doing back at your hotel room my love?"

A flash enters my head so quickly I changed my mind to the thoughts prior to Nicolas emerging into the hotel room where I was plotting. You have been alone so long; you need the tender touch of a man. He may not be your dream man but he wants you. Will you ever find your ideal? Does anybody? Nicolas is rich, why not give it a go. Perhaps it could turn into a lifelong relationship, I do hope so.

I can wait it out for a couple of days, pick a fight, then tell him it will not work out between us. That would let him down gently, he would never need to be offended by the truth. I could act uncouth and spoiled, be everything he doesn't want in a woman. Claim that the speed of our progressive relationship terrifies me. I would just be a letdown. I must repel him. I have plenty of time to make him not want me. I will be everything unsophisticated and unladylike. I must act like a lowlife in his presence of course, not in public. I could not stand the shame of people actually thinking me lower than I am. No that would be a stretch too far. There is respectability and there is utter nonsensical behaviour. As he walked into the bedroom where I had become frozen onto the spot where I stood, startling me. I was that entranced, deep in thought overlooking how long it was taking me to respond.

Walking into the bedroom with its blood red walls and white coving, cream curtains, deep dark heavy oak furniture, I was standing by the four-poster bed which was said to be over one hundred years old. As he was speaking I was hoping he did not pick me up and throw me onto the bed, I didn't think a bed that old would be able to stand the pressure. Wishing I was more of a nun. I knew I should have been more religious. Trust the god damned priests and catholic school teachers to repulse me and make me sick by their condescending ways with their degusting lies, when I used to be a catholic. Always hating them for what they pretended to be. What I was forced to endure by their deplorable hands. Innocent blood drips from their lips and hands for the masses of wrong they have committed.

"Darling, I hope you like the engagement ring I picked out for you. Impractical me I forgot to ask your size before leaving this morning. Becoming greatly excited, ending up forgetting the important things. I told you, you have a powerful effect over me. You make me tipsy on you. I rarely ever forget anything. Considering you are a small and petite woman, I got the smallest ring size they made. I do hope it fits. If it does not we can have it changed. I'm sorry I was so long, I had to wait at the jewellers while they resized the ring for me. I did not want to return without it. That wouldn't be very romantic."

"I'm sure it shall, Nicolas. I know with your tastes the ring will be beautiful. Absolutely perfect. I hope I suit it and I don't let it down by not being a good enough showcase."

"Don't be silly, dear, you are more beautiful than the ring. Any ring. Let's go for dinner now I'm starving. I haven't eaten all day as there were a lot of arrangements to take care of. The ring, licence, the church and so forth. I shall surprise you with the ring later, alright, my dear?"

I stood there in further shock than I initially was! Astonished. He really is serious about getting married. He had started to sound as though he was going over the top. My gut niggling me. I should have left. I fucking knew it.

"Don't worry about all the arrangements I can do that. After all, that is a woman's duty to prepare her own wedding. We have plenty of time to reserve the church darling. You don't need to start worrying about such things right now. Let's just enjoy ourselves, get to know one another better firstly – at least for a while. Perhaps next year at the earliest we can make it legal, how does that sound, my love?"

"I have reserved the church already, my sweet."

Unable to speak for a moment, even breathe. My blinking froze. I stood there before him. Stunned. Doubtful at what my ears thought they had heard.

"Already?"

Letting the word out in more of a shout than I intended.

"Why yes, of course, we didn't have much time to get things organised for Monday."

"Why, what is happening on Monday, Nicolas?"

With trepidation I asked, with an overwhelming feeling of knowing the answer filled me. I knew it. Instantly I knew what he meant and had done. But I didn't want to believe it. For a moment I hoped.

"What, Nicolette? You're silly sometimes but in the sweetest possible way. Monday is our wedding day."

"We are getting married this Monday, in three days' time, Monday?

Saying with not only shock in my voice, apprehension and unadulterated annoyance.

"Yes, Nicolette. What is wrong, you seem stunned?"

"That is because I am. I have every right to be. I cannot believe you have done this. Do you honestly not think this is totally crazy or that you should have consulted me at the very least?"

"Oh, I know most brides enjoy arranging their weddings, but we don't have much time. Why should wanting to marry you be crazy? I was trying to be efficient and romantic. The sooner we are married the better. That's the start of our lives together. Why wait? I didn't want you to be like a billion other brides stressing out, I wanted you to be able to relax; you are too good for that. Are you angry, Nicolette? No, you couldn't be angry, baby. You want to marry me as much as I want to marry you. You couldn't be angry, there is no reason to be. By Monday lunch time we will be husband and wife.

Husband and wife for life."

"No, not at all... I'm not angry, what I am, is surprised."

It was a brawl to bury my annoyance knowing I needed to. There was a spark in Nicolas's eyes which indicated to me not to travel down that road. Unaware exactly what could happen, I knew I did not wish to find out, I could relate it was not a good journey to undergo.

"I mean I didn't think you were that serious about marrying me in the first place after only meeting me. Assuming for the most part it was the alcohol speaking. As for the proposal, the mere idea would have vanished from your mind once you awoke. Then feeling you needed to think up some idiotic story for calling the entire show off. Embarrassed possibly for thinking up such an idea. Along with the aspect we didn't speak about when we would get married. I thought you were only going to get an engagement ring today, that was the only thing you mentioned doing. Presuming we were going to have a long engagement, giving us a chance to get to know each other better before taking our vows. Not planning and organising the entire wedding in one day, only to be married three days later. Why are you in such a hurry, my love?"

Struggling to get "my love" out without crying. I recall that day so clearly, I was never as angry in my entire life. I couldn't believe he had done all this. To me there was only one word for it, not captivating, not adorable or charming. Insane. On one side of the coin it was flattering, nevertheless a lunatic thing to do. No part of me thought it romantic. I could detect in his tone he understood it was not romantic either, he was being a control freak. Sugarcoating lies with dribbles of honey. A most dangerous combination. A combination not to be crossed. It was an amalgamation between jealousy and anger. A cocktail for disaster, death possibly prison. Whichever came first it was certain destruction was about to follow.

"Oh, my sweet child! You are silly but in a kind way. How could I not genuinely want to marry someone so closely mirroring perfection as you? I am an old man who may not have long to live. Not that I neither intend nor plan on going anywhere yet, but I am much older than you, I do not want to waste any time on starting our new life together. I have wasted too many years in my younger days. I was futile, thinking I had plenty of time to meet the right woman and then I would marry her. Never meeting the perfect woman, now almost fifty years later I finally have. I cannot wait to marry you now. If we are going to get married, why does it matter when we marry? The sooner the better is it not? You're the most perfect woman I have had the privilege of meeting. You are the most perfect creation. Are you getting cold feet?"

Nicolas asked in an enraged voice, with furry in his cool blues, attempting but failing gravely to come across as nice. Nice was not a word to describe Nicolas Beaumont. On account of my negative attitude for the first time, perceiving a sense of tension in Nicolas's manner, to an extent a degree of sharpness, frightening me. Giving me a chill of a bitter winter's night and goose pimples standing on my delicate pale skin. I don't know why it did. I could feel something in his voice, the tone he decided to use with me. This told my instincts not to fight back, not at this time, capitulate. In that instant I let out a nervous frightened laugh, with a forced smile intended to calm Nicolas. As I sensed a look of horror, disappointment and what I thought at the moment in question, a slight hint of disgust. Seeing sadness and offense in Nicolas's eyes, at once I responded with a word of encouragement. In turn I responded in a soft intimate voice, my aim to reassure and sooth him, and me. It was the only card I had to play. At that time I truthfully felt bad, bad to mistreat him. He was being kind. I could put myself in his position after spending thousands of Swiss Francs on a diamond ring, I would be infuriated too if I was being let down immediately afterwards. There is a time and a place. This was not it. This morning before he left was the time, another perfect time, I left it too late so I must wait for the perfect opportunity, seize it and confess. It was my fault and I was woman enough to take full responsibility. I should have informed him earlier, as soon as we woke this morning, regardless. I knew he would make it out to be my fault if I had told him earlier. I will make everything alright. I'll fix everything. Never before have I seen a mix of emotions in one person's eyes. Such a combination isn't natural.

"That is not what I mean, my love. Let me clarify. We've only just met, already done the deed shall we say. Four days after meeting for the first time you want to marry me. We know absolutely nothing about one another. It's not that I don't want to marry you, but do you see where I am coming from? It's fast, isn't it, darling".

"Honestly, Nicolette, you appear angry."

Picking up on Nicolas's dismay and hurt, not wanting to be responsible for breaking his heart I felt it wise to be kind, even if it was for that moment.

"Forget about me being angry, you're overlooking the importance of what I am trying to explain. I want to marry and start a life with you immediately. I'm not getting any younger myself. Thank you so much for taking care of everything. You did all that today; it is all taken care of? What church will it be, Nicolas?"

Responding in the nicest tone I could muster, opposed to wanting to react in the fashion I felt fitting for the occasion, ripping his head off. Immediately, Nicolas's face filling up with relieve, a healthy pink colour restored, rendering him speechless only for a single moment. Regaining his composure, his self-control and managing to let out a few words.

"It is only the most perfect church you will ever find; it is located in the heart of Genève. I made reservations at only the best hotel looking over the picturesque lake. You will adore it I assure you. It has a spa and a Michelin Star restaurant. I know we will be living right here and it won't be a faraway honeymoon, even so it is the greatest hotel and I want you to have the best. This city is magical; I want you to enjoy its splendour."

Now speaking with exhilaration to his voice and with it wrote over his face.

"I have no doubt that I will ,my love, love it so please don't worry. I cannot believe you did so much in one day. You are a superman if ever there was one. I am very proud that I will have a husband as efficient as you. And as romantic. For a man you are very concerned and involved."

With a slight giggle he instantly carried on with the rest of the plans. My mind had one switch, off. I was hoping they would all switch off, but I understood he would be asking me questions relating I would need to reply.

"Tomorrow you must get a wedding dress, we get married in three days. I have already made an appointment for you at West more Boutiques. You don't have a great deal of time; I want our wedding day to be perfect for you. Mr. Cusack has promised me that he will take your measurements and have any adjustments taken care of by Sunday. Of course I had to pay extra for that service or else you wouldn't have gotten the most wonderful dress, and not just anything will do for such a special occasion. He will have the dress delivered to the hotel the morning of the wedding. I know you will make the most beautiful bride. The reason I know this is because you are the most beautiful woman. I am a very lucky man, I will be proud to have you on my arm. I will show you off with great elation. You must come with me to the registrar's office to collect our marriage licence in the morning. You will need your passport and birth certificate. Don't forget them. If you didn't bring your birth certificate with you on holiday I will bribe the office. They will do anything for me. They know the power I have and what I can do if I am displeased. I know a great deal of important and influential people, jobs will be lost if I don't get what I want, when I want. We are legally bound to have an affidavit signed that will be done tomorrow at two. The solicitor is a friend of mine he won't ask any questions. Just put his signature to a piece of paper and hey presto. Most weddings take a minimum of three months to organise, with an abundance of paperwork which makes many people rethink the idea of marriage as it is a strenuous task. But I have all the right connections in all the high and important places. I also have more than enough money to buy anyone and anything I require."

Being the smart woman I was as life taught me harsh lessons I was forced to learn, using my body to get the situation back on track, despite the blaring alarm bells going off in my head. Taking his hand gently and passionately kissing it, going onto suck his fingers seductively. It worked, it always did. I was never a failure. As I sucked his fingers I could see the stirred up look in his eyes. Within a few seconds I could feel his manliness pulsating into my thigh. Yeah, I was good. I was damn good. It always worked. He thought himself the tyrant. I knew I was the dictator, I take control and I rule. A smart woman does this in silence, without divulging her system to another soul. That's what keeps me on top. This world is filled with too many people who talk too much. The negative and disapproving look which coated his eyes had quickly turned into erotic pleasure. Sensual sparks of sex flashes through his body. Embers his manliness. His need to fuck. Grabbing me hard by the back of my head, roughly pushing me onto the floor, in front of a lit fire in the bedroom, which was roaring and healthily ablaze. Abandoning all notions of dinner he went straight for the sweets. On a regular basis this would not be recommended. In a brutal manner ripping off my long royal navy blue dress from my body, only to find I was wearing black stockings, a suspender belt, a thong with a matching black lace bra. Instantly turning him on further, moaning as though he were already inside me, now unable to conclude until he exploded once again. That empty relaxing feeling of sex just had he must feel. Like any man unable to discontinue while in play. Arousing him more, sending him to heights making it a struggle for him not to come in his own trousers. Aggressively tearing off my lingerie, destroying the fragile and sexy lace that masked my flawless body so perfectly turning on anyone with a heartbeat, women could be included it would not have been the first time. Within seconds shoving his finger into my mouth demanding I lick it, treating it as though I would his erected dick, once he could manage to remove his trousers. Licking his finger in a sensual way, using the middle finger of his left hand to penetrate my vagina. Tonight I was rather dry not as provoked with sexual desire. To stimulate my arousal he commenced fondling my clit, leaning over me whispering smut into my ear. Telling me what he wants me to do to him. On occasion licking my ear in a distasteful fashion. All of a sudden he ran his right hand slowly up my body, starting from my right thigh, working it up to my waste this giving me multiple shivers. Slowly manoeuvring his hand to my tits, nibbling my nipples making them stand. Moving onto my neck squeezing my throat for a brief second, causing me to feel concerned, once he let go, oxygen inhaled and carbon exhaled I felt relieve. For a moment my body flexed unsure what would happen. For another time slowly he directed his hand up to my jawline, running his index finger along my bone, once again forcing his middle finger into my mouth telling me to suck. I sucked his finger as he rocked me compelling. What he thought had stimulated me believing it was semen, instead it was blood. Too much of him too often and hard was hurting my body. I couldn't take it. With every thrust he gave me I felt a throb so intense it was unbearable. Breath robbing would be more accurate. I attempted many times to tell him I was in agony, unfortunately either his finger or tongue were down my throat, progressing, squeezing my throat to the point I found it challenging to breathe. At this juncture, Nicolas was more concerned about his rhythm, shoving his erected penis into his wife to be, simply the best piece of ass he had ever devoured. With every thrust Nicolas pounded into me and furnished my vagina with a rigid dick I felt nauseous, almost certain I was going to vomit.

Too preoccupied to notice I was crying in despair, unable to cope with his profound conquering of me. I was exhausted, certainly chafed. I could feel the usually veiled area of my body was burned. After a lifetime or so it felt, Nicolas finally climaxed and my harsh punishment had now zenith. For Nicolas it was a good moment, ultimately feeling satisfied. For me, on the other hand, this was my climax not down to multiple unbelievable organisms, but due to the pain Nicolas unintentionally inflicted. The ending was the best part for me. Finally ceasing, punishment concluded.

"Fuck, that banging was the best piece of pussy I've ever possessed and dominated. To give you a forewarning, my lovely, from here on out that succulent and ripe cunt of yours belongs to me.

I govern it. I hope that's understood. How do you smell so good after taking your husband's dick? You smell sweet like spring flowers. You smell of a woman, a real woman. I have never fucked a cunt as juicy or ripe. It feels so good I could eat it. It feels a cross between a perfectly seasoned peach and a sodden watermelon."

Laying on the floor unable to neither speak nor move. In too much pain to muster a word, to move an inch. Knowing without looking my skin now had abrasions and lesions. I could feel them, the smarting and stinging sensations inside. I was not quite able to cry, yet out of nowhere a few tears rolled down my cheeks. Without moving I let them flow freely.

"What's the matter, my love, are you alright?"

I began to regain consciousness. I felt drunk. Everything was spinning.

"I'm not alright, Nicolas; you have really hurt me, look." I point to my groin.

"It's one thing to use and abuse me making me your piece of play, as you so tactfully word it, but I'm bleeding. This is where I put my foot down, I can't take being physically abused. I won't. I WON'T, NICOLAS, I WON'T."

I yelled as loudly as my vocal box permitted.

"Do you understand me, Nicolas, I won't take it anymore. You have to shop this madness!!!

Undeniably I had gone into a fit of rage induced by violent pain.

"Not while you have the time of your life, while I suffer, Nicolas."

"CALM DOWN, CALM DOWN–

I'm sorry, baby; trust me when I say I did not mean to be rough. I thought you could take it. I thought you wanted it the way I was using you. You sounded as though you were enjoying me, like you were losing your mind with pleasure, wanting me and wanting more. I was going on your reaction, giving it to you how it seemed you wanted it. When I manhandle you I cannot control myself. Losing all self-control. You and your body have a hold over me. Once I get my hands on you I must seize the opportunity and shag the life out of you. It is as simple as that."

I was in too much agony to respond or to argue my point. Instead of cleaning me up as I lay naked on the floor by the fire, which was no longer ablaze. Reiterating in my mind how long I was being occupied and made use of. My mind was the sole part of me starting to function again. Laying there that second night limp and lifeless. As I lay there I wondered was this going to be a daily or nightly performance, with fear beginning to embed in my heart and mind.

213

Fear of sex, too much sex, what had my life come to. At one time I used to be frightened of snakes and spiders even clowns, but sex holy god. I knew I had three days to make my final decision, if I couldn't take him stuffing me with cock every turn around, I was an adult so I could walk away. I had that option. I made my own decisions; I am the key to my destiny. He is a pitiable man; I do not need the permission of any man. All I must do is choose my moment carefully.

I fell asleep, when I awoke my legs were still to east and west, pain was present. Nicolas was kissing my face, fondling my nipples. I could not feel anything other than pain, wanting to get cleaned up, but still unable to move. I could smell the sex taken. The smell of sex wanted was potent in the air also. This man was not letting up. I was not safe while in his presence. Nicolas not noticing the blood, or quite simply didn't care while I was much too cataleptic to make him aware for the second time. My patience was now nil.

"Nicolette, you are beautiful. I will treat you more tenderly never hurting you again. Please forgive me, my love, I sincerely did not mean to inflict pain upon you? Your way of being and your sexy body do something to me, things I am unable to control. If I am entirely honest with you I don't want to control them, I desire to go with those feelings and surmount you."

Wakening up the next morning I was just about able to move, if I took it slowly. Baby steps. I hoped it was a dream, an awful merciless and shameless nightmare. I tried to shower but my open and raw cuts still smarting from the attack the night before. Bloody water ran down the insides of my legs washed down the drain. Seeing last night as an attack as I tried to scream and tell him to stop. Saying aloud, in attempts to accept what had happened to me, starting to feel embittered.

Nicolas he did rape me. He bore down on my windpipe making oxygen unattainable that was an attack. But he did say how much he loved me, that I was beautiful and promised never to hurt me again. Everyone deserves a second chance and he did reap remorse. But

214

that was his second chance. Two attacks in two days. He finds me irresistible. That's a compliment not anything for me to be alarmed over. So, I found him overpowering and overriding me, but that's a good thing, meaning he finds me alluring and captivating. It is hard to find a man who wants to get married as well as use a woman the way he uses me. The wife typically is the woman who gets the straight sex, the boring typical stuff, while the mistress gets the good stuff, the hot steamy fucking. The dirty fucks. The exciting rides. I am a lucky woman I get to be his wife and I get the bloody great rides. I will have him tone it down that's all and give me a rest for a few days too. Becoming excited, overwhelmed by our marriage and how prompt it was all occurring.*

I'm getting married to a man who performs like a savage animal because he cannot resist me, how lucky am I? What a compliment.

I started to go into my excited little girl mode. This is never a healthy or wise move for any fully grown and developed woman. It is these acts of unwise immaturity which can get one caught up in a web of unescapable danger.

Nicolas walked into the bathroom from behind me.

"Good morning, my plaything."

"Morning, my savage animal, god you have rid out my entire pussy. You are a bear, a tiger and a shark all in one. I wonder what that makes you. Is there a name for somebody like that, or do I need to make up a special name for you? There's nothing left for our wedding night!"

"There's plenty left, darling, don't worry your pretty little head about that."

Nicolas sharply responded.

Yeah he didn't care whether I could take it or not, he was going to give it to me nevertheless.

"I'm not. I'm just worried about how much more shagging you expect to give me, that maybe as fierce and unruly as what you have been filling me up with. I am only a woman of flesh and blood not in destructive steel. We get married in two days, can you please let me rest and recover until then, or else no sex on our wedding night. We can't have that, we won't be legally married. It will only be twenty-four hours; I am sure a cultured man like you can control yourself for one full day."

Forcing an innocent girl laugh, the kind where no harm was in me or intended. Detecting annoyance strike up in his eyes as soon I breathed the words.

Nicolas laughed in response. A fake and unhappy laugh. It wasn't deduced very convincingly. I thought to myself, his laugh is ferocious as his way of taking me is. His laugh was as insincere as an American.

"When I'm inside your body, darling, can't you see I'm in my natural habitat? It is where I belong. Just, like I belong with you."

As I stood naked looking in the bathroom mirror at my reflection, Nicolas came from behind and holds me, cradling my body as though he was the tenderest man in this world. He held me like he owned me. Like I was his property at that very moment I understood his insolence. He was used to owning things he admired. He simply took them.

"Look right here, right now, at how beautiful you are. How could I not find that reflection, this body tempting and not lose control each and every time I handle it, handle you? I'm like a vampire. The scent of blood, the sight of blood I transform into an animal. Savage, unmerciful. I see your face, your body I have to feed. I have to have it. I just have to. I'm sorry I hurt you, I never will again. I will be sensitive, easy and more aware of you when I'm occupying this masterpiece from here on out. I swear it, my darling. Trust me, believe me."

"Please do, Nicolas, I'm in abysmal pain today. I could barely shower, it was agonising. Now I must go out to buy a wedding dress, when it's too much to walk like this. I'm walking as though I've been raped."

"I am deeply sorry, please forgive me, please don't hate me? What else can I say?"

Frustration in his demeanour and furry sparking in his eyes.

"I don't hate you, Nicolas. Don't be stupid. That isn't possible. I understand you found me irresistible unable to control yourself, that's a compliment to me, isn't it?"

"It certainly is, Nicolette!"

Throwing me a cheeky, flirtatious smile.

"Then don't be thinking I hate you. If I hated you I wouldn't be marrying you. Just please don't ever bear down on my windpipe again, I couldn't breathe properly, it was frightening. I know you meant no harm but what if you had gotten carried away not noticing I wasn't breathing. It could have happened and that frightens me."

"You're right, I know I was wrong, insensitive and selfish. Never again! I would never want anything bad to happen to you. Do you believe me? Please you must."

"Of course I do, Nicolas. I know you want to protect me – that is what husbands do."

"Exactly, baby. Good. Don't ever feel fear again, I will always protect you, keep you from harm, never inflicting it. I feel ashamed now, my beautiful woman. I only want your love."

"Oh, no you mustn't. We all get carried away its human nature. I think the world of you already, Nicolas."

"I do love you, deeply love you. I hope you know that even though it has been fast. Now I'm certain that love at first sight exists, no longer sceptical, it's not a cliché."

"I know you do, thank you for loving me. I hope you never fall out of love with me, Nicolas, I honestly mean that."

"That is not possible, baby. The love I feel for you is like no other love anyone has ever felt. This love is real. This love is never-ending that I promise. I love you greatly that if anything bad were to happen to you, my life would end right there and then."

I looked at my husband-to-be in a very touching way. At that one particular moment I have no doubt he believed the words he spoke. I was starting to believe him. In retrospection of our life why did I have to listen to those endearing words? Because that's all they were meaningless empty words. I was a foolish, stupid girl not at all the intelligent woman I prided myself on being. Women are rarely out for sex alone, we long for love and affection. I became carried away by all the wrong things. Filled with joy and security, happiness I had never experience before. The feeling was potent; I was assured that the atmosphere was filled with devotion, love, affection and everything that is pure. My eyes filling up with tears of pride. Pride for my husband-to-be. He loves me, he truly undeniably loves me. Yet feeling awful as though I were the worst person alive. I didn't love him the way he appeared to love me. Yes indeed I was falling, the emotion was currently in flight, not yet landing, wherever it is that love lands and situates. I was in a state of confusion. How could he love me that much this quickly? How can he be this definite? I was never as sure of anything in my life even till this day, than right at that moment in time I did not love him. I was wanting to, but I didn't. I thought I was falling, instead I was drunk. Drunk on imaginings desiring to be happy, being lonely made me go somewhat crazy. I was drunk on dreams, pink champagne and being in love, but not actually in love. Nevertheless, knowing I must marry Nicolas. Something from deep down in the pit of my soul was telling I had to marry him. The reason why it did not indicate. I knew I would marry Nicolas in two days.

I was lonely, desperately needing the touch and companionship of a man. I had isolated myself much too long. Being lonesome had started to affect me. I was much too young to be so alone. Deciding, in that instant I would go through with the marriage. This being to Nicolas's advantage. I was currently unaware of that crucial fact, yet I would be awakened to this exact same fact in the very near future, for right now I was ignorantly in bliss. The ignorant bliss I would take comfort from only to become my adversary.

After a rather hasty proposal rushing to systematise the many arrangements for his perfect wedding. Nicolas unconventionally taking care of every part, while very unconventionally the bride-to-be not lifting a finger. Completely shut out of every plan. In fact the bride-to-be being entirely pushed out of all provisions. He was eccentric to the point I did not choose my own gown. I didn't get to see my gown until the morning of our wedding. When I arrived at the bridal boutique, assuming I would try on a few dresses and choose the one I wanted. The typical way it is done. Forgetting that Nicolas was anything but a typical man. No. It was not this simple with Nicolas Beaumont in my life. He had already chosen the dress for me the day before. The women who was going to fill the dress the day before that. When I arrived I was blindfolded, before helping me into the gown Nicolas had already purchased. I was simply there for the fitting. Mr. Beaumont being his customary overstated and verbose self not giving me forewarning. Taking too much for granted. I let myself down at that point. I should have made more of an issue about the matter. That could have been my salvation. If I had shown myself to be a strong-willed woman, he would have cancelled the wedding. I would have replied him. It doesn't pay to always be nice. Sometimes being nice cuts one's own throats. Nicolas leading me to believe I was going there to choose my own gown. Needless to say everything which was planned, was how Nicolas wanted his wedding to be. He had spent years waiting for this day. Thus reminding me of the characteristics of Tom Cruise, or how he is said to be: overpowering and demanding. Whether this is true or not, I believe he would be more romantic. I wasn't asked if I wanted anything in particular on our special day. My hair and makeup was prearranged, I think this was more like Elvis. My jewels were delivered to me in their boxes the morning of the wedding; I didn't have anything old nor borrowed. Everything was brand spanking new. When mentioning this to Nicolas he attempted to flatter me into becoming happy and more obliging with his organising, that he was my something old. The perfume was chosen, my lingerie purchased hand delivered to me on the morning of the wedding in the hotel I spent the last night being a free woman. Becoming Nicolas's project.

In the time I knew Nicolas he had made it clear he was not a man to settle for anything other than perfection. He was a man to take control, being in charge at all times never halting. With his wealth he wasn't forced to settle. He was influential in many means and with his attitude, "I'm better than everybody" strong and dynamic. His impertinence frightened people into submission and capitulation. The only thing Nicolas understood was how to buy many things, even more people. To him people were nothing more than objects to manipulate, simply because he could. His technique mastered in oppressing people endorsed those people into becoming mere acquiescence, distaining themselves from being friends. A man like Nicolas Beaumont is too similar to Hitler, a man such as he must roam life alone. He had the money to buy whatever his inclination. He had the money to buy people and whatever they could provide. Bearing in mind he did not make his money not by his own hard work nor efforts. His adoptive family bequeathed every penny, every million he owns including those businesses he doesn't run, but hires others to run them for him. He wouldn't know where to begin. Later on finding out about his most disreputable businesses that was the biggest shock of all. He was intelligent, he was educated but he educated himself in everything which did not pertain to business management. Making him a weak link, giving him his inability to operate his families' corporations. His strengths lay in ideas, paying for those ideas to come through by others hard work. The fact he did not accomplish his own success did not faze him, he was richer than most this being more than enough for Nicolas to rub in other people's faces. A man this powerful would make enemies wherever he goes. Enemies they would never be, not to his face. This man did not need friends. He did not want them. That would involve a certain degree of loyalty. Nicolas Beaumont has no loyalty for anything but himself. When I learnt he had bought the proprietor from the wedding gown boutique, it made me feel I was marrying into the Italian mafia. Not an improbable conspiracy when taking into account that people ski over the border on a daily basis from the Matterhorn in Zermatt. It was within easy and high-speed distances to travel. Could it be too much of a stretch, was I becoming paranoid? It could be as farfetched as a declaration of accusing the Queen of England, for not being the authentic Queen of England, because she seems like a much nicer person these modern days and because she smiles more, opposed to the times of the Charles and Diana disputes, when she was thought to be much more unapproachable. Now seeming like a lovely woman. It's not that inexcusable, when in view of the Chinese who pay lookalikes to do their time in prison for crimes they have committed. Was I starting to become pessimistic, driving myself mad with conspiracies? There are conspiracies about everybody and everything. Everyone has an opinion. Not everyone is correct. I was no Princess Diana, I would not marry an older man purely because it was imposed. I will marry because I am trying to be happy because I happened to be lonely. I just didn't know which road to travel to find it. I was presented with this road. If I were to have other motives then that was my affair. At least I am trying. Admittedly the proposal from Nicolas petrified me. Wanting it, but caught off guard, nevertheless. I expected it to have taken more time to have persuaded him. This was almost too easy. On reflection, there is no almost about it, it was too easy. At least somebody in all actuality wishes to spend the rest of his life with me. This statement brought me little yet some comfort. Many men will admire a woman, but how many will in reality marry her? This was a gamble; believing it to be a gamble worth taking. If it is not a winning marriage there is always divorce. Divorce and death!

CHAPTER THIRTY-TWO

Marriage

Marriage is the vows we take,
The vows to always love.
Marriage is the love we give,
The love that will never stop.
Marriage is the heart we give,
The heart to never stomp.
Marriage is the wife we take,
The wife we will never break.
Marriage is the husband we accepted,
The husband we will never detest.
Marriage is a quest you see,
The test to be failed or passed.

CHAPTER THIRTY-THREE

Marriage Sex & Champagne

Our wedding day arrived much too quickly for my liking. It wasn't a dream like day filled with butterflies, doves and princesses. Horses and carriages, with white just married ribbons. Confetti and waltzes. I had started drinking day and night for almost the past two days. My liver could not stand anymore alcohol, from that perspective I was glad I did not have longer to wait. I would be taken my vows inebriated; like most brides with desperate secrets to hide. Starting to shake with fear, or was it an overabundance of wine and brandy? Gin had never been my poison, yet I was consuming anything which would numb the fear and make present a false illusion of unflustered anxieties. Whatever it was this wedding was starting to get to me. Glad no family or friends would be present to witness my shameful deed. My family alone would have a feast of my embarrassment. I was guilty of thinking as I was slipping into my Italian handmade wedding gown. A pure white gown made of silk and lace accompanied with a graceful cathedral veil, made from Italian lace and silk, with real diamonds hand sewn on the edges to add some sparkle and glamour. "No bride ever looked so exquisite" was what Nicolas told me; he was never more correct about anything. I could not believe how beautiful I looked. My flawless ivor- skinned body wrapped around and caressed by a stunning fishtailed gown, tightly fitted around my breasts, the veil embracing my entire body thus escorted by a pair of Italian leather and satin shoes. He unquestionably chose the optimum gown for me to wear on our historical day. When I saw the end result I could not have faulted him. Though I was still guilty of thinking how nice it would have been to have experienced the picking out and trying on of my dress. Baring a slight grudge. This I could not refuse him. The dress he chose displayed in a tasteful yet elegant way, my best assets, the outline of my ripe and blossoming breasts and amazingly shaped hips. My husband-to-be in approximately another twenty-three minutes knows exactly what he wants and how he wants it displayed. He knows precisely how I should be and that can't be a bad thing. The more I thought about it on the way to the cathedral, because he was right about his choice, I really didn't mind him taking full control over everything. I suppose it added to the excitement an element of surprise. A nineteen-fifties wife. If he is right why should I mind? Instead of wakening me up, telling myself to run in the opposite direction and to get far, far away from this man, I was credulously flattered. Age is a killer.

Enclosed within a gift box made of navy satin fit for a queen held a diamond tiara. Finding out on our wedding night it had belonged to his adoptive mother. A story so sweet behind it, it should be made into a Walt Disney cartoon. A tear of blissful romance welled in my eye. It was a replica of a German queen's tiara. It flaunted a staggering five thousand diamonds. It was certainly elaborate and heavy causing me a migraine. He was making me his queen. This wasn't merely my wedding day but also my coronation. His adoptive mother wore it on her wedding day; her husband had it specially made for their wedding. Now that is amiable. On our wedding night after hearing the story, I thought how romantic he was and the sentiment behind it, therefore making me passionate and yearning for him. My body couldn't fight the romance any longer. Whoever said romance was not the way to win and land a woman? Any woman who maintains this is an utter fool. But Nicolas had an amazing fuck from my appreciation for what his ancestor did. Not for his endearing gesture.

Nicolas thought as he awaited his bride how beautiful I always looked. Knowing he would not be disappointed. Today I was even more radiant, striking and alluring. Exiting the carriage driven by two black beauties, Spanish Lipizzaner horses. I set my foot out of the carriage and stood on a red runner which ran the entire way from the carriage to the altar where he stood patently awaiting me. Outside there were locals standing and cheering. Not knowing any of the people, yet they so thoughtfully shouted kind annotations as I entered the church. From left and right the doors of the cathedral to the altar were pews decorated in my favourite flowers, white lilies. Gold altar candles alight, with silk white rose petals sprinkled on the runner, as I walked slowly and in sequence to take my vows and take my husband. I walked down the aisle to greet him, I could smell the most beautiful smell of roses and a mixture of other flowers. The effects soothed me. I felt as though I was getting married in a meadow.

Nicolas had incense burning at the back of the church, adding a more romantic and powerful atmosphere. The burning incense kindled an intent emotion, making me feel more in love with this man I was about to marry than I really was. It wasn't Nicolas I was in love with, it was the wanting and longing to be happy and in love. To be a wife. To be loved in return. Have someone of my own. It was the idea of it all. Nicolas stood at the altar; I slowly yet nervously walked down to be with him. Beneath my gown my legs shook. Part of me was glad nobody was giving me away, they would have felt my fear; it would have projected into their body feeling what I was feeling. The other half of me wished I had somebody to hold me up, I was that nervous. Nearly collapsing. My heart pulsated loudly in my small chest.

Nicolas was feeling rather proud and satisfied within, knowing he made me his personal preference share. Receiving his dividends in excess, opposed to every year; I'd be paying him on a daily basis. I was the greatest decision he has ever made, knowing I was the greatest investment he had purchased. I was the investment he was more than glad to collect when my owing was due. The only investment out there so great there was zero risk, through his ignorance he believed. Not realising I would turn out to be the highest and riskiest investment he had ever invested in. How wrong this man was. How wrong I was about this innocent naive older man. Both of us taking each other as fools when the both of us were anything but. When I play games, I play them perfectly or I don't participate. There is too much risk involved, a life along the way will be taken. I was going to be the asset which brought him prestige. It was written over his face he was unprepared to hide his glee. Now marrying the most beautiful woman he has ever been privileged to have laid eyes on. When I was walking down the aisle to be with him, Nicolas felt blown away, formerly never feeling this emotion by any woman. Beautiful was not a strong enough word to describe me on our wedding day.

On our wedding day like any other husband convinced that this marriage would last for a lifetime. No prenuptial decree in place because everything would be safe. Trust was intact. There was no risk as far as Nicolas Beaumont was concerned. I did not have such a strong standpoint about our marriage. Never-ending happiness, love and passion would linger with us until one of us were to depart this world. No divorce. I decided on my way to the church we would not divorce, overlooking my concerns that morning attempting to convince myself. I don't want to be in that category. At this point in our life together there was no reason for either of us not to believe this would occur. It was only the beginning. Nicolas felt this was an infinitive love. When a marriage starts off with trepidation it is destined to fail. Doomed. Figuring I was woman enough to possess the ability to smooth out the roughness he embraces. All it would take would be patience and time. Using my body to manipulate. Like a child, Nicolas becomes interested whereby losing pursuit within a week. Having notions, impulsive whims, this was what Nicolas's life had been erected from.

Nicolas ardent for the wedding night; "I must taste her, feeling her sweetest again."

Being more excited today, thinking she is now my legal wife, forever. She will taste much sweeter tonight and every other night until the day I die. When someone belongs to you their juices taste intoxicating; like the most exclusive brandy, becoming compulsive once the first sip passes the lips, hits the stomach and reaches the brain. The brain unable to ever forget how wonderful it tastes. If its sampled once, once will never be enough needing more and more. An addiction forever to be feed. If one runs out, craving it like a heroin addict and going out of one's mind until it's disbursed throughout the body.

Half an hour after our wedding arriving at The Kempinski five star hotel which looked over Lake Geneva, it is such a stunning sight

I conveyed to my new legal husband as we drove up in his impressive bronze Bentley. Skipping up the stairs slowly as the train of my wedding dress was long and proving difficulty to walk in. Once entering the lobby every male and female eye was on me. I was not skilled in neither being exploited nor being the centre of attention in this fashion. This was completely different to how I paraded myself. I was aware that men found me attractive but graciously over the years of being admired, attained the ability to ignore and on occasion snub men who would gawk at me. For many years until I was capable of ignoring these men who felt the need to drool over me, I was awkward in pubic, easily embarrassed, having no choice but to deal with these incidences granting me the right to socialise without difficulty. I had become accustomed to this, but today for some reason I felt naked. Something was absent. The cards. The games had now concluded. There would be no more cards, dices, royals or aces. The minute I said "I do", I won. Today these strange people I couldn't stand to have their eyes on me. Interpreting their unwanted attention as a incommode stepping on my privacy. Was it because I was now a married woman? I was a woman who in the beginning took my vows seriously. I was serious about our marriage after taking this man. As I took my vows a compelling feeling entered my body. Our marriage I was determined to give one hundred percent of myself to ensure it worked. If it did not, then I would give up. But give up easily I would refuse. Nicolas being his egotistical self, disregarded my awkwardness being publicised the way he was doing it, like I was something special, when this was not how I lived nor chose to think of myself. Nicolas was unconcerned I had lived my life not wanting to parade myself like a floozy. Instead Nicolas saw me as a prize. Winning him admiration and resent from other men. I was a walking exhibit. He prided himself as most rich men do when owning rare things. He already owned the best properties throughout Switzerland, France, Austria and Germany including vineyards. This wasn't enough anymore. He wanted more and better, hence why he conquered me. Nicolas was very happy, sincerely happy. So much so he gave the porter who was in his early twenties with blonde hair and blues, wearing a red and gold uniform, who brought our bags to the suit, a generous tip of five hundred Swiss francs. That alone indicated he was very, very happy.

A honeymoon suite decorated for a happy couple to celebrate our historic day. A day of a lifetime. Rose petals covering the floor like a pretty carpet, sprinkled over the gothic style four-poster bed. There were more altar candles, scented candles with their romantic and sweet odour. Sex was present in the air. A royal blue and gold duvet cover on the bed, with wooden panelling on the walls and ceilings, with long royal blue heavy curtains and sheer gold panels. Champagne flutes already filled with the chilled contents of an expensive bottle of Pernod-Ricard Perrier-Joet. Nicolas paid fifty thousand dollars online to have the bottle shipped. Purchasing this particular bottle three years ago, when he was still wife shopping. I must have been a class A purchase for him to open an extravagant bottle of champagne to celebrate our wedding. It was the most exhilarating day of my life and it just kept getting better and better. Nicolas had money to burn, when he would pay such obscene amounts for a bottle of alcohol. Only the best for the Beaumont family. I am now rich. Rich for the rest of my life. No more worries to cripple me, only a life of luxury, a life of bliss. Budgeting long gone. Sales, no more. If only my family could see me now. I'm sipping glasses of Pernod-Ricard Perrier-Joet, a name they would never have heard of. I'm honeymooning in the most exclusive hotel in all of Genève. A country they could never afford to even holiday in. Homes across the world I now possess. Multimillion businesses. Luxury cars. Servants. If my family were on fire I wouldn't spit on them. This was a proud day for me. I've succeeded in life. My wedding and security is the equivalent to PHD for me. A marriage of the highest degree.

Within seconds Nicolas had me naked and on top of the bed. I wasn't at all shocked rather I was not expecting anything less from him now, while part of me dreaded it. A husband and wife should make love, especially on their wedding night. God only knew what kind of sex I was going to be inflicted with. I knew he would consume me. I wanted him to. I had two days to recover, this I did, barely. My body was now pain free and yearning to have my husband consummate our marriage. For the first time, he was gentle and tender. That I was surprised about. Lovemaking was what I could call it. His soft and soothing touch made me feel not only loved but safe. Teasing my flesh before entering me. His touch was like Aloe vera putting out the fire. The fire life foisted me with. This

228

was the kind of sex I wanted. I was worrying over nothing. He fondled me gently from head to toe. Caressing me tenderly, stroking my face, my back and my arms. As I lay on my stomach he ran his tongue up and down my spine, kissing and licking every part of me, making every inch of me legally his. He took his time to put his body into mine; for the first time. Every so often, his cock poked into me. At first I found it a little embarrassing for some unknown foolish reason. After a few moments I became sexually stirred up, I yearned for his touch. The notion came over me to take control. Bare on top of him and straddle my husband the way a wife ought to. I wanted his body as far inside me as he could assemble. I was falling in love with him, he was taking his prize. I was falling in love with my husband on our wedding night. He was my god, my king. My body felt things that particular night I have not since felt nor felt before. I suppose it must have been the power of taking our vows. The power of our vows sex and sweet, sweet champagne.

I laughed softly and blushed. As he whispered into my ear in a kind of dirty tone of voice sending me to heights of wildness I never before knew existed.

"I love you dearly, my Nicolette. You're mine for the rest of my life. I will keep you satisfied in every way. Sexually, there are no boundaries between us. I will have you whenever and where ever I wish. You will take whatever I give. Understood, my precious?"

Under the impression he was only teasing, attempting to get my blood boiling and me horned up, therefore in a flirtatious manner returning the gesture accepting his demand. While thinking, *why on earth did he bother spending two thousand Swiss Francs on a bridal negligee?*

All the time laughing slowly and innocently. Not once laughing in an adolescent way, in contrast laughing in a naïve fashion, to Nicolas there was a definite difference; knowing this would stir him up further. This in no way failed to work on older men. In turn drove him out of his mind, while sex drove him insane. I learnt a multitude that night, positions I did not have the imagination to dream up. I was being well stretched, used and filled. When having enough of foreplay he rolled me over; gaining my trust, relating it was now time to have his way with me. After enticing me, making me feel it inside, making me need him. Exchanging positions with me on top, now he taking me and everything I had to give him. Nicolas taking it merrily. Finally, both of us were exhausted. Trying to come back down off our roller coaster, both of us sweating our hearts racing, out of breathe. I lay on top of him attempting to catch my breath. In a low voice, telling my new husband of approximately a mere two hours, especially now that it has been consummated. Now legally his and in every other capacity, now there is no getting away for him, unless he dies.

"Darling, may I tell you something?"

"Of course you may, I'm your husband you can tell me anything. There are no secrets between us."

"I don't want you to get upset but did you realise the first night you had me you scared me?"

Diving up quickly to shout. "WHAT!!!"

Saying in an aggressive tone with spit pouring out of his mouth, this nicely landing on my face and entering my eyes. His DNA was now inside me just like the DNA from his semen. We really were one now.

"YES! Really you did."

Talking to my husband in a soft voice to enlighten his mood, which was not effective.

"I didn't know that was going to happen when we returned to your home. I believed you when you said nothing would happen, Nicolas, I had faith and entire trust in you. I thought you were going to show me your chateau, perhaps have a drink or two over more intriguing conversation, like you told me. I didn't know. I should've known better. I was contemplating on giving you an innocent kiss on the cheek. I still wasn't certain. Before I had a chance to say no, I have your tongue down my throat, you have me on the floor and you were on top of me."

"Bull fucking shit!!! Don't give me that story, you wanted it as much as I did. I could feel it in your pumping tits. They were pulsating with sex and wanted to be sucked. You were drenched between the legs. Your panties were soaked with wanting sex. I could smell it coming of you."

"I was horny for you yes. That much is true I won't deny it. But that was it! I didn't want to sleep with you the first night, darling.

You were forceful, it scared me. It is as clean cut as that. Accept it or not, that is a fact. I do not regret you having your way with me. That is not what I am saying. It is too late for that now even if I did. But there are no two ways about it, you frightened me. I didn't tell you before, nervous of hurting your feelings, regardless I refuse to start of our marriage on the wrong foot and with lies. That is the truth so respect it please, stop arguing with me on our wedding night."

"OK, OK!!!I'm sorry. I was shocked by what you have just told me. I had no idea. I honestly believed that was why you accepted my invitation. I know what I said to you, I assumed you knew what I wanted. I was only being a gentleman by telling you what you wanted to hear. Men say those things to get the chance to ride women. Now you tell me this on our wedding night, making me feel I forced you to marry me. If we hadn't fucked that night it would not have been the night I decided to proposed, do you understand? But I don't believe you. I could feel how much your body wanted to be fucked."

"Yes, my husband, I do. I'm sorry I told you but I did not want to hide it any longer, because I knew what you thought. I did not want you to think I was that easy, I am not. I have never been that kind of girl. It had been difficult for me to keep my mouth shut for the past two days. I just had to tell you and get it off my chest. It has been bothering me a great deal. Now that I have told you I feel much better. That isn't the kind of woman I am, to sleep with someone at the onset. I wasn't looking for that when I went out. I'm grateful now that you took me when you did, the way you did. It frightened me at the time, but it was the best thing to ever happen to me, because now I am Mrs. Beaumont. So thank you, my darling. I just needed you to know."

With a tender smile and a passionate kiss and more wild sex everything was alright again. However, I held it against him for telling me he didn't believe me. I was happy we married, no longer worried. Life with Nicolas would certainly be exciting in the bedroom. This time I was pleased that I was generously profuse with Nicolas's girth instead of oxygen. Nicolas Beaumont was the proud owner of the thickest cock I have ever seen, or had inside me. Undoubtedly, life wouldn't be conventional. Conveying to Nicolas as he was showering, I was left on the bed to daydream of our impending future together. I was glad that fear had dissolved.

"Nicolas, you remind me of a relentless bounty hunter. Instead of wanting to take a criminal into custody, his urge was to capture me, bringing me back down to earth after a climax. Arouse me to heights I've have never seen, felt or went before, or even likely to go again."

"I'm pleased you understand how life will be. No nasty surprises in that department, sexy baby."

Both satisfied until the next round of games commenced.

Despite the fact he didn't really get me hot and bothered the way in which I felt he ought to have, not to my full potential, I did enjoy getting it the way he gave it. It was different. It was dangerous. Exciting. Thinking someday I am sure I will love him all the way, for now I will take it one day at a time. If it doesn't work out there is always divorce, as I attempted to keep myself on the straight and narrow, attempting to make myself not feel trapped. Such a thought on my wedding night, only a few hours ago I was convincing myself our union would never end. Doomed. Destined to end. Doomed. I was disgusted with myself, it was a mere six hours seventeen minutes and twenty-nine seconds prior, I was certain we would never get divorced. Fickle. When did I become an American? Divorce was not for him or me. It was not in the hand we were holding. It was only six hours seventeen minutes and thirty-two seconds ago I was overwhelmed with happiness, as I stood before the padre, taking my vows and looking deep into my darlings eyes. Even in church Nicolas was incapable of subsiding is animalistic nature. Flashing a wild look within his eyes he wanted me right there and then, in front of the padre. Deep inside I was sure I could see his heart inflating and the veins within this Iris pumping rapidly from exhilaration and anticipation. Whether I was going to be happy or not was yet to be discovered. What I didn't know wasn't able to wound me. Ignorance is bliss and bliss is contentment. Ignorance and contentment equals danger.

After consummating our marriage repeatedly, now bought and paid for, it was the first opportunity to fully take the hotel room in. I will be the best wife he could ever have sought after. I am truly grateful for this second chance. This is a chance to be happy. I will gladly spend the rest of my life showing my new husband of a little shy of seven hours, how much I appreciate him, love him and adore him. This will be the marriage to last all my life through, or his life through whichever it may be. I've chosen the path for the rest of my life, partially it's thrilling and partially fear-provoking. Admittedly I was not in love with him but I loved him for wanting me and for all he wanted to give me. I did love him in some strange way but I certainly wasn't in love. I had no doubt I would come to fall in love with him at some point, hopefully it was not too far away. He wasn't Charles, or was any other man for that matter, I trusted I could encourage my heart to melt.

The sweet champagne he filled me with on our wedding night made me feel merry, lightheaded and bursting with happiness. Laughing constantly. I was about to explode with happiness. It was the sweetest ecstasy I had ever felt. For the third time that day we made love, the stimulants I felt by the hands of this lover was like none other. We actually made love, it was compassionate, warm with his moist lips and soothing touch, all of which made me feel wanted and special. Drunk. Drunk on marriage, sex and champagne. I felt as though I was the most tempting woman on earth. He owned that ability. The power to control one's beliefs. I could not get enough of him. Based on the fact my new husband did not wish to leave me alone, he could not get enough of me either. This added to the frenzy. We made love in bed on satin sheets, slipping all over the bed, we did not care nor did we stop. My body wanted him regardless if we had landed on the floor, I would not have been apprehensive. I would have still fucked him where he lay. Now I know how some of the most embarrassing sexual experiences end up having accidents and end up in hospital. Being carried away by sexual enjoyment the feeling which cripples the body, abandoning the mind and common sense. When he became too hot I poured sweet pink champagne over his body. I thirsted for him. Licking it from his manliness as I devoured his cock and balls. I pushed open the hole at the end of his cock, poured more sweet pink champagne over the head and licked it out. I licked every dribble. None was wasted. That night I got drunk on cock champagne. I poured it over my body too, he licked it from mine. He then consumed my pussy with his mouth and tongue. Giving me as good as I gave in turn making me want more. I was starting to become raw from so much sexual attention, I did not want

233

to stop. I fucked through the discomfort. The pleasurable sensation was worth it. When having champagne sex he leant over to the bedside table, opening the drawer and producing an expensive looking gift box. Before that night I had no idea how real diamonds truly sparkled, how much more they shone when being bathed in champagne. On our wedding night I felt such closeness to him, I had no doubt I was falling in love after having sex with my darling husband the fourth time. We would be happy until the day one of us died. That would not happen before I was old and grey I had no doubt, with that thought of attempted reassurance a sinister thought entered my mind. A thought I dare not let cross my lips to any soul. It couldn't possibly be true, could it?

It can be exciting when the right amount of thrusting is provided, with the right amount of passion allocated. It can even result in being pleasurable. If each participant is given the same amount of leverage, this can lead to being repeated. The earth will move. The bed will creek if not break. The pussy will be stretched, soaked and well used. The cock will bulge then explode like a bomb, louder than any bomb in Iraq. The spunk which escapes will envelop the pussy it played with like fog. Even the Matterhorn could be pushed out of Switzerland, across the ocean to the Canadian Alps, if the thrusting is hard enough and the earth rocks sufficiently. Naturally this would require the perfect ambiance, the perfect night. A flawless day from the morning sun, considering there is no bickering, no tension or bad vibes. Unless the philosophy is, make up sex is the best. With your husband paying his delicious wife enticing and generous complements. An unspoiled gourmet dinner at the most exclusive restaurant in town, with the precise bottle of Krug'Klos Du Mesnil, from the year 1995 with a price tag of approximately $750. Going home to the large open firelight, roaring like a gentleman's wife soon would be, but wanting her to roar so loudly the roars of the fire and the crackling of the wood would be drowned out. The perfect scene for that perfect day, for that wicked sex to be had. Or perhaps creating arguments purely for the sake of wanting that great makeup sex, could be included providing the two parties involved understand it is only a little pit of foreplay. But a dream and wish is solely a dream and wish. Dreams and wishes are limitless.

CHAPTER THIRTY-FOUR

A Future Filled With Mystery

The day after our wedding I was still wonderfully happy, however, I felt a little sadness. I knew it was stupid but I could not help it. I had started to fall in love with him, I was more than happy to fall deeper and deeper. No turning back. A future filled with mystery. Having fallen into a hole, a well more like, so deep I will never be able to dig my way out. Climbing impossible I will surely fall. Situated in a forest filled with heavy foliage and monumental trees. He was a gentleman, not for one moment would I have thought he'd treat me badly. I felt safe in his arms, he would be my protector. I felt a moment's sadness when I awoke in our hotel bed, as I looked over at my sleeping husband our wonderful day had gone. It was over. I knew that it wasn't the end, instead it was the beginning of a new life. A happier life. I just wanted our wedding day with all that happiness to remain. To endlessly be relived. Not realising it did not have to go away; I would be living in bliss every single day of my life. When bad times come I will use my body to make things better. I would seduce him with marriage sex and champagne.

CHAPTER THIRTY-FIVE

The Crushing By Brutality

When one is at home in their own bed, one is inclined to feel relaxed, safe and solely themselves. Traditional feelings. One should feel free to dream and hope. Dream of one's future, becoming a politician even a superstar. We can all dream for anything that is something people are unable to take away from us. Conventional expectations for one to long for. No pretences, no faking of any kind. No makeup upon the face hiding the flaws we all have, instead a clean blemished face. Blemishes are the components which make us beautiful. It is the apparatus which makes us individually unique. At home it is acceptable to have blemishes. It is the one place where it is satisfactory. The place where one covers them up when necessary. Yes when one is at home we can simply be ourselves. Be who we are and what we are without explanations or apology. We can do anything we desire. The four walls which lock out the world. Secrets being made and kept from preying gossips eyes and where safety is found. Home is said to be where the heart is. Home can sometimes be the place which must be escaped.

In so doing one does not expect to become a sufferer, least of all a victim. In spite of these desirers some become what they never thought they would. I became what I never expected to. I became the sufferer. I became the victim of the evil doers. This is when family becomes the utmost nemesis. Family can be the cruellest of them all. The husband who was supposed to protect, love and make his bride happy becomes the predator. A man who does not cherish his bride how he promised and ought to. False promises made. Vows of lies. To make him feel in control at all times over every aspect in his life, reducing once again to raping, beating, starving and humiliating his wife for his own indulgence. This egotistical bastard born to a rich dejected whore, who needs to see his fragile scrawny wife beg for mercy then for death. When the time comes for him to dispense with my services he will want me dead. That time will come. It's an inevitability. My gut knew this after five months of marriage. Instead of facing it I lied to myself. Trying desperately to drown out the fear the truth was causing. Not doing myself any favours. Wanting to be happy in some way. I walked into this new life with eyes wide from innocence, all the time they were shut. Shut tight to the truth and what was happening. I could not face reality. I wanted to run away become the free once more. Unfortunately I could only run away in my mind. Over time I became many people, living many different lives only ever in my mind. I had no key to lock or unlock these many doors inside my head. I went with it. In fact I wouldn't have wanted to get rid of the different rooms which existed in my brain. I was happy to permit these dreams and imaginings, because it was my only escape. These rooms took me away from this life which was too tough. I lived in a fool's paradise and I was more than happy to allow it to carry on. In its end I would be alone. Terribly, terribly alone.

Relentless pain, abuse and sex is what husbands are not designed to be notorious. Thus giving rise to the sick. The tying to the bed with legs and arms forced apart, to left and right. The whipping of my tiny fragile back. The same back where ribs were visible of a young defenceless woman. Leaving bruising and cuts, the telltale signs of the handcuffs, which have dug into and around my skinny, bony wrists and ankles. The bite marks which have left their scars on my chest, breasts and the insides of my thighs all to mark his property. Like a vampire, claiming his chattels, with his bites and manipulative ways. Like a dog that pisses on trees and lampposts claiming his territory. Men are no different, they aren't any more advanced than a shaggy dog of six months. Animal instincts! The alfa male. They yearn for to be superior and respected by any means necessary. His slim and small framed wife weighing ninety- eight pounds, forced to listen to his ramblings that I was fat and out of shape. Therefore making me unattractive to him, using this as a legitimate excuse to starve an already underweight woman for his enjoyment proving he is in control.

Nicolas Beaumont is the tyrant all men yearn desperately to become. Nicolas Beaumont simply had more guts than others to demonstrate his authority more ruggedly than most. His guts came from his sickness deep within his brain. Perhaps it was more stupidity opposed to bravery, either way he was unstoppable in his quests. Successful when abusing. The more he would succeed the more he abused. I have come to recognise that it is only the sick-minded who become a tormenter. It is always about control. Rape is not about sex or the feeling of passion, not even lust, it is only about control. To be in control is to feel power. It is about the breaking down of a person, the humiliation inflicted. The power over another. When a man rapes it has nothing to do with the explosion his cock needs to feel. The release of adrenaline which indicates to a man he has conquered wet pussy. The sensations against the woman's uterus wall pulsating sex and organisms into his body. It isn't about finding the victim exceedingly attractive. The sick individual who needs to feel adequate, knowing he is not. Nicolas was desperately seeking to prove his worth to himself, by instilling fear in others to demonstrate his ability to intimidate. Hence why certain mental disorders occur, they can be traced back to stemming from an incident in life, such as being the bullied party at school or within the home. Being the underdog: the useless worthwhile one who needs to be on top, becoming delusional to the extreme that they will kill for to be classed as the autocrat. The man who will do whatever it takes for a lifestyle upgrade. A life filled with beatings, domination, sex and even more champagne.

PART TEN

Life
After Marriage

CHAPTER THIRTY-SIX

Midnight Snow

Wakening me from my sleeping bed, Nicolas rips off my Gucci negligée. Roughly rolling me over onto my stomach. No foreplay, no words spoken. Forcefully pulling my wrists together, it took place so quickly the breath was knocked out of my body. Pushing my head into the pillow with one hand, while holding my wrists with the other. Slapping my ass. Two big spanks, making me gasp. I couldn't believe the sound my ass cheeks made, thus arousing him more. I could hear his breathes becoming quicker and deeper. I could tell though I was unable to see, he was stroking his hard engorged cock. The next thing I feel is a slight sharp pain as he pushes his finger into my ass. Finger fucking my ass for a few moments, becoming so thrilled he dribbling drool on the side of my cheek as he leant over me. My mind rushing with adrenaline, blood, fear and panic with the anticipation of the abuse, pain and pleasure of what was to come. With the next moment came the depraving sniffing of his finger, savouring the scent my ass had left.

Flinging me over his shoulder, carrying me to the snowy balcony, with rope he tied me to the pillars in-between the balcony. I was laying in approximately a foot of snow. My body quivering from the immense pain shooting into my limbs from the cold. Hoping distraughtly I could fall asleep or go unconscious. I wanted nothing more than to be unaware of what was happening to my weakening body. Finishing his play. He did not cum. More was to come. What, I had no idea. Nicolas was too unpredictable. It was impossible to assume what he could come up with when it came to sex and being depraved. Five or six minutes passed, he returned untying my ankles and wrists. Blindfolding me.

"Get on all fours," he demanded in a rather hostile tone.

Kissing my ass. Rubbing my ass cheeks. Then ramming his finger in once again.

"You might want to hold your breath for a moment, you will feel pressure." His tone changing from dominate to callous.

The ungodly being with no mercy gave me an enema. With freezing cold water, only to fuck my ass once more. At intervals stopping only for a moment to push pieces of ice and snow up my ass, progressing to rub it around my pussy, then continuing to fuck me. My knees felt as though they would fall victim to frostbite. My temples pulsating. Heart speeding up frantically. My insides ached. I saw stars. I never before felt such coldness. Certain I was on the verge of a heartache. My chest fell victim to multiple tightness and crippling pains. Nicolas fully dressed with his cock hanging out and bursting through his trouser hole. It looked swollen. He didn't have the courage to stomach the cold he forced me to endure. Slapping my ass for another time then pulling out of me. Leaning over to grab a handful of snow, pulling me by the face to manoeuvre me into a better position to push it down my throat. With the third handful he shoved it between my legs, holding it to my pussy. Stealing from me my ability to breathe. I started to panic irrepressibly. I felt I would faint. Shaking my head in every direction it would bend into, he let me go. I was then unchained for one more day. Wakening up a few hours later. I was naked yet soaked through. I did faint from the cold. Shivering uncontrollably. My skin had turned blue and purple. Relieved as I stood under a piping hot shower feeling drunk and dizzy, affected by too much cold air, then all of a sudden by the heat. It wasn't a smart idea but I didn't care, I needed to warm up. I was thankful, however, that tonight was not the worst of them. It was just hard to stand beneath the falling midnight snow.

CHAPTER THIRTY-SEVEN

Cleopatra

Friday 12 December
A Wedding Party

Our first event after becoming Mrs. Nicolas Beaumont was a party hosted by the wicked witch herself to celebrate our lifelong union. No, it was not the aunt I recall from my childhood who had the face of Satan, with the tongue which waged filthy, vile fabrications; and owned the soul that was lost in a black well of evilness where only badness lingers with echoes of cries of misery to be heard. In my adulthood I had come to discern that there is more than one wicked witch in the world. The world indeed is made up of them. Nicolas loved to be the object of attention and gossip, good or bad, so long as he was being recognised for something or other. For this our first night as a married couple he had bought me an abundance of wildly expensive designer gifts in preparation for the party of the year. This was bigger than all the awards in Hollywood. Tonight I was a bigger star than Catherine Zeta Jones. Clothes, shoes, handbags, jewels and fragrances for a party especially thrown for us "by an old dear friend." This was the way he worded it to me that sunny winter's day. I recall a strange emotion of some name or other, as the sun shone throw and reflected upon Nicolas's hair. This was the only moment in our life together which made him look angelic; making my heart melt. Angelic as his tongue spilled lies. In saying this my gut plagued me with concern. From Nicolas's tone of voice I could recognise when filling me in about Sophie he was hiding something, lying. When it came to this one woman he was incapable of being kind. His true self was on view for the world to see. Nicolas was a good liar I found out during our marriage. It didn't take me long to figure out when he was trying to be deceitful. He had unique giveaway traits. The rubbing of the ears, his breathing increasing. Significantly. An uncomfortableness displayed in his demeanour. Fidgety. His eyes would blink more, struggling to make eye contact. Looking everywhere and anywhere. Failing the majority of the time. Trying to smile. His face becoming stiff having to force a fake smile. The harder he tried the more I knew. Nicolas's tone would change from hostile to calm, attempting to patronise my womanliness. Stroking my stomach like the feline I am to demonstrate affection. Luring me to believe his bullshit. Wanting me to believe what he was doing was for me and only me. Like a wine his lies grew better with age; but they were never polished. Whatever happened between the witch and him, Nicolas was almost proficient with his lies about her. I couldn't quite establish if he liked this woman or not. Was he fighting his real feelings I frequently wondered. He seemed to have a spite towards her, if that was so I couldn't comprehend why he would remain friends with her for all those years. Was this something the rich do when they have too much to lose?

"Keep your friends close and your enemies closer," preferably not too close.

There was some sort of history between them and many unscrupulous lies. It was his fault and her fault. Exactly what he was hiding I was still ignorant to. I didn't much care to find out the answers; knowing it would prove screwy. The situation between them was too odd for me to want to know. The moment my eyes seen and my brain registered the witch for the first time I understood everything. There was an underlining current, how tremulous I couldn't ascertain. As she walked towards me it felt like a hurricane was about to spiral out of control, blowing me fiercely like a ninety kilo samtex bomb. The only thing I could establish was I could feel the erratic tension from her body for Nicolas, making my blood not quite boil to an inferno but effervesce with a kind of misunderstood fear. I felt fear of what I did not yet comprehend. In fact I did not know anything when I had taken my vows to Nicolas. I was currently learning many unsettling truths. Truths I wished did not exist.

Nicolas had to impress by dressing me like I was some kind of foreign queen. Buying me everything and more than Elizabeth Taylor could have desired with her extravagant fancies. I was his Liz or perhaps his Cleopatra. Dressing his new, young, stunning but above all charming wife in a long white Greek style evening dress, designed by Alexander McQueen, with a split running up the middle, which would reveal too much if I wanted to be accepted as a lady. Consequently needing to take extra caution when sitting down. Legs crossed. No abrupt moves. Certainly no dancing unless I wanted to do an Angelina Jolie stunt. Supplementary I was the showcase for an 18 carat white gold pear-shaped drop earrings, holding a staggering five hundred diamonds per earring and a nine carat Columbian Emerald. Big and heavy they were giving me a headache and being guilty of making my ears throb. I only hoped the guests would not detect my ears turning red from the weight of these unmerciful features. A matching pear-shaped neck-let, with an even staggering fifteen hundred diamonds with another nine carat Columbian Emerald right smack in the centre, a matching diamond bracelet, which showed off nineteen hundred and fifty-eight diamonds. A queen I indubitably looked. Finding everything nice however it all looked too much. A wedding gift presented to me on our wedding night. As beautiful as everything was this was not me. This would never be me.

On the night of the party I found out it wasn't the sweet sentiment behind giving me such lavish gifts, he knew ahead of time about the party taking place. Thereby he wanted to parade me around like I was some sort of trophy. This was the night where it all began. Not in the church, not when we married. But the night of the twelfth. They were only a few of the flamboyant gifts I was showered with four nights ago. He was proud with himself for being in a position to purchase many beautiful gifts, such as these ostentatious possessions for his young darling wife, from the Omega, Chartier and Rolex boutiques on the streets of Genève. His pride was too pretentious for my liking. Tonight I couldn't respect him. Until Nicolas, I had never had the disadvantage of knowing such a narcissistic human being.

Admittedly my new possessions were impressive, regardless, it is not the sole way to impress and satisfy a woman. It takes much more than gifts to keep me pleased. Not many husbands can claim they have bought over one million two hundred and thirty-five thousand Swiss Francs worth of jewellery, for a wedding gift in one day! I Mrs. Nicolette Beaumont being the exhibition to bring Nicolas his credit, the admiration he had longed for since his first wife Gabriella was inactivated as his wife. Since then he had waited ten long gruelling years for this night. Tonight was not about the both of us; even though he claimed it was at the start of the evening. It was not about introducing me to his friends. Not even to the friends he hated and wanted to destroy their lives, rubbing me in their faces, knowing they would hate him for his new collection, on top of everything else he owned. It wasn't solely about showing me off. Tonight's party was only about people patting my up market husband on the back, cheering him. Congratulating him on his whirl win, me! Tonight was my official first day at the office, tonight I started work. I was briefed beforehand about ensuring my etiquette was perfection. Nothing less would be acceptable. I had to start paying off the debt I was now in to keep my husband happy; or he would have no alternative but to collect. When Nicolas was not happy the penalty was ruthless. It was about him being celebrated, not essentially the event which transpired. Our wedding day. At that time I was unacquainted to the importance this night held for my husband, or its relevance. To my horror this night held more value to him opposed to our wedding day itself. Four days after our wedding the second most special day in my life, abreast of Charles and my wedding. No day could ever replace the importance and relevance my marriage to Charles had. I loved that man like I had never loved before. Sadness came flooding back to haunt me. Now I could see ever so translucently the selfishness within Nicolas, the destructive and self-destructive streak which I would come to hate. This man was drowning within his own ego. He was beyond help. And soon so would I.

With finding out the meaning behind the expensive gifts, me and my beauty was to be rubbed in Sophie's face, it was exactly like Nicolas to stoop so low. The scenario was like something from a pair of teenagers trapped in a love triangle because the coolest guy in school was caught out fuck both girls. Childish and pathetic. His overall objective was to hurt Sophie making her feel worthless.

Retaining a wicked streak to his character. The streak which was so strong it destroyed his life and others who he decided he wanted to harm. In fact nobody but Nicolas and Sophie were conscious of the meaning behind this party. For over a decade playing sick twisted mind games with one another. Reminding me of a salsa dance. With one kick forward and a twist, two steps back and an even fancier twist, hands flung into the air, representing the upper hand. Nicolas tried with passion to make Sophie feel she was the lowest of all women. Not satisfied with just hurting her. His main objective in life was to destroy her; both her being and everything she stood for, which wasn't much. It was his daily goal to think up new ways of wounding Sophie.

Sophie hosted the festivity especially for him, longing to make everything perfect and complete for her secret love, the man she was desperate to be with. The man she would do anything for. With every breathing moment Sophie longed for his love. His time. His attention. The warmth of his skin. More than anything wanting to be near to Nicolas as she once was. Nicolas, he wanted nothing to do with this sad pathetic creature. A life and time sucking creature. Sadly he took great pleasure, too much pleasure in crippling her, simply because he knew he could. In turn, making Nicolas feel powerful. Fuelling his eccentric ways. It never took much to impress him within his own mind. Each evening while in her elaborate gold leaf bath Sophie would pine for Nicolas and the animal which swung side to side between his legs once set free. Playing water games with her body, trying to surmount the sexual urges she yearned for any time she thought of him. Her body could feel Nicolas on her, over her and in her, if she imagined hard enough. Thinking back to the time when Nicolas actually was using and abusing her mature cunt. Make believing ever so transparently Nicolas was inside her body, filling her up with all the girth her uterus could procure. Feeling great and getting better, with each drive of his stiff and ready to burst cock was giving her. Sophie's fluids running out of her body, floating on the water, as her own finger attempted to replicate the job Nicolas's manhood once allocated. The longing her body beseeched. The impulse within her body which cried for his entry, the begging she did when Nicolas was not around, wanting him to be near, to fill her up how he now fills me. I now owned her leftovers. I now had his girth filling me for the past week. Sophie did not want for Nicolas to be her leftovers, she wanted him to share her bed now and forever. She repulsed him. I repulsed her. All women did. Sophie was unable to bare their separation needing strongly for them not to be apart. Hating with a very definite perilous passion how he now shared my bed and above all my body. His tongue would now enter my mouth, my pussy, and my ass when eating me out. He now fucked me. He now owed me.

All Sophie is left with is the old used up memories and delusional imaginings of things which will never be. For nine years guzzling antidepressants downed with red wine. Three bottles a day on a good day. A day when she could manage to get up out of bed. A day when she was able to function normally at least for a few hours. The bad days brought double dosing and six bottles of wine, on top of the spirits which were kept in for parties she would through at the last minute when someone came on the radar who needed to be impressed. When Sophie heard of our marriage a part of her heart died. Understandably. I know what it is to love and lose. I know the pain. The crippling never to recover pain. The slow long journey of pretending to be alright. I could see this in her the first time we met, as her eyes projected immeasurable sadness and hurt, even hatred for me. This hatred I could also empathise. She looked a broken woman. I felt somewhat sorry for her. I could feel her pain. It vaporizsed from her existence into the room. The air was heavy. The sadness deafening for Sophie maddening. This woman is a lost embittered soul. Nevertheless I could see such evilness within her precarious eyes. Brining a lot of her sorrow onto herself. Her eyes were deep and bursting with abhorrence. This evilness I had not seen in anybody since I last lay eyes on my wicked aunt as a child. Over the years I have been haunted by evil faces, meeting an abundance of revolting people, the nightmares still protract. I didn't like nor trust my aunt, based upon experience I knew not to like Sophie. Not that Sophie was a likable character. Inside she was falling apart, but still trying to demonstrate her eternal love for my husband; chancing her arm in case he may ditch me for her if I proved a disappointment. Highly impractical, delusional, triggering further grounds to be wary of this irrational woman. It was a little thing called hope. It has a strong marvellous way of helping people through the toughest of times, including those we believe we can't possibly endure. We won't make it. The more dangerous a person is, common sense should prevail watch out. Sophie simply did not grasp reality; needing physiological help. Her demeanour was one of a woman who would not think twice about taking her own life if she could not have Nicolas to herself again. If she allowed the truth to sink in. Then I thought maybe she should have Nicolas. She loves him with all her heart, what is left of it. I don't. She deserves him more than I do. It was important to her that hope remained. It is important to everyone if they wish to get through this world. If it is gone entirely, her life she would surely take. Not that Sophie ever really had him. This fact Sophie has not been able to fully absorb. Living her life in hope, devoted faith for something which will never be. Dreaming for a love she will never have, from a man who does not want her. A man who is incapable of knowing what he wants.

With all female bitchiness aside, what an unfortunate soul. A part of me felt unsure how she would cope with this new revelation. Initially I was concerned in case there would be trouble of some kind for me. Not knowing if she would practice being a thorn in my side, attempting to destroy my marriage, or if she would be woman enough to be a thorn silently. Medalling with a smile and considerate tones. Misleading her prey with a very definite intention. All I was able to concede was that Sophie had a heart of unadulterated evil. Exuding revolting sinful qualities. Plus Nicolas would never stand by and permit her to make my life a living hell. I could never be her friend. Firstly she would not permit it; she despised my existence too much for that. My hands were tied, I could not help her. The only person who had the cure to fix her was Nicolas and that he would not do. He turned his back on her many years ago. Now laughing at her from a distance.

Regardless of how tough this charade was for Sophie to perform, forcing her to put on a fearless face, this I respected her for. I could see her heart was in a billion unfixable pieces through her eyes of ace. Coal and coldness. Continuing to throw the party she knew Nicolas would have wanted, thus giving Sophie balls of steel. She's more of a woman than Nicolas is a man. He had done the most despicable deed by marrying another woman, injuring her terrifically. So much in fact at that time she was certain she would not recover. Nicolas did not give a damn. Planning to kill herself by the end of the night. In his whole life he has never cared about anybody, yet was involved within a maze of exultance knowing her love for him. A puppet on a string. Nicolas pulls, Sophie jumps. Similar to Michael

Douglas taking his wife for granted, the only difference Nicolas was not man enough to admit the harsh reality of his actions. With a great deal to be ashamed of; he just doesn't have the heart or a conscience to be bothered. To me, the party was a strange thing for her to host, a thought unable to conclude any reasonable answers to. They were both highly complex creatures, perhaps nobody understood them or their actions. Not knowing if they could have been helped.

During the course of our marriage learning firsthand that Nicolas Beaumont was a cold, calculating man. Acting as though he cared about people, enticing them, intriguing them but it was nothing more than a game for his amusement. A pass time for when he was bored. Boredom is something the rich suffer too often. A purpose to get something from people. Mostly something he benefited from. Nicolas did not fall in love. He couldn't. He did not own a heart. Nicolas's game was to choose a target when he did not have anything better to do; living his life as though he were in constant play. Not once stopping to take his prize nor to start a new game, instead jumping from game to game. He loved toying with people, enjoying being able to make people react in particular ways, pushing there buttons, taunting, humiliating, pushing them harder and harder, further and further making him feel like a God. The God he was not or will be.

If Sophie could not have the love of her life she would settle for being close to him in any way he would allow. If it meant it was only in the same room, even if it had to be on the other side of that room. Sophie desperately yearned to make Nicolas proud of her, thus throwing elaborate parties to invite him to have him somewhat near. Spending lavish amounts of her husband's hard earned cash to fund the feeding and intoxicating of people he abhorred, especially Nicolas Beaumont. Nicolas was Frederic's utmost nemesis. Nicolas understood this, her devoted loved he thrived of, knowing how much it wounded her husband and not daring to touch her shattered Sophie. He was the tree, a strong and tall tree not prepared to be pushed down by wind or earthquakes. Not even time. She was the feed smothered with vitamins and nutrients to keep him flourishing. The more he thrived of her demonstrations, the more he detested Sophie's face. Hating the sound of her hoarse and aging voice. Finding it like gravel or nails being scraped on a blackboard, cringing with displeasure. Not wishing to waste his time thinking about her. That was an insult to his intelligence and abilities. Until he felt the urge which he could not resist, rubbing the truth in Frederic's face; *I've had your wife. I no longer want her dried-out cunt,* only to sneer at both of them, to their faces and behind their backs. She loved Nicolas in spite of his taunting and Nicolas her, in completely different ways, unexplainable ways, for entirely different reasons. Nicolas loved her but far from a conventional love. He hated but loved her, she simply loved him. Their relationship or rather lack of it was far from comprehensible. Through the strongest hatred ran the oddest love. For Nicolas it was an inexplicable foreign cocktail he hated strongly, to him it was a type of love. To love the conventional way was impossible for Nicolas Beaumont.

Sophie desired to leave her businessman and entrepreneur husband Frederic Von Mirkowitsch to be the perfect wife to Nicolas. Despite the fact Frederic had been the perfect husband to her during their marriage, who any smart woman would have been lucky enough to have captured. Omitting this, Sophie understood Nicolas was a tortured soul yearning to ease his pain, his grief. She would have done anything for him, given him anything whether it belonged to her or not. Sophie was not beyond stealing whatever it took for Nicolas's affections. For years she teased with the idea to murder Frederic by her own hand. In addition to doing whatever filth Nicolas demanded in bed. She was the only woman he had ever met who would do anything, there were no boundaries. There wasn't anything too much nor too smutty, too disrespectful or painful. Being indecent was what she did best. Sophie like the Chinese, Russian and Ukraine women were the furthest away from being ladies. Screwing their way through life to attain their aspirations. Their cold, selfish ways sometimes gaining them everything, while at other times similar to Sophie getting them nowhere. In turn, this would force these women to become vindictive to the more successful women. These particular women always hate genuine ladies. A venomous circle. Sophie and her husband drifted apart after she fell for Nicolas, shortly afterwards Nicolas threw her over. Her filthy ways being the reason he loved being with her, but also the reason she repulsed him. In so doing anything wild, dirty, vile if not illegal she destroyed herself with Nicolas. Not that there was something wrong with her, it was simply too easy a task for this man to conquer. Nicolas was nothing more than a petulant child. When he wanted something he would do anything it took to attain it, when he attained it not wanting it any longer, this proving a very dangerous way to live. Scores constantly being notched up. Points proven. His dick measured and documented. She was too similar to who he was and the whores he screwed. Needing for at least once, that one time many years ago, someone to understand him and his craziness. A person who had no frontiers, someone he could exploit, thrilling him beyond belief. The knowing that there are women out there who will do anything to make a man happy. Neither wanting nor needing a person who is alike to become his. A mere five minutes with Sophie was more than enough. With her there isn't anything he can break down, anything he can change and no way of humiliating her. It is the shame, the pain and the disgrace he is to bring onto a woman which gets him off. Hence why he has to have innocent women. Women who have not had the opportunity to develop their own minds, it was a target easier to manipulate. Making him weak. It was their weakness which give him power. This power he fed off. The very reason why a real woman he could not bring himself to be with. Any strong woman knowing her mind intimidated him. This was Sophie through and through. Nicolas had for all time been the type of creature who loves to destroy and belittle, it wasn't solely women but with women he took the greatest pleasure. The greatest pleasure was the woman who was his wife. He felt this was the ultimate of sins, the supreme dishonour. Especially considering how much a husband is supposed to love his wife, making his pleasure that much sweeter. Later finding out Nicolas would take contentment in luring defenceless women into a false sense of security to leave them stranded, making them believe nobody but he wants them. Nobody but he could or would be willing to love them.

At the start of a whirlwind romance telling the women he set up, how much he loves her and is proud of her. Later when he feels the time is right he sets out to break her heart, seeing the hurt in her eyes as the tears well, when he tells her; "I hate you. You disgust me." It is the metamorphoses which a human undergoes when devastated which thrills him the most. Making Nicolas feel as though he were the oppressor he worked hard to be. He had the guts to conquer a woman. The weaker species, those who were not a tough fight. Not having the nerve to take on the world. Unfortunately his mother did not help encouraging his delusional ravings and beliefs, telling him he was the most important man in the world. How capable he is of doing anything he wants. Nothing is beyond him. Reach for the moon. So he did, he was already educated, achieved much in intelligence but there was no doubt there was something wrong with his mind. There was something which was harming him, accountable for him hurting others. He believed he was a bigger, better and a stronger dictator than Hitler, Stalin, Saddam Hussein, and Gaddafi were. What do all these tyrants have in common? They are all bloody dead. Each and every tyrant, particularly those in their own right and mind, with only self- recommendation deserve to die. Sent to a place where no more innocent people are slaughtered. Unfortunately not all oppressors are within the public domain. Not all tormentors are known for their cruelty. Most of these tormenters appear within society to be the kindest of people. It is the unknown oppressors who are the weakest, incapable of having their dictatorship publicised. Their work inconsequential. Nicolas was a mere wife beater, a woman hater, thief, and a killer. His mother was the lowest of the lowest, an idol gossip everything evil, the worst kind. I could see where he got his badness from. It's in the genes. My philosophy over the years has become if someone is too sweet to be true, they are too sweet to be true. People in this world don't give without wanting something in return; more than what they have given. Everything no matter how little it appears to be has a price, be it monetary, morally or life. Absolutely everything has a price. Somewhere along the line we all pay. Usually paying for more than it's worth and by the end we won't be the same.

Sophie had spent a decade in its entirety waiting for Nicolas, the love of her life, to say; "leave him, be mine. Marry me." By the third year she was in no doubt, those words would never be spoken to her by Nicolas. That day of utter pleasure would never arise. Not for her. Unable to fully accept the facts in all areas of her brain, hope was still embedded within her heart, but the more sensible part of her brain had alarm bells trying to get her to face the truth. Her stupidity would be her worst nemesis. It is impossible to help those who refuse to help themselves. Face the truth and stop wasting her life in vain over someone who will never love her in return. This wasn't altogether an insult or a negative. This in fact saved her life. Sophie was too strong of a woman to be Nicolas's ideal. She had balls, balls of steel and balls of fire. With a tongue which could cut through steel. Sophie was certainly a fiery woman who would not hesitate to fire up like an uncontrollable ball of fire creating an inferno, if the occasion gave rise. Destroying everything in its way. Sophie being a heavy drinker with deep wrinkles upon her worn-out face, neck and chest, too much sun and too many Cigarillo Cigarettes, with Scandinavian blonde hair, like the majority of the women in Switzerland. Her eyes were as cool as Nicolas's and each were as self-centred as each other. For the time being I was fresh faced, new and clean. Unsullied! At this time my face was not detailed with life. Although my eyes were starting to indicate some unhappy times within my previous life, as Charles's loss had hit me hard. The silent truth about Charles's death was slowly killing me. Confessions they claim is good for the soul. My confessions about Charles and the particulars surrounding his death would be the key to my ending. In the face of it, I still could not confront what I had done to destroy the love of my life.

Sharing a week of solitary, well-balanced, fiery, furious and bizarre sex. It was all about dick and pussy loving, nothing but those two compounds. He was the best ride she ever had enter her, subsequently falling in love with him and what he could do when playing cowboy with his horse. He had the biggest cock she ever did see, never mind being able to fuck her with those cool piercing blues by merely looking at her. Sex was forever on his brain. When her eyes met his, impure thoughts in HD imagery flashed through her mind. Hearing the moaning, feeling the shocks of ecstasy. Tasting the kisses and sweat. It felt real. It wasn't, but Nicolas was that good. He owned the skill of controlling women's minds. Dictating what she sees and thinks. A dangerous skill to master. These two factors gave Sophie a weird yet desirable emotion of which she could not associate, it made her feel she was having an orgasm, yet at any given moment he was going to kill her. Both incomprehensible and outlandish! Getting this look in his eyes, it was like his being had been abducted, swearing he was either going to choke her until her last breath had drawn, or at any moment as he was coming he would pull out a knife and stab her. Sophie had no doubt at certain times as they fucked each other, she would end up in one of those snuff movies being played on *YouTube,* after her body had stopped kicking. It was a weird sensation though she loved it. This was her orgasm. It was better than being high on the crystal meth Frederic's business associates would sometime consume in her home at private parties. Getting high parties. Dear sweet, stupid Sophie was too in love to consider that Nicolas would not think twice about killing her, even if it was for five minutes of sexual heaven for him. And only him. She was nothing more than a diversion while he was on the search for his perfect companion. He was having a little bit of fun in-between searches. All work and no play would never do for Mr. Beaumont.

During that week in May 1991 when her husband was away on a not so innocent business trip to Germany, picking himself up a whore. Men and business trips are always masquerades for sex orgies. While Sophie was busy fucking Nicolas, Frederic was busy fucking his whore, a Russian nobody transported to Germany as new cliental. All in all it was a good and eventful week of pussy and dick. Everybody was being serviced. Everybody was enjoying orgasms. Orgasms they cannot enjoy together. Nicolas didn't exactly fall in love with Sophie he was more smitten with the no boundary sex they shared. The wicked, dark and nasty. He knew he could do anything to her body and she would take it. She wouldn't exactly like what she was exposed to, nonetheless, she would stand it proving herself to the man who stole her heart. He loved this but by no means did he respect her. How could any respectable human being respect a whore like her? In so saying Sophie could not take that aspect too personally, considering Nicolas Beaumont didn't respect anybody but himself. And he was a man whore. This appealed to him and his sick, twisted mind. Not many women would endure the crazed fantasies. Beating her with whips going as far as using kitchen utensils. Sniffing her unclean ass. Running his tongue in between her crack. What stuck in his mind the most was fucking her rather disappointing large cunt with a wooden spoon, but the best was the fist fucking. It was big enough for that. Yes, Sophie's cunt was so large that his entire broad manly fist was rammed into her wet pussy; it being wet didn't help much. It could have been this very same factor which repealed Nicolas so greatly. This alone made her anything but a lady. The hypocrite fraud, Nicolas enjoyed every moment of taking advantage of a woman in all ways he had forever longed to do. The selfish part of Nicolas made him wish if only he had a woman he actually wanted to invade in this manner. No one can have everything, not even Nicolas Beaumont. He used, abused discarded walking away after taking what he wanted, laughing his ass off at his used up piece of ass. Classing her as an older woman trying to remain young. Young only in heart as her body was not weather, sexual and cigarette worn. A piece of pussy he would never touch again. It didn't end well either for Sophie. She gave him all he required. To say goodbye he didn't hold her for a little longer, kiss her extra passionately, send flowers or surprise her with a gift. He was gift enough for her. Nothing to soften the blow. To degrade her further, to make her feel like an animal who should give up and die, ending their own life, Nicolas tied Sophie to the hotel bed, refusing to free her. Threatening to allow the maids to enter and see her naked body, with wrists and legs handcuffed to the bedframe if she refused to do what he demanded. Aware that if that happened the news would make it back to her husband faster than the speed of light, as she would be arrested for such conduct in such a high-class establishment. She made many enemies. There would be somebody out to get her back for all the badness she had inflicted onto other people's lives. Building up countless enemies. Thereby conceding. Allowing her bladder to be set free, golden showers Nicolas adored. The smell, the taste, the willing to do anything debasing to satisfy his urges. More than anything what really made Nicolas climax was the bowels being released. Shitty, filthy certainly. After the first time, after seeing how much it pleased Nicolas, Sophie didn't want to stop. They continued to fuck on a golden bed sheet.

Sophie felt a mixture of emotions for her best ever lay. A mixture of feeling sorry that his wife was supposed to have died on a romantic skiing trip while in Austria during November 1990 for her birthday. Six months prior to their sexual lunatic experience. Not that she didn't want Gabriella out of the picture, she wanted nothing more, not merely to land Nicolas but Gabriella's beauty caused her to be snubbed. Not solely by Nicolas but her own husband, not to mention within their social group. Sophie and Gabriella just like Sophie and I, Nicolette, were the complete opposite. Sophie was cool and unapproachable. Mind games she plays, crazy games with her crazy over-the-top sex. Gabriella and I warm, kind natured, soft natured, real, calm not to neglect peacekeepers. We were the type a man takes home to mother. The type a man marries. The type a gentleman stands by and appreciates. Sophie not so much, she was more the kind a man fucks only to fuck off; just like Nicolas did. He was far from the first man who treated her in the same fashion. She asked for it. Conducting herself like the whore she was. If any man is dumb enough to marry her kind, he'll spend the rest of his life if he doesn't get divorced first paying for his terrible mistake. The mistake which may make a man bankrupt. To Sophie's distain and hatred. Of course at all times being socially polite and the biggest hypocrite God had put on this earth. Being nice to Gabriella's face, going as far as to complement her, only trashing her behind her back, there wasn't anything this woman would not debase herself to in order to attain male attention. Any man would do. Attempting to have people cast Gabriella out of parties isolating her, Sophie's overall aim was to make her depressed, dejected and hoped she would be weak-minded enough to kill herself. Not to put her out of her own misery, but to put Sophie out of hers. Sophie did not have the courage to end her ordeal until later days, therefore wanted to take the easy way out, by treating people unforgivably in order to attain what she wished. She was the type of woman to make things happen, sometimes as a consequence with grave repercussions. The typical behaviour from trash who think they are something they are not. Sophie like the rest of Geneva was uninformed about the true circumstances which surrounded Gabriella's death. If she had known the facts she was so screwed up she would have continued secretly stalking Nicolas. He was in her blood. Toxic. Dramatic. Excessive. Nicolas had never confessed that Gabriella died in her own bed at home in Genève, on April 25 1991. The only other two people in the world who knew the facts of the elapsed five months were Nicolas's closest allies, Philippine and Emilio. Treating Gabriella the way they had subjugated me only a few months after our marriage.

Shinning like an angel, a very successful movie star. Nicolas could not have been prouder of his precious find. For the time being like everything, it was only for the time being. Peace does not remain long when Nicolas Beaumont is present. Taking me to Sophie's house a friend I never had the pleasure of meeting, until that night. Nicolas briefed me before setting foot in the ten thousand square foot home which was more condescending than the owner. Discarding her bony, flat ass and no boobs ten long years ago. The moment I laid eyes on her I did not care to learn anything. She was without reservation the most patronising person I had ever met. It was present in her demeanour. Her demeanour was as off-putting as she was. She wasn't good at acting, she was even worse at pretending to be nice. Thus being the reason she wasn't liked by her own guests, perhaps more significantly why she wasn't a professional actress. Then again if Kathleen Turner can be successful and rich from being an uninteresting actress, then Sophie had every capability, she should have taken lessons from Angelina Jolie. People simply attended her parties because everybody important went only to see her husband. It was a safe place to get high of heroin meth, anything they could get their hands on. Frederic was admired and respected by the people of Genève. Although he did have affairs as did Sophie, he was not a man whore. Frederic had traditional values, a pillar of society. Based on the fact his wife was the whore and treated him like a piece of crap, something he never was. In reality he was a gentleman, yet longed to feel love. Not merely sexual but genuine heartfelt love. Pining for many years for a real marriage. As rich as he was, love he learnt the hard way could not be bought. His parties were the perfect place to make contacts for the guests and to make even more millions than they already possessed. In later years he came to love his bank balance over any woman. A tough life had turned him into a switchboard, one to be turned off to people, his circuit board possessed no on switch. Unable to find the perfect match to share his life and fortune with, feeling sorrow at this embittering him into a state of lack of enthusiasm for life. He took love from where he could find it, money could not hurt him. In turn finding safety within his assets.

Sophie's head in the air overly wiggling her nonexistent hips, acting as though she was the Queen of Sheba, if not the resurrected Cleopatra. Sophie's nonexistent boobs on display making her look more a cross between a five-year-old boy and a scarecrow. A flat chest in a dress made for cleavage was far from the best of looks for anybody; especially not an ugly, quickly aging, used up cunt which wasn't capable of getting wet anymore. She was over-the-top in her manner, too flamboyant to be likeable. Too much makeup upon her wrinkled face, dried out like a prune after too much sun, too much jewellery, her perfume too strong. She tried too hard to be nice, tried too hard to do everything, still managing to fail. When someone tries too hard there's a purpose. Even to be the centre of attention, when the party was held in honour of her dear beloved friend to introduce his new sweet wife. Instead she acted as though she had won some impressive award. Her aim to make me feel inferior. Everything dramatised, so much so I could read Sophie's character as soon as she commenced in our direction. She was rather self-absorbed to state the most obvious factor. As we came through the front door of the most unwelcoming and uncomfortable house I had ever set foot in. One could be excused for believing that it was a bachelor's pad, opposed to a family home. Everything was dull and cold, neutral, boxy. Impersonal. Lack of character in every sense. Not at all family orientated or homely, not even comfortable. Modern it certainly was. Tiled floors, grey walls, no family pictures, no anything that a normal warm family home would possess. No, love did not dwell here.

Not wanting to remain by the time the guests had overloaded my brain with an abundance of drivel, rendering me with the most frightful headache I have ever endured, reducing me to silence. My ears couldn't take anymore shouting. God these people are loud! The higher they became the louder they got. The more intoxicated they became, I was rendered to becoming deaf, then my ears rang. My lean feminine fingers massaged my temples which pulsated, feeling as though any time now they were about to explode. Showering this god forsaken grey box with a bit of colour, red. The conversations were as boring as the décor and the hostess. Between companies going bust, wanting to murder the CEO of some big time multibillion Euro franchise. Good God I couldn't take anymore. Instead of a party it was more like a business meeting. Tempted to get high myself for the first time in my life just to quiet the voices. The loud voices, the sharp voices and the squeaky voices. Everyone. I wanted silence. My head needed peace. Sophie's voice I detested, she talked more like a man than a man. Without any bias Sophie was the most unfeminine woman. Nicolas was talking with business men, while I sat beside an unattractive plain white wall mounted fireplace, which hung on a grey wall. Breaking up the dullness and the coldness of the colour. The colour triggered off a thought reminding me more of a colour found in a prison. No character, no anything. Simply clinical! My attempt to escape the vultures went unnoticed or so I believed. Foolishly. I continued to drink a tall glass of champagne in despair, drowning my sorrow and boredom. Drowning out the annoying voices with each sip I took. It was the cheap kind, the kind that was actually drinkable with no bitter bubbles or fizz in the mouth. No salty after taste. Figuring Frederic must have put his foot down with so many parties, she would have bankrupt him if she gave out expensive free champagne at every part. I couldn't blame him. As I clutched a hold of myself and my quickly depreciating emotions, forgetting where I was as I mouthed to myself, attempting to jolt myself back into reality unlike a spoilt little brat:

"You are a very lucky girl don't be selfish. He's put a lot of effort into making you look as beautiful as you do and showing you off, be appreciative. Look at what you are wearing. Make your husband proud, stop hiding away in the corner. As we came in all eyes were on me, people want to see me. Blag it. "

Instantly fixing a fake but believable smile upon my angel-like face, attempting to enjoy myself the very best I possibly could. Fixing a false smile was what I have been forever good at. Pretending to be alright on the exterior when inside I am dying, not indicating this to anybody as being weak can never be forgiven. This my injurious and insalubrious family taught me. Being weak will get one nowhere, it will either get one into trouble, or into an early grave. Perhaps there's no difference between the two.

Looking over to my far away husband who was standing across the room, unfortunately his attentions were on everybody but me. I accepted him to be no better than an inflamed quickly spreading rash, stuck to my side like glue. I was the one person his eyes should have been on, considering that this was not a business party but a special occasion. It was our party; it was supposed to be about us. Not purely him. Never wasting an opportunity for his own glorification. Not that he was admiring other women; he was simply taking in his glory. This was his moment. I was aware there was no other woman at this party which came close to me in looks, manners and respectability. Counting how many admirers who were admiring me, filled with lust and envy, the delight was advertised in Nicolas's eyes. Going onto count the men who would have loved nothing more than to steal his glory away. At least by tarnishing it by fucking me to prove a point. I was no longer his piece of play, I was now his. He owned me, all five foot two inches, every strand of hair, every piece of dead skin which falls from my body each morning. Every molecule which makes me who I am, is his. Down to the clothes I would now wear to please him, the food placed in my stomach providing he okays it. I was bought and paid for. I would now do everything I was told. Nicolas who was the king of the chateau. I Nicolette, no I was not the queen of the chateau or ever to become the queen. There would never be room for a queen in his chateau; there will never be a coronation. I am the lady who was no better than a servant and I am not even a Virgo. The only difference was I Nicolette had a marginally better sounding title, a title was all it was. Words. Empty meaningless words. Being a wife did not give grounds for promotion. EVER!

CHAPTER THIRTY-EIGHT

I Held My Breath

I didn't dance the night away. I wasn't high. I wasn't drunk. Though how I wish I were. I was glad to have left those prison walls of grey and white. As soon as we entered the marital bedroom Nicolas yelling and entering a state of insanity, literally shaking my heart with fear.

"You've let me down immensely; you made a fool of me. What have I done to deserve this from you? What, Nicolette? Look at what you are wearing for fuck sake! Look at your home and everything I have given you. I had no idea you were this selfish. You are not the person I believed you to be. You are a fraud. You led me to believe you were someone better. Someone I could respect. Someone who would make me proud. How could you let me down this gravely? You made a fool of me this night. Nobody makes a fool of Nicolas Beaumont. Nobody. You have made a laughingstock of the both of us, the first time I show you off. You've disgraced me. It has taken me all my life to build up my reputation and in one night you swan in and away with it. And you're a nobody."

Astounded, unable to reply with my voice, only my eyes as they stared at my husband with horror, his eyes were bulging from his head. Cold! His cool blues turned black before my very eyes. His complexion turned grey. His tone of voice, well it was evil. He shouted so hard with so much essence spit was being splattered all over on my face. Nicolas's saliva entered my eyes landing on my lips. Rendered wordless when he did not kill me. I was positive he was going to kill me.

Pausing for one split second to look at me as though he already has the noose knotted and ready to hang me for my grave sins.

"Answer me, you dumb bitch."

"I don't know what to say, Nicolas, I'm shocked. I didn't think I did anything wrong. What did I do? Why are you so upset? You were fine with me until we arrived back home and your friend Sophie's house is thirty minutes away from our home, why the instant change of heart and temper now? You did not speak one word to me in the car. I thought everything was alright."

"What did you do and why am I so upset? You have the impudence to ask me two obtuse questions, when you of all people should know the answer to those questions are, as you are the only person who caused it. I did not speak to you in the car, I was fighting the urge to beat the shit clean of you, you worthless whore. The only reason I refrained with grave difficulty I must add, is due to the fact you are beautiful. I need you looking your best for these parties we have to attend for the next month. I cannot show up without you, that would create gossip and scandal and I certainly cannot have you bruised and cut. That would defeat the entire purpose for marrying you and flaunting you in this fashion. Consider yourself fortunate, you lucky cunt. Trust me when I say you have no idea how lucky you are, and what pain I can inflict onto you."

Moving close to me. My heart rate increased. Holding my breath, bracing myself for the unexpected. Bending down to whisper in my left ear as I sat on the bed. It was clear to see the wickedness which lived within this man through the key to the soul.

"After this month of parties has concluded I must inform you, do not be so comfortable. Bruises will have time to heal and cuts time to disappear before anyone will see you again. Scars can be concealed. Punishment for selfishness must be bequeathed for the youth of these days to learn."

Abruptly turning and walking away from me. Relief fell over my entire body. I felt light as though I would fall to the floor. Inhaling the deepest breath I had ever at one time breathed. It was like it was my last gasp of life. It was fearful. Intense.

"Caused what, baby? Just calm down and explain to me please, I don't understand. It is so important we are able to talk to one another. I did not wish to upset you, not now not ever. I thought you had fun and enjoyed yourself. I was sure the party was a success. If I did anything wrong, please understand it was merely from nerves and not at all intentional. I was intimidated by so many strange people. My voice quivered, my hands shook. You know every single person who was there tonight. I didn't know one. You were my support you were the only one I knew, yet you weren't with me the entire night until we were leaving."

Nicolas walked over to me (walking slowly, holding himself in a tense and ominous manner causing me to become frightened), grabbing me by the throat and squeezing as he said;

"Don't call me baby. I am not your baby. I am a man, a strong man, the man of everything. You are my selfish, ungrateful whore of a wife. You embarrassed me tonight. You caused me shame in front of all my friends, including Sophie of all people."

Extra and harsh emphasis made when speaking her name, with spray of spit discharging from his mouth. Wetting my face.

"She will laugh at me behind my back for all time, I will never be able to live this down. Great shame you have caused me. For years I have been able to degrade that cunt, now you disable my leverage. You have no idea how long I have waited for tonight. This was my night, my time. You took it away from me. I'm too old now to wait another decade to remarry. How could such a laughable idiot take such an important night away from me? You're nothing. You're a no body. I've given to you and given you a hell of a lot. You rob me. You stole my admiration and you're nobody. I married below myself. I should kill you for what you have done. Do you understand me; I should fucking kill you, you CUNT. If there is any justice in this world you would die this very instant from guilt and shame. That way I would have the sympathy from those same people tonight and attention would be all mine once more. That is the only comeback from this. You should die right now, this very moment to make it up to me. That is the only right thing for you to do. GO ON DIE!!!"

Grabbing me by the back of the neck, dragging me from the bed to the dressing table, shoving my head into the glass. Certain the glass was going to break, disfiguring my assets for life. Fear filled me. After a few moments which felt like an hour after shaking my head in every direction it would go and being disappointed I was not an owl, he finally let me go. Left in tears, involuntary tears, not knowing what to say or how to fix the situation. My body was not going to be enough to mend matters tonight. Not this night. His unhappiness was a much greater issue to him than what my body and open space between my legs could fill. I was left in an absolute loss. This was the night the first signs of abuse shone through. The first tears which dropped, the first shaking my body underwent. I had no idea how to make things better, how to fix it, how to fix him. It was this night, this very same night, I knew he was a sick man, sicker than I originally realised. It was this very same night realisation hit home, I had bitten off more than I could chew. I was way in over my head and before the end, the long dreadful end drew near I would drowned in mourning, mourning for my sombre mistake.

CHAPTER THIRTY-NINE

King Nicolas

A day of cold, blustery winds blew howling like a wolf. When night fall casted over the Beaumont household, Nicolas sent the maid to come for me. I was in our marital bedroom where I was reading a book out on the balcony. For modesty purposes I threw on my matching silk robe to cover my sheer black negligee. Completely oblivious as to what would occur as I entered the study. I was still learning. Nicolas was naked, sitting at his desk. In a dominant tone demanding me to come to him. When I drew near ordering me to kneel before him.

"Who am I and what am I, Nicolette?"

"You are Nicolas my husband, baby."

Banging his clenched fist upon a solid mahogany desk with zest of anger and hissing through clenched teeth...

"WRONG, WRONG!

"Are you completely stupid?"

Raising his right hand and planting a stinging slap on my left cheek.

"I am not just Nicolas Beaumont... I am King Nicolas. I am king of this Chateau."

"You are King Nicolas, you are my king... What can I do to pleasure my king?"

"Exactly and don't you forget it. I am your king. Thankfully you are learning. You do whatever I demand. Now suck my cock, peasant.

After approximately five minutes of blowing my husband, he pulled my hair, in turn, my head away from his cock. With a dirty smug expression on his face looking down at me and saying:

"Kiss my feet."

After kissing his feet I continued to suck his cock for another five minutes or so, deciding he would turn things up a notch. Standing up from the desk chair, telling me to remain on my knees he wanted me to suck his balls. Sticking my head underneath and between his legs I start to suck and lick. He started to moan. Looking down at me with darkness in his eyes. This man is never happy.

"This can get better."

Turning around, sticking his ass into my face ordering me to lick the crack of his ass.

"Lick it until it's soaked."

Was my order. After an hour of this being replayed multiple times, he finally came over my face and hair.

"Lick every last drop out from the head of my dick."

Immediately after my midnight feast, he told me "go to bed." Just how all kings throughout the ages are renowned to do with their mistresses when sex had been had.

PART ELEVEN

Presents Bestowed

CHAPTER FORTY

Viennese Waltz

Saturday 13 December

As a romantic gesture Nicolas thought out his Christmas present meticulously, for our first Christmas together he had to get it perfect. The first year is always the most important, it indicates one's true feelings. He could not accept anything other than perfection. Therefore putting his entire heart into making sure whatever he decided upon would be fit for a queen, his queen. Since he had married me in December, every day spending lavish amounts of money in such a short space of time should be considered criminal. Because Nicolas was as affluent to the degree he was spending money was what he did best. It was his job, his career, his hobby. His aphrodisiac. Going through large amounts in short spaces of time he did even better. Spending money thrilled him, earning it bored him. He had no interest in working, given everything his entire life. Nicolas could be considered a cross between Celine Dion who is said to be a self-confessed shopaholic, with a supposed in excess of two thousand pairs of shoes; her husband Rene, who has been said to lose in excess a million dollars a day in Las Vegas when gambling, hence the move to Nevada. With funds like theirs and Nicolas's, I guess if you have it you might as well spend it, especially if it is going to keep right on rolling on in.

Nicolas was certain with the four and a half million in jewellery he had purchased that month, that more bobbles and lustre would be too much, considering I had never been accustomed to this kind of life style. Pleasing me, considering how I quickly became sick of looking at diamonds. In the beginning I was entranced by the lustre expensive possessions had over the cheaper items I had once been familiar. Very quickly I became sick of the over-the-top outfits and jewels. The layered on makeup. The strong potent perfumes. Undeniably I had habituated to a comfortable lifestyle, but to this extend no. It did not seem right somehow. Not watching every penny, budgeting, being smart with money, I had not yet become accustomed. Four and a half million in a space of two weeks. Madness! Comfortable yes, I was used to comfortable; tragic was even more normal for me, but not being spoilt. I the girl who only knew sadness then all of a sudden, now I am being showered with millions worth in jewels. My, how life changes sometimes in a blink of an eye. Life can be unfathomable. The unexpected only to arise, the much needed never to appear. Until December 2001 I did not know how it felt to be showered with gifts, being spoilt was foreign to me, it wasn't exciting, it wasn't amazing; I didn't like it, this I came to know without reservation. Perhaps I was guilty of being crazy or ungrateful, either way it was not for me. I was used to budgeting, being prudent. I was used to being cautious with most things in life. Being cautious is being wiser. To lose oneself within spending vast amounts of money is an evil. Somewhere along the line, there is no alternative to one losing themselves and who they are. The devil in sheep's clothing. When one grows up without knowing what it is to have everything one desires, with no surplus cash and to have everything one sees, it is common place to yearn for the things you want but cannot have. The things you want but do not need. When one has money all bills are paid, no worries financially, heaven. Having money all one's life, this is not a blessing altogether. Having too much of anything can be a moral hindrance. The more one has, the more one wants. After a time it is only normal to lose sight of oneself, morals and one's own character. The less one has the more lessons learnt the richer one's life.

Clothes, no clothes can be bought anytime, something special, something unique. I need something tailor-made for the most beautiful woman in the world. A spa trip, with chocolate covered strawberries, the best strawberries needless to say. Champagne the most expensive, lavish dinners, a spa trip for a week. Massages, facials, manicures and pedicures. No! Nowhere near good enough. A car. Can she even drive pondering for a moment? It could be a contender. Perhaps a Bentley! We have a chauffeur, we have Bentley's ...

Pausing. Screwing up his face, rolling his eyes around his head as though to get the blood within to flow properly, biting on the inside of his cheek. Rolling his neck around in circles. Tapping the desk with his fingers. Debating. Deciding.

... No, she doesn't need a car. I own ten. I could get her a maid, a maid to do her hair, dress her and carry out her wishes. All Queens have maids. My wife is a lady she doesn't lift a finger. She doesn't carry, clean or lift. Lady of the manor. No, that won't do, I do not want anybody in this house who does not need to be here. I have too many things to keep secret...

Delaying a moment, rolling his eyes around in their sockets again, encouraging his brain to think deeper. Tapping his fingers of his lips and slightly on his chin.

... I've got it I could buy her a lake house, some kind of holiday home, one she could go to whenever she wished with or without me, if she gets bored with being here all of the time. A place she could entertain friends once she makes some. An opportunity to throw lavish parties or it could be a place to escape. She is too beautiful to hide. A house it is, she can use it for whatever she wants. Nothing under a million. She has standards to uphold. Immediately going on the net to check out listings.

Good question where? Should it be in Switzerland or another country she could actually travel to, making it feel more like a holiday, after all Switzerland is a small country? I've got it! Sweden! The country is said to be an intriguing place to be and live. Fun, freedom and liberal. No political bull shit. Stockholm is nightclubs galore. There is much more life there compared to the sleepy streets of Genève. This will be the place for such a beauty to receive all the attention and admiration she deserves. Nobody like the Swedish appreciate beauty. The country is filled with it. Everybody will notice her there. Pleased she is dissimilar to the Swiss or the Swedish women, with the majority being blonde-haired and typical blue eyes. My Nicolette will be rare even there. My dark raven. In so many countries I can take my bride she will be different, this making me prouder than I originally was. I have met many beautiful women over the years. I have never had the privilege of meeting a beauty who reaps as much attention and veneration as my sweet Nicolette.

After three hours and twenty-eight minutes spent looking at every lake house he could find, finally finding the perfect one. It was wooden – the traditional style with a wooden decking, a separate sun room, a place to barbeque and entertain outside. A deep green forest with ten and a half acres of land surrounded the house. Reminding him of pictures he had seen in Canada. Booking tickets including a five-star hotel in the heart of Stockholm. Hotel Barriere. It was a contemporary hotel for a contemporary city. Stockholm was thee cosmopolitan; it was the place where it was all happening. New York weep your heart out. Knowing I was traditional and far from contemporary hoping I would enjoy it, nonetheless. A change, a fresh exciting change. Needless to vocalise it was the city to be. Forget LA, California, forget Miami, Stockholm was the place. The place where Abba were still alive and beating, as though no time had passed between their breakup and current time. Still fashionable. They were still as loved today as they were at their peak. Four beautiful people, who made up the greatest band in the world with none other to compare.

Starting to Google for a few other pieces of information, an ad appeared on yahoo advertising tickets for sale. The Viennese Christmas concert. Starting at seven in the evening, the concert lasting for two hours. Instantly planning which evening dresses I would need, which necklaces would match which outfit the best, with which clutch I would carry. Going online to the official website to purchase tickets, picking the most extravagant package. Nothing less could be expected. The Vienna Christmas Concert, first three days prior to the opening of the new house he would buy in full before leaving Genève. Rearranging his schedule with excitement. Marking on his computer calendar the dates and events which would now take place, to ensure my eyes would not see my thoughtful surprises. Leaning back on the leather office swivel chair with a satisfied sensation and smile, kicking off his shoes, knowing he has done himself proud. Flinging his legs upon the desk stretched out before him, taking a well-deserved sip from his brandy glass. A sigh of pride escaped from his thin lips.

CHAPTER FORTY-ONE

Christmas Trees

Certain if I closed my eyes tight and perhaps held my breath I would drown out the pain. The pain perhaps numbed but what I didn't count on was the smell of his breath, a mixture of peppermint and garlic with an undercurrent of bitter gin. Desperately trying to envisage the sight of a living room beautifully decorated. I dreamed while he violated me.

Beneath my breath words seep into the atmosphere:

"Please, lord, let it be your wish, your merciful and fatherly wish to end this all tonight, my torture and dismay. Be it I die, or they die, either way someone must or else this will never end. I am weak of body and mind, destroyed, reduced to nothingness, on my hands and knees I implore you grant my prayer. If I am truly your daughter and you my father, grant this prayer I pray."

CHAPTER FORTY-TWO

Vienna Christmas Concert

21 December 2001

On the train from Geneva to Vienna Nicolas was in a rather appalling mood, the usual for the past few days. With a deep frown on his forehead there was silence the entire duration of the trip. I knew not to utter a word, if I did I would have released a demon. Having many doubts about our first Christmas together, I had been dreading it. Putting that daunting thought out of my mind to deal with the task at hand, my moody unpredictable husband. He blew as hot as the Sudan dessert sun, as cold as Antarctica with his blaring words of fear blinding me like the Moroccan sky. His threats and slaps giving rise to my hairs standing upon the back of my neck and arms with chills of fear running through my body like electric shocks. I knew they weren't just threats. He executes what he avows.

Sitting on the train enjoying the ride as much as I possibly could. Heavy weighing on my heart. Train rides are wonderful. Adding extra sprinkles of magic during this Christmas time, all was not lost. I sat with pride as I wore my new fur hat and coat, elaborate, beautiful but pleased they looked real but weren't. I didn't own the heart which could enjoy flaunting death. It was a sandy coloured full-length coat, accompanied by a pair of tan leather gloves and chocolate coloured leather boots. Elegant. Sophisticated. Above all sensible. As soon as we crossed the border I knew without needing to see the signposts we were now in Austria. As cold as Switzerland gets in winter Austria has an entirely different type of coldness, its sharper, harsher, breathe robbing. Such as the Texas heat, no oxygen is attainable.

On arrival at the Hotel Ambassador in the heart of Vienna. Nicolas racing to the minibar in our room to down his needed stash for the day. Raiding it from all alcoholic contents. Afterwards phoning down to the bar to have a bottle of Dom Perrion and a large bottle of brandy sent to the room immediately. I left him to fester in his bitterness about life and his overprivileged lifestyle. Taking time out to chill indulging myself with a hot shower and the much needed time to relax and pretend to be somewhere else. The mind is a splendid structure with a spectacular ability how it so magically allows a person to pretend they are somewhere else. Imagination is the greatest invention. Ten minutes passed feeling only slightly relaxed; I had every reason to believe tonight would pose more turbulence than an airplane flying in the sky as a tsunami hits land below. After my shower with entering the bedroom I was grabbed from a blind spot and flung onto the bed. I wasn't certain if it was Nicolas or if a stranger had gotten into the room. One does hear many frightening stories about tourists being attacked in their hotel rooms by gangs following them from the airports; not to mention crooked receptionist. Their occupation is sitting at airports twenty four seven seeking out the rich, listening to the instructions the taxi driver will be given, or bribing the prearranged driver to which hotel they will be brought to, giving them a cut of the findings. Giving them an idea how much they are worth and how much they could abscond with. Somewhat thankful when I saw Nicolas's face and that nobody else was in the room, from out of nowhere I am graciously greeted with a smash. An empty wine glass was thrown at my head, cowering like a yellow belly I froze for a moment, waiting in anxious anticipation of what may happen next.

"Remove your towel."

Grabbing me by the wrist my towel fell from my body, he stuck a tie into my mouth which had been already rolled into a ball.

"Suck on that if you must. Roll over, Nicolette, I want you face down on the bed."

"Yes, my king, anything you say."

I mumbled through my gagged mouth, not very successfully. As I rolled my eyes I knew to stroke his ego. It was the only thing I could do. The only thing which was effective.

Nicolas removed an altar candle from his case which sat by the large window, lighting the wick, waiting a few minutes for wax to melt around the top. Rolling it around as a gentleman does his brandy glass releasing the aroma and encouraging them to flavoursome the contents. When enough wax had melted around the wick and built up in a pool of hot shiny wax, pouring it over the middle of my spine, from top to bottom, then in reverse. Pouring it down the crack of my ass, screams then needed to escape. On my spine the burning sensation hurt but only a moment's amount, then I felt a dirty minx of a thrill. In effect the wax was the key unlocking the lock of which I hide behind. Ladylike prim and proper. Turning out not to be the hell I first associated the experience to be. When poured on my ass, it was a little too painful to give me any sexual pleasure, that feeling was substituted for badness. Sheer delightful badness. When Nicolas spilled it over my tits, my soaring nipples, stomach and my pussy I loved it. My body was going mad craving for more, for dirtier. For him. Going mad for love to be made. Turning me on like never before. Now the kitty-cat was purring for much, much more.

The Vienna Christmas concert was the most romantic gift Nicolas had ever planned for me. It was a special gift. The night was magical with so many amazing memories to hold dear my entire life through. A night to remember. Wearing a gold and ivory ballroom gown, off the shoulder. A Princess style dress. With delicate gold sandals, which weren't very comfortable to walk in, but were very beautiful to look at. I felt very important. Admired like never before by the highest of society. Sat in between Kings and Queens of Europe and Duchesses and Lords, from billionaires to actors. I would return back there one day I knew as I exited the building. The evening started off with me being pampered at the hotel spa, getting dressed up as though I were in some colonial movie. The singers were magnificent, the corps de ballet more so. Music from Mozart and Strauss was played. The scent from outside the palaces of mulled wine, gingerbread and Christmas cake vaporised into the air and into the concert. It truly smelt like Christmas, the sensation could not be misunderstood. The most wonderful Christmas I have ever known. With each symphony performed I got lost in a melody of my own. With my head tilted to the left my eyes open but shut off to the crowd which surrounded me, I was in dreams. Imagining I was dancing with a princes in one of the exquisite ball rooms of the castle. Later dinning at Meditena Neo enjoying a three course dinner. Royalty and other aristocrats were present, treating me as though I were in their league. Dancing the night away. After the evening concluded I was left heartbroken. It was like my wedding night all over again. Feeling like Cinderella longing for midnight to stay away. My bubble had to burst and it did. I could not face going to bed, I did not want tonight to become a dream just yet. A precious memory to recall. It had to be here and now and still in current time. Still being savoured. Nicolas granted my final wish, we walked the streets of Vienna until three a.m. Instead of seeing Santa, like that first night in Zermatt we walked and walked the cobble streets. Singing and dancing down alleyways and squares. This time we window-shopped. There were too many exquisite Christmas decorations on display in the shop windows, decorated with pine twigs and silk ribbons. Other windows had little ornaments and nativities. There was one in particular I will always recall, displaying many little villages, rooftops kissed by snow. Iced paths and grass covered in winter white. Windows a glow. Candles and fires ablaze. People wrapped up in clothing no longer worn, gentlemen with their waistcoats, top hats and chained watches, women with their modest dresses and pretty bonnets. Children running around, playing innocent games children ought to play, throwing snowballs and patting their precious puppies. Sleighs and horse drawn carriages. There was never a more beautiful sight. I had completely forgotten about the rough start our marriage took. Making excuses for him. Putting it down to not knowing each other and that all marriages suffer hard times, more so when two strangers undergo a union meant for life. It's natural. The first year is the hardest. The New Year will bring happier and meaningful times. We will make our own family and warm-hearted Christmas village for next year, instead of ornamental it will be very much real.

CHAPTER FORTY-THREE

Raven the Shark

Raven of black secrets to mat and match
Mysterious with rightful clandestine
Woman of dark and sight of lark
Upon a throne of gold with pride does sit
Won't forever be silent when she comes out in the dark
Seduce and deduce
Smart and opaque
Garden of dances entwined
Shadows of beasts back and forth streak
Back and forth sway
When she's out, she's out to become the shark
Her world is the world of lessons learnt toughen and taught
Melted, broken down and destroyed
Low misty clouds walk through and veil dampen
Raven of black eyes of coal and hair of deepest darkest black
halfway down her back
The raven is not a bird instead a mysterious and dangerous woman
She lives behind yet moves fluently and elegantly within the
darkness
Souls, no souls know when she's near

Spying, lurking from behind the darkness and mist
Watching for the beast
Pounce and kill
There's no time for her time of year
No season is dear
A knife in the back of the back of he who she selects
A dance to her is the death kiss given, a dance till the death
Don't dance with the raven
The raven is not a bird, instead a mysterious and dangerous woman
She lives behind yet moves within the darkness.

PART TWELVE

Revolutionize

CHAPTER FORTY-FOUR

A Husband's Betrayal

Tennis Clud de Geneve

Following Sunday lunch at the Tennis Clud De Geneve I met more of Nicolas's so-called friends. I state so-called friends based on the fact I could distinguish they hated the sight and the being of Nicolas Beaumont. With each breath he exhales hoping it will be his final. If Nicolas ever turned up murdered it would be a long and strenuous job for the Swiss police to determine and eliminate possible suspects, with the large amount of enemies Nicolas Beaumont has made over the past fifty years. Most would give the guilty party an air-tight alibi, ensuring the greatest gift the world has ever been bestowed would be safe from consequences. Creating enemies everywhere he went. Glad when the afternoon was concluded; from being winked at by the waiter, the very handsome waiter with the dark black swept back hair, six foot one, perhaps two. With a strong and very manly nose, with long and lean hands. Well used and worked. He was everything a man should be.

Being thrown onto the marital bed violently to certain couples maybe considered an act of sexual foreplay. "I want you now!" If this is a mutual feeling between the two sexual partners one can only hope. Wanting to be occupied by the man who I think the world of, if he's the hopeless romantic type. Or the man who turns me on in the dirtiest and most delicious ways. This could be all one needs for a fuck out of this world. Nicolas lost my heart many years ago. There was no love between us anymore. Not in this heart and not in this home. He became my gravest mistake and regret. Wishing silently I could start anew. All there was between Nicolas and I in the later days of our marriage was sex. Not regular I find you attractive sex; I cannot keep my hands off you. I love you so much until the end of time. Instead it was the crazy violent sex. No closeness, no breathless need to keep riding one another when it hurts too much, and the rawness becomes more and more skinned. There was no bond. To Nicolas it was only about pain, making me feel not merely his manhood, not merely his girth. Nicolas Beaumont wanted to reduce me to nothingness. In my debasing as a human being, a woman the weaker sex, this made sex for Nicolas an undreamed dream. Nicolas was forever guilty of wanting the greatest of everything. In short he was a selfish bastard. In order to attain the fuck which silently would be considered the fuck of one's life, both parties must enjoy. Feed of him to feel your heighted pleasure. Be it the countless positions demonstrated or the hardest fuck your body has ever been exposed to. But when the man who is my husband attacks me aggressively, repetitively tying my hands behind my back, shoving me onto my face upon our marital bed, pulling my hair from behind, pulling lumps from my scalp my heart beginning to race each time. Fear soars through my body. Barely able to conduct breathing adequately, feeling as though I were smothering. Smothering in fear, smothering in sex. Is my husband destined to end my life by asphyxiation? Is this what my life has come to? Was I born into this world only to leave it as I am being fucked senseless? The most disgraceful way to leave this world for all time. I see stars in front of my eyes and it is not the night skies twinkling above. It could not be this, I am faced down upon my bed. My bed, the place where I ought to be safe to sleep entering pleasurable dreams, instead it becomes my prison, my hell. What am I to do the thought enters my mind, how am I going to get oxygen into my lungs. Desperately attempting to push myself up upon my arms, only to be pushed down harder he next time by Nicolas, onto my throat. I feel dizzy; I begin to panic that much more. That wasn't a smart move; I can breathe less now. Powerless to become free. As I am being fucked relentlessly from behind like a bitch, the dog is in his sexual element. Through fear I am unable to feel pain. If I survive pain is all I will feel tomorrow. My life could be ending slowly, yet in the end certain I am going to die this night while I am being exploited and used like a common cheap whore. A whore I am not. Then again in an unbiased review of me and my life, perhaps that is what I have become. A whore is what Nicolas has made me. I knew before he ended his play, I would be in immense pain. Knowing it would not be inconceivable to be left in a pool of blood for another time. It is never great sex for Nicolas until he leaves me bleeding. The knowing that I am in colossal pain added to Nicolas's climax, this made him harder. Meaningfully injuring my uterus making him a sick and mentally ill brute. Enjoying my ass too much not to be gay. Nicolas did not just like to fuck his wife, he liked more than anything to rip my insides apart. Leaving me in a heap with arms behind my back unable to set myself free, realising I was at his mercy hence making Nicolas feel worthy. Laughing at me once he concluded his play, because I had no choice but to hop and place myself in many awkward positions to try and become free. Grateful I was flexible after investing all those years of yoga and Pilates, finally they have paid off and saved my ass when it came to the crunch. There were many questionable traits which would cause alarm with the way Nicolas lived and the dreams he dreams up.

In his own mind he was only worthy. A born again Nazi in my eyes. Nicolas took momentous gratification and amusement in seeing me incapable of moving and in too much pain to cry. This night I am startled. Why, I am not sure. Nicolas taking me by surprise with the sexual experiences he has put me through. As he pulled his explosive cock from out of my body, slowly he shoves it into my ass. Searing pain shoots into the back of my head causing me to cry out in agony, as he forces his dick in and out as hard as he could muster. While he pushes my back down exposing my ass in mid-air, suddenly gasping for oxygen once more as he pulls my hair, in turn snaps my head back sadistically. With each thrust I feel nauseous; vomit emerges into my mouth and up my nose. Less oxygen and more fear. I can't breathe; it feels like an eternity before I gasp for air. All I could feel in the meantime was a pain which resembles swords being shoved into my body. It was a pain I never felt before, the sharpest pain I have in my life known. Once I could breathe and when the pain subsided, shamefully I must admit even to myself I enjoyed the antagonistic lunatic sex. I was becoming Nicolas. Sick. This I was shrewd enough not to enlighten Nicolas of. I knew, he would have become more assertive in his fashion of exploiting me to these unthinkable acts of sex. His desire was for me not to enjoy his rides. They were designed to be my punishment. Punishment for what he felt I did wrong. I could feel his thighs tighten and his breathing becoming heavier and more staggered. I hear the loudest groan. I knew in that instant he was about to come inside me, again, to my dismay. To my surprise, to my embarrassment he pulls his engorged cock from my ass, pushing me fast and hard onto my back he straddles my face as he strokes his own dick in front of me until he cums over my face. Seductively on his hands and knees moves down to my crotch with a rather sadistic look in his cool blues. A look which indicated he was about to murder me. I was too shocked to feel anything. No fear, no fear... body limp and paralysed. Ever so dirtily licks my wet pussy. Wet not from my own pussy juice, there was no outflow from sheer enjoyment, instead wet from his own cum and my own blood. Then reality hit me, it felt like a hammer against my fragile skull. So much fear made me feel faint. Delayed reaction I wondered or was it stuck halfway up my back and couldn't quite reach my brain to send the signals my body requires to respond. Passing out again that night I live to be demoralised for another day.

CHAPTER FORTY-FIVE

Who else is in This House?

Nightmare or real? All around me I hear breathing. Heavy, sleeping breathing, but there is no one present but me. I can see through the darkness before my eyes. I lay in bed my legs the only part of me covered, half sitting up, there is no one but me in this room. Faraway voices I hear, they aren't in this room of which I am present, instead somewhere else in the house. Women's voices. The only people present in this house is the three of them and me. Do ghosts of the past wander in the shadows? Who else are they harming? Who else is in this house?

CHAPTER FORTY-SIX

Dinner at Eight

As usual we dinned out god forbid the people of Geneva would not be blessed with seeing the ace, King Nicolas. By three months into our marriage he had started to drink too much. Hell I started to drink more too. Drinking day and night. We had both transformed into alcoholics. I drank to numb the pain. To be able to deal with another day. For courage to seed and multiply. Why Nicolas drank I have no idea, possibly because he could afford it. His drinking was in excess as to what is socially acceptable. Not having a job perhaps it was the only way to get his days in. An endless party. Nicolas was on every chat room created, whether it was in English, German or Arabic. Sleeping apart now in separate rooms. My only blessing. A marriage was not what we had. Of course he did not create scenes in public, this was beneath a gentleman, never giving an opponent a chance of the upper hand, a card stolen from his hand weakening his comeback instead they occurred on the way home in our chauffeured driven car. It was at home mercy was never granted. Arguments which resembled tornadoes. The charm veiled by anger.

On our way home from the Cottage Café, where we dine every Thursday at eight, a place where we are on constant reservation, I ordered for dinner cittadella, the best I have ever had. By this Nicolas was enraged. It was this night he started to complain about my weight. Ordinarily I was not considered to be out of shape. With Nicolas there weren't any excuses not to be sexy when the sun shone

286

or the moon glistened. For Nicolas it was another thing to complain about if I was not in proper attire when he would call on me for a good time. I had not turned into one of those wives after getting married becoming comfortable. Homely. In fact I had lost weight. Barely eating and mostly drinking. Burning up a magnitude of calories from the tears I cried alone. Behind closed doors secrets and shameful things occur. No home is exempted.

"You haven't had a baby I don't want you looking so well feed. I spoil you too much, I'm too good to you but no more. I can't allow you to show me up, people will wonder why I bothered marrying you with the way you now look. Everything is stopping until you look attractive again. Ugly, fat women do not deserve the gifts I give you. You have half of a contract to adhere to. You're forsaking your legal responsibilities. If we weren't living in a democracy I could have you stoned to death for dissatisfying me. I did not marry you fat so stop eating until you get that weight off. Don't make me tell you again!!!I can't bear to look at you and both your double chins. It's an insult to my eyes and not to mention most disgusting. How dare you insult me like this. A woman like you should have more self-respect and dignity than you appear to have. God what's happened to you?"

Too disgusted by the words which vaporised out of his hellhole mouth rendering me unable to reply, I couldn't fathom his declarations. My mouth fell open, nothing uttered. I had lost weight since we met and married from worry, stress and fear. There was no pleasing him. In the back of the car he lit a limited edition Cohiba cigar, costing an absurd four hundred and twenty dollars each. Imported from Cuba. Waiting until long hot ash had formed neatly at the bottom, flicking it at my legs and arms, hands and face. Grabbing my head coarsely, threatening to press the hot end into my face and my eyes. Promising to blind me. Temptation was evident in his eyes. My breathing increased, I became uneasy. My heart didn't pound like normal. I was used to his abuse and exploitation. Looking in his eyes I was sure he would do it; I wouldn't dare push his buttons I would be crowned the loser. Exiting the car to enter my impending prison, running upstairs to get out of my destroyed evening dress which he had burned multiple holes into. Jumping into the shower to wash away my fears and the night I wish would come to an abrupt end. Hoping as the water ran down and off my skin I would never have to see Nicolas again. Praying silently he would die in his sleep. Humbling myself to my knees I pray;

"If anybody is to die from a heart attack this night please, Lord, please let it be him. Don't take another good soul from this earth when evil people like he roams it still," I implored.

My gut niggling at me, telling me there was more to come this night. I waited an hour and a half forcing myself to remain awake, fighting the sleep my eyes craved. Shortly after when I was starting to fall off to light flimsy sleep. Hearing the bedroom door open, the overhead light blinding me before I had the opportunity to protect my eyes. The next thing I feel is burning, I hear a crash, it happened immediately after and in total three times. It was three cups filled with hot coffee. A strong smell of French vanilla coffee materialised. Through half opened sleepy eyes I see Nicolas standing by the doorway. I hear the most sadistic laugh. It was all about to start again.

CHAPTER FORTY-SEVEN

Red Cross Gala

39th Anniversary of the Geneva Conventions

As we sat eating our dinner listening to the entertainment provided, and the many important speeches addressing the state the world is currently in, at the Red Cross Gala Ball, there were cameras everywhere, taking photographs of everyone, mainly Shania Twain. Until Nicolas donated a million Swiss Francs claiming the attention to himself. Yes, Nicolas associated with some of the best known entertainers in show business. The photos taken indicate a naturally happy Nicolas. A man of kindness. Consideration for others. No reasons evident to doubt this man. What the people did not see beneath the elaborate dinner table was a sore and red staring to bruise calf belonging to me. The least famous woman in the entire room. In public view he was demonstrating the perfect husband, while beneath veiling his actions, demonstrating to me of what was to come when we got home. Many men asked me to dance, so I did. I was determined to have a little fun before I went home and pay with the spillage of my blood for the smiles, laughs and looking into men's eyes whom I didn't actually despise. Completely forgetting what it was like to be held tenderly by a man. Any man. How good it felt to be in the presence of gentlemen who knew how to treat a woman. Counting twenty-two men in total who thoughtfully expressed endearing compliments to Nicolas about his enchanting wife.

Smiling in reply and shaking their hands, exchanging kind regards in return. While I simply smile and nod in response, flattered to be noticed. Seen and taken in. Nicolas insisting on looking at me in a way which would indicate he was extremely proud of his woman, including me for one solitary moment was fooled, until he perhaps inveterately flashed me that glare of contempt. Relating I misunderstood. I drank and I ate, both actions was against my king's wishes. Drinking to kill the pain my body will soon undergo. Eating because I could. I wanted to disobey. The one thing my dear husband desperately needed to learn is that he is not the only person who knows how to prove points. In the department I am the queen.

On our way home I was flicked by the ash of a highly expensive $750 each Gurqha Premier Cigar in the back of our indulgent black Bentley. This one was chiefly used to impress and dazzle when attending grand parties, and this was the part of the year. Another five thousand Swiss Franc dress destroyed, now used to this, only wearing an evening dress once, a second occasion was beneath me. I was Grace Kelly in the movie *Rare Window* only wearing an item once "only because it's expected." In the back of the car this night, humiliating me further. With the modesty window rolled down between the front and the back seats, Emilio, able to see me being forced to suck my husband's dick. Emilio's instructions were to watch. Nicolas bending me over to fuck me in the ass. Moaning from Nicolas, sneers from Emilio and muffled screams from me.

CHAPTER FORTY-EIGHT

Grand Theatre de Genève

Sunday 21 December 2001

Handing over our opulent gold leaf personalised invitations, at the entrance of the Grand Theatre of Genève. The Theatre towers over the Place Neuve, evoking a thought of how Nicolas towers over me. We were there to attend a new French Opera by the name of *"Snowdrops in the Night."* It was about a beautiful deep feeling of romance of modern day sparked by a single encounter only to have a love lost. Reminding me of my marriage. The difference between the play and my life the couple truly and passionately loved one another. The man lost his wife in a war, while the woman lost her life with the ending of her love. Throughout the entire play in our private booth which cost six thousand Francs, up high and overlooking the largest stage in Switzerland and the audience, Nicolas who was nipping my hand and arm only doing this because I was wearing a red ballroom gown with long laced sleeves with a matching lace shawl, to cover my inflicted red marks.

Having more than enough of Nicolas's constant public yet private torture, as he was talking with Duchess's and Lords of England, an empowering erg came over me, running down the steps at the front of the theatre and ran across the road to the grounds of the University of Geneva. Running as fast as my legs allowed, on entry through the gates I felt like a child escaping from my disciplining parents. Playing the role of the rebellious teenager and not indeed an adult or wife. I felt alive. Exhilarated. Emancipated. A joyous smile crosses my face, my blood coursing with excitement and adrenaline, yelling at the top of my voice: "I am free, I am free!"

Spinning around in circles and shouting as though I were a five-year-old little girl once more. Wearing my ballroom gown I looked like a princess or perhaps Cinderella escaping her captives. Strolling along deep into the grounds on the left I notice the Reformation Monument, honouring the main people of the Protestant Reformation. Stopping for a moment to take in the many precise detailed carvings, laughing to myself as I think what they and I had in common. Rebelliousness. They were rebellious against the Catholic religion and me an abusive husband and once before the Catholic church myself when I married Charles, both of us with the potential of facing certain death. What Nicolas's punishment would be for my short-lived escape I couldn't care less tonight, because for a moment in time I was free. Breathing in the night December air, cold and getting colder. Snow fell upon my hair, veiling my sadness tonight.

CHAPTER FORTY-NINE

Notre Dame Cathedral Genève

Friday 19 December 2001

Christmas time arrived, the city was magical like a story from a children's book with all the hustle and bustle, as families shopped for presents to place beneath the lovingly decorated Christmas tree. When I was guilty of thinking Genève could not look any more sensational how wrong I found myself to be. I had never been blessed with seeing Genève at Christmas time before. The beauty of the Christmas lights twinkling on the water, bringing the night water to life. Santa clauses standing on every street corner biding family's warm Christmas sprits. Orchestras playing festive music, spreading joy. The theatres filled with their Snow White plays. Churches with choirs singing hymns about Christ and goodwill. The morale, be friends to your neighbours, not solely the people who live near but everyone who one comes across. They are there for a specific purpose, don't be blind, reach out and lend a helping hand. We all need help sometime. Restoring a rebirth of goodness we humanity ought to feel and demonstrate for longer than the Christmas period. But as soon as the trees and decorations are removed, packed away for another year, left in storerooms for dust to gather upon, so is the goodness we found in Christmas. The warmth we feel within our soul, reminding us we have a soul, it wasn't lost like it was perhaps feared. It is the time of year for a revaluation of oneself and inner being. The paths we have taken in life starting with a new year a new way to live. Inspiration for the better.

Before the Padre Nicolas and I along with a filled congregation, listen to the sermon from the Old Testament. He preached in French, making the service somewhat more special. The padre explained how the world will change. As I sat absorbing every word inspirational bliss and serenity moved me, leaving me teary-eyed. I was never before more grateful to Nicolas for anything than taking me to mass. That evening I felt I had power and control restored. I could turn my life around. Perhaps my husband and I could be happy. Perhaps he may change too.

Things not staying good for terribly long; I had been hoping for too much. After mass we remained until the cathedral had emptied. The confessionals were not occupied. The padre exited to the back of the church, after giving us a wave indicating goodnight. I believed Nicolas was touched by the same spirit I was, as I noticed glee in his eyes. I had unadulterated thoughts while Nicolas had the most impure of imagings. We exited the pew, walking to the altar to bless ourselves and take one last look at the statue of baby Jesus displayed in a nativity. Pulling me into him by my waist. Holding me tightly. More than I was comfortable with. I could feel the inappropriate stirred up erotic tension to his body. I couldn't believe it. Not even for God does this man have respect for. Wondering why he would bother going to church at all. Walking towards the front door, before we made our exit, Nicolas whispers "come here," pulling me to the left-hand side, pushing me into a confessional. He barely had me fully in, before he started squeezing my tits and snogging me aggressively. It felt like a stranger from the street was attacking me. Without seeing or feeling him he had opened his trousers, dropping them to his ankles and shoving me to my knees. Grabbing me by the head forcing my face into his cock and balls.

"Suck them, suck me off in this confessional you naughty girl. I bet I'm not the only man whose been blown in one of these things, but I'm certain I'll be the first who wasn't a priest. I should blow all over this box, leave a surprise for them in the morning, they're masters in cleaning up messes I'm sure they won't mind. God will never forgive you for this. You're too bad to be granted absolution,

Nicolette. But it feels so good don't stop, we're both already doomed we might as well enjoy it now."

Ripping open my blouse, I can hear tearing, buttons fly everywhere he pushes my bra down and from my tits. Naked breasts revealed. My hands were shaking from the possibility of being caught and knowing that God was watching. I could never show my face in here again. Within five minutes of me sucking his erected cock and pulling him off as quickly as I could manage, wanting to get the hell out of there, he came over my tits. Dripping down onto my long dark brown fur coat. Shame and relieve captured my being. Grateful nobody came before we snuck out of the cathedral. As we exited there were many druggies laying out on the manicured lawns, many begging for money. Nicolas must have felt more generous than usual or perhaps it was more guilt, considering he threw over one thousand Swiss Francs on the ground. Frist come first severed. "Merry Christmas to all and to all a goodnight."

Tossing and turning after this evening's events, I was guilt-ridden. What sins I have committed. Feeling I was stuck between a rock and hard place. This night I need comfort. I could do with a hug from someone who really cares, reassuring me I will not burn in hell. Reaching my arm out from the covers placing it behind my head, a warm sensation came over me. It was the assurance I crave. Knowing now before I fell asleep I can still be saved. If priests can abuse little children from decade to decade, voicing their deceitful lies I will be perfectly fine. Rolling over and threw the gap in the curtains I deliberately left in them to let the moonlight shine in my mind was rested and at peace.

CHAPTER FIFTY

Christmas Day

A seven foot Christmas tree stood in the stunningly decorated formal reception room. Garland on the fire place where old looking stockings hung. No children running around the house, the one thing which truly represents Christmas. No laughter, eager anticipation for what Christmas is designed to bring. No seasonal music playing, no smell of festive cooking. If I had not gone into the reception room there was no other sign of Christmas anywhere else throughout the house. No presents under the tree. Our first Christmas together seemed aloof. I had no idea what to expect for our first Christmas but it certainly wasn't this. He wouldn't permit me to go into town to buy him any gifts, telling me in a rather assertive tone:

"A man with as much money and as many possessions as I own, could not possibly want anything, especially when I have everything I could hope for in such a lovely wife."

Such sweet words but similar to cheap Easter eggs each word was hallow and easily shattered. The present I decided I would give to not solely him but to both of us, was trying harder to make our marriage filled with sexual ecstasy. Tenderness. Everything a successful marriage requires. Raiding my lingerie drawers picking out a naughty little number. Not much was left to the imagination, which was precisely the idea behind it as Nicolas did not tend to use much imagination. Predominantly he was an open and closed book. Downing a large glass of red wine, false bravery. Filling a large glass of white wine vined in Genève for me and a triple brandy for him. Seductively I walked in my ridiculously high stilettoes to the study where Nicolas spent most of his time. For his eyes only. As I entered the room he was talking on a chat line, as usual, even on our first Christmas Eve night together. Not very romantic. My heart was crushed; I was hoping for a little more from him at least tonight. Dismissing this entirely though I was devastated, otherwise knowing I would go mad defeating the purpose of my efforts. Looking as stunned as I was, once his cool blues reached me I was sure I could feel his dick stand up and hear a ping when it reached the top, when I saw the stirred up look in his eyes. Placing the brandy glass on the desk, I was just about to take a sip of wine from my glass before I had the time to execute this motion, Nicolas had me on the desk, biting my neck and licking my earlobes.

Once we concluded our passionate rampage, Nicolas wrapped me up in a throw he had flung over the sofa in the study. It felt warm as soon as it touched my skin, the heat from the open fire made it cosy for me. It felt like caresses of love. We snuggled close, after he opened the French doors we walked through to the porch, looking at the twinkling stars. The night air was so cold, we could see our breaths; it was dry like ice. Perhaps tonight we gave each other what we needed to have an everlasting love and perhaps our Christmas together will be special after all. Giving birth to the deepest of loves.

Christmas day came like it was destined to; I woke up in the arms of my husband. The day could not have started off more right. Like a child Nicolas had stars in his eyes as he stared endearingly at me. It was only ever Christmas day he was at his happiest. It wasn't about the presents given or received, it wasn't the party season, it was the feeling captured from his childhood being a creature of attention he was. Leaning over to kiss my head he asked me tenderly to close my eyes and not to move, no matter what I heard. My head turned away with my hands covering my eyes. I hear rustling of some kind. A few moments later I was permitted to open my eyes, before me were a few small boxes wrapped in Christmas paper. Box one, covered in silver foil with white snowflakes.

"You are going to love this one."

Nicolas said to me as he looked deep into my eyes, it felt as though we were sharing a special moment. Bonding. More excited than I. To Nicolas it was the offering and the giving of the lake house in Sweden which made him feel his proudest. Opening the box a set of keys were inside.

"I know people claim one ought to keep the best till last, but I couldn't resist, I had to give it to you right away. Forgive me."

His face illuminated with the brightest smile I ever knew Nicolas's face to project.

Box two, a flat box the size of an A5 piece of paper, taking off the lid, inside were photographs of the new house. My house. It was beautiful, I could hardly wait to visit it.

"When can we go see it in person, Nicolas?"

"In spring, you will see it for all its glory. With the ripened, flourishing deepest green leaves, mature vast and strong. Buttercups, daffodils and daisies fully grown and in their masses framing the house in its true splendour. What better time to see a new home?"

"I will count down the days until we leave, thank you so much, my love. I can barely wait. It is lovely and traditional-looking, exactly what I would have chosen. You know me so well."

Without changing from our bed clothes, Nicolas took me by the hand leading me out of the bedroom, we hurried down the stairs to the Christmas tree. As soon as Nicolas opened the door, I could see through the crack at the side of the door, there were presents beneath the tree, big and small boxes perfectly wrapped in traditional paper. Santa did come last night. Today I only had my love to give my husband. Despite the fact he would not allow me to buy him presents in return I felt terribly ashamed, foolish more like, he had spent hundreds of thousands on me. I was given everything that Christmas day. Everything but what I truly wanted. The real things in life, the things which matter. The love from my husband I desperately craved.

CHAPTER FIFTY-ONE

Abuse

Abuse it happens.
Abuse cannot always be seen.
Abuse is violent, but not always silent.
How does the victim come clean?

Nobody deserves abuse.
The bully, the abuser deserves to be punished.
Punished for what he has done.
Made to feel what his victims have felt,
What he made them feel.

Abuse it happens,
Abuse is rampant.
Abuse is negotiable, but dished out despite.
How does the victim repeal?

Nobody deserves abuse.
This is what the abused must recall.
The bully is the tortured soul, not that this is an excuse.

The abuser needs the help.
The victim needs a new life.
The victim is the innocent they must always recall.

CHAPTER FIFTY-TWO

Sexual Sadism

People claim makeup sex is the best sex of all. Some proclaim that the idea surrounding the wild passionate act of fucking, while in a rage and baring a grudge is the whole enjoyment behind the crazy idea of fucking one's brains out, until one moans their head off. When the sensation is too intense but amazing despite, a person's spine just isn't able to take anymore tingles shooting up and down, and being directed around one's body. Or one screams in pain. Or until one yells to stop! When one yells to stop, no matter how angry the other is, or how much he may be trying to teach his bitch a lesson, the "STOP", "NO" or "NO MORE" should be respected and adhered to. When the other party with whom one is moving the earth with neglects this bid for cease, automatically that party, in turn, becomes the guilty party, the wicked party. It only seems to make sense when usually the female party sharing this act feels vulnerable, as though she were being raped. If someone claims they love you, then they ought to love you enough to yield when asked or told. When the continuance of shagging a woman's pussy is asked to conclude and it is not, then it is rape. Baring down on a woman's windpipe or binding her arms restricting her ability to become free, then it is rape. Not willing and non-complying is the definition of rape, not overlooking being taken forcefully in turn made to feel terror. There is never any room for selfishness when it evidently involves two persons. To be selfish without regard for the person is unfair, unforgivable. When this path is crossed, how can that person be trusted again to feel safe to go down that avenue once more? What

Nicolas neither understood nor cared about is trust is a major factor to having amazing sex? When spoiled with anxiety, understandably the sex goes downhill. Not rocket science it makes perfect sense. These are the rules most men neglect. Not caring enough to neither listen nor respect. Out for their own pleasure simply fucking the woman they are with. The alfa male who must be in control, who must have his own way constantly, even when he is wrong. The man with the unhealthy oversized ego, the same ego which is greater than the Matterhorn and the Mont Blanc put together. When these rules are broken repeatedly, hence making the matter worse, especially when it comes from a husband. Once could perhaps be forgiven if the man of course can design a good enough story (whether it is true or false), a good enough lie, or simply makes it sound true and complimentary. Complements are the key to absolution.

The story best used to recoup some absolution:

"You were just so hot, too sexy for me to resist. You drove me mad; I couldn't control myself, that was some grade A sex, baby."

A compliment to soften the blow if charming enough it can be successful, though it really shouldn't, only if the woman is shallow enough to accept such a hollow excuse. No woman should be forgiven for being that susceptible. The majority of men know how to lie, if they haven't mastered the charm appeal, they still give it a damn good go.

A husband is the man who is supposed to protect his weaker spouse. The love of his life. The husband is the party who is expected to love his wife unconditionally, to make her happy without thought for his own happiness. The man is the party who makes sacrifices for his family. The person who is duty-bound to kill on his wife's behalf, her honour if the situation ever arose without hesitation or trepidation. Natural instinct. Women being the weaker sex; this is what men have declared from generation to generation. Particularly pertaining to the older generation, as the younger men these days just aren't men. The Italian lovers who prim themselves better than most women from facemasks to nail polish, to waxed eyebrows and plucking. An apocalypse is sure to happen if a hair is out of place with an outburst of temper, like babies requiring their dummy or their mother's tit. Spanish men in their tights, the picadors on horseback who fight bulls with a lance, and the Matadors in his traje de luces (suit of lights) the bullfighters. As they tease the bull within the ring. This must be where men's preconceived ideas about teasing women for their amusement stems from, able to toy with them until they get bored. Causing the first cut which is the deepest right into the heart. The deepest and the most deadly.

Not many men are attracted to women who are as masculine as they are, or who tend to be every bit as combative as men are inclined. Men have a tendency to be more attracted to fragile women. Women who are women through and through and nothing but; thus making Chinese women complacent to the stage of being unlistenable. Taught to be submissive. Taught to do as they are told – having no opinion, no say, and treated like the whores they are. In exchange for a man's money, an upgraded lifestyle they spread their legs. No morals, no respect for their bodies. With women who have opinions, with a say who have had an education, they are real women. They know a little something about making a marriage work, as intellectual conversation helps to boy caught boredom in between sex rampages. These women do not bow to men and degrade themselves for an easy life, where men do the work as that is what the money grabbers desire. What is more ridiculous is the men who do not mind they are being used, so long as they have a woman who will do anything they demand. No self-respect, no consideration for anything but what they can get, hence why many men toy with them, discarding of them as though they were yesterday's trash. Real women are those who have ambition to excel in life, to amount to something and to earn the right. Causing this to be another factor in men's minds, making them feel that the female sex is inadequate. In turn making mankind feel they are boss. Hence the phrase "It's a man's world." It's true so true. Giving rise to their unconditional disrespect towards all women, classing every female as a whore. Despite our predecessors having fought and demonstrated throughout the world for women's rights, as far back as the turn of the nineteenth century. Men still believe they are in command. Lesser wages for women still in these modern times does not help for to make men realise women are not here to be a pushover, they fight back they are no longer weak. A woman does not need to have a body of muscle to prove she is tough.

"The taller they are the harder they fall," this is consistent for narcissistic bullshitters with their immodest ideas about being superior.

Sex seven times a day, a raw and dry vagina not wanting any more Nicolas, not wanting to be filled up. My pain reducing me to feeling drunk, wanting the world to stop shaking or is it just me who is shaking?

I had become so filled with Nicolas I felt sick. It wasn't just nonstop sex which I became sick off, it was the tools he used to degrade and hurt me. It was his stench. His personal unique odour made me gag. The stench of his sweat even more so. The smell of him was the most nauseating reek I have ever been subjected to. It was worse than death. The repulsive stomach-churning liquid he would submerge me in, from the inside out as it dripped into my mouth, eyes and every opened cavity. Initially his broad and out there excitement, his need to feel constant bliss from a climax made me want it too. I loved his crazy ideas. That was exactly what they were crazy, and not anything more than ideas. Making his ideas real, making them happen, I felt powerful. Fulfilling his fanaticisms made me the staring actress, the one with all the attention. Never having that before. I was the star of my own movie. Thus making me feel valuable. Having unadulterated attention from my husband faithfully is the most powerful feeling a woman can experience. Not requiring an affair because I had adequate attention from the man I once loved. I felt like I was a good wife. I used to feel like a good wife. I liked feeling that. At that time it was important to me, I wanted to make it work. For a time he made me feel like a goddess. I made him happy too, I think. Gradually like all men, at least all the men I ever met, he became ungrateful not appreciating what I was doing for him. Opposed to respecting what I did for him sexually, our marriage persistently got to the point where he automatically expected it. Not only what I was giving him, but what I was permitting him to do. What I was doing was allowing him to do the filthiest, nastiest things imaginable without complaining. I would let him throw me into any and all positions, no matter how much they hurt or were uncomfortable for me to endure. I let him do all of these things and more, simply because he was my husband, it was my duty to make him happy. It was my duty to make sacrifices. To satisfy him I wanted to do. But what about my happiness? I didn't have any. I deserved some too. Eventually my power declined, subsequently making me defenceless. I was then feeble as a woman, as a human being more so as a wife. The more I gave the more he wanted, the more he wanted the viler he became. It was then I began to hate him. Yes the hate started to seed, my wild crazed ideas of murder commenced. Before the hate I tried to talk to him, mistakably thinking this was a conventional marriage, that he would take my needs and concerns into consideration. He would stop hurting me. A conventional marriage with the best sex any married couple would share. The kind of sex one has prior their wedding night, when all is new, lust is burning an inferno in a woman's breasts and pussy, needing to have that out of control sex to keep that attraction fervent. The lustful sparks in the eyes indicating I want your feminine fruits, juicy and sweet bursting with mouth-watering, tantalising flavour.

I understood in the beginning we were not equals. We would never be equals regardless how long we would remain married, and how much I proved myself to be a devoted wife. During the passage of time, believing I had gained some leverage to be given somewhat of a promotion. I categorically believed I proved it, I earned it. Not meaning to hurt me, not meaning to cause me pain, in any capacity that would be the traditional marriage. Our marriage was not traditional by any means. My husband's goal was to cause me pain. His objective was to expose me to as much pain as he could inflict, not how much I could withstand. What this is called I do not know. It was at this time my eyes were open. It was during this period I learnt many things.

When the horse cocked size dildos were introduced, then rammed up inside my body, the coldness was breath robbing. Then when the hose pipe he used to give me an enema was lodged inside me, shame started to fill within. I was humiliated. When my own husband is mentally ill to the extent he would leave me for days on end tied up to a bed, unable to become free, not permitting me to use the toilet, not feeding me. This is when someone is mentally unhealthy, desperately requiring physiological attention. Becoming one's own toilet is the most appalling thing to be subjected to. It is one thing when one is ailing or elderly, accidents occur, that is both understandable even acceptable. When one is young, healthy, willing and able, it brings a person absolute ignominy. When one thinks no more indignity could fill one. When my own husband goes further from the line of acceptability, I wanted to die. Praying for death to claim me, saving me from this nightmare. In the same moment he whips me with his Italian handmade leather belt he had purchased in Millan. Untying my wrists, instantly I feel pain shooting into my hands then my fingers, it was the most intense burning sensation as the blood flowed back into my fingers, coming alive. My arms were weak. Coldness decreased. Tingles diminished

Without giving me adequate time for my upper limbs to recover, Nicolas demands I sit on his foot. Yes the idea which popped into my head as to what he wanted me to do with it came to pass, he fucked me with it. My mind telling me "no," my body not wanting to move. My brain incapable of analysing his command, certain it had misunderstood. It was my mistake. This command just could not possibly be correct, it is too wrong to be. In that very moment it is as though my brain decides not to absorb his command, neglecting every word because that wonderful complicated machine knows this isn't right, it can't be right. My brain wisely abandoning to send my limbs and body the automated command, wise yet dangerous. When I would not do what King Nicolas directs instantly, anytime delay engrossing his rage, his chronic fury. Demonstrated in his tone of voice; "you better do what you are told," consequently I obeyed. Fear becomes my new brain. Fear of the pain which will be inflicted over rides the signals my brain wouldn't send, my brain was relatively normal, understanding this is not what is done. The deepened frown and dark look which fills his eyes signifies, do it or you will be sorry. "You know you will be sorry."

The consequences will be worse and more painful than being fucked by my foot, only because his cock is too raw from the unremitting shagging rampages. Fear is a mechanism which is more wonderful, more miraculous than the byzantine machine called a brain. Doing anything one is commanded to do out of fear, objective to avoid the worst scenario. Realising no matter how bad I imagine his punishment to be, it is something incomprehensible.

Unimaginable to the healthy mind. Hoping and praying I did not chomp down and bite my own cheek from shock. My body shook. My limbs twitched. Tears escaped my eyes and ran down my cheeks. After a brief shag by my husband's foot he pulls it out from my body. By this time my neck was soaked from tears of discomfort and humiliation. Nicolas quickly with excitement covering his face, opens his trousers letting them fall to his ankles. To my astonishment, I presumed his cock recovered and I would be fucked again. Unfortunately no! Nicolas's next command was for me to kneel on my knees. Doing this without delay. Pulling my hair at the top of my head, pulling my head halfway back taking his dick which is not erect and pisses on my face. His stinking urine floods up my nose and into the back of my throat. Golden showers had become one of his favourite depraved things to subject me to. Ultimate humiliation! Far from the pleasantest experiences but it didn't actually taste of anything, certainly of nothing bad. It was just warm, it didn't taste as wretched as I would have presumed. I must admit I wonder what it would taste like with ice, nice and cold. I'm starting to become as mentally ill as Nicolas to wonder such lewd things. Would it taste like Bud lite, that pissy beer Texan men drink just like the pussies they are. Men they are not, Bud lte, beer it is not.

I did not mind the cucumber, I did not mind the carrots, even my mother taught me vegetables were good for a person. She just did not elaborate in what form, masked, steamed or pouched or into your person, deep and plentiful and raw. Making me suffer severe nausea. Vomit soaring up from my stomach and into my throat, they would turn me onto my side very kindly indeed to let it run out. The whole experience scarred me into a panic as I almost choked to death many times. Certain one night when they are playing with my indisposed body, they would let the show get too far letting me die, choking on my own vomit. Dreading their faces being the last faces I ever would see, smiling at me laughing their asses off while I take my last breath. If things ever got to that stage the only thing I could do would search for a corner of the room which they did not occupy, close my eyes and seeing darkness before I departed this world. No mercy was granted persuading them to cease, even for a short time. With vomit in my mouth, flowing up and down my trachea, inducing a ruthless headache. Sharpness stabbed my head.

It was Emilio's time to step up to the plate, commencing the second act. He was no Shakespeare. He couldn't act. He couldn't fuck worth a damn, to my advantage. His post was to fist fuck me. To add to my misery, he did not have refined gentleman hands like most Swiss men. Hands like a Canadian lumberjack: rough and chunky, causing me impenetrable pain. Hating every second; with every moment which passed I hated myself and what they had lessened me to. When at all times I had dignity, courage and gentleness about me. They took it all away; they stole so much from me. They stole who I was. Philippine, Emilio and Nicolas recognised how much shame they brought onto me by hurting me, how it crippled who I was. Thus causing me agony as a consequence giving Nicolas utter ecstasy. In my dying his life elated. In my tears his satisfaction appeared. Within my pain his cruelty burnished.

CHAPTER FIFTY-THREE

Fire and Ice

As soon as the morning sun split through the clouds, waking Nicolas with his daily hard-on. Racing to his wife's bedroom to empty his sack, like Santa on Christmas Eve night. Instead of spoiling children, he was spoiling himself with pleasures of too much sexual relish. Frosted sugar cookies. Sweet, indulgent and yummy. Racing down the hallway with a bucket of ice from his fridge. Which Philippine puts freshly in his bedroom fridge every day for his nightly drinks. Waiting in bed with trepidation on what was inevitably a daily ritual. There is no getting away. Throwing the door opened to my bedroom, storming in like a bat out of hell, naked, with his engorged cock and a bucket in his left hand. Racing at me, I jump up, lashing out and slapping my face, I whimper in pain. I fall back onto the bed from the pressure of his slap. Pulling my hair roughly, telling me: "open your mouth," knowing to do as I was told, Nicolas stuffs ice cubes in my mouth, as many as would fit. It sounded as though my teeth were breaking. Feeling as though I were choking. Grateful I had a small jaw. Holding his hand over my mouth, the cold sensation freezes my teeth, tongue and throat as the ice melts and the cold water hit my gag reflexes, feeling I were drowning, or is this called suffocation? It was only when I gaged, Nicolas let go of my mouth. A few moments later, pulling me from the bed, merely to stuff two or three ice cubes each in my ass and pussy, forcing his hard cock into me and begins fucking. For me it was a mixture of fire and ice.

PART THIRTEEN

No Divorce

CHAPTER FIFTY-FOUR

No Divorce for Him, No Divorce for Me

I am incapable of understanding why Nicolas would not just divorce me. It would have been that much similar. No one needed to die. No cleaning up necessary. What were his secrets? What was it he did not want to be exposed for? Or was he simply just that evil? And in the end no divorce for him, no divorce for me. Only secrets and lies and dust to ashes.

CHAPTER FIFTY-FIVE

WHY ME?

They are going to kill me! I have no idea why. Why would they do this to me? Why? My life has always led me to the distraught and the dissolute path with no reason given. This wasn't meant to be, my life was not meant to go down this path once more. This path was supposed to be the first path of happiness and joy. For the first time I was supposed to have these things. For the first time! I shall laugh last, not they, not they. It is nonsensical. What is the meaning of this, why would they do this to me, why, why, why me?

CHAPTER FIFTY-SIX

My Impending Death Sentence

Life is a hell we are forced to dwell,
Till the time comes to bid farewell.
I pray for a bombshell to indwell my every living cell.
My brain feels like a nutshell, I'm terribly unwell.

I don't want to live to tell the tale.
Being forced to inhale life, while being blackmailed making living
stale.
I want to unveil the black tail, making my life unreal.
I appeal to end this misdeal.

I peel the world's hell from my body, exposing the seal apposed
and refusing to conceal the truth any further.
How do I reveal the black tail, which is willing to tell tales and
destroy my life?
How do I show the demon that condemns me to a living hell?
I don't know yet but it will be done.

An untruth destroys my youth.
A half-untruth destroys my soul.

Instead of enduring this hell, I take a stand.
I'm in control, I'm ending the misdeal and I'm living the life I
was given.

No more living in hell.
To that I have already bid farewell.
I don't want the bombshell to impel,
I am no longer unwell.

My brain still feels like a nutshell.
I have inhaled life and I am going to tell the tale.
The black tail will be unveiled,
My misdeal is now his misdeal.
No mercy will be granted, as he granted me none.

PART FOURTEEN

THE GAME OF LIFE

CHAPTER FIFTY-SEVEN

PURE

Why can't you leave the pure to be pure?
The good to be good,
And the righteous to be righteous.

Why must the bad be bad?
If they must be, then let them be.
If they must affront, then leave them alone.

Why can't they leave the peaceful in peace?
Let the happy be happy.

Why must they hurt the innocent?
Hurt the righteous,
And sully the pure.
I let you live
Let me live,
Let me live.

CHAPTER FIFTY-EIGHT

From Lovers to Players

Players are notorious for playing games, hence the name "players." Mind and physical games are their specialty. Men want what they can get; even those precious things they cannot have. Being as charming as one can manage to attain their deceitful desires. If they are unable to succeed, they become irate to the extent of becoming abusive. Destroying everything pure. Players only play games. Acquisitive games. Their life is in constant play. Players are the ultimate bad losers. Their expiration date not advertised on the packet. False advertising! Nonetheless they have a very definite run out date. Their aim is to fool, however it is branded within their brain for only them to know. Thus giving the player who is in play the power to delude the unfortunate soul they are swindling. Consequently becoming guilty of misleading them at the controller's mercy. If the game is more exhilarating than one expected initially, that expiration date may extend. If their game becomes jaded the date brought forth. Moving on to another competitor and yet another game, the hand and the rules remains the same. Being the player and never a lover gives one the ability to control by the reins. Manoeuvre the direction, have supremacy over the intended loser. To be a player and not a lover all emotional personal feelings must be eliminated for a chance to win. It is merely their pastime. Players are void of emotions, the victim feels too much. There is no other intention than to destruct. Harming an innocent soul, a gullible being for having a foolish moment, enticing their prey, knowing they are probing for love, making the instigator the unhealthy one. Fooling another just because they can. The player is the equivalent to a bully. The bully and the player both are the victim having to create victims for inner worth. Subsequently, the reason they are cold and unfeeling. At no point having clemency for the party they wound. Players are narcissistic. It is not about having fun, it is about causing destruction to another. Proving to themselves there are weaker people out there who are weaker than they. They are the most selfish creatures of them all. Something unrecognisable within encourages them to be detrimental and injurious. The object of the player's fascination is for them to become emotionally involved. It is only at this time they rule. When emotions are invested pain can then be felt. When the victim falls the player finds the ace. The game has concluded. A new game must begin with a new victim to be sought after. No more time of the aloof injurer can afford to be invested, or else boredom will commence. The more years under the predator's belt the more games played. Their technique mastered, their charms that much more artificial, their smiles fraudulent. Their intentions that much more dangerous.

What women are notorious for are playing mind games more so, but with greater ability! Women can use love and their body as inveigles giving them more to play with. The more cards in the holding hand, the better the chances of winning. Women are better at twisting, men are merely colder. A man never seeks love, a woman's heart rules her life.

What did Nicolas and I have in common? We were both physiologically dysfunctional. The making of a unique game! A game which has never been created until now that is. A nameless game! A game without rules or limitations, one which could go down any avenue at any given moment in time and without notification. It was our game. Unwritten rules changing as the clock ticks. More mysterious than any other game known to man. Both players are searching for the aces, not having what it takes to be royals. A cocktail of the ultimate deadly game! The winner wins it all. The loser goes to his or her grave, the winner lives on. The ultimate Roman style game: fight to live, win for life, fall and you die. No in between. No if, ands or buts. It is what it is, or what it will be. It is about self-importance and self-gain; it is about being the most selfish human being it is possible to be. Cold, calculating, voided of all emotion, is what this game requires. The last mixture to the cocktail is not the result. It is in fact that both players come from an insensitive unsympathetic past, overflowing with cruelty, these additional sprinkles upon the blood red cocktail of heartlessness, makes it that much more unpredictable. As to which court the ball is in. This is the most volatile game in modern times. It consists of violence to the extremes. Unless the other is smart enough, cunning enough to allure, not permitting the other to ensnare at any time. It is about me, myself and I. Both of us possess the requirements, but who possesses the most of these traits? Who is strongest? Neither of us will know until the end. Until the last breath. It is an unpredictable game, standpoints changing all the time. The winner may think he or she is home clear, while the competitor draws near, much too near for comfort and to remain alive. It is anyone's game. The winner cannot be announced, until the loser is lying in a pool of his or hers own blood. Then the ace has been found, the crown placed and the trophy secured. Pride can then be felt.

When true love is on the cards it is not about who will win or lose. Even with true love there is a winner and a loser but in two completely different concepts. The rules surrounding true love is fake. More deep minded games are in play. It is too complicated. When it comes to lust, hate, power, or winning then it is only about destruction to win. A couple who love one another deeply are willing to capitulate to each other's needs and wants, to make the receiver of one's love indeed nothing other than utterly happy. When winning is the only card among the game then death has no alternative but to follow. The black ace must be found, the answer lies within that card. Perhaps a dribble of blood from the heart may drop. This is when lovers become players. The husband now out to win by any means necessary. The one party who may be fooled. The one party who will definitely fall. Both parties want to live; both parties are prepared to fight till the death. The most proficient noxious one will say goodbye to the lifeless one. Bestow a kiss on the dead lips, while the greyness of death takes over the corpse. Then the ace has been found and the winner announced. Some believe that winning is by chance, pure luck and nothing but luck. Some believe this, but not entirely with more complexes, such as the moon and the zodiac signs, some speculate that it depends on the day. When exactly is the right day to play to fight for your life?

In the blink of an eye, or the following second the games will commence.

CHAPTER FIFTY-NINE

His Whores, His Bitches

It is commonly known that most men enjoy watching porn, looking at magazines of women who are risky. Men are fickle. Those women who tend to be raunchier than the woman they are with. Perhaps they do the things their wives refuse to in bed, or dress more provocatively with more on display. Women have come to terms with this fact over the decades, as long as their man only looks refraining to touch most women are happy to settle. It is always classed as an insult to the female sex when her man does this but they will do it nevertheless. Regardless of the woman playing the role of mother demanding they cannot look at anybody but them. This is never a smart idea.

Failure one – when a woman starts to talk to her husband as though she was a mother figure. Men are the more dominate force, this insults them. Pouring fuel onto the fire. This is when a man is inclined to lose all interest in his wife, starting to window shop more than he would have done originally. Finding the one woman who is better than his wife. Followed by the window shopping comes the affairs. The dirty weekends away or if he is daring enough to claim he's working, taking a week away here and there with his bitch, his whore.

Failure two – a woman's nagging is the fuel to her own destruction. Keep the mouth shut, compliment a woman who is attractive to highlight one is not jealous. Hold oneself with pride, highlighting one is comfortable within their own skin. If one is not fully comfortable, never emphasise this fact, it makes one appear inferior. The minute one demonstrates inferiority to a particular woman; passion in the relationship goes downhill, like a speeding car traveling one hundred and fifty miles per hour straight into a brick wall. Slam your dead! Left with a lot of damage to be cleaned up, as a body lies flat out upon a road, no limbs in tacked. With no limbs there are no cards to play with. No leverage remains, standing solo without one's man. But there is only so much a woman can take before being pushed over that dooms day cliff, smashing into rocks the end is nigh.

Many men fantasise about buying the perfect woman. For hundreds of years if not thousands, men wishing there were mail order books, inside only to be found are beautiful women who fill every criteria imaginable. Scanning the catalogue hey presto, a man has found and bought himself the woman of his dreams. Providing he has the capital to pay, allowing all his wildest dreams to come true. Came on. Along with modern times this invention came to pass, it is no longer a dream for the ideal world, as the ideal world was then indeed invented. This is when mail order brides who debase themselves by being more than willing to be bought and paid for to some weirdo of a guy they have never met. This is when one can pay thanks to the Russian Ukrainian and the Chinese women, rendering men to think little of all womenkind because of these few whores. Putting all women in the position where they must fight back harder and tougher than they had to before. These few debase the rest of women race. In turn suffering insults because of the whores we have never and will never meet. Making it that much more problematical to find a gentleman in this era. Men these days believe it is acceptable to treat women as they do these mail order brides. Treating women as though they were all whores and bitches.

I begged him to stop. He refused. Instead he laughed. During his laughter my tears fell. Philippine came into the bedroom that morning, as I had stepped out of the shower. I was smelling clean and free from sex, above all, free from Nicolas. His scent I finally managed to get rid of after spending hours scrubbing his odour from my flesh. I did not smell alive; my flesh had not had the opportunity to recover from their abuse the night prior. My soul was lost. My heart gone. My flesh smouldering in death. I could only manage to smell a bit better.

"You have to get ready for your husband. He is in the mood to fuck you some more." Philippine instructed in a hostile superior tone and glint in her eyes of pleasure at my expense.

A feeling of doom filled me; I hoped I would die from a heart attack before Nicolas entered the room. If shame was enough to kill me, I had enough to kill the world. No such luck I would be granted. It was mid-December in Genève, snow and ice was on the ground and covered the balcony attached to our bedroom. Philippine pulled my wet towel which was wrapped around my bruised and fragile body. Without forewarning I was pushed out through the French doors. Standing naked and exposed as my small, delicate feet were standing on freezing snow. With cable wire Philippine roughly tied my hands, this time for the first time to the front. What was going to be different this time I quickly thought? Any small change to my presentation meant massive changes to my treatment. Fear grew before Nicolas entered. There was something in Philippine this morning more hostile than usual. More rough. I knew from experience this was not going to end good. With the handle of a Philips Head screwdriver my husband rammed it without lube into my dry and unwilling cunt. My screams went unheard by anyone who may have helped me. People tend to count sheep when they are trying to sleep. On that December morning I counted thrusts. In total as I lay upon the snow with my legs tied to the balcony and apart and my hands tied to the front, Nicolas stuffed my cunt one hundred and fifty-nine times. Each shove got harder and deeper. With each shove Nicolas's vindictive expression upon his face became that much more alarming.

As he concluded his fun for the morning, Nicolas leaned over me and whispered: "till later my whore. I have a surprise for you. I know you will enjoy. Whores like you always enjoy what I have to give." Rubbing the side of my face like a dirty sweaty paedophile would with an innocent child he is taking advantage of.

323

CHAPTER SIXTY

Confessions of a Husband

The honeymoon was well and truly over, left forever in the past. Memories will eternally linger like shadows lurking around on one's footsteps spying. That honeymoon period in all relationships, the feeling of sheer celestial and marital bliss does not usually reach their closing stages quiet as dramatically as ours had, considering that our relationship was a new and existing one. Having recently met our honeymoon segment becoming once upon a time, forever to linger. I still do not know how it ended as quickly as it occurred; the more I think about it the faster it seemed to come to a close. Then again it is quite absurd to believe one has fallen in love as quickly as Nicolas maintained he did with me. This was all one massive mistake I need to get out of. Of course the happy days of excitement and anticipating ecstasy would rapidly conclude. I heard about these types of marriages before, I did not believe I was entering into a marriage of such kind. I thought he loved me. I could not understand how he could love me as quickly as he asserted, be that as it may I was sure he was passionate about me at the very least, even if it was only my body he longed for. Along with our vows being taken real life had sharply emerged.

I lay on our marital bed of one hundred and fifty years old, in a bedroom furnished with antiques. Antiques were Nicolas's hobby. A thought crossed my mind about how many happy sexual memories were made on this bed before I existed. A strange thought no doubt. I was searching for happiness. Happiness was not on my path. Taking pleasure in others' contentment. I did not want to become one of those atrocious people who are embittered by other people's success because of my own shortcomings. No I do not take that quality from my family.

While Nicolas was working downstairs making his phone calls and sending emails in between watching porn on YouTube and other unruly websites which should be against the law; I started to feel smothered as though I were dying. Reminding me too intently when Nicolas squeezes my throat during fucking, giving me the feeling I am about to die, before releasing the pressure desperately gasping for much needed air. A psychological state came over me; it was the strangest sensation I have felt. My heart started to not only race but pound, then stopping for a split second only to pound more. My shoulders felt as though they were being forced down. I could feel immense pressure throughout my entire body. I never experienced it prior; I haven't experienced it in quite the same way since. At that particular moment a powerful force, a force of negativity and sadness wanting death to come and claim me abducted my being. My mind. This emotion was overwhelming. Was it my sixth sense warning me, because this feeling of wanting to die I had not felt since Charles's passing, since I lived at Lake Garda. The brutality by the hands of the Beaumont family had not yet commenced. I was still a young bride. I was supposed to be on cloud nine, dreaming dreams of our life together. Cooking dinner, deciding which shirts he would wear and running romantic baths. Massages, sex and red wine. Marital bliss. Heaven sent. In the back of my mind I knew something was going to happen. I knew it was bad. That gut feeling niggling from within. I just did not know what it was or when it would take place. Many people have claimed when one loves somebody more than their own life, or one may have a special bond with someone, they can feel the very moment when pain or death has found them. A connection twins proclaim. A cold chill which radiates up and down the spine, I believe people describe it as. So I did not know for sure if it was to come to find me. With that thought entering my mind it evoked yet another.

God do I love him more than I believed I did, do I already love him in the way I ought to as a wife, even after all this madness. Have I loved him for longer than I've known?

Many questions for me to ask myself, no answers to give bringing reassurance. I lay in bed bemused, trying to figure out how we got to this stage as quickly after being idyllically happy for the past few months. Yet for the past month, things have been different. The years which followed did not change.

I simply figured that life was starting to become normal, a typical married couple where we have our moments of wild passion and our days of normality. People can't be happy all the time. At other times conversations had to be forced. Nicolas had been different. He had been distant – at times dreary. As a result making life tough, to be around him was tougher. Making me glad I was locked up in my room. It was the only peace I had for all those years. But it drove me a little mad. Instead of being relaxed the usual easy going man he mostly had been with me in the beginning. This Nicolas was long gone. Making me upset frequently. When I would become emotional, genuinely emotional, instead of being the attentive husband he once was, now telling me:

"Stop sniffling, your crying is giving me a headache. Why must you cry? SHUT UP, SHUT UP!"

Followed by throwing crystal brandy glasses at me, smashing them off the back of my head, providing I was lucky enough for them to pass me smashing against the wall. Or flicking cigars or cigarettes with long hot ash, they always had to have long hot ash at the ends. Going further when he was excessively annoyed as to threaten me with the most unimaginable punishments one could fathom.

"I will throw you down the stairs, smashing your brains on the hall floor if you do not stop your sniffling, you Cunt! God you are such a cry baby. I do not know why I married you. Why can't you be a real woman taking a little slap now and then to make me happy? You selfish fucker. What kind of wife are you? It is only a slap, it is not as though I am killing you. Not yet! Sometimes your crying makes me want to kill you, one day I assure you, my wife, I will not be able to and will not want to resist the temptation of feeling your life slip away between my hands. I will silence you for all time. And it will be your fault for driving me to it."

326

Initially I did feel something towards Nicolas when we married, it was not love that much I realised in the aftermath. It took me many battles to figure out what I felt. I just was not in love with him. I was certain when the abuse started I never would be. In the beginning of our marriage I lied to myself every day, telling myself, "love would come in time." How can a woman love a man who harms her? Betraying her trust invested. Prior to our wedding I predetermined that if we spent enough time together doing things together, forming a bond, closeness, falling in love would come naturally. I would not have to encourage it. It would be real, it would come freely. I still had not fallen in love with him because when I was starting to after falling the tiniest amount he changed, consequently stumping all growth. For the first three months I was in heaven. For the past four years I have been miserable. In a well of darkness never to see the world for its beauty ever again. I married into a hell because I married Satan. Starting to get to know Nicolas better with each passing day, I've come to know he has never been truly in love with anybody. He is too in love with himself. He is not in love with a real person, more an idea of them, the idealistic aspect of what love and marriage is supposed to bring. Nicolas was not ready for what marriage brings. Unable to understand why he would want to get married. The feeling of wanting to be married does not last long for him. It is no longer the era where marriage is expected. Being from Geneva and living in the playground for the mega rich. The place where a man can buy a woman, multiple women if he wishes for the night, the weekend no strings attached. No words spoken. No promises made. It would have been healthier for him to remain a bachelor buying a woman's touch when he craved it. The heat of a body, the scent of floral on the skin. The softness of moisturizer. His ideal perfection did not live up to reality, as a consequence disheartening Nicolas. He does not have traditional views on matrimony, the type of marriage which lives in Nicolas's head does not exist. At least I hope no such union exists. Periodically I thought Nicolas loved me, instead everything Nicolas does is an act. I think it was more the feeling of excitement to conquer was what he was out for. Some men get unmovable ideas into their heads. Ideas which can harm others so long as they have their moment of excitement they do not care about the consequences their actions brings.

What I have become now certain of is that I am his slave. I was his sexual object. I was no wife, he wouldn't let me. It is one of those peculiar things which can be construed as odd which makes me laugh, perhaps a nervous laugh. How did I get into this insane episode of life? More importantly, how do I get out of it? The only time Nicolas would be inclined to spend with me was when he required a sexual release. Pussy loving. A typical man. It has all become so disconnected, indifferent and unemotional. I am just a pastime; I suppose I was nothing other. As I thought deeper, maybe not even that. Perhaps I was just convenient. What he or the law could not deny I was his wife. At least I was considered something of significance. I hate myself for needing desperately his gentle touch at the start. A hand to hold, a shoulder to lean on, someone to snuggle up to at night when in bed, to feel his breathe on my skin. To send my libido soaring. The breath of a man who loves me, making it more appealing trying to convince myself of an untruth, unsuccessfully.

When I was young and foolish I wanted nothing more than to have a man's body next to me in bed at night, every night, more so when winter came. I couldn't stand being alone. The silence. I couldn't stand my own company. I needed to be distracted from who and what I am. The romantic ideas youth brings can be staggering. When adulthood hits real life can be harsh, knowing these dreams do not come true, these things do not exist. Lying in bed together, warm and feeling loved, making love, listening to the rain or the snow falling, the wind howling outside the bedroom window, sounding like a hurricane about to destroy everything in its way. True love feels like a tornado. Passion feels like a hurricane. The exhilaration that once was there, now gone. Our life had been good. He treated me well, apart from the night at Sophie's when he scared me for the first time, on a slippery slope we went. An icy slope of heartache and bruises. We went to lavish restaurants on nightly bases, never wanting me to ruin my hands cooking and cleaning, the reason for the home help, or so I believed. There is always a precarious reason surrounding every aspect. But I wanted to cook; I wanted to be responsible for taking care of my husband. He desired me to dress up every day for lunch, as he would take me to golf clubs, lodges and tennis club restaurants. With every evening wanting me to dress up in evening dresses, with diamonds to go to the most expensive most elite places in town, or have Emilio drive us into one of the cities such as Zurich or Bern to be near the rich and famous. He spoilt me, showered me constantly with gifts, making me feel like I was a queen. He spoilt me to spoil himself.

After five months I was restricted; I had not been out of that chateau in over four and a half years. Initially he took pleasure in people admiring me, complimenting him on his finest possession and his greatest accolade. After a brief time he began to despise me for attracting the masses of men I did. People not once tiring from seeing me, watching every move I made, each breath I took. Somehow somewhere with the passage of time, he became bored of it, or resented the fact I was the person on the receiving end of the admiration. My beauty was supposed to bring him attention. I was the bait. I was well and truly caught; reeling in the attention, like Nicolas had never witnessed before. His plan was initially designed for me to catch the eye, for him to receive the compliment. Nicolas was too narcissistic to be in the company of such beauty. Therefore locking me away, keeping me hidden from the eyes that once admired me. Feeling kidnapped because that was precisely what I was, but I was happy for a time. I had my man, in-between losing him to other women. Without hesitation or turbulence I took my punishment in silence to prove a very definite and profound point. To get it throw my husband's head that I did not want anyone else. Treat me right and I will for all my life long remain true. I was giving our marriage all that I have. All that he would permit me to give. However, he kept throwing my attempts right back in my face. Not wanting to know. It was the other women he wanted to focus on. But all he ever cared about was sex and getting his own way, whether he was right or wrong he could not stand to lose face. My husband did not care about my feelings. I did not care about other people, my Nicolas was the man I longed to make happy. I had a beautiful home. I once had his love (or so I thought), even if I was just lying to myself. Perhaps in all reality this I never had that, but at certain times I did have his attention, at other times I had his time. It's strange how ignorance can be bliss when the cold imprudent truth appears to show its callous face, with it breaking one's heart. It's funny when I really think about it, how loneliness made me feel things which weren't there, which aren't true. My mind only wants it to be true.

Every so often I recalled that day once upon a December in 2001. The beautiful chill in the air made me feel loved. He held me close making me feel warmth, making me feel safe as we made love on a snowy balcony attached to our bedroom. Granted it was freezing but his body, his blood pumping and the sexual stirred up tightness to him covered me like the warmest blanket I have ever been covered in. That was a special night; I had his attention, his time, and his physical love, with a softer look in his eyes that particular night. Those days are far away, gone and left behind. We don't have anything anymore. Things I hoped used to be now hard to remember. Things I wished would be, never am I to have. I am his prisoner, his captive. How did I become a captive I still am unsure. Still astounded by my position within our marriage, in my life, not knowing how this occurred, not knowing how to escape this torment. Staying in bed all day, every day thinking of ways to mend my broken life, knowing if I could mend that, in turn, it would mend my broken heart. Somewhere along the path of our marriage, I fell in love with him, it happened that night on the snowy balcony, now at the darkest corner of our life together, I had no doubt I would regret doing so. As I would lie in bed I was reduced to thinking:

I'm so desperately depressed. I'm so very alone.

CHAPTER SIXTY-ONE

A Mind inside a Mind

The sunshine missed
While winter caresses our minds.
The fire flickers,
The people are fickle.

While frantic lingers,
Optimistic no longer mystic.
The lyrics and lipstick of the lovesick.
Whilst the firebrick reflects optic music.

The traffic in my mind toxic, tragic, cowardly,
Condemns me to hell, endure the mayhem.
Life no longer a gem,
The present dwell never to be a farewell
As I rebel no one to hear my out yell.
I'd gladly resell my present hell and impel,
To be free.
Never angry or catty but,
Possess beauty and to be by nature carefree.

PART FIFTEEN

NO APOLPGY

CHAPTER SIXTY-TWO

Do What You Must

2006

I would cry out but there is no one to hear me. The servants hear they will not help. Nobody in this house cares if I live or die. In fact I suspect they would prefer I died. I do not know what is taking them so long to get rid of me. I am in their way. There is a plan and I'm not in it. I am impeding their progress. This will not be stood for much longer, I can see it in their eyes, the way they look at me, the way they don't want to look at me anymore. My end is approaching. I am astounded I have not as of yet left this world, this life and met my new me in another dimension. That is of course if there is life after death. Or shall I remain in a worm infested black damp hole for all eternity? These people are cold. No hearts, no blood in their veins to make them human or capable of feeling. At that time when I did not know the truth I believed.

Nicolas had paid the servants too much to disobey his demands. Or perhaps they were too frightened of him, as Nicolas owns a very powerful demeanour. The vibes which ooze from his pores are enough to make one submissive. Instantly one knows not to speak back like a disobedient child hanging the head with a big lip. Cursing him but never to his face. Wanting nothing more than to speak back some unruly insult, knowing not to as the discipline would prove too uncomfortable for the worth of one moment's glory. I have no way out. In that same instant I realised. *Death, I have death.*

In death he could not hurt me. Knowing Nicolas he would try. He is evil enough to try but death is beyond him! Despite believing nothing is above him. Death is! Death is beyond any human man. Nicolas Beaumont is only formed of flesh and blood, a heart which pumps the blood around his body but has no feeling in it. A brain which gives his body instructions, veins which could burst. Arteries which can clog, he is as superhuman as the rest of mankind. He is a mere man like any other man, he is as in destructive as the rest. Nicolas would probably keep my corpse and wound that but I, my soul would not be aware of pain anymore. So I do not care. How could I do it? What would be the least painful and quickest method to escape this unreasonable man? Thinking even if it hurts it would only be for a moment, then that would be it? What is a moment's pain to give me peace and salvation after years of it?

I fall to my knees with tears trickling down both my cheeks, "Oh, God, I pray, I have never felt as powerless."

Crying uncontrollably. Through tears I managed to sob.

"How can he do this to me, why must he do this to me when I have been a good wife? I've tried and I've tried. I've given all I have. I've done things I did not want to do only to put his happiness before mine, show him my devotion at the expense of my own dishonour. I have been a selfless wife."

Uncontainable I cried myself to sleep. My tears would not stop, not this night, they just kept on flooding. Each morning I would wake my pillows stained and soaked from last night's tears. By 2006 every night I would cry till the tears ran dry. Till my cheeks were scorched, until my heart felt as though it would burst with one more beat. My frown line increased and deepened. Becoming painful from too much pressure of being scrunched up. During my solitude the isolation becoming too much for me to tolerate, I would often speak to myself to feel comfort and not so alone. Nicolas and Philippine had succeeded in making me lose my mind. The sound of my voice broke the silence; I was reduced to pretending to have conversations with myself. Just what exactly had I been reduced to? All I know was my mind was slowly, no faster than that, it was quickly abandoning me. I was losing grip of reality. I was losing me.

Six hours later I awake after the best night sleep I had since before I was married. My body better rested than it had been for a terribly long time; however, I was still mentally exhausted. Crying always ensured I slept well, draining myself, dehydrating my body. For me it was like the glass of wine I had as a night cap, it was the key to a goodnights sleep. "It was only a dream," I mumbled to myself, in a low and tired voice as I lay under the covers, not wanting to rise. One of those dreams one has when they are exhausted, one's brain desperately requiring sleep. A long and terrible dream. I slept soundly, dead to the world and everything in it, but I was not dead. I could soon be if I wasn't very careful. Waking up confused, dazed even believing my dreams were real. When in fact they were not, they were only dreams. I was not safe. I got up from bed to have a hot shower drenched in sweat and smelling vile. Fear has a way of messing up the body, making one's sweat smell different, stronger nastier. Fear has its own odour. For the first time I actually had pleasant dreams. As I ran the shower Nicolas brazenly rushing into the bedroom, startling me, so much so I jumped letting out a scream. The bedroom door banging against the wall making a staggering sound.

"It wasn't a dream, it wasn't a dream."

I thought as soon as I seen his face.

"This is my life."

I had only just awoken to more violence.

Instantly grabbing my small throat and squeezing it brutally. Lifting me off the bathroom floor, all the time carrying me by the throat. Throwing me harshly onto the bed. By this time I knew it wasn't any use to scream. Firstly, no one would hear, the staff who did hear would not come, they would not help. Finally and much more importantly, it would enrage Nicolas, making his savage daily and nightly attacks greater in agony for me. There were times I was pleased when I did not have the energy to scream. Yielding any temptation my brain may have had, preventing all signals to be made.

Nicolas quickly placed his body in the best position for him that day, the bulldog then the jack hammer, permitting him to take the upper hand of his wife's body. Until he stimulated my libido, he knew it was probable I would resist for a time. He did not realise I had to force myself to go with it, closing my eyes and making my body want it to prevent excessive pain. I pretended he was Claude. Envisaging his face before me. His hands on my body. Claude's lips of mine. I did not want my husband to be close to me. Not that close. Not that he would have cared about me forcing it. He would not have taken it as an insult like most men, providing he had an enjoyable ride and his urges were dealt with successfully. Once having me worked up and saturated throwing me about in many different positions for his pleasure. I felt like a rag doll during our correlations. Each night would be different. Every night Nicolas could not flout his urge when it came to fellatio and T. square, deck chair and fuck face. I was sure he must have read many books about sexual positions, based on the fact he knew all their names and how to demonstrate them. His particular favourites were basset hound, bridge and cross, very fitting. The cross I hated. There were many ways to invade a wife's body, but having my vagina in a back to front method intensified his ejaculation. This hurting me excessively, he would become more brutal and rougher than in any other position. This position he found limited my ability to restrict his access. I had no alternative but to be submissive. I had to pretend to be that Thailand whore he spoke to on the internet. The one who put many naked pictures of herself online to entice my husband. The one he enjoyed visiting in Bangkok on those fake business trips away. Whimpering in pain infuriated him. Over the years there have been countless times when he was doing me from behind, I had my face in the pillow cringing with pain ever so careful not to make a whimper, not to make a sound. I wanted it to be over as quickly as possible, if I had made any noises to signify I was not enjoying what he was giving me, indeed in grave pain, it would have lasted until I passed out. Nicolas was sinister enough to hurt me more. It would not have been the first time. He would shag me repeatedly, then leaving our marital bedroom to work in his study. What I believed at that time to have been work. If one considers human investments and flirting with slutty women a job. Importing and exporting in an illegal and immoral fashion. It had been years since we cuddled up in bed together, or went to bed at the same time, even shared the same room. The normal things married couples are known to do, in a traditional life a traditional marriage. Simple things such as having breakfast and dinner together long since ceased. His work was more paramount. Money and other women was his ultimate supreme.

CHAPTER SIXTY-THREE

The Arrangements in Process

Wednesday 13 September 2006

During September Nicolas had the largest bedroom suite within his house redecorated and newly furnished. A room he did not use a great deal of. Formerly it only stored boxes of business documents and other personal information, which looked as though he was trying to hide. It did not make much sense to me at the time, since then becoming perfectly transparent. Long ago I had started to become weary and felt fatigued after being used for sexual desire. I was not a wife, I was a slave. A mere child who does as she is told or I would be chastised quite viciously. There was meaning in the redecorating. There is a plan and I'm not in it. It wasn't meant for me.

I had always been thin. Thin but healthy. My frail and weak body had long since shown. Born with anaemia. Since being held captive I had lost a good deal of weight, resulting in saggy skin upon my small delicate face. My eyes sunken into my head and temples collapsed. Dark circles under my eyes, brittle, dull hair. Consequent to my anaemia I felt the cold very easily due to my thin skin, where every vein in my body could be seen. My flesh was like art with splattered paint in the colours of blue, green and purple. My hands and feet were red from bad circulation, the lack of food and being kept in a cold room every day and night for years did not help my blood flow. I had broken red and purple veins on my face and by my nose. In addition to dry dehydrated skin from being malnutrition, broken nails caused by biting them due to stress and strain. A habit I never acted out before this life and sad state of affairs inaugurated, an inclination which newly developed. For me it was like smoking. Being a non-smoker, although smokers claim that they smoke as a means to distract themselves from their worries. Under strain very few people act rational. We all go a little crazy sometimes.

That night I was finally relieved to get to sleep. The cold night air during that harsh winter made my body that much more difficult to relax and settle. I was exhausted whilst in pain. I had fresh cuts around my wrists which kept me awake. Finally drifting off to the land of nod, my only escape, I was awakened by Nicolas's engorged cock being pushed into my mouth. Out of shock my first reaction was chopping down on the head of his dick. With that came the biggest slap my left cheek was ever subjected to. Slapping my face a further six times, my entire face throbbed. Cracking the skin by my left eye. A few drops of blood trickled to the surface from beneath to Nicolas's amusement. The tears which trickled down my cheeks without actually trying to cry, inflamed the pain my cheeks suffered. Nicolas automatically became angry. Understandably, with the pain he must have felt by my biting on the head of his cock, this would encourage annoyance but it should not be at my expense. From out of nowhere he pulled out a bright red lipstick and drew over my lips and teeth. Screaming at me to open my mouth wider, shoving his dick in as far as it would fit, demanding I suck him dry. I couldn't breathe. He forced his cock all the way down my throat till I gagged and choked, yet he still would not ease or stop. Saliva dripped out of my mouth over his cock and onto my chest. Somehow I had clear juice dripping out of my nose. I don't know if it was because I was already tired that made this night seem to last forever, or if this ordeal indeed carried on for as long as it felt. I thought he was never going to cum. To speed up the process I stroked his cock and pulled it back and forth to stimulate his orgasm and intensify the sensations as I could not stand anymore. This needed to end fast. I sucked and nibbled his balls. This technique was my friend when helping me to get him to climax faster. I pulled slowly from base to head, I treated his shaft as

I loved him dearly. I made it feel good, making Nicolas feel even better. Thank fuck. When he eventually gushed his load into my mouth, his final demand for me that night was to swallow. Although it was only a mouthful, it was bitter and thick. Swallowing he knew I hated. Nicolas's cum was much too salty for my liking making me thirsty. It was a good excuse to down a straight brandy, washing every part of him away. Insisting I lick his cock head clean, which consisted of sticking my tongue as far as I could into the hole at the head of his dick. Telling me:

"Don't miss a drop." Kissing me upon my cheeks and saying, "Goodnight. It won't be long until tomorrow's fun. If I can manage more before then I will wake you. You will tend to my every desire. It won't be long until the next round of games, petal."

As he neared the bedroom door turning around to flash me a wink. My face stung, feeling like a wasp had injected its stinger into my skin, inflaming the wounded area with a great deal of sharp pain for near a week. I had the print of his fingers branded onto my skin. I was his. Only his.

The next day I awoke in an oversized two hundred year old Spanish bed alone, this made me feel safer. After checking the garden from the balcony, I observed Emilio doing his usual morning gardening. Peeking my head out of the bedroom door to make sure Philippine was nowhere to be seen. She was not. There was only an empty hallway decorated in golden silk wallpaper, with an impressive one thousand crystal chandelier hanging in the middle of the hall from the ceiling, with ten matching wall lights unlit. I was no longer permitted to go about the house, forced to remain within the four walls of my bedroom. They did not want for me to become informed of their business particulars, nor their plans for me. I was the mess which needed to be cleaned up, before the greater plan came into play. There was a greater plan designed for better things, a plan I was not in. Every so often and being me, I would wonder about when the coast was clear. Tiptoeing to the head of the stairs I could hear two voices: one was Nicolas's the other Philippine's. They were talking about me. I knew from their tone of voice it was not thrilling. I could not believe what my ears witnessed.

I could hear Philippine's voice announce.

"It will take a matter of hours before it starts to work, Nicolas. Then it will work gradually. We will give her breakfast, lunch and dinner for the next two days, shortly after that she will be dead. In between times we will butter her up so she has no idea about anything. If not she will most certainly be too weak to fight us, or pose a threat of harm. She is fiery enough to throw something. But someone like her does not have what it takes to fight to the kill. She's too much of a wimp. If I were to spit on her she would cry from pain. Either way she will be made ineffective. Plus she has no idea we are planning to kill her. Nicolette will be dead long before she had the chance to figure out what is happening. I will bring up her breakfast now. She won't taste a thing or be aware she is being poisoned. After a couple of meals she may feel faint maybe nauseas. I have been rather generous with the quantity. If she is a lightweight for the poison she could be dead sooner than we have estimated. The very reason for keeping her skinny, it takes affect faster. We knew the day would come when we would do this again. Mama always plans ahead of time. The sooner she is dead the sooner you can be happy in your new marriage. Count yourself lucky we do not have to worry about people reporting her missing, considering nobody knows she is here. People haven't seen her in over four years. Remember Mrs. Suti asked me about three years ago if you would consider remarrying, as your young bride did not return to you. She suspected Nicolette ran off with a younger model, possibly the body guard. That you attained a divorce and you were left brokenhearted. Not to forget about Mr. Alonso who presumed you were widowed again, he sent his deepest regrets. Our plan is genius, my son. Don't worry about a thing. Dear old mother is taking care of everything. Doesn't mother come through for you, never failing her dear precious child who she loves and would die for?"

"Great. Yes, you do, mother, you are amazing, you always clean up my dirt, and straighten out my bed. You know how to take care of these matters amply. You take care of your son better than any woman could. They don't make women like you anymore, mother. Women are just dirty whores who should be used, abused and killed. I'm glad we aren't killing her like we did Gabriella. That was too much hard work, especially at your age now you wouldn't be fit for

341

that again. That was fifteen years ago, you are not as agile as you once were. Age is not on your side not to mention your arthritis, mother. Your fingers are slowly becoming deformed. Their strength weakening."

"I know, do not worry this time around. We have had years to improve our tact, with many girls in-between to practice our different methods on. Women who were not wives to eliminate any connection between us and them, wasn't I smart to get you to do it that way, son? Furthermore, she has had no contact with her family she has no friends – there is nobody to interfere. This could not be more perfect. When have I ever been wrong? There will not be anybody to create any issues for us later on; with no possible way for this to get messy. There is no doubt this won't work, especially how she is uninformed of our plans. When people are ignorant to the fact they are going to be attacked, it means the attacker has the upper hand. If one does not know how the game goes, how can one win? Nicolette is unaware you are remarrying Yana. For you to do so, you must get rid of her immediately. You go away for the weekend like we discussed, I will take care of everything. I will observe how she is reacting to the poison. If she is alive tomorrow morning or another couple of days by the latest, she will be dead by Sunday night at the outside. I will finish her off, be sure of that. You *know* I can't stand that skinny bitch. I can't stand any of them. No woman is good enough for my dear boy. We will still have more than enough time to have everything cleaned up. Your wedding can go ahead in Norway next week. Don't you worry about anything, my dear son."

Kissing Nicolas on the cheek and patting him of the shoulder as though he were a good little boy who did well on his school project. It was a weird sight. Philippine kissed her son on the cheek for longer than would be acceptable for any mother.

"Thank you, mama, I feel better for being reassured. Your words always bring me great comfort. You know how to make things right when I am stressed and panicking."

"What are mamas for but to take care of their children? You don't simply have a child, when they turn eighteen leave them to their own devices. A good and loving mother, a caring and devoted mama, spends all her life through looking after the one she loves. That is our job. Children are a mother's life. Now give your dearest mama another hug and a kiss."

"Mama, how long should I keep Yana for? You think I kept Nicolette too long yet Gabriella not long enough. So how long is it too long?"

"It is hard to tell, Nicolas, it depends on how good of a wife she is to you. If she can keep you interested but above all satisfied those are the main obstacles you face. You know how quickly you change your mind about most women. You lose interest in women much too quickly. Nicolette was the longest so far. I do not think you ought to keep any of the rest of your future wives anywhere near as long. We will see. When Yana arrives, and I determine how much you are into her, I will tell you how long."

"Thank you for your advice, mama. Other women would send me astray but not you, my happiness and freedom has forever been your most significant concern. Have you received the translated documentation for the marriage? You know the documents translated from Ukrainian to Norwegian for the wedding to go ahead."

"Yes, son, I have. They are in your desk draw, in a manila envelope marked Project Ukraine NO 5.

After what my ears fell witness to I knew what I must do. I had to pick my method of motion. What exactly I was going to use to kill them, more importantly when. The clock is ticking I haven't much time. Both Nicolas's and Philippine's words rang through. I had no alternative. I was in shock regardless of knowing they were going to kill me someday. Someday always seems so far away. Especially when year after year passes by. Yet there was something different in them recently. When the words are heard; the confirmation knocked me on my ass, making me that much more determined. I will die someday. We all will that much is certain. There is no escape from that. I will not die this weekend that much is also certain. They don't realise this yet. The Beaumont family is completely oblivious to the fact that their expiration date is fast approaching. That is an undeniable fact, an ultimate promise. Realising I was not prepared to die after all. That was the only reason I had not succeeded in killing myself over the past several years. I really do want to live. Finding a strength from within from somewhere. I don't know where it came from but it was marvellous.

I started to plot. Plan A, plan B, plan C. I didn't know how. But I have to know how. Returning to my bedroom directly to the balcony to breath in some air, needing something to reduce my nerves. A stiff brandy right now would be ideal. My mind had clouded. I did not feel fear, I was merely surprised. I felt something; yes it was a strange sensation. I don't know the name of that particular emotion. It was new to me. Perhaps it was more a lack of sensation, deadness. My mouth, my nose, I felt I was being smothered, as though someone was holding a pillow over my airways. From where I stood I see Philippine walking down the back garden approaching Emilio, giving him his instructions for when I was dead, I suspected. Advancing in the direction of the bathroom to throw freezing cold water on my face, frantically needing to come awake, to think methodically. My brain had started to shut off. For a brief few moments I entered a state of shock unable to shake it, until the coldness of the water collided with my fair skin. Immediately jolting my brain back into action. As soon as I came to, I was ready for combat. This was going to be messy. I wasn't naïve enough to doubt that factor, or to try to sugarcoat a harsh truth. Before my life was safe to live, I had dirty work to undergo. I have three people to kill. Then I must clean it up. The clean-up will perhaps be the dirtiest of all to endure. I had a dark path to journey down. It was time I took control. I had to design a plan, a most definite plan. Minute by minute. I had to start killing them today. If only I knew where the poison was kept, what they are using on me, I could use it on them, a double-edged sword.

I struggled to compose my breathing; I knew that Philippine would be up within the next three minutes. My heart was racing much too quickly for me to control it now. I was shaking all over like a guilty paedophile, it would give me away. I could shake later when she thinks she has poisoned me. It would then be acceptable. Deciding to jump back into bed, covering my body up to my neck with the covers to obscure my shakiness. Concluding I will tell her I feel ill. If I feel ill, my logic was Philippine would be lured into thinking the poison will take affect faster. My immune system would not be strong enough to fight back. I would pose no predicament. A false sense of security they would be lured into, making her believe it was a job too easy, and without awareness I will have her trapped within a web. Thereby not expecting me to be running around to house in preparation. My objective, was for her to let down her guard. Complacency is a self-destructive force, making my job that much easier. Her worries and my life would be taken care of as far as she would be concerned. They will die by my hand, through her lack of knowledge and arrogant ways. I must do what I must do. This will be the performance of my life.

CHAPTER SIXTY-FOUR

Hidden Agenda

With no other alternative but to kneel down past the country white hand carved French style kitchen cupboards, only to run when I reached the hall. At the same time needing to ensure Nicolas did not walk out of the library. In-between talking to his whores and bitches via internet. In a rush to get back to my bedroom I ran just as fast as my poor weary legs would carry me, down seventeen doors to my bedroom. Just in time. I was flushed, yet within forty seconds Philippine opens the bedroom door, walking into the bedroom carrying a tray, with an extra-large portion of lunch upon a very fancy china dinner plate. The cheapest cut of beef, the fattiest portion for me, keeping the good tasty succulent stuff for themselves. On the tray was a crystal glass filled with milk. Philippine looked like a matron from the nineteen-sixties movies, with her German-looking head as she entered the room. She may have been Swiss, but there was no doubt she had German if not Austrian blood with those chiselled features. Making it obvious that something was different. They barely fed me in all the years I have lived here. They have given me different food to what they eat for all that time. When anything is out of character, always question it. There is always a hidden agenda. ALWAYS! Insisting on giving me the evil eye, not so different, perhaps not wanting to give too much away to her prey. I would try and be passing, after all, it is our last day or two together. Despite wanting more than anything to rip her throat out from her neck and beat her German-looking head with it.

"Philippine, why so much, you know I will not be able to eat all that after all these years with very little food? My stomach has surely shrunk."

With annoyance Philippine's eyes answered, this time uneasily, but for the first time answering me by using her mouth in a softer and more fake tone. Confirming what I already knew.

"You must eat it all, my girl. You have been getting too skinny recently. Your husband would like more weight on you. You were once out of shape looking as though you had given birth, hence why he does not touch you as much these days. And cannot stand to sleep in the same bed as you. You must make your husband happy by any means necessary, doing whatever he desires. You can start now by eating every bite. That will make him happy. I have noticed it too, I would not want for you to get ill. If you are ill you cannot be a good wife. Illness takes away from the attention you must pay your husband. A truly wonderful wife never gets sick. You must eat every bite. Don't waste. When I say every bite, I mean every bite!"

Said with a more assertive tone to her voice.

"I would do anything to make my husband happy, absolutely anything. Is he here?"

"Yes, he is in the house but he is busy working. He could not possibly see you today."

"I understand. Would you ask him to please find five minutes for his wife who loves and misses him dearly? Now that I am no longer out of shape, just the way he prefers me. Please ask him… Tell him I love him, please."

"I will pass the message on. I cannot make any promises, but don't hold your breath. Emilio and I have a lot of work to do today, we do not have time to waste passing on messages. You know your husband is a busy man. NOW EAT!!!"

The fakest smile any witch encouraged to execute crossed her face, with a very honest wickedness in her eyes, not at all well camouflaged. One would think with the amount of years of practice she has had, she would have perfected her profession of lying and deceiving. Complacency dominance and badness was holding her back.

"I must get on with the rest of the housework. There is a great deal to do in a house this large. I cannot talk all day. I will be back in an hour for the tray. Is there anything in particular you would like for dinner today? I know I never ask you what it is you would prefer, but you must know everything is going to change from today onwards. You will enjoy the changes I am sure."

The sinister comment with a sinister snigger, I knew exactly what she meant. Realising no matter what I was given whether it consists of poison or not, they were ensuring I die hopefully today. So I must not eat or drink anything. Not one thing will cross my lips this day that is prepare for me by them.

"No thank you, anything you are making is fine. I like everything you prepare. You are a very good cook. I appreciate all you make for me. You have worked hard all these years and been dedicated to your job. I am very sorry that I have not thanked you before. When you say changes, I hope they are good transformations and we may be friends this turn around. I would like that."

By the way she looked at me, Philippine knew I was lying and that I was aware she deliberately over salted and undercooked the little bit of food I was given, as a means of added torture. This was one of the biggest lies which had ever crossed my lips. Her cooking was worse than the food one would find in prison. Although I was trying desperately not to actually find out firsthand how dreadful prison food is said to taste. Friends with Philippine NEVER! I knew I was lying and she knew I was lying. It was a day filled with games of playing cat and mouse. Not in this universe or the next.

"Keep your friends close and your enemies closer."

The wisest advice which ever was said. In my fight to live I must be wiser than wise.

"My, aren't we a sweet girl."

Sounding more like an evil granny who was poisoning an innocent child simply because she lost her marbles.

"Thank you very much. I just would not want to put too much on you with taking care of such a large house as you say. It is large. You

348

have more than enough to get through without worrying about me and what I enjoy eating. Take it easy and relax each chance you are given."

"Thank you, Nicolette. I will see you at dinner time. Just leave your tray outside the door as usual, instead of me coming in."

Unable to advertise the happiness in her eyes Philippine certain she was cunning, not distinguishing she was giving away much too much to her victim. To my advantage. There are more of them than me. I am only one against three. They are the gutless having to do it underhandedly there is no glory in the way they do things. The dice has been rolled and in play we currently are.

CHAPTER SIXTY-FIVE

The Wicked Witch of Switzerland

The servants knew everything about Nicolas, not because they snooped and stole, but because Nicolas told them everything. I overheard him many times. I used to be curious as to why, now I simply do not care. It is odd, however, to confide in one's home help as intently as Nicolas chose to. Nobody in this world can be trusted. Never knowing what could be used against you, or when a poor person decides they are brave enough to attempt to become rich. They will no more live life being poor. Seizing the perfect opportunity. Blackmail is too easy a trap to become tangled up in when one is wealthy. A web of smothering, leading to only one thing, certain death. Especially considering his pretentiousness and pomposity. Rich people who are in Nicolas's league look down on anyone who does not come from the same background as they do. I found it peculiar. There have been times I have thought Nicolas relies on them too much. He was unable to function without the wicked witch of Switzerland. Somehow Philippine had managed to control him, when Nicolas is the man who lives to be in control. That was the strangest accept of all. Could she have been blackmailing Nicolas from the start, from before me coming into the scenario? Is this all her doing? Did she already have dirt which could destroy my husband? Whatever it was, she did have the greatest power over him. It was a bizarre set up. Philippine could control him like a puppet on a string. I have been incompetent when it comes to decoding their relationship, her clutch over him. When the two of them have been alone together, without Emilio and when they believed I was a good girl hiding in my bedroom, I often thought they looked like a couple. The way they spoke to one another, the way they would hold each other. I have never known the master of the house in any mansion to hug his help. Charles never did, especially not as fervently as Nicolas held Philippine. Unable to figure out how he could find a female attractive who looked as manly as she did. Philippine was the most unattractive woman I have had the misfortune to lay eyes on. Even worse than Sophie. They are creepy, all three of them. I found it odd how the wicked witch of Switzerland felt the need to constantly attempt to reassure Nicolas, like a new born baby. I will end their intrusion in my life. All of them are going to die. The world will be a better place without delinquents such as those three. Life's a bloody bitch, I will do what I must with it. The position for a new wicked witch of Switzerland will be up for grabs, perhaps Sophie will take the trophy.

CHAPTER SIXTY-SIX

Revenge As Sweet As Pink Champagne

8 November 2006

Nicolas returned home on a bright winter's morning, after being away for the weekend on a business trip to Hamburg, German. Unaware it would be his final. Silence was the key to my redemption. The sun was dazzling. There was no intense heat projecting from the orange circle above, it was merely blinding. It glistened upon Lake Geneva just meters from our chateau, making it resemble a little like summer. Though it did not feel it with the bitter coldness drifting in the air. I needed the coldness on my flesh today. It keeps me awake, aware alert. There was a slight breeze present, blowing from the north as he exited his Bentley. His tie dispensed in mid-air as the breeze reached his being. The water shimmered like the diamonds I wore around my neck, and the dangling earrings which hung from my ears on our wedding day. Making me look like a queen before I stood down, or so Nicolas once maintained, that was long ago. The rich blue coloured water, with the sailing boats lined up side by side by the deck. Summer was far away, it would be quite a while until those boats sailed. It was the wrong time of year. It was merely the breeze which triggered a memory. I closed my eyes envisaging what they look like during spring and summer, sailing on the ocean like water. Remembering how alive Lake Geneva is that time of year. How alive I once felt. It's a stunning sight to behold. A sight when one is lucky enough to experience it, the beauty is so intense it is never forgotten. I remember everything from that day. How the air smelt. The breeze felt like it embraced my soft baby-like ivory skin. The coldness of the air has forever had a way of motivating me. I would experience such an exhilarating sensation. There was nothing quite like it. Everything from that day reminded me of the nicer times. Weighing heavy on my heart. I did not want to do what I knew I had to. I truly didn't. But I had to. Truly I did.

Whilst Philippine was in the garden giving Emilio his instructions, I crept downstairs to the kitchen, where she mostly had the television on, listening to the local and world news. The lady advertising the weather today, claimed that the weather was taking a turn for the worst this evening. She had short red hair with a fringe. Not the kind of red that reminded me of a ginger cat. The kind of red which was deep and vibrant. Really enhancing her looks and her eyes. She was pretty and spoke with a strong French accent. She gave me the delightful news I required. It was essential I knew this information. I knew there was a reason why I loved winter. My plan was always going to revolve around it, although I did not know it that particular morning. I did have some idea how it would be accomplished. I merely had to fill in the details. Link up the lines. Dot the T's. No breakfast together, no kissing his wife hello on return home. No tender kiss upon the forehead, nor a passionate kiss on my lustrous lips. Morning sex to celebrate his return ended with all good reason. It was not because I refused to have sex with him, I had no say in that regard. It was because he had no energy for me, using it up on cheap whores and bitches. The pathetic lies also ceased. We were both beyond caring. There was no zeal in his cock and balls. There were both sagging and lifeless when it came to me turning him on these days. He just took me. He had younger and better models than me now. He used up my youthful years. When he would occupy me, his mind picturing other women. I could tell. A wife knows these things. I could feel it in his touch. Taste it in his kiss. My husband was a condescending fucker who had forsaken his principles, if he ever had any, mistreating me daily. He thought more of fucking his German and Russian whores on those long business weekends away. A few months ago I was guilty of thinking business weekends, bullshit. For that I really ought to apologise. Now I realise those German and Russian whores were his business, in more ways than one. They were helping to make him wealthy. It was all in aide of determining which harlot he would bring home in replace of me, which would be sold and which would be kept captive, doped up constantly until there was no risk of them fleeing. Depending too greatly on the dozes they were given. Given but not from kindness. Forced to become an addict, for their benefit. Men in control destroy the world. Taking liberties with them, teasing them. The best were sold. It was not exactly a compliment to whoever took my place. If Nicolas had not been drained already, after emptying his hot white loads into strange stretched wet disenchanted Russian pussies, I his legal possession he would still have mistreated, like a dog. Nicolas was a brutal animal. Rough and ready. Brutality too egger to provide. He had beaten me often to great extremes, there were times he could not bear to insult his eyes by looking at me. Unable to view the bruises he had left on my body, and the scars he had implanted into my skin. He went as far as to claim he could not stand my voice, the sound of my crying or the muffled sound of my whimpering, as I tried to catch my breath after each beating he felt the need to subject me to. Nothing between us occurred which resembled a marriage. Only distance was present these days. Distance and hatred. This, the both of us were mindful of. Both parties were more than aware of what we had to do, in silence and in secret. I was more than aware that I would have to fight, fight hard and fight to win. Nicolas underestimating the task. Underestimating my ability, my determination. My will to live. A wise man is a man who does not underestimate, never, not once, only analysing facts. During his trip away he was plotting and having my death arranged. How it would be done and when he already knew. I knew what I was going to have to do now too. Foolish notions of murder pervaded my brain, causing me to feel obtuse. I am a breathing corpse. I felt foolish that my life was in danger. This never happens to me, it is always to other people. It happens in movies, one hears about it on the news or reads about it in the newspapers. It is never me who it happens to. But there is always someone who is in danger. Why couldn't it be me, because it is me?

On a wet and blustery Sunday evening I humbled myself, going onto the balcony I knelt beneath the large bright moon. Blessing myself, crossing my hands I prayed to God.

354

"Dear, Lord, I pray it will not be me who is killed this time. I will die one day that is true, my time has not come yet, surely? When my time arrives I will leave and with great pleasure. It just doesn't feel like it is my time yet."

Explaining my story, the story he knew too well. He witnessed every part. Every yell, every threat, every slap. It made me feel good. I felt I had cleansed myself from brutality. Confessions cleansed me. I prayed that darkness never falls over another innocent soul. I pray for myself and for them. The families whose daughters have been taken by men with empty promises and abused. I ask him to grant me a way out. For a short time I grieved. From somewhere deep down, a place I did not know existed I asked for forgiveness. I felt shame, sadness and despair. Every human emotion at one time. An overabundance of sadness and inspiration. Requiring a release, I cried. Uncontrollably. It was exactly what I needed. Suddenly from nowhere I felt the strongest feeling of forgiveness, before committing my crimes. Illegal and immoral. Then I felt an even stronger feeling building from within my heart, from a place where I think the soul exits. A profound feeling of ability encouraged me. I was embraced by warmth and kindness. I realised within that moment, regardless of the arduous tasks I will face, everything will be perfectly fine. Having no doubt what I was doing was right. Even if I died losing to them, the probability was against me in any case. There was every likelihood I would be defeated. Three against one. I must not defeat myself. It would be alright, I would be a winner, because my torture would be concluded. There isn't anything else I could ask for. I would be unconstrained from their grasp. I went into that phase again, becoming delusional, not knowing reality from my dreams, unconcerned about being able to decipher. I tried frantically with a sincere heart to determine why the Lord above who I believed in fully, would not end my misery. Why allow the continence of my cruelty and exploitation? Why would someone I love dearly want me to suffer savage attacks? Starting to doubt, is there really a God? Faith lost. Hope obsolete. If there was he would save me. If there was not, I would not have felt forgiven. Taking that as a sign. Convinced I was destined to live through murder. I would kill them and save other women. I will help who I can. This is my predestined path. My purpose. I have found what I am good at. This was all in design to make me stronger. I must be stronger for myself and for them. Immediately feeling dishonour and the need to repent. I prayed silently. I misunderstood. God had not forsaken. He had granted me strength. I was empowered to survive. For a brief time I spent searching for answers to my many questions. I did not want to kill, unless it was absolutely necessary for my survival. There was no other way out. This was it. This was my life. An intelligent person apprehends, badness and murder avoids those who deserve it most. It was then I tasted the thought of revenge. Revenge as sweet as pink champagne.

During the time Nicolas was taking his extra marriageable rights with escorts, I valued my alone time. Time free from torture, rape and ignominy. I put my time to good use. I planned different scenarios of fighting back. Once my freedom was attained I dreamed of rebuilding my life. Where I would go, what I would do. Endlessly changing how I would live again. Catching myself. Don't look too far ahead. Focus on the here and now. This is battle time. This house is the battlefield. I am a solider. I am a mercenary.

CHAPTER SIXTY-SEVEN

Mother the Deceitful One

November 9 2006

As a means to reboot my brain into working order, to structure today's murders meticulously, deciding to snoop around the study. I needed a slight distraction to get my mind in the right mode. But what is the right mode for committing murder. At the same time there was much information I needed to uncover for my best interests. Searching for weapons I could use was paramount. Nicolas has an impressive collection of Swiss army knives and Swiss military riffles with live ammunition. I had not yet designed my final draft. Throwing around in my brain different ways of committing murder. I resulted in confusing myself and drawing a blank. Reduced to feeling like a writer unable to create anymore, the best days are gone. Ensuring I use the best method for me. There are many ways to kill. I was searching for weapons of inspiration. I must choose carefully. I was not a strong woman, even weaker since being brutally abused for five years. Wondering what else I would find. Would the truth be more disturbing than I could imagine? Nicolas was a suspicious man. To be suspicious to the degree he was meant he was far from innocent. It is only they who have dark secrets to hide who behave like Nicolas Beaumont.

The drawer to Nicolas's desk was locked. Of course it was, when are desk drawers ever left opened? This is Nicolas Beaumont, drawers belonging to Nicolas Beaumont had to be locked. Secrets to hide and interests to protect. A reputation to keep pristine. Money to be made. A lifestyle to maintain. Orders to be carried out. Subsequently why was there no password on his computer? This was sloppy for such a dubious creature. Something I could not accuse him of in the past. Was he slipping up in his old age? Or was he becoming more complacent than he originally was? Hearing a noise from the hall. My heart jumped. Scanning the room as fast as my brain was capable. Quickly dashing from the desk, hiding behind the floorlength velvet curtains. They were closed and heavy disguising my silhouette. It was a blessing it was mid-winter, the early evenings were casting over fast as it was only 05:16. When murder is to be committed the darkness of the sky is forever a murderess's best friend. The one component which can be relied on for discretion. The one thing which will not bear witness against me… Darkness and the wind. There wasn't anywhere else in the study to hide. All the walls had built-in panelling, with only one door which lead into the hallway. The direction from which the noise came from. I did not have enough time to get through the white French doors and abscond on the other end of the room. I've come this far, I was not about to take unnecessary risks of being detected. I had no other alternative but to wait inaudibly in expectancy. I stood there waiting, my mind flowing wildly. Ready to be attacked at any given moment. Adrenaline galloping through my body, like the wild horses I once rode. I had to control my hands from shaking. Vomiting in my mouth, forced to swallow, in order to keep my presents undetected. The nerves were searing strongly from within, making me pee a little in my own underwear. Crossing my legs to tense up my bladder muscles, trying to prevent an accident showing my position. Nicolas's computer was bugging me. Nicolas never leaves his computer on without having to enter a password. This isn't right! For Nicolas this is unheard of. Something more than murdering me is going on. I've known it all day, I could feel it in my gut. My gut is never wrong. Absolutely never. Call it a woman's intuition or just knowing my husband well. What is his game? Or should I say what is his business? What is he hoping to gain? They know I am unable to escape, regardless of my efforts in the past, for which I've paid for with my blood. I must think out of the box. I must think the way they think. I must think like a sociopath. I have to be one hundred steps ahead of them, that way I can corner them in. Attack before they know what's happening. That way I can win. How often does a woman of twenty-five have to fight for her life? It is not a bad thing to be unaccustomed to decoding murder plots. Unless one is faced with being murdered. It is in Nicolas's nature to abuse women. The Beaumont family have now made it my nature to kill. I have been put in the position where I must kill, so I will and without regret. My only regret is that things had to come to this. This is there doing. This is there will. Not mine. It was never mine. But I will do whatever I must to survive. Survival cannot be a regret. If this is truly what they want this is precisely want they will get. I am prepared for whatever it takes. Blood will spill, breathes will seize and life enviably will end. This is the time where evil ends.

It is now early evening the poison should be taking affect, or so Philippine would be expecting. She has not checked in on me as frequently as she normally would in a day. Wanting me to die alone. I'm surprised with her sadistic streak she would not want to witness me gasping my last breath. Laughing her fat ass off at me because she lives on and not I. Wanting me to know she has won. Finally getting rid of me once and for all tackling her new conquests. Or was she too busy with her other preparations? I look at the clock which hung on my bedroom wall, it is almost time to strike. Slowly but with each tick of the cuckoo clock their bodies are preparing to give in settling for all time. They just don't realise it, yet. I believe with conviction that when a soul knows the end is near, it prepares in advance for its journey. While the brain plays catch-up. With a heart of pain I went over in my mind my definite plot. Yes, I had now figured out how I would do it. I just needed to replay the scene over and over in my mind for it to become second nature. Until it was time. Committing it to memory. Like going to the toilet, no need to think about it, one just does it. The lighter feeling of junk removed once finished. I need it to be that easy. I had my self-defence figured out too, just in case the unexpected transpired. It is the unexpected which very definitely will get me killed. The obscured angle, the shadow following me. The shadow lurking patiently until I let my guard down. The person I did not realise was on my tail. It is the unseen which plans to be seen at the last second. No time for the victim to respond. No time for the prey to move. Barely enough time for death to register. The noise from outside the study subsides, thankfully before I have the chance to move an inch Philippine walked into the room. Sitting down at the computer, motionless for one moment, commencing to type. Unable to see details from the distance. I was short-sighted. All I could observe was Philippine was on a chat room. The only thing I was able to do was wait until she had finished. Twenty-nine minutes later and many self-satisfied giggles to herself, finally making her exit. I rushed to the study door which leads to the hall to listen if the coast was clear. No noise was being made. No voices. I felt comfortable enough to open a small crack to peak through the gap in the door. I must safeguard my location. The coast was positively clear. Rushing to the computer. Conversations were on display. I felt my skin crawl as though a snake was slithering over my body, with each line I read. Philippine had messaged some of the girls Nicolas had been talking to and luring. That was one thing. It was an entirely different matter when I read further, discovering she was pretending to be Nicolas. Not that this was weird enough, but an old woman like her talking about sex and what she would do to them once they arrive from Russia and Ukraine. In-depth detail. For a woman of her years that was as wrong, as wrong can be. A granny pimp, my god what has this world come to? She enjoyed herself too much, I observed from the French doors. Why mislead them? What is this all about? Why would an old woman who is also her employer's mother wish to talk raunchy to young foreign girls? Mother the deceitful one. Yana was the girl she spent the most time talking with. More sweet, innocent and intriguing conversation. More interest focused on her. Why? The girl Nicolas is getting ready to marry. Why marry her?

Philippine to Yana:

"My mother will love 2 meet u.

She is a wonderful woman.

I no u both will get on well when u come over next week."

Yana to Philippine:

I cannot wait 2 meet her.

She sounds lovely.

U r lucky 2 have such a gr8 mother.

I wish I had sum1 2 love me like she loves u.

Philippine to Yana:

O but u do my pet u do.

U have me and I have u.

U will always have me and mother and I will love u.

U will never b alone again.

I like u so she will like u 2.

Yana to Philippine:

I will make u a good wife.

I know I will.

I will do anything u ask from me.

Anything u desire.

Ur wish is my command.

Philippine to Yana:

U beta, otherwise we will not get on and I will have 2 send u back.

U don't want that do u?

My mother is a Queen in my eyes, u must get along with her.

Yana to Philippine:

No I don't.

That is not gonna happen.

I will not prove a disappointment 2 either of 2.

When I leave here I will never return.

I will make you both very happy.

If I do anything wrong just tell me so I can improve n not make any more mistakes.

Philippine to Yana:

Then I could not b more sure I have made the rite decision in acquiring you.

Yana to Philippine:

U r the man of the house.

U r in control.

I will b a good wife, a good daughter in law.

I will not once let you regret picking me out of all the girls on these websites.

I cannot thank u enuf for given me this chance 2 come 2 a new country n have a chance of a life.

Philippine to Yana:

I have a great deal 2 offer.

I am wealthy beyond reproach.

I can do a lot for u.

If you are good to me you will never want for anything again.

Yana to Philippine:

I have dreamed 4 yrs about going 2 Switzerland.

I never imagined it 2 come true.

Now thanx 2 a gentleman u have made all my dreams come true.

Thank u.

Philippine to Yana:

U r welcum.

Yana to Philippine:

I am excited.

I can't wait.

I wrote in my calendar when I come 2 u.

I am count down the days eagerly.

Philippine to Yana:

I am plzd 2 help u.
U seem like a sweet girl.

Yana to Philippine:
I didn't realise men like u actually existed.

Philippine to Yana:
U r 2 pretty 2 live in a prison.
I only ask 4 love and 4 u 2 understand me.
Do as u r told we will get on well.

Yana to Philippine:
I don't no how a man like u hasn't been married before.

Philippine to Yana:
I never had the luck of finding the rite woman.
U will never have 2 c Ukraine again.

Yana to Philippine:
I will b whatever u want.

Philippine to Yana:
I have 2 get bak 2 work.
Talk later.
Think about what we will do when u get ova here.
Husband 2 b xxx.

Yana to Philippine:
I will b here waiting my love.
Hurry bak r I will b lonely.
Xxxxxxxxxxxxxxxxxxxxxxxxxxxxxx.

My gut feeling told me to get back up to the bedroom ensuring everything appeared routine, in case Philippine could not resist her compulsion to see if I was lying dead, or still hanging on for dear life. Sometimes that family were too predictable. Other times too unpredictable. It was easier to play it safe because I just don't know. I wonder if she would have enjoyed it as much if I was pleased. If I was willing to die. If she thought she was doing me a favour, would she have kept me alive? I spend every day in my bedroom – today cannot appear any different. They are not aware that I know what they are planning, what they intend to do. It must remain that way, until it's time. Be smart. My life is hanging from its very last quickly wearing out threads. I think as I glance at the cuckoo clock checking how long it will be until it's time. Not long now! I must get prepared. Remembering before I left to take a gun, magazine and a silencer. Disguising them beneath my bra and panties. From the liquor cabinet I remove an unopened bottle of Napoleon brandy. Something to help keep me calm when it came to the crunch. For an alcoholic, too much alcohol would diminish accurate aim at the intended target, as a result of constant obdurate shaking. For me, I needed something to steady out my hands. I had too many nerves soaring and taking over. For a non-alcoholic it has the adverse effect. Edging out in silence from the study, I felt like a French Special Forces Commando creeping up on Afghan rebels, getting ready to pull the trigger. Running briskly up the lavish stairwell, past seventeen doors to the right, to my bedroom. For an old house I was grateful the floor boards did not creek like most old houses allowing me to move about unnoticed. Giving thanks to Nicolas, who claimed he had all the floors throughout the house re-fitted, and the entire house rewired in 1999. Saving me money on house renovations after they are gone. For now the floorboards with the wind and the night will keep my secrets. This will then be my house but never to be my home. The luxurious staircase evoked a memory from when I first moved into the chateau in 2001. I used to be fascinated by that staircase, with its elaborate and specialised hand carvings and how glossy crystal like clear water it looked. Seeing my reflection glistening back at me. Like a most extravagant mirror. It was like something out of a nineteen-twenties movie. I have never laid eyes on anything like it in person before. They don't make carvings like that these days. It certainly would not be found in Ikea. That could explain why Nicolas paid almost forty thousand Swiss Francs for such a creation. He knew beauty when he seen it. I cannot take that away from the man. Nicolas once told me it was two hundred years old, buying it in bad condition having it restored to its former glory. He claimed he could see the beauty it held. I still do not know why the staircase was so vivid in my mind, that day of all days. Maybe my spirit was preparing to say goodbye to the world and hello dear lord. Perhaps it was the unknown, the possibility. After all the probability could not be denied was against me. Three against one. The stairway seemed to play a very potent aspect. It meant something more to me that November's day. Was it to do with dear sweet Charles? Would it be the component which would give me my victory walk?

Curiosity filled me, my mind battling with potential ideas. Were Nicolas and Philippine not only mother and son but business partners in luring these foreign girls to countries far away from their homeland, using them to make money? Money to support this opulent lifestyle Nicolas has become much too accustomed to. Not simply feeling but utterly convinced he deserved nothing less than the greatest of everything this world has to offer. As intelligent as he is he had no idea what the real world was about. How tough it can be. The answer to the question which puzzled me the most, why would Philippine play the role of an average cleaner. A low paid, uneducated nobody all these years, if there are making masses of money from these poor unfortunate girls? How could she settle for that? What else did she get out of it? Was it a cover-up? Tax avoidance. I don't know what the hell is going on. Was this just her role in the business so people wouldn't find her too interesting? As for the constant cleaning up, excessive, this is a mask to conceal the fact cleaning is what she is employed to do. All I am sure of is there are many questions and many answers to those questions which will be alarming.

Yes, I have murder to commit today, cleaning up to take care of and much snooping to undergo. Perhaps people to call off. How dangerous will these business acquaintance be? Acknowledging my foremost mistake. I was thinking too much about things which did not at this particular moment take presidency. One task at a time. One bullet, one body at a time.

And as I blinked before my eyes was that country road once more.

I had an hour to prepare myself, body and mind until the time approached for me to become a killer. Jumping into a freezing cold shower. An attempt to calm my nerves, more so to keep my hands still when I aim. Taking deep breathes, envisaging where they would be when I do it. How it would feel when I squeezed the trigger. I knew to expect a pull, a bang I was not expecting. I would be using a silencer. But a hole with blood inevitably will flow. How much blood I would have to wait and see. I suppose it depends on where I shoot. A tear of blood fallen from the eyes of the loser. Three large gulps of brandy the good old-fashioned way, the peasant way from the bottle and straight. With each gulp I swallowed, I felt the Napoleon kick. Nicolette Beaumont now ready. I rolled the dice. Six and six. Time for me to throw out my first card of this game. The card I no longer required. The queen of spades. The kiss I intend to bestow. The winner takes it all.

CHAPTER SIXTY-EIGHT

Muddy Road .

This windy day will become even more tempestuous. Violence would take place outside and in. The wind will be my friend. My only friend. My confidant. Disguising my actions. Every move I take. Each breath I expel. A howl and a bang, a tree may fall, doors may slam. An innocent and honest day. The ordinary kind of mundane day. The coldness of fear felt as though it was somehow burning me. Fire and ice. This weak bodied twenty-five-year-old woman who nobody loves or wants has found her strength, the will to continue on. On this windy day I have found my voice. I scream aloud: "no more, no more. This is finally the end."

For some reason with the inner strength I found came along an image. Each time I blinked before my eyes I could see a country road. A place I do not recognise. In my gut I knew after I freed myself I will find out the meaning to this constant flash of tall green trees and muddy roads.

CHAPTER SIXTY-NINE

Blood Flows

The Games Start
9 November 2006, 18:30

Dressing in a blood red, skin tight mini dress. Not much was left to the imagination to envisage what was beneath to play with. The entire point. This evening I was not blessed with an abundance of time. I had to move swiftly. Two minutes of foreplay, two seconds to pull the trigger. To winter I was grateful. Night lasts longer. Many more dangerous performances can take place unobserved by inquisitive eyes. Accompanied by black slutty strappy stilettoes. Trying desperately not to break my neck, yet walking in a seductive fashion. Now that was a task hard to do. Bright luscious red lips. Eye makeup painted on in the style of cat's eyes, Egyptian Queen heavy black eyeliner. I didn't have time to squander on suspender belts. Spraying Channel in the alluring areas. Twice as much as I would usually wear. The dress, shoes and the fragrance had to do more than eighty percent of the work this evening. I had to focus on the important things. Only spraying where I want to be kissed. A man like a dog will sniff. Going wild for the scent of his bitch. Making up on the time I did not have to waste on suspenders, merely pulled a pair of lace rimed stockings on. Easier to remove when the time came, but just as effective for a man's fickle mind. For the first time I would be the one to seduce my husband. Beneath I wore a black lacy teddy, sheer so he could see exactly what he was prepared to have murdered. Fool! Men never identify what they have until it's gone. Too late for any reconciliation. Death is no better way to ensure this can't happen. Men then live in misery for the woman who got away. Carrying a bag filled with Anne Summers' raunchy toys, wanting him to believe they were going to be especially for him. This aspect was true, but not for the reasons I wanted him to believe. They were the tools I needed. The pleasure was going to be all mine. Although I did have a surprise for him. In all reality it was more than one surprise. This night was designed for my freedom. In the conquering of my freedom, I was damn well going to have a little fun. At Nicolas's expense! He was my husband nevertheless, I earned the right to say goodbye privately and properly once and for all. The thrill of the end. Giving me tickles like it did in the beginning. I was happy but I could not allow myself to become too happy, just yet. I've learnt much from dear old mother. Seeing how her overconfident self has hindered her ability to see the important things. Things which should never be overlooked. The things that will come back and bite one in the ass. The main killer of a collaborator is not a sniper shooting, and entering a bullet into a body, it's not even poison like the Russians are inclined to use. It's not any of those manmade weapons, its arrogances. When one is sure they know everything, but do not. When one is overconfident they categorically refuse to listen. When one believes themselves to be a king or queen, incongruously. Then they have committed suicide.

Nicolas was in his bedroom drinking heavily. A common occurrence. Ideal for today's events. When I opened his bedroom door, disbelief was in his eyes. Lowering the brandy glass from his mouth, without taking a drink. I must've looked good if his reaction was anything to go by. This sex Goddess before his lustful eyes, he knew was going to devour him, every inch of his body was to befall the mercy of his concubine. Slowing walking in his direction as he lay on the bed. Pretending there was music playing, my body moved in rhythm. I felt like an elegant cobra getting ready to pounce. Like a bought and paid for whore I danced. Stripping. From head to toe every garment I wore was now lying upon the floor. Everything exposed. I noticed as I started to seduce him, there were two brandy bottles empty which sat on the bedside table. A third bottle half drunk. His body seemed to become accustomed to an overabundance of strong alcohol, considering he wasn't completely out of it. Yet. Although he was on his way. Quickly opening the zip to his trousers I pulled them down and off. He was already inebriated and in my control. Pushing him back onto the bed, climbing over him making him believe I was going to fuck him long and good. Treat him like the king he believes himself to be. Instead I kiss him. Starting off tenderly then wildly like a panther. Making him believe I was about to eat him whole. He couldn't get enough, the pathetic overbearing male chauvinist pig. He was thinking this was going to be the night of his life, not knowing that this was going to be the last night of his life. Once and for all he would be gone, no more to suffer his degrading abusive sexual depraved ways. Peace will be mine, life will be mine. Leaning over him I whisper ever so softly and alluringly, "Close your eyes, my love, close your beautiful eyes. I have a surprise for you."

Able to feel his stiffness between my legs as I climbed off to get his surprise. From my big bag of toys I removed the rope which would bind him, restricting his movements and my bathrobe belt to gag him. Silence is golden. Tying him firstly to ensure he posed no problem to my safety. All the time speaking in a soft sexy tone of voice, whispering of all the nice and naughty delights I am going to grant him this night. Smart enough to let him feel the entire time he is still in charge. It is vital I ensure he does not lose sight of this, as at any moment he could erupt robbing me of my escape. My final and only chance. Not once a sudden move. Moving in slow enough motion to make him feel safe, relaxed. Allowing him to see every move I make, where my hands were at all times. Not acting suspiciously. Leading him to a false sense of security, only to pounce like a black widow once he was firming in my trap. With a blink of an eye letting down his guard this was my time to act. Reminding me of a mouse with its head fully secure beneath the trap. Broken. Gone. Dead. Leaning over to the bedside table where his already awaiting tall glass of brandy stood. Taking a gulp, only to lean over Nicolas letting it flow into his mouth. Keeping his alcohol level up and my stress levels down. Gaging him next to make certain no call for help was heard. Any call of help must fall onto deaf ears, like they did when I called for help and mercy. Tonight no mercy is granted. Treat others as you have them treat you.

Kissing his face, neck leading to his nipples I had to keep him aroused, all the time stroking his engorged hard cock. Knowing I had to face the prospect of sucking it one last time. Knowing it was the last time made it a little easier to endure. I sucked it knowing I had him under full control. For the first time I ruled. Making the end taste that much sweeter. In all men the small head rules the big head. I heard the telltail signs of his breath quickening and felt his thighs tightening. In my mouth I could feel the head of his dick swelling. Tonight he wasn't going to cum in my mouth. Those days are long gone. I pulled him off all over his stomach. Seductively whispering, "How was that, my love, was that to your expectations?"

Nodding sleepily. His head turns to the side and he begins to snore. The alcohol and orgasm had taken their toll. Working like a sedative. His own self consumption was an aiding hand for me. I stood up and over him making sure he was asleep. It was now my time to leave and carry on with the tasks at hand. I will come back to the son of a bitch when everything else has been taken care of firstly. Nicolas has more to endure. In his death comes my emancipation.

CHAPTER SEVENTY

Rose Bed of Blood

The Roll of another Dice
19:19pm

Looking over the balcony from Nicolas's bedroom, the day was darkening and quickly giving into the night. I didn't have long. There he stood...

Removing black leggings, a black roll neck and a pair of black boots from my big bag of toys, I briskly got dressed. Understanding I would need clothing that would allow me to move easily, without rustling giving my position away. Chiefly without hindrance. Nicolas laying on the bed unconscious, unaware that his family was about to be decreased. Instead of three, there will be two. Instead of two, one. One to none. The wind was howling. I could hear it increasing as I ran down the hallway. Reaching the top of the stairs to put on a raincoat I had hid in an antique chest, wrapping the gun up inside. Checking the gun, no magazine loaded. Pulling the slide back checking there was no bullet inside. The weapon is empty. Seating the fifteen round magazine. Pushing it in hard making sure it was in place. Grabbing the top slide pulling it back. Letting it go quickly. Pushing the .22 round into the chamber. My weapon of salvation now loaded. Safety on. Silencer attached. Ready to go. Placing the gun in my pocket. Keeping a firm hold on it. I was not about to let my last chance of living escape. All those years spent watching

Nicolas behave like a child playing with his guns, at the time bored me. If I had not taken notice of him playing with boy toys I would be dying tonight. Running quickly into the kitchen. Needing to stop for a moment, having to take everything in. Where their locations were. Where mine would have to be. I could see Emilio sweeping leaves, his back turned in my direction. He was wearing a heavy charcoal coat and a thick woolly hat. Thankful for this. I knew it would help muffle the sound of my approach, and what I was going to do. As I stood outside, the rain began to fall heavier. Colder. The wind blowing more harshly. The leaves being lifted and blown in mid-air, disguising my approach with its rustling. Looking like a modern dance before my very eyes. Elegant, smart and flexible. The sound of the gales creating a unique symphony. Never before heard, never again to be heard. Pushing myself forward through the wind with grave difficulty. Slowing me down but giving me a little longer to focus. Exhilaration began to soar through me stronger and stronger with each step closer I took. Walking at a normal pace. Having to hold myself back from running. I walked confidently and steadily. Taking deep breathes, controlling my limbs, controlling my breathing. Within three feet of Emilio I stopped. Because of the harsh wind he was completely oblivious. Unaware I was now standing behind him. For a few moments I stood watching every move he took. It all seemed to be in slow motion. Tunnel vision. I didn't feel like me. I felt some strange sensation within, not knowing the name of that particular emotion. Not knowing why I felt I was in the middle of a nightmare, hoping I would awake. But I was a wake. My brain understood what I was doing. Some other part of me, however, was playing catch up, lagging too far behind. Needing what I was doing to be explained. Dumbed down. Taking the gun from my coat pocket, leaning forward placing it to the back of his head, as he pulled weeds out from the flower bed. Without hesitation or emotion I squeeze the trigger. I felt a small kick from the pistol, Emilio falling forward. Dead among the flowers. Whatever sick and perverted thoughts Emilio was thinking, the last thing to go through his mind was the bullet. The only sound that was heard was a dull thud. Taking a couple of steps back. A couple of deeper breathes. I needed a drink. I needed something. It seemed easy but altogether too hard. I was astonished how quickly a life can be taken. A life can be gone faster than a blink of an eye.

I knew Philippine was only a few yards around the corner in the garden shed. I screamed as loud as I could muster and my lungs allowed and waited. Pulling my right hand behind my back. Philippine appearing with shock on her face, looking at me for a few delayed moments. Giving me time to catch a breath. Composing myself, I point at Emilio. I felt I was about to cave in. Philippine like the devoted mother she was, rushed to her dead son's body.

"I think he has taken a heart attack," I announced.

Proud I did not have quivering to my voice. Despite my knees starting to feel like jelly and Santa's big belly. Philippine falling to her knees to check Emilio. Moving as fast as my feet permitted before the truth registered. Reaching out my arm for the second time. Aiming for her head, pulling the trigger. Feeling the familiar small kick of the pistol. Philippine was dead. Laying over her son. The bitter end was not bitter at all. It was more joyous than I expected. In fact it was so sweet I could feel my teeth ache. The end was the sweetest thing I have ever experienced. Sweeter and tastier than chocolate fudge cake. Mother and son in amongst the flowers. Red blood flowed into the earth's ground polluting the beauty of what would grow. It was a rose bed of blood.

Standing over their lifeless bodies, looking down on them knowing finally that my torment from these two deranged monsters was over. I suddenly felt myself begin to shake, my heart to pound, my breathing erratic, confused to what this was. I realised it was the adrenaline leaving my system. My body profused with new oxygen. I had to fight a little to gain my composure. This took a few moments. Clearing my mind I had to concentrate on the task of dealing with Nicolas. Having pulled the trigger and taken their life's I now knew that I could take Nicolas's without a second thought. And I would.

CHAPTER SEVENTY-ONE

The Walk to Freedom

17:26pm 9 November 2006
Part Two and Body Three

Slipping out of my boots after leaving four muddy footprints on the back hall floor which lead to the kitchen. Pulling off my drenched coat, I let it fall and lay upon the kitchen floor. The heat hit my skin as soon as I re-entered the house. I was shaking. At first I thought it to be from the cold. Then perhaps the shock. To find out it was freedom soaring through me, welcoming me home. Welcoming me back to life. It missed me as much as I missed it. I was almost across the finish line. The thunder rolls for one last time. Currently in second place, slowly taking over and passing. Taking a deep breath, wiping the sneer off my face, I rush to be by my husband's side for the final time. Philippine's face stuck in my mind. My heart starting to feel relief. My walk was to bring Nicolas's death, giving me my own sovereignty. As I blink that muddy path with tall green trees I could see again. Entering the bedroom, Nicolas still unconscious. My second raunchy outfit for the evening would be my final. The death veil will then cover the third and final lifeless body. I changed into a red lacy bra and matching thong, in record time. It was the skimpiest thong I had ever seen. If I had pulled it on too fast or hard, it surely would have ripped. The colour red, an intended mockery of blood to flow. Nicolas's last sight would be one of a sexy woman. His wife.

The woman who was about to kill him within the next four minutes. The cuckoo popped his head out from the clock one last time, as it hung over the fireplace in Nicolas's bedroom. For five seconds or so it played a traditional Swiss tune. With a little family in its chalet, popping out to dance on the balcony. It was a charming hand carved Swiss clock. A sweet creation, which only belongs in a loving family home. It was out of place in Nicolas's bedroom and in this house.

Kissing Nicolas and running my tongue over his neck and earlobe. I climbed over him. Enticing him. Whispering: "Wake up, darling, wake up and fuck me again. I hope this outfit turns you on half as much as your hard cock turns me on. We cannot waste a minute. There is plenty of time for sleep."

To my advantage he did not yet understand the depth of my words. Reluctantly he was like a child first thing in the morning, refusing and hating to get up for school. Nicolas was always the child. Dramatic. Spoilt. Kissing his lips, grabbing his dick. Yeah he was beginning to stand. That stance never failed to be effective. Lifting Nicolas's hands I put them on my tits and tell him to squeeze. Running his left hand down to my ass.

"Squeeze it hard and spank me the way it turns you on. Spank me like the bad girl I am. I must be punished. Or am I too good and you want to introduce me to the darkness. To the adulthood of pleasure?"

He was starting to come alive now. Fast. For another two minutes and thirty seconds he had life in his body and pulsating in his cock. And blood which did not run free. Teasing him. Playing with him. Encouraging my husband to follow me onto the balcony.

"Come, fuck me on the balcony like we've done before, then we can get into bed and warm up, fucking each other till we can't fuck anymore. We won't feel the cold air when you're pounding my hot, wet cunt. I'll let you do ANYTHING you want to me tonight. ANYTHING."

"Oh you will, you bitch. I know you will. I'm going to taste that ripe succulent cunt first. It might be the last time, for a while anyhow."

The biggest cheekiest smile filled both Nicolas's face and eyes. Within two seconds he was through the French doors. I now had one minute and forty-nine seconds. Time was closing in. I knew the meaning to his statement but he did not know the meaning to mine. That was the most important aspect of all. Adrenaline was increasing. My heart was prepared. Not once taking a moment to realise, when propositions are made which sound too good to be true, they usually are. Wife or no wife. When there is a change in character, there is always a purpose. Usually a significant purpose. Telling Nicolas: "Hold on one second. I have to get a pillow for my knees, your cock is going to have such attention paid to him my knees will need support. He is going to be well used tonight. I am going to love him so good right now. He won't know what's hit him. By the time I'm finished with you, you will never be off me. You will want to fuck me every minute of every day and you shall. I am going to make you the happiest husband who ever lived. I have so much wildness in me. I feel like a panther. I feel like going a little mad. Do you want to go a little mad with me tonight, husband dearest?"

I could hear him mumbling something or other, I wasn't particularly interested in knowing what he said. As I return to the French doors, Nicolas wide awake, leaning on the balcony balustrade, stroking his bundle of joy with one hand, holding a brandy glass in the other. He was always so proud of his cock. He acted as though he owned the only cock in the world. As sexy and seductively as I knew how, I walked with the pillow covering my stomach. My right hand behind my back. Dropping the pillow to the ground by his feet. Manoeuvring my left hand on to my hip. Flashing a naughty schoolgirl look, one which suggested you're going to have a whole lotta fun. Cancel all appointments here I come. I take two steps back in the event that he would lunge. Pulling the gun from behind my back and aim. I left enough time for what was about to occur sink in. The fear of what was about to come advertised in his disbelieving eyes. The realisation in my prey's eyes was amusing. A delighted fulfilled smiled was advertised on my face. Both of Nicolas's hands raised in response. The brandy glass breaking on the ground spilling its contents. I did not blink, not a flinch I did not allow it to disrupt me. In the blink of an eye the cards can change hands, too easily and too quickly. I learnt the rules, I live by the rules. Lead by example. A typical yet unproductive attempt to save his life. No words spoken. He froze like an icicle found on a windowsill in deep winter. No longer the tyrant merely a wannabe. Now reduced to a quivering begging mortal. Still thinking himself the god he never was. God was an entity he would never meet. Spit trickling out of his mouth. Tears falling like a child who fell off his bicycle, crying for his mama. Finally managing to scream: "Mama, Emilio. HELP ME, HELP ME."

Reduced to the coward he always has been by a woman he had robbed everything from, including trying to rob me of my own life. I was the weakened being who fought back. The tables are turned. I have only one ace to find. The black ace. And then the kiss of death can be bestowed upon the motionless lips.

"Don't worry, poor baby, your mama and Emilio are waiting for you. In HELL. I have a bullet each in their heads and blood flows into a rose bed of blood like yours will now. Goodnight sleep tight."

Laughing as evil as I could manage. Like a witch, like Philippine, like my aunt but not quite as good. She had more years to practice than I. Ensuring I kept my promise. The one I made to myself. Their last sight would be of me. The last sound they would hear would be of glory. My glory. As they close their eyes to never open again. I take from them. I win. I had twenty seconds left. The clock was ticking away. The closer the time approached the louder the ticks became. Hearing nothing else but a clock. And heartbeats. His and mine. My hand did not tremor. Not this time. Seeing nothing else but red. Red blood which was about to be drawn. As Nicolas moved to fall onto his knees, to beg me for mercy which I would not grant, feeling the familiar kick for the third time this day. No more fear dwelled in me. Falling over the balcony. For this I was grateful. Making it easier for me to dispose of his corpse. In his death he did one half decent thing for me. I could not ask for much more than that. The Beaumont family now reunited in hell.

I took two steps forward I looked down over Nicolas. All I could feel was blood. I felt blood flooding through me. I could hear the sound of the glacier water flooding downstream into the village of Zermatt. My blood sounded just like that. I felt hot. I felt weak but strong all at the same time. Reality was now hitting me. My body, my brain was under some kind of new transformation. Attack. I suppose I was the equivalent to a blind person. A person who once had sight, abruptly losing it. Sounds become more defined. Smells heighten. That was me. My mind kept flashing back to the Matterhorn. The Snowboat. Claude. The Glacier Express. I think I felt like a pregnant woman: emotions all mixed up. Feeling everything at once, but nothing at all. Before today I did not know that blood smelt like metal. Copper to be more precise. The clean cold wind was tarnished by the potent smell of copper. The nauseating smell of death. And evil. I could taste it. Not needing to compose myself this time. Rushing downstairs to the garden in my red lacy underwear. I didn't need other clothing, despite the coldness of the gales which blew and the rain which fell. I neither required a coat. I didn't require shoes. The games had to conclude. There was no time to waste. I hadn't found the black ace. The winning card I have all day been searching for. I hadn't won until I bestowed the death kiss upon my dead husband's lips. Standing by his head I fall to my knees. I lean over putting one hand on his forehead, the other to his throat as I held a Swiss ragged army knife against it. Just in case. It is always the just in case which could too easily turn the tables. Rolling the dices once more, when they should be still, the games should be ended. With trepidation in my heart but no fear felt, gently and delicately I kiss his dead lips. The death veil shrouded his face now for all time. The game was now won. I knew what Nicolas's death brought. It brought the start. The new birth of Grace Van Burge.

CHAPTER SEVENTY-TWO

Soul

I stood beneath the fresh falling snow unsullied until it touched my flesh. My abused and poisoned flesh. I close my eyes and breath in, holding my breath I have found my soul. Snow speaks my language.

CHAPTER SEVENTY-THREE

Burial

A funeral to bury a loved one in sanctified ground. When a person is not a loved one, no funeral needs to take place. No kind words spoken about the lifeless body from when they once lived. No tears fall to symbolise the sadness felt. Does everybody deserve a funeral? I do not believe so... We all have to be put somewhere that much is true. A person should be gotten rid of in the manner of which they once lived. If one is not religious or believes in God or anything for that matter, they will not believe they will go to heaven in the next life. Go to heaven or go to hell, whichever it may be just get the hell away from me.

CHAPTER SEVENTY-FOUR

From Bodies to Ashes

12:54am 10 November 2006

Drinking wine and celebrating my newfound freedom and fortune. I ate like a pig. Everything that was in the fridge and cupboards consumed. I cleaned up blood and burned bodies. Out with the old and in with the new. I felt like a brand new person, because that was what I had turned into. I was a new woman with a new name. A new history, a new future. After I've tended to them, I will tend to myself. I will restore my body mind and soul. I will have a new identity. In my new life I must not resemble what I once was. I must look in a mirror and only recognise Grace. Grace Van Burge.

Dragging their bodies to the shed, out of sight. No eye witnesses to confess my dark secret. All three were now ready and waiting. Lifting up the floorboards inside the garden shed. My goal, to dig the deepest and biggest hole I was humanly capable of producing. Burying scum into the cesspit of the earth. The earth under the shed was softer than the earth exposed to the elements in the rest of the garden. It was easier to dig, regardless of the gruelling task of digging for seven hours. Now was not the time to be lazy or to take the easy way out. Every muscle in my body ached, including muscles I did not realise I owned. Multiple blistering had formed on my hands. My hands were crippled as though I were an elderly woman inflicted with arthritis. So much so, it was harder the second time to drag their bodies from inside the shed to the hole. Pain from my hands caused sharp pains to flash like electric shocks around my body, primarily into my neck. The hole was approximately six feet deep, by six feet long and four feet wide. Deep enough for three bodies and all their belongings to be burned. Dragging Philippine over to the hole, enthusiastically kicking her in. Standing back for a single moment realising how final this was. This was really happening. Glory I reaped. Throwing Nicolas on top of her, then Emilio. Pouring petrol over all three of them approximately five gallons, which was stocked up for the lawnmowers inside the shed since last spring. Striking a match with great pleasure, flicking it in on them as I stood a good four feet away by the shed door. There was a deafening whoosh as the petrol ignited bursting up into the air. Reminding me of a black magic spell, from the movie *Bell Book and Candle*, there was pure evil in them after all. I set them alight at twelve that night. I could feel the heat on my skin as the flames raged. Evoking a memory of a Halloween bonfire from when I was a child. Almost immediately I could smell the acrid smell of burning flesh. Repulsive. I exited in a rush, an attempt to stop myself from vomiting. While I was waiting for the bodies to diminish, I filled up and brought wheelbarrow after wheelbarrow of their belongings down to the shed. Throwing them into the blazing flames. Instead of thinking of the best way to do this, I had to be dynamic. I had to work with what I had. Going through the kitchen with the filled wheelbarrow, taking a tea cloth I ran it under a full blasting tap. On return to the shed I had to tie the damp cloth over my mouth and nose, to prevent the smell of burning flesh and petrol which was making me gag. I spent four hours and twenty-three minutes burning them and their belongings. I was amazed how quickly bodies burn into nothingness. If anybody had told me how quickly this can transform I would never have believed them. Seeing it with my own two eyes I could not honourably deny it. One moment flesh and blood, a form known as a body. The next moment ashes are left. No similitude of the person who once lived. Their belongings helped to suppress the flames from soaring out of control. All resemblance of bodies had to be burnt. Only nothingness could remain. At four thirty-six in the morning a pile of ash lingered. Every trace of the Beaumont family I was satisfied was now gone. By eleven minutes past five I had closed the door to the shed. I had concluded raking the ashes to level them out. Placing the shed floor back into position. I moved a lawnmower on top of the boards I had moved and other garden tools. One look nothing would seem to be out of place. There wasn't anything suspicious. Just a fowl stench. Everything was as peaceful as it was before their cremation. A regular garden shed, in a regular rich garden in Geneva. I was confident no telltail signs were exposed. I was confident I had seen the end of the Beaumont family. I would now live. Live in peace. Only a house remains, the battlefield cleared of blood and bodies.

PART SIXTEEN

Ultimate Sinner

CHAPTER SEVENTY-FIVE

Sinners to Winners

Nicolas believed with assurance he would win. Believing he will kill yet another beautiful young wife. Nicolas Beaumont was an inadequate man. He was a weak and worthless individual. Cockiness is a disadvantage for one's ability to succeed. Slowing down one's senses to act and react. Automatically taking for granted they will win. Because one has won in the past, does not mean they are the best. It doesn't even indicate that this person should have won. It could have been pure luck. Most likely from being underhand. The moon may have been in the perfect position on that particular day. One's star signs may have indicated they shall win, lending a helping hand. The following day the winner could have lost everything to the loser. Being positive is a good motivator, being complacent an inner evil. I had to win because I did not wish to be the next victim of the Beaumont family. I did not win from pure luck, nor the moon or the stars. I won because I played the cards right. I waited, timing my defence perfectly. I moved in sequence to the music playing inside my head. I used the cuckoo clock as my motivator. Keeping me within the time I allocated. Throwing enough cards out to confuse, luring my opponent into a false sense of security. To become the winner in such a deplorable plot, it was inevitable all involved had to become a sinner. To become a sinner and do what it was I must, winning, in turn, would be the glory for the living to take. To become the winner we must all become the ultimate sinner.

CHAPTER SEVENTY-SIX

Sovereign's Day

I fell asleep beneath the moon, stars and falling snow. I fell asleep for the first time without feeling pressure, fear or a combination of negative thoughts. There was no panic in my blood that night. I did get wet and next morning feeling the symptoms of a cold starting, but what is a cold when I now had my life back. It made me feel alive because I could now feel. The deadly disease which overpowered my body now cured. There will be no more days of playing the pessimist, my later days will be more affirmative. When I awoke I was not as certain. Breakfast was served each morning at seven sharp. It was past breakfast, nobody came. No noise was made. I did not want to become elated prematurely. I couldn't believe it, fully accepting that they had gone. What I had the ability to achieve. I knew it, at the same time I didn't. It was the just in case niggling at me. Yesterday was like a dream. Did I really murder three people? Did I really burn and bury their corpses? Doubting reality. Was this just a dream which confused me, one I believed was real? Did I dream my plot? I'm always getting confused between dreams and reality. Is today the day I am meant to kill? If I have already killed them, I thought I would feel more the next morning. I was sure I would feel something. All I needed was to get this day past, then reality may sink it. I was the typical battered wife. The feeling of being put down constantly, needing permission for everything. Not able to be me. Not able to be my own person. I had much adapting to undergo. I was now what I should be, free and my own person, to make my own choices. I no more require permission. I can do whatever the hell I desire. I can do anything. Waking up on the sun lounge I looked over the gardens, peaking over my duvet like a nervous child, no sign of Emilio tackling the usual morning gardening. Nor would there be any sign of him there again. There would be no more breakfast at seven sharp. There would be no more pinging on the computer, indicating there is a message waiting for Nicolas to respond to. Another whore. Another bitch. There would be no more lurking around the landing for me, hearing what I could. Running around the house on the sly like I once did. Like a disobedient child. That is in the past. I chose what I do and how I do it. It's finally over. No noise, no movement throughout the house, unless I create it. Yesterday I said goodbye to the old. Today it a new day. Today is my sovereign's day.

PART SEVENTEEN

TRUTH

CHAPTER SEVENTY-SEVEN

Project Ukraine No5

10 November 2006
08:10

Realising I must take a crucial precaution. Becoming caught up in everything which took presidency, I cannot let an urgent matter be overlooked. Especially one which has the ability to become as detrimental as the Beaumont family were. I hope it's not too late. How could I have forgotten? It is these stupid slip-ups which will get me caught. I commenced to panic. Only for a moment. I couldn't afford any longer. It's human nature. Hands starting to tremble. The first sign of sweat appeared since I shovelled up the earth to which was their transportation to hell fell from my brow. I could feel a deep enraged frown form in-between my eyes and fury building up within. Sure my eyes looked like a reptile seething with immense anger. Angry with myself for being sloppy at this stage. It was the unknown which frightened me. It was the potential danger which could lurk. I needed to take care of them ASAP. The unknown people who demand a reply. The unidentified strangers who I knew I must communicate with. My gut nagging at me, a little voice in the back of my mind telling me there is more danger to come. Take care of it. The computer still clear from a password. Looking at Nicolas's contacts and reading messages to and from his business acquaintances. No names were stored on his contacts, odd. They were referred to as No.1, No.2 and so forth. In total there were five. In the messages to each other, no names were given, ever. Apart from Nicolas's. I did not know everything which was going on, so the prospect of somebody calling to the house panicked me. This could be the aspect which sinks me. Scanning conversations with my eyes, they moved a million miles an hour. My brain struggling to keep up. Fear has a way of speeding up one's senses. Yes there were many daunting messages. Many which required replies. Too many for my liking. Prudently reading, vigilantly wording my sentences. Glad I observed how Philippine and Nicolas spoke to one another over the years. I had to respond. I had to buy myself time. Just a day or two. In my boredom I observed. Allowing me to present myself as Nicolas or Philippine if need be, appropriately, to fool who is on the other side. It is those who are on the other side who could perchance destroy everything I have fought for and gained. My freedom cannot merely last twenty-four hours. It must last for the rest of my life. I must move quickly. Until I am that old lady on my deathbed who owns a useless body. Not a young woman of twenty-five. That is much too young for death.

As I made a pot of percolated coffee French vanilla flavoured beans I grinded. The strong coffee which kept my mind alert, while the vanilla soothed me and like a scented candle permeates the air. One particular conversation haunted my mind, so much so as I went to pour coffee into my cup, spilling the contents over the worktop, dripping onto the kitchen floor and burning my left hand. I did not clean it up right away. I did not hold my hand under cold water for the advised ten minutes. Alternatively, I rushed into the study to reread those daunting messages, articulating some kind of acceptable reply. It was the sort of message which did not deserve to wait for an answer. It was that imperative. It was that chilling. I was glad I was not too naïve to read between the lines.

Project No 5 Ukraine to Project LG

10 November 2006 19:28

(Project LG), let us know immediately once your wife has left. I have Yana ready to come. She has her papers to enter Geneva. Furthermore the Commissioner of Immigration is to allow twenty

Russian and Ukrainian girls through. It cost two million Swiss Francs. It is now your responsibility to ensure that the girls make that money back. FAST. Don't make me wait, or I will arrange a visit to see you and your family. I don't care to do so. I prefer when I don't know the faces of the people I communicate with. It makes for a better business relationship. If you force my hand I will be very displeased. I become short-tempered, I don't listen. I want results, that's what I am paying you for. It is dangerous to make me wait. I'm never happy when things do not go my way. I hope this is understood.

Project No 5 Ukraine to Project LG

10 November 2006 23:01

(Project LG), has your fucking wife left yet or must I send someone to pack her things for you????? I'm starting to get angry. Albanians have no patience.

Project No 5 Ukraine to Project LG

11 November 2006 02:46

Why the fuck are you not answering me?????????

How long does it take the Swiss to complete a task??????

You must understand Albanian people do not like to wait!

I will not say this again. Now fuckin hurry up ...

Albanians NEVER take this long and are not this sloppy.

Answer me fast or there will be reprisals.

Project LG to Project No 5 Ukraine

11 November 2006 08:33

Sorry to take this long to reply.

I was occupied in completing the designated task.

I was trying to avoid being sloppy.

It took longer than I had estimated.

She has left. Forget her.

When will Yana be arriving?

Two million Swiss Francs won't be a problem raising here in Geneva.

I would estimate that would be raised by the two of them in less than two weeks.

Perhaps a week if I work them hard.

That's why you recruited me.

I have the contacts, I possess the fear factor.

I like getting my own way and in Geneva I do.

In turn will get you your own way.

Then we are both happy.

Project No 5 Ukraine to Project LG

11 November 2006 8:35

It's about fucking time.

When I say get back to me in three hours, you get back to me in three hours.

If you have to stop in the middle of a job to update me, then you stop.

You NEVER make me wait.

I DON'T LIKE WAITING.

It is I who dispatch orders, you are simply the little person who jumps when ordered.

Don't forget your role.

Project LG to Project Ukraine No 5

11 November 2006 8:37

Of course I did.

Whatever you say goes.

I understand. I will not prove a disappointment.

Project Ukraine No 5 to Project LG

11 November 2006 8:39

Yana will be arriving in Geneva 14 November at 07:30.

Collect her at the airport with your chauffeur.

Take her to your house.

Make her believe you are going to marry her.

Show her the wedding plans, the emails about the church and honeymoon arrangements.

Let her see the cost of everything. Keep all quotes. Take her in.

Once a Ukrainian woman sees the vast costs of these things, they become more the whore.

They will eat right out of your hands.

Then blind side her on the 24 November.

Between the 14th and the 24th wine and dine her, but not in public.

Give her some of your wife's most expensive belongings to wear.

Make her think you bought them especially for her.

She won't need them now. Wrap them up.

Make her feel special.

You can take liberties with her, but do not I repeat, do not rough her up.

The other girls will then arrive on the 24th.

Between now and Yana's arrival arrange for the girls to start work from the 24th onwards.

Get bookings. Confirmed bookings.

Have all the shackles and locks setup.

I know you can't have them at your house. It isn't safe.

Never shit where you eat.

Which address will they be staying at?

I will send you details throughout the day for Project Russia No 149, Project Russia No 162, and Project Russia No 201.

Having no idea what the arrangements were prior, having no choice but to scan over old messages to and from Project Ukraine No 5. There wasn't anything in that folder. I looked through the hard copy of Project Ukraine No 5. Nothing. Searching frantically through conversations under folders Project Russia No 149. Nothing. Folders Project Russia No 162 and 201. Nothing. What the hell am I going to do? Searching through folders stored in the filing cabinet. A very thin folder titles Project Russia 149, a slightly thicker folder titled Project Russia 162, but a very thick folder titled Project Russia No 201. Still no indication of any other premises. The clock was ticking. I could feel my shoulders weighing down. My heart pounding. Sweat pouring. I smelt vile. When the cuckoo popped out his head, it made me lose all strain of thought. My left ear becoming hot. The superstitious wise tail of being talked about. I was sure I could hear typing of Project Ukraine No 5. Getting ready to give me a grilling for taking too long to reply. I searched through drawers and drawers of papers, folders titled dubious names. I was at a loss. Where do I go from here? Trying to calm down, having to reduce my heart rate knowing I could then think better. Standing at the bar I take a small brandy. Pouring myself a second glass. Taller. Hell what have I to lose? I've got three days to get my things and leave. I have three days to sort myself out. Fuck these Albanians. I can't be bothered anymore. I'm more interested in me, myself and I. I have a lot to take care of. A new life to start living. Just abscond, I could get away with it. There is no signs that any murders took place her last night. They believe me dead. I will check through every book, every shelf and every cupboard ensuring nothing is hiding between the pages or at the back of anything that will give my identity away. Wedding photographs must be burnt. I do not know for certain that they don't know what I look like. I can only presume. Until I know differently I will plan my escape under the belief they know me. I have adapted the will of changing the things I can, neglecting the things I cannot. I can't put the house up for sale. I cannot sell. That is not important right now. I merely need a distraction. If I put the house up for sale today, when they arrive they may assume Nicolas and his family fucked them over by leaving. I will refuse all offers and in a year maybe two, if it is safe to do so I can then come back. But right now there is nothing more certain, Geneva must become my past.

Lighting a fire in the study, I start to look through papers getting rid of the majority of them. Filing cabinet, done. I start to look through the desk drawer. Three hours and forty-two minutes later there was my answer. In a file titled "The first to go" was the address of the house. The house, Project Ukraine No 5 was asking for. I go onto the chat room immediately. I can buy myself a little more time.

Project LG to Project Ukraine No 5

11 November 11:31

Not to question your authority I know the address but would it be wise to put it on here?

Why the hell didn't I think of that hours ago? I am starting to fuck this up.

Project Ukraine No 5 to Project LG

11 November 11.36

I was testing you...

You seem to be acting somewhat differently since yesterday.

I know your wife has left but you're like us, heart of stone. Women come and go.

No feelings.

So do not claim you are mourning her.

No you should not put it on here.

That was our first rule of engagement. Have you forgotten?

If you had messaged me the address you would have been fired before noon today.

I may be in Albania and untouchable.

The AM have contacts in every city and major town throughout the world.

Don't fuck with me, because I guarantee it will only end badly for you.

The police won't touch us. They are scared of us and our families. We're relentless.

We have access to weapons beyond the ability of the police.

They can only imagine our resources and then still not fully grasp the magnitude of our abilities.

We are a God of our own.

We are a government of our own.

Considering we can buy any government, considering we own the government.

They want to get rich just like us. Just like you.

We are more puissant than the Nazis ever were.

There is nowhere to hide.

There is nowhere to run.

    There is only us to run into.

CHAPTER SEVENTY-EIGHT

Albanian Robots

Bleaching the house from attic to basement twice a day for two days. Burning papers, boxes, books, clothing, anything and everything which could leave a trail. Anything which was handwritten had to go. There could be no trace back that Nicolas Philippine or Emilio did not sell up and move on. Even if it was abrupt. If this really did happen, then there would be no indication of them left in a house they no longer own. When I was in the attic I was looking for things which may have belonged to me. Finding many boxes with women's names written on and woman's belongings inside. A lot of the boxes were titled Project something or other. Were we all a project? I hadn't seen my passport in years. Everything I had in my case when I first came here to live as a bride, was taken from me six months later. Searching for my passport. It was paramount. The most important thing I needed to find. Without that there was no getting out of Switzerland. Finally after two hours and eighteen minutes I found it in the bottom of a box. On the outside of the box was written 2001? What the significance was with the question mark, I did not know. My initial thought was the year I arrived, questioning the year I would die. He'll call me paranoid! My passport was still in date, only just. I wasn't certain how much longer I had on the damn thing. I had my old name on it. In fact it wasn't updated to my married name. That's okay. I don't require Beaumont to be on anything belonging to me. Its better I'm not associated with the family. This aspect kept me free from knowing them. When we married they did not take my fingerprints, they did not take a photograph, only a signature. A signature which will not be attached to me any longer. When I change my name, my appearance I will change everything. It only takes one small thing like a signature to explode into a great by thing. Rending the name and the new appearance unproductive. I will have my new identity all put together soon. The passport I now hold will be long gone and the person it belonged to. No old signatures to creep up on me, only the one indicating we were married.

I packed my most beautiful clothing, jewellery and other possessions. I was given many beautiful belongings since being married to Nicolas. It's a shame Nicolas wasn't a better husband. It could have been the perfect life. After I had my belongings packed, I revaluated my scenario. I did not want to stand out this time. Five years has passed since I went everywhere to be noticed. I was freer then. I didn't have too many tales to hide. Things have changed. I have changed. I must blend in. I must not for the longest time bring attention onto myself. The AM have contacts all over the world. I must play it down. Taking all my most beautiful belongings out of my case and repacking. Feeling sad. Knowing it was vitally important. Glamour or no glamour I must be smart. I am almost out of this. It's almost behind me. I could leave a young and beautiful looking corpse or grow old and somewhere in this messed up life find happiness. This time packing leggings and jeans, T-shirts and jumpers. There isn't anything wrong with being ordinary once in a while, whether one's life depends on it or not. No evening dresses, nothing bling, bling. I packed my beautiful possessions into bin bags. Accumulating forty-seven. That was a lot of clothing and jewels, considering I have not been out of the house in years. I took them to the bottom of the long garden, down by the Virgo rose bush. I dug ten deep holes. Burying them, keeping them safe. I had every intention on coming back for them. I didn't have children, therefore to me they were like my little babies, I had to keep them safe. They are all I have now. Hopefully it would be safe after a year, two at the most to come back. If not, I would come in the middle of the deep dark winter, in the middle of the night and like a thief take what was mine. I earned those things. Although I did take a few pieces of jewellery just in case I was short on cash and needed money fast. That was my backup plan. Always have a backup plan. I did have Nicolas's money and credit and debit cards, I would be okay for money. Trying to minimize the chances of being traced. Committing

Nicolas's bank details and other house addresses to memory. I could not have any paper trails or trust a computer. Modern technology is said to be our friend, it is only the smart and the fraudulent' friend. Everything that has been designed for a good has been proven to aid a criminal better.

I threw out food from the fridge, canned food from the cupboards, toiletries which weren't wanted, everything had to be bare. I did not want any indication that anyone had lived here for a while. Taking an extra precaution of putting the rubbish in the neighbour's bins during the night. Leaving the house bins empty. Cleaning, packing and repacking. A woman's work is never done. Setting out to place doubt in the Albanians' minds. Wanting them to doubt and to think perhaps Nicolas was contacting them from elsewhere other than Geneva. As long as they could not pick up on the IP address this illusion would prove ideal. Presuming they knew Nicolas had many homes around Europe. I would expect them to know thoroughly their employees, regardless of meeting them or not. One does not need to meet the boss, these types of organisations have many little men. Men right here in Geneva. Men who I must make sure do not find this building interesting until after I have gone. Men who meticulously find out the information one takes for granted to be protected. With the technology they would own, bank details, the size of underwear one wears, the secrets hidden that if revealed will destroy a life, if not multiple. If somebody has changed their name, if they're dead or alive. If someone is dying from an incurable disease. This and more is the information which is at the fingertips of the people we should fear the most. This is the age for wars between Muslims and Albanians. Both fighting to rule the world but in different ways. For different reasons. The Germans are long forgotten. What a distressing concept.

They probably knew about the log cabin in Sweden Nicolas bought me for our first Christmas together. The cabin we never did visit. I had my doubts if he purchased it at all. Or if he did, now I'm thinking was it a place where he kept his captives, or to bury their bodies deep in the woods. It was remote. It's possible the Albanians are working from there. Is Sweden destroyed too by these vultures? Isn't there any corner of this world which is untouched, pure and free from the grasp of scum? It could explain why he never took me there. It could explain a great deal of things. But I do not have the inclination to be concerned about these matters. I am not James Bond. I am not a secret agent, nor am I being paid for putting my life on the line. I am a woman who only wants to rebuild a life. As boring or selfish as that may sound, I do not care. I will not meddle. If they come after me, I will do what I must until they kill me. I am not a stupid woman but I do not possess specialist skills to take on an army of brutal beings. Could I even call them people when they lack so many essential human emotions? I think personally I will consider them Albanian robots. They have no minds of their own, they have a dictator. Disciplined like a robot. They are told how to be, how to function, who to kill when and where to do it. When one does not think for themselves what else could they be considered but a robot?

CHAPTER SEVENTY-NINE

Albanian War Lords

I could not believe my eyes as I searched through Nicolas's emails and documents. He had documents in every room in the house, hidden behind things and within things. At the back of shelves, behind cabinets, with false bottoms in display cabinets and chests. So many secrets to hide. I found a great deal that would have incriminated him and many others. People I heard of and knew, others I didn't. Important people. Rich, famous people. This was my leverage. Without leverage there wasn't anything to bargain with if they came after me. If I put my findings in the public domain, a great deal of politicians, judges, solicitors, doctors, accountants and police officers, even a few singers here and there would be shown up for what they truly are. What celeb could suffer such shame? Nicolas Beaumont was a very bad man. I felt that Switzerland was a faithfully pure country. Untouched. Masses of beauty to be found. Mountains of high Geneva Lake of deep with the colour of ocean blue. A godsend. One of those places which had not moved on in morals and standards since the 1940s. Perhaps the very reason for attracting many rich and famous people to move there over the decades. Peace. Tranquil. Safety. Sadly like the rest of the world it has moved on. It is a new time. The time we now live in is filled with evilness and danger. Money and murder. Rape and prostitution. Drugs and trafficking. What has this world come to? On November tenth 2006, to my horror, I found out Switzerland was not as pure as I formerly believed. If I had found this out on November ninth 2006 or earlier, I would have been heartbroken. Dismayed. Instead I found this out on November tenth, since then I had murdered three people. I have cleaned up their mess, burned their bodies. Any sign that they once lived within this house has been erased. I had no more ambitions or hopes. The truth I found about Geneva did not disturb me. Nothing much does once a person has taken a life. I now figure, well that's life. The world is as tough outside as it was in here. Perhaps I had it easy compared to many out in the big bad world. I have come to believe we are all treated badly. My world was just smaller. Who really is in charge of their own life? We are all dictated to in one way or another, be it by politicians or religion, the law of the land. There is always something or someone to control us. One thing for sure is we all die. It isn't necessarily the world or the country we live in, it is very much the people, not who we surround ourselves by but those who impose their will onto our lives. Until November tenth at ten past eight a.m. I was merely living in a fairy tale. A life that I wished was true. Perhaps a story created by Walt Disney in HD. I was mesmerised by the bright colours which a dream can have, which the world just does not possess. The world is only filled with grey clouds, thunderstorms and hail. I was merely waiting for it to be my turn to become the princess, wearing a beautiful ballroom gown and for my prince to come along and save me. This rarely ever happening. Our only savour is ourselves and a gun. I was disgusted when I found out by reading an article online that it had been reported by the Geneva-based Daily Tribune De Genève, that a Geneva Deputy Public Prosecutor Yves Bertossa had announced:

"The Albanian mafia is one of the most powerful ones among nine identified mafias in the world. The criminal organisation is laundering a part of income in Geneva economy restaurants, bars, real estate and cabarets."

According to him the drugs which the Geneva police found were transported from Afghanistan through Turkey, Pakistan, Iran and the Balkans into Europe. Switzerland is already a wealthy country and with Zurich as the financial capital of the world. Geneva is considered to be a rich man's playground. Millions are made there each year, millions are spent there each year. It is far from a cheap country. Is it then considered perfectly fine to spoil a wonderfully splendid country with so many riches, in so many ways, including losing respect from people like me who loved their country faithfully? Basically dressing up a façade of its purity and excellence with cowbells and traditional outfits, with sleepy streets and peaceful villages. Luring the world into their territory under false pretences. Is supporting gangs considered fair when they do not need blood money? Are people really so unimportant as long as the rich keep getting richer. They drink their fine wines and smoke their Cuban imported cigars with ridiculous price tags, while people's lives are being taken away from them. Does wine taste sweeter when blood has been spilt from a teenage girl who made them their money? Who ideally should be at home with a loving family in a warm, safe bed? Or does a cigar taste stronger and more intoxicating when a twelve-year-old girl has been sold and raped, on occasion married off to a pervert? It is far from the dream I once had. The truth disappointed me, thankfully I was not too disappointed. Along with taxes, hurricanes, crooked politicians and broken hearts, the world is filled with disappointments. I have come to learn how the world is run. How cruel reality is. Since learning the rules I now stand a chance.

Nicolas never gave orders he jumped to them. He wasn't high up. He was basically a puppet on a string. A jockey. When told to take a piss, he takes a piss. When told to be at a kidnapping point, one can rest assure he was there. One can also rest assure that when the Albanian Mafia demand they get their way. They are no better than spoilt children, crying until they get what they want. Instead of crying they shoot bullets. Taking pleasure in breaking another fellow human being's will just because they can. There is no difference between them and dogs pissing on lampposts and street corners, robbing what once belonged to someone else, claiming it to be theirs. When opposed, a bullet, sledgehammer, or an axe will then embed into the flesh of whom they consider the lesser. The offensive one. It is not beneath them to piss on a corpse. Enjoying every second they spent taking a life. When one of them are killed, the uproar the world will hear. Because they feel hurt, they expect us to morn with them. There filth of the earth. Vengeance they will seek. I felt I had no more innocence in me after the abuse of the Beaumont family, after being forced to murder again. But this, this I am naive to. After reading the masses of emails of Nicolas's transactions to and from these gang members. Locations, times, where money would be ready to be collected. Who to ask for, what to say. What colour tie to wear, what signal to gesture. Hotels to wine and dine in, to be seen at, people to make contacts with. Who to manipulate. And who's ass to kiss. Which explains perfectly the reasons for all of Sophie's unimportant parties, where people went to improve their businesses. Build a larger clientele. I did not know what I had been dragged into. I was way over my head. I couldn't figure out how I ended up in the middle of all this. There were many disturbing emails, one in particular which specified exactly their order. Descriptions of girls to set up for a kidnap, down to their size, their height and hair colour, nationality. Clearly a common occurrence considering how the email indicated a particular place to go back to. Details about this particular project was fifty of the world's richest Arabs were looking to buy young white women. The purpose; sex slaves. They were prepared to pay millions for the right girl. Making the Albanian Mafia millions, making Nicolas millions. Albanians have to pollute the earth, destroying everything. Every country, every young person. Every woman of course who is good enough. They rob, launder, murder and so many more illegal immoral despicable things. Everyone has to make a living, but to go about it the way they do is nothing less than outrageous, immoral not overlooking criminal. Who gives them the right to dictate? Stealing people, demanding they reduce themselves to shame and utter humiliation in order to make them rich. To make them feared. No one has that right. No one should. We are born into this world to become a unique individual. We have the right to be who we are designed to be, when forming in that very innocent place named the womb. But that is in an ideal world. A world we simply do not live in. How the hell did Nicolas get mixed up in something as perilous? Was his opulent lifestyle worth all this? The danger he would surely face if he failed. I'm surprised with Nicolas being as dominate as he was, the god he believed himself to be to reduce himself to a mere slave. A secretary like the police who have no authority, taking their instruction by hierarchy. This is very much out of character. The money must have been great.

Once my eyes fell upon this grievous information immediately going online to research. I needed to know exactly what I could have been placed in the middle of. I needed to know if another fight was about to commence. In my life here is always a fight to be fought and won. We all have to lose sometime. This time I did not delude myself, I would not win.

The Albanian Mafia (AM) or Albanian Organised Crime (AOC) are active in not solely Albania but the United States and throughout European counties. Involved in a varied range of treacherous and threatening enterprises including: Drugs, weapons and human trafficking. Passport theft, Prostitution and smuggling of human body parts. It is unbelievable. It is preposterous as to what these people can do and will do. There are strong and powerful, but reckless. Anybody is powerful in a gang and who hide behind guns. Cowards when they stand alone. And weapon free. I thought Nicolas was deprived from all human emotion, but these families who form gangs spreading their fear around the United States and Europe are nothing compared. I can fight the Beaumont family and win, but these other families whose names I cannot pronounce I do not stand a chance. No matter how tough one is, one is never strong enough to fight a war of hundreds of thousands as their competitor. An army couldn't successfully win something like this. Especially when they are radical, no morals, no humanity. When there is nothing to bargain with, no leverage can be found. When one faces the Albanian War Lords one must kill. Kill one, you must kill the rest. Unreasonable, impossible. I Grace Van Burge incapable. One man, one woman can stand alone, one man can kill many, never them all. Their allies are the Sicilian Mafia. Despite the Italian Mafia originally stemming from the Sicilian families and moving across, the AOC have reduced the fear the Italian Mafia once secured. In London the Italian areas now feared by Albanians. They are classed by the governments of many countries as ultraviolent. There is no talking to them, there is only killing. They are radical beyond recognition and comprehension. The history of their creation is said they have been brutalised by conflicts in the Balkans in the 1990s. The Mafia Shqiptare are believed to have taken over the sex trade in London's Soho district. The gang rulers and its members are formed by small families with a strong unbreakable bond, held together by a code of honour and blood feuds. These war lords have become the government's worst nightmare, of course only those politicians who are not involved and genuinely want them seized. Most if not all of the Kosovo Liberation Army members skills were taught to them by Al Qaeda. The Kosovo war played a major role in the rise of the Albanian mafia throughout Europe. Even so, they have become an overawing challenge for the world.

CHAPTER EIGHTY

People

With people around me who don't understand me,
Making life intense to get by, as they always demand.
With people around wanting to drag me down,
Making me sad and wanting me to cry.

With people around wanting me to fail,
Making me stronger much more stubborn to win.
With people around me wanting me to die,
Making me that much more willing to live.
When people are negative,
When they are vile and conceited.
When people are making life awkward,
Tell them to leave you alone.
Stay away.
Tell them to get out of your life, never and to return.
Good riddance to the foul.
Tell them their badness will be found out.

Go to hell and remain.
Be murdered or abstain.

PART EIGHTTEEN

VALEDICTION

CHAPTER EIGHTY-ONE

Power Is Mine

They wanted me dead, dead I am not.
They wanted me gone, gone I am not.
They wanted my life, but my life is mine,
They cannot take anything that's mine.

They were never my family, friends or anything for that matter.
I feel no mercy for them, as they did not me.
Recouping my life, I am recouping me.

Power is mine and they can all die!
Burn, burn till the end of time.
God forgive them not, like I will not.
My life is mine.
Power is mine, go to hell and let the church bells chime.

CHAPTER EIGHTY-TWO

The Stars

I was hoping to fall off to immediate and deep sleep, but the past few day's events started to sink in, too quickly I might add. I had been more robotic, getting on with the tasks at hand. No emotions thus invested. Knowing I had to do it and complete it as quickly as my body permitted. I did not have the time to think about anything. For remorse or regret. While I was snuggled up in bed wearing a long white lace gown with a split up the left leg with boobs revealed, looking sexier than I had done in four years, making me feel uncomfortable but exhilarated. I felt daring. I also felt I didn't suit this kind of outfit anymore. I had too many scars. Telltale signs. Now allowed to wear what I wanted, when I wanted. I am now my own dictator. Relieved I had finally once and for all attained my freedom, no longer being treated like an animal. I snuggled up in bed hearing heavy wind almost like an owl crying, attracting my attention to outside. Too exhausted and in too much pain, after all, it was a hard day's work. Blisters had formed on my hands bothering me greatly. My body desperately needing to sleep, yet my brain was dragging me up out of bed into the cold night air and perilous darkness. I put on my long white lace robe which matched my gown, white bedroom slippers, which had hardly ever been worn, rushing out onto the balcony. I walked into the night, under the large falling fluffy white snowflakes and crisp clean snow. The air was cold, yet fresh. The smell of evilness and death had gone. I ran down the stairs with butterflies filling my stomach and glee filling my body. As I went through the library into the garden, running up and down and around the acres of land like an uncontrollable two-year-old. I lay on a sunlounger on the bricked porch by the library. As I lay there, I gazed at the night sky. It was so very dark, black, it was a starry night the longer I remained gazing, the more stars had become present. I was about to get up, run around for as long as my weary legs could stand it, as I did I stopped for one split second. Fear stopped me. I was certain my knees would cave in beneath me landing on the bricks. I was in no doubt that at any moment Philippine would be coming out to manhandle me back upstairs to the master bedroom. Only to beat me relentlessly. Like a parent would with their disobedient child. Like my father once did. Then realising it was all over, all the demanding and dominance it had gone, because I got rid of it, I got rid of them. No cachous is in my life anymore. I made them go away, forever. I burnt their bodies, I cleaned the mess. I cleansed my sins and found my soul. This was merely the first opportunity for me to think. Really think. I've been occupied by cleaning, searching and researching. It is now time for acceptance. When I leave this house, I will have undisturbed sleep. No more nights of wondering will Philippine be coming for me. Is Nicolas ready to rape me? When reality finally hit home I felt happy that I was able to be myself and nothing but. This was the first feeling I had which indicated I was going to be alright. It will all be just fine. My life has only just begun, again! Life is mine.

We are all born into this world with a purpose predestined for us. Some of us are unaware of what is in store. Others are deeply in touch with their being, their life even as far as their death. Knowing in advance how they will die, when they will die and where. Uncanny? Yes. Useful? Debatable. It can be plausible to ponder that it depends on how much one accepts life, loves life and loves living it. How happy one is within it. It falls down to personal choice. Contributing factors are known to be, age, life style, depression and one's environment. Whatever is meant to be, will be. If it is good enjoy it while it lasts. If it is not so good take a deep breath look to the sky, if it is night then look for the stars. Stars give the strength to live. There is magic within those faraway little white things up high in the sky. Lie beneath the snow, watch the stars until you fall asleep. Answers will come, they will guide you through.

CHAPTER EIGHTY-THREE

Gabriella

Finding photographs of an attractive woman packed in a box, inside a secret panelling in the study wall. Thinking to myself how predictable it was to have a secret panelling in the study. Only in movies I thought they existed. So typical of Nicolas. "Wife" was written on the back of a few of the photographs in conjunction with the year. Thinking how odd it read just "Wife," opposed to a name. She looked like a short woman. She had a small bone structure and petite features, long brown hair, dark brown full of life eyes and olive skin. She was very beautiful, much more beautiful than I. I can see precisely why Sophie felt beneath her and wanted her gone. Finally stumbling upon a photograph with a name, it read "Gabriella." Such a beautiful name for such a beautiful woman. How did she end up making the same mistake as I? Beautiful women aren't always the smartest. Finding a journal which was in Nicolas's handwriting, outraged by what my eyes were exposed to. Taken aback to find that he had admitted murdering Gabriella, the meticulous plan as to how he would kill her and even so heartless as to specify when. I had assumed for quite some time that he had murdered his first wife, but not certain of this prolonged thought until the day I found out they were planning on killing me, finally once and for all, now disturbed by the cold hard truth. I have been too busy for reality to hit home. Whoever said that truth was the best policy, when it is this macabre? Feeling emotional that such an attractive woman had been murdered. I wished I could have helped her. My vision becoming obscured by tears. Feeling guilty, almost shameful for surviving. Pondering over the potential magnitude of women who may have been murdered by these calculating people. Feeling remorseful Gabriella certainly did not receive a sanctified burial. I was even gladder they did not receive one either. They didn't deserve it. They have reaped what they have sown. Taking it upon myself to take one of Gabriella's photographs which was captured from seven years ago, placing it at the end of one of the many gardens along with some flowers and a set of rosary beads. Burying them and saying a little prayer to remember her and laying Gabriella to rest, the only way I could.

"I will remember you and pay respect to you, Gabriella, it is the absolute least that I can do."

It was the only thing that I could think to do. I didn't have any other belongings of Gabriella to pay an honourable tribute.

The next day buying plants and setting tulips above Gabriella's photographs. It was an attempted token of respect which still did not feel enough for me. What could be enough? NOTHING....

CHAPTER EIGHTY-FOUR

The First Flakes of Snow

The first flakes of snow commenced after twenty-four hours, this time landing and remaining on the ground. With the snow it justifiably became colder. I took advantage of the cold air in order to get my body and mind back on track. With each passing day I was slowly getting better; my state of mind improving. I only went out once. I had to remain under the radar. When I did go out it was to purchase hair colour and new makeup. I had a new me to put together. I did not want to stand out in anybody's mind. I came to identify that all I needed was food, rest and peace. Glamorous belongings were simply materialistic making me a shallow person, taking me long enough to relate. These three things would not materialise at once, I was well on my way to attainment. Following eating as much food as my body could abide. Regardless of how little it may be, I had diversions to keep my mind occupied. This was precisely the vital key my mind starved for, preventing me from going completely out of my mind. Following each day since I killed for my freedom, I have had ice baths, submerging my head in its entirety into ice buckets, to tighten my skin bringing life quickly back into it. The shock of the freezing cold ice cubes, started to work within no time at all. The whole house had now been taken care of. I was now taking care of me. I had to look different before I left. Finding Nicolas's bank details figuring out ways to spend the money. The law would claim I had the rights to his capital as his once legal wife. I was starting to see improved changes in me, in many ways. My life was starting to fall into place.

In the middle of the night I went as far as to start redecorating. There were paints I found in the shed where they now lie, when I was searching for things which would benefit me to discard of. I painted the kitchen and bathroom walls and Nicolas's bedroom. Any signs which may indicate that Nicolas, Philippine and Emilio had been there recently I believe I successfully erased, along with my finger prints and DNA. The smell of fresh paints lingers for weeks, if they come and break into the house, they are sure to smell the fumes. Hopefully placing doubt in their minds. Focusing their time on searching for Nicolas instead of me. Looking for them elsewhere. A place I was not.

I had dinner and three tall glasses of wine, I was feeling tipsy, I was feelling mischievous. I remembered we had a sauna in one of the bottom sheds. The large expensive kind that crazy people looking for punishment put outside when the snow is falling and laying on the ground in these European countries. The same kind which are seen in brochures advertising Switzerland and Austria, Sweden and Norway people high up in the mountains, wearing skimpy bikinis laying in and relaxing as the snow falls over them. I was not concerned about getting changed and into a bikini, I ran from the kitchen in my bare feet the snow crunching beneath my small toes. I was glad I had drunk three glasses because one would not have been anywhere enough to mask the coldness which darted up through my entire body. Alcohol gives the impression one is invisible, capable of doing anything. After what I had been through, I did not mind that feeling but I understood it would not be a friend if I felt it too long. Throwing open the wooden doors to the shed, I dragged it with grave difficulty out into the garden. I managed to finally get everything connected; pouring water from the power hose to fill the sauna. Starting the machine up by which time I was more than enthusiastic to jump in, my feet felt like frostbite was starting to take effect. Sinking into the hot water my toes tingled. Heaven.

CHAPTER EIGHTY-FIVE

Haven't A Moment To Waste...

Standing on the balcony relieved that everything had been taken care of. No sign of murder. No sign of anything criminal. I glance to the vivid blue sky. Snow clouds were present but none had fallen since last night. Flocks of blackbirds flew above my head with ease and in groups. They appeared to have time on their hands. No worries. I envied them. Reminding me of the movie *"The birds"* by Alfred Hitchcock. Instead of the terror felt by his characters, I seen the birds which flew above me as inspirational. They roam the world season after season. A new country. A new nest. A new way. I knew what I must do. I haven't a moment to waste...

CHAPTER EIGHTY-SIX

The Phone Call

02:00

In the dead of the night a noise woke me from light and flimsy sleep. I always slept lightly when I was about to travel; and tomorrow's events were very special and important to me. It has forever been a habit of mine to travel on the early planes and trains. That way I have more of the day to enjoy my new surroundings.

The noise ceased. I could tell it was a mobile phone. Location unknown. About two minutes later it rang again. Hanging up. Beginning to worry. There was cause for alarm. Location still unknown. I got out of bed, left my bedroom to go to Nicolas's old room. I think it was from there. Two minutes late for the third time the phone rang again. I was correct. It was in Nicolas's room. That was a certainty. But there was nothing but furniture in there now. The bed was bare, the wardrobes and drawers emptied. There wasn't anything remaining. For the final time the phone rang, I listened carefully. I understood it must be important when someone would phone in the dead of night and be so persistent. It was under the floor boards. I ran to the kitchen, grabbing a knife. I prized two floor boards up. There was a very old Nokia phone laying there with a stash of cash. I counted it. In Swiss francs there was eight thousand.

In Euros twelve thousand. In Kroner one hundred thousand. Removing the contents, I placed the floor boards back into position. I packed the money in my bag. I checked through the phone, the name displayed on the screen under missed calls was Ukraine 11. I froze in fear. The thought crossed my mind, it really is happening. They do exist. In the darkness I ran and threw the phone into Lake Geneva.

CHAPTER EIGHTY-SEVEN

Goodbye Audrey

It was the day before I left Switzerland. I planned one last wonderful day. A day to recall when I thought of its magnificence. I didn't want to allow the Beaumonts to spoil the special feeling I once felt. When I first came I was a tourist. I wish to leave as one, with many fond memories. When I think back how hard I tried not to be seen as a tourist. How naïve and pompous I was. I had a list of places I wanted to visit and things to do, which I wrote out when I was in Lake Garda. At that time I had enthusiasm in me. I was trying to find it again. The place I wanted to visit most, I did the day before I left Switzerland.

Waking up at four a.m. dressing in a lace dress I had not yet buried. It was the only dressy item I was taking with me. I had my new hair, with my new makeup painted to perfection on my face. I looked completely different. I felt weird. When I looked in the mirror I did not recognise Nicolette Beaumont. I truly was Grace Van Burge. I walked into the city and through the streets. Nobody seemed to be on my tail or taking any notice of me. I visited the old St. Pierre Cathedral and the Notre Dame Basilica where I visited once before Christmas in 2001. Walking by the flower clock. Strolling through the empty streets I seen the beauty I once did. Recaptured. It was the city which had not forsaken me. I had forsaken it because of personal bad experiences. But under the morning sky I fell in love with Geneva all over again. It felt like the first time. Unadulterated. I strolled down by Lake Geneva and walked the length of the entire path. Taking a moment I stood crossing the street, on the corner at the pedestrian crossing by Rolex, where I had the ideal view to watch the Water fountain (Jet d' Eau). Things seemed normal. Life seemed normal. The many people around me did not appear to be trapped within a hell. They all seemed content.

Briskly walking to the train station. Taking the train from Geneva, second class; not wanting to stand out, despite being able to afford first class. I was rather dressed up but it was a special occasion. I excited roughly thirty minutes later at Morge. I walked through the station and down the platform, I left the station by a square. Walking directly across the street I sat on the bench at the bus stop waiting for bus 703. The signpost indicated I had a twenty minute wait. While I waited I felt thirsty, the air was cold and my nose pinched by the harsh air. Ordering a hot chocolate, perfect on a winter's day. The smell of cooked food attracted me. I looked right, then left. I saw a McDonalds by the train station, tucked away in the corner. As I placed my coins on the counter worktop I heard the bus approaching. Rushing out I ran over. It was the wrong bus. By the time my bus did arrive I had the drink fully consumed and my toes were restored back to a healthy temperature.

We stopped at an out of the way stop sign approximately fifteen minutes later. I got out and checked my map locating my bearings. Deciphering which direction I needed to take. A signpost on the other side of the street read 'cemetery', I followed the signposts. Crossing the road I went under a bridge, to the left-hand side there was a car sales place. That was the one thing I noticed from the bus, there were many car sales places in that one small area. One which stood out for its particular name 'Dotti'. I wondered could it be? I kept walking straight and entered the cemetery with great pride and feeling privileged. After walking around the snowy cemetery for forty minutes, looking at each headstone for a very special specific headstone, to no avail. I asked a woman in the office which was located at the entrance. I was deflated when the woman who spoke broken English told *me:*

"A lot of people come here each year looking for that grave, but it is not the right cemetery. Where she lies in only a short walk from here."

Giving me the correct directions and drawing on my map the route, I left. I was sure this was where she lay. I was close, but not close enough. I went under the same bridge and crossed the road, passing another car sales place and an industrial estate to my right, I walked up multiple steep hills. Passing many stunning homes along the way. The woman told me it was only a short walk and on the map it didn't look far, but it felt never-ending. I was now close, almost close enough. The road finally came to an end. It was the longest road I had ever been on. Before me was a hill and slightly to the left was a cemetery. On my approach there was a tree to the left, beneath it sat a delicate little bench. Snow covered it like kisses. Wrought iron gates which stood tall at the entry. As I pushed the gates opened disillusionment soaring. Creeping of the hinges. I whispered to myself: "please be the right grave yard this time."

When I entered there was thick snow beneath my feet. Nobody had been there since the fresh snow fell. The snow was untouched. I was surprised how small and quaint it was for such a star.

Although I was freezing I dressed appropriately for the occasion. No less would do. An occasion like this doesn't come along every day. I wore a tan fur coat, long tan leather gloves, a black lace scarf, and a black furry Russian hat, like a movie star I looked. Beneath my coat a black lace dress, high up to the front and in a V neck at the back. Accompanied by pearls. I wore my hair up like she did in the movie *Charade*. I dressed respectfully and in honour of her. I found her grave to the right-hand side and at the back. It wasn't spectacular like one may expect. That's alright because it was modest like Audrey Hepburn. I blessed myself, tears filled my eyes. I prayed for a moment. This was the proudest moment of my life. I almost met Audrey Hepburn. I lay down the white lilies I brought especially for her. I took a moment to take it in. I was close, very close.

Saying, "Goodbye Audrey."

I turned and walked away. Stopping after a few steps. I didn't want to leave. Stopping again as I approached the gates. I looked back one last time.

"Goodbye Audrey, goodbye. The world misses you as do I."

CHAPTER EIGHTY-EIGHT

The Snow

Along with the snow cleaneth sullied souls. My soul had gone, disappearing with the evil I had done. Here on out I would have to face each day as it comes, without too much sentiment or thought. There was something in the stars last night which changed my perspective about life, about living and no more giving into death. Death is the easy way out. Death is not the answer to anything. It is simply for weak-minded fools. For a time that was the person I turned into. The one thing I have shown myself is that I am not weak. If I had truly wanted to die, I would have let them kill me. I did not so here I am. Safety will be found, I have no doubt. I might have another path to travel down to find it but it will be found. I accepted I had many miles to travel before this would become fully my past. Precluding disappointment. Within the upcoming days the most pressing issues for me to tackle will be successfully getting away from the MA. After I am across the border, I will then be just another woman, another tourist. Another face. When I have a new identity assembled I will be a new name, occupying and displaying a new face. Just another stranger in the crowd. Life is definitely an endless holiday. An endless battle. I considered myself lucky as I was on the boarder of many beautiful counties. I could have my pick. If I didn't like one particular place, this is Europe after all I can always hop on another train, taking me to my new life. I could be a tourist on an endless holiday. Become anyone I want to be. I have Nicolas's funds, I have the time. There isn't anything holding me back. This could be the very thing I need to rebuild me. The world was now my oyster.

There are so many promising things which could now be mine. Finding my personality and character would have to wait. Nonetheless it will have to be found. I cannot afford to have weak, unsteady legs like Bambi. I had to remain strong. At some stage I will have to socialise in some capacity. Socialising was going to prove my toughest task. This time around, low-key is the only key securing my safety. I had been locked away for many years. As a result I had become unnerved by people. I had never been a lover of being around masses of people. Crowds have for as long as I can remember intimidated me. Unfortunately I had to be around crowds in the train stations to get me out of here. There was no way out of that. Masses of people coming at me from every direction. I wondered if my heart could stand the stress. It was winter time and large amounts of people are everywhere to be found. It was December in Switzerland. December in Switzerland was the equivalent to Paris in summer. The skiing as the main attraction. I will use this to my advantage to blend in. To be overlooked. Being unnoticed meant I could not be associated with anyone or anything. Granting my safety. Ensuring my escape. I had to face it. This part of my escape seemed more difficult than killing and disposing of three bodies. Panicking like I had never panicked before. I knew I had to leave this house, there was no other way. It was never my home. I wanted to leave and run away from the haunting memories. Knowing I had to walk down the driveway and through the six feet tall security gates into the world. The world where anything can happen and too often does. The world where danger is lurking. It is not necessarily lurking for me, but danger finds those who are innocent and alone. When I walk through those gates once more I become vulnerable. This very same vulnerability is what could make me a victim. I felt smothered by fear, of the unknown again. I felt alive, but the feeling of not being guaranteed safety made me want to hide in this house which had been my hell, forever. But danger would surely find me here. From then on I will have to listen to everything, watch everyone. The nice, the precarious. Trust nobody. Trust not even myself. No one is nice. No one is safe, nowhere is safe. It is only them to run into.

The second flakes of snow commenced. There isn't anything colder than winter on a train. The windows were steamed up from people's respiration, cancelling out the beauty of the snow kissed mountaintops. Heat was not apparent. With the snow it justifiably became colder. Night skies and falling snow tranquillity can be found. What is it in the snow which brings such cheerfulness, liveliness and goodwill?

CHAPTER EIGHTY-NINE

Shadows of Her Mind

I needed a break from this life,
I needed a way to survive.
When life is filled with strife, how do you survive?
Where do you find the strength to fight?

Through all the pain, pounding down like rain,
When it's your tears you hear.
When you've lost the one who made your life
Bearable, to endure,
How do you deal with the unexpected?
When the sufferable is intolerable.

Life can be joyful but also so awful,
When tinged with evil.
How can you make it blissful?
When forced with the dreadful?
When life is no longer tolerable?
And, when you've already bade farewell to mortal
Existence.

When it has made you become empty and
Obsolete.
How can you change the hateful to the grateful?
When it's not as easy as a command?
How do you make the fearful times in that life,
More breathable?
When you want to goodbye the world.

It's not a puzzle anymore. When you've given up
On life.
Why would you want to awake?
How do you say it's not the night, when laughter
Has gone and in flight?

When the darkness surrounds my mind,
Do I dress in my death gown, get on that boat
And leave the shore to sail?
Do I goodbye the world and hello dear lord?

Or do I fight to survive?
Remain the righteous?
Be the winner and burn the sinner.
I'll murder to survive,
I'll fight to recover,
Salvage my life.
I will live and I will be unbound.

PART NINETEEN

PIECES OF MY LIFE

CHAPTER NINETY

Pieces of a Life

I don't know how it began. I don't know how long it carried on for those other girls. I will never know, but I am glad it's over.

Why do people commit murder? I always thought it was due to a mental disorder mainly prompted by hurt in the early years of life. At least that is what many American psychologists proclaim. Many state that it is within one as a child, we don't just become killers in adult life. How correct that is I do not know. I have never studied the mind. The only thing I discern is it wasn't in me since birth. As for the Beaumont's, I am not so sure. I do not know how long ago it began, I don't know how many they murdered. I am only glad a long tough fight is finally over. Proud that I ended it, that I had the balls to see it through. In turn protecting others like me. Knowing what I have done that I was able to achieve something of such magnitude, killing predators of Switzerland.

Becoming mentally conditioned, becoming an agoraphobic. It's always the craziest names given to these disorders making one feel sicker than they are. The tags attached to being a little ill, or a little afraid. A little lonely or a little depressed. We all get lost along the way sometimes. We only grow older not altogether wiser. I never imagined that I would turn or be turned into a murderer. This isn't the life I chose for myself. After the abuse I sustained by my father and brother as a child this I did not need to go through. Why do I have to be exposed to so much mistreatment? I wanted a happy life filled with love, joy, a husband and a child. No fame, no glamour just a wholesome regular life stability consisting of a routine. Murder wasn't in the cards. They were the cards I was force fed. Murder for right now has become my life. What I have become good at. I was forced to commit murder to prolong my life, as they were the crazies. But where do I go from here? This is not the end for me. This is only the beginning.

I was a victim of a man who gravely let me down. I was a thoughtful wife who had given him love whenever he craved it. Trying and trying but forever time being shot down. I supported him. I was a shoulder to cry on. Even when he was wrong I would let him win in arguments. Winning to him was more important than it was to me. When we met I was simply a girl. I had my choice of me with everything going for me. I even had brains. I didn't need to get married, I chose to. Now I am lonelier. Sicker. If the truth be told I was on the lookout for a good man, he didn't necessarily have to be vulgarly rich, or considered to be in high esteem socially. Instead a man who knew how to treat a woman, who would respect me, love me for what I was, without changing me into what I wasn't. Making love to me passionately, wildly. With lust for my body forever in his gut. I didn't realise this was such a tall order. It has been a terribly long time since I felt love. When I had it from Charles I didn't appreciate it. Charles gave me to greatest love of all. True love. When one is young we don't understand these things. It is forever the unimportant things which seem more important than they are. I am glad I am not that young anymore. With age comes wisdom to a certain degree. With wisdom comes appreciation and understanding. With wisdom and understanding together comes a richer and fuller life. And broken hearts. But with broken hearts comes strength. Men tried to strip not only from me the clothes on my petite body but my pride and my respectability, including my cruel brother. Even he would call ne a whore as a child. A whore before I was ever touched by a man. I only ever wanted my heart to be filled with love. I miss Charles. It used to feel so good, I was happy then, I wanted it back. I want Charles back. If I wake up tomorrow with him beside me in bed, in an instant I would snuggle up to him all day long and never let him go. Never. We would have happiness, the best sex of all as it came from the heart, the love we would share and sweet, sweet pink champagne.

I knew my beauty wouldn't last forever. Once I hit thirty it would quickly wilt. One day I would be overlooked by younger and much better. For right now this was my time. I wear the crown of beauty. I needed to get a move on to find a love for life. He could never be the love of my life, that man is gone. I had already found the one. This time I would settle for companionship. Every day I would attempt to look my prettiest, enhancing my best features. Some have told me my best features were my eyes and lips. Painting my lips red, seductive red. I was confident I oozed sex appeal. My shapely hips seen to that. I naturally owned what I needed, allowing me to be blessed in life. I was confident because I took note of what men desired. Not only did I ooze it, but I used it. My adopted mother or so I would like to believe, Sophia Loren taught me how to make it work to my benefit. When my body begun to shape into a womanly figure, I watched her movies and I learnt a lot from her about being sexy, about being a woman. If only I could have known her in reality, she could have taught me so much more. I never used it to have sex. I was never stupid enough to be premature with regards that. I didn't need to have sex with every man that caught my eye, for that matter every man whose eye I caught. I only had to make them think I was going to. Embedding the thought in their head that I was going to allow them to make me their piece of play. This guaranteed them eating out of my hand. When they believed this they would do anything. Absolutely anything. I was not the type of woman to have meaningless sex, one-night stands were not my style. I would tease them in a ladylike fashion, being dignified at all times. If I treated myself with a lack of respect, why and how could I expect or demand they treat me accordingly. Never provocative. I would speak to them in low, deep sexy tones, moving my body slowly and exaggerating my movements, touching my body, my leg, arm or face, licking my lips slowly and in a way to suggest fucking. SEX. Plenty of sex... Putting thoughts in their heads of things which they believed would take place, things that would never happen. A dangerous game which had to be played just right preventing it from blowing up in my face. Men, sex and egos is a combination of disaster if not constructed properly. A bomb ticking gently when they have hope. When all hope is gone, explosions like fireworks demolishing my plans. All this whilst in public but still in a non-smutty way, getting them aroused. Hard. It is never difficult to get a man aroused. If a cold wind during a summer's day brushes against their skin, they are

431

horny for hours. Whispering dirty suggestions into their ears at dinner, before the waiter gets back to our table. Toying with men, luring them to believe the unbelievable was too easy. I enjoyed a challenge, but men, my God men are docile like sheep. Some are cute but oh so dumb. Even the educated ones. Touching my gentleman's hand, gently stroking his finger, using it to roleplay his juicy dick. Telling him I want him to take me. Put me down and force himself into my wet and tight pussy. All the time he is aroused and me – well not one little bit. Telling him only he can make me wet. Only he can make me come, make me reach levels of exotic desire I have never experienced prior.

Of course, being a man this always works, they can't help but fall for it. I would tell them anything I think they wanted to hear. It sends them right of the rails even in their own trousers. Never using the actual brain the lord gave them, instead using their sex machine to get them through life and a mountain of women. I have found in my life it is the easiest thing in the world to lure a man into a false sense of security by using the body. Women are more blessed by being a woman. It makes life easier. For getting through life having tits, the bigger the better, having curvy hips the curvier the better and dressing to enhance those famine assets, the easier it is to get by. Picking myself up, dusting myself off. I must find the will to fight through each day. This time I will never have to kill again. Unfortunately in life there is forever a fight of some kind. I have so much to live for, so much to give and accomplish. I am still beautiful, I must not waste what I have going for me. I only have to pick up the pieces of my life still remaining, attach the useful pieces to the new and the future.

On the train at Lausanne we stopped for a few moments. While I was waiting I closed my eyes envisioning the past. Replaying my techniques. I didn't have sex with the men I lured and teased. I wasn't going to start now. I hate what men have turned sex into. A game, a meaningless and impersonal game. A smile came across my face, I was thinking over the good old days.

PART TWENTY

Released

CHAPTER NINETY-ONE

Forgive it's The Right Thing To Do

I should forgive it's the right thing to do, but I don't know how.

My heart is unwilling, my head even more so.

It's my soul, the humane, the realness to a person that tells a person they are wrong.

A conscience. The good part within.

Maybe someday when I can accept the things I've been through.

When I've settled my fear,

When I'm safe. When I've found me.

Then I can be the better person and forgive my wrong doers.

Maybe I should forgive it's the right thing to do.

But right now I just don't know how.

CHAPTER NINETY-TWO

Emancipated

Bitter sweet memories are what I have to start over with. A barely filled case, a heart overflowing. I must find a way to put them in the past. Put them in a secret room deep inside my mind. Formulate a key to keep the memories locked away from the world. One day, I must forget how to open the door, the key forever lost. I pray that in time everything becomes dormant. Formulate a key, in time which will become incapable of unlocking the door to let those memories flood. I have a chain of broken dreams. I am back on the journey of life. It feels magnificent yet terrifying. If only there was some way I could find the time to when I was a little girl, a baby in my mother's safe and untouched womb, long before the problems and strain of this world, this life entered and filled up my mind. Weighing me down. Why must life be such a melee? With every turn around, crossed roads I am faced with; bridges and bodies to burn. It's been inordinately long since I've felt sincere and genuine tenderness. It has been so long since I've kissed and touched Charles. I hope my new life can bring me this with another, as this is all I am wishing for. I believe I have earned it. Either way here I go again. We all make mistakes, particularly when one is young. My mistakes are drastic there is no doubt. I am no angel; I am far from innocent myself, but there cannot possibly be any worse than the Beaumonts. I was still a victim of a husband who let me down. And a mother-in-law who was the cruellest of all them all. I have made all the mistakes I am going to. I am starting off observant, vigilant, ensuring I don't mess up. I shall roll through life alone, for a little while anyway. Everyone has a life, live the life were given. Forgive them I never will!

When Nicolas and I married that was supposed to be me starting over. A move from Italy to Switzerland. Everything fresh, new and exciting. Five years later, I'm doing it again. It doesn't feel like before. Where does one begin when one's dreams are shattered and the world does not care? When nobody cares if I were to die? There are a great deal of complexities in the world. Can anyone actually survive in it? One may be able to win fight after fight, but there comes a time when we all fall. We fall and goodnight to the world. Hello dear lord.

It has been one of those days which reminded me of the unhappiness they brought me. I don't want to remember but I know in my heart I always shall, against my will. There will be a person with facial resemblances, a familiar walk, voice, the same name. The brain is a wonderful creation remembering a vast amount. Sometimes it is even selective. This was what they wanted. They wanted to haunt me all my life through and all my death through. Making them important, making them the tyrant they fought so frantically to become. With the remembrance of them, they have won. Against my will they held me in what was no home, a brothel perhaps would be a truer description. I would consider it a prison of hell. A home, no not in any regard, never a home. Now a graveyard of bodies, bones and ashes, letters and many killings, how could this ever be a home even now? Now that they have gone, they were the ones to "farewell this world, and hello dear Lord," not I my dear, not I! Not this time. That game I surely won. To me that was the hand of most importance. Therefore a few scars are to be expected. Like wrinkles, scars tell a story. A very nefarious tail. Every night I will pray to God, find a way to forget and that my prayer shall be answered. I shall thank him for my survival. If God cannot forgive me for fighting and repossessing what was rightfully mine, I truthfully and faithfully do not give a damn. But I have faith that if there is a God who exists, he will not be dishonest by telling me I have done wrong. He surely must be grateful I eradicated filth from this earth, protecting his children from what I and Gabriella suffered. I merely acted as an apostle. Cleaning the world. An eye for an eye. I piss on you and I shit on your family! May you all burn in hell for all eternity, this I pray for with all my heart, soul and all that is in me. You are now where you belong. Body to ashes, ashes to earth. I am now emancipated.

CHAPTER NINETY-THREE

Her body lay there still, so still

Her body lay there still, so still,
She never told me she was ill, so ill.
I did adore her that much is true,
She said goodbye, I made her blue.

Frowns and tears,
Heartache and fears.
Couldn't carry on
Couldn't sing a song
Ears to the world, my love deaf.
Her eyes to me blind,
My heart has broken,
In tears, regret and fears soaken.

She never told me she was ill, so ill.
I never told her how I felt, the truth or confess to my regret.
All she asked for was the truth, to her own lifeless regret.

CHAPTER NINETY-FOUR

Condescension

There are times I should be strong – more significantly smart, but the sudden blows of life have brought me rapidly to my knees, causing tears to fill up within my hallow eyes. Causing the crushing of my heart by the crippling pain bestowed. I will never let any man watch me die. No woman either for that matter. Regardless how important any other man may become to me, whatever the case may be prudency is the best policy. Not the truth. My truth could never be the best policy. If my next relationship does not work out successfully, I will walk away and cry my tears alone, before I let another man see me brokenhearted. When I was growing up, I heard the phrase many times "It's a rich man's world." They spend their time throwing money at women, buying them possessions to impress and trying to buy a woman's love. When the presents start, they've got a woman where they want her. A gift! The giving of something unselfishly, the definition is considered to be. The one exception to the rule is when the gift is from a man to a woman, then the games commence. She's caught. Dead prey. Hunted and caught. May the best man win, because not very often does the woman win! I am in control of myself principally my body. I decide who I become romantically involved with. I choose who I fuck, who I use and throw over. I determine who I am. I am out for me, everybody else can burn down in the maggot soil of hell. I will please only myself. No longer the weak, the one who stands by only to be used. The strong the unmoving, this is who I have become. Mess with me now, die you will. This I promise all the world.

CHAPTER NINETY-FIVE

I Could

After all you have done
I could wish you ill harm.
After all you have done
I could wish you hurt.

After all you have done
I could wish you resent.
After all you have done
I could wish you ache.

After all you have done
I could wish you death.
After all you have done to me,
All the times you have, harmed me.
After all the times you have hurt me.
All the times you have done so much bad to me,
I could wish you all of these things and more.

I would wish you all of these things and more
But I am not you, I am a good soul.

I could, I could, I could, I could.
But I shall not wish you any resent, ache, not even death.
All roads lead to one place, we all await death

PART TWENTY-ONE

Nonconformist

CHAPTER NINETY-SIX

Wicked Echoes from My Past

Cerebrospinal fluids which surrounds my brain acting like a warm blanket, its purpose protection. Protection from external forces, infections even cleaning away the debris, the dead cells within me, cleansing my body. My heart pumps clean new oxygenate blood. But when the past haunts, it haunts assiduously. Unwilling to die like a festering cancer. When the evil poignant past grabs a hold of me, it refuses to let go. So being tortured and beleaguered still remains. I'm becoming Annabelle. Like tenacious; the annoying high-pitched ringing inside the ears. Until one welcomes it, until one deals with it, it will literally drive a person out of their mind. Making them crazy within their own body. Making me crazy within my own mind. Wicked echoes from my past has the exact same way of driving me insane from the inside out.

CHAPTER NINETY-SEVEN

One O'clock, Two O'clock, Three O'clock Cuckoo

Switzerland is famous for a multitude of exceptional wonderment. Their worldwide celebrated and loved wrist watches, army knives, chocolates, and cuckoo clocks. Cute and adore. When one is slowly going out of their mind, how detrimental can a cute and adore cuckoo clock become? These little wooden clocks are to be found throughout the country and within most establishments, hanging them with pride. They are on sale in almost every souvenir shop. Most Swiss and European citizens have them as decoration within their homes. Sweet at first, when every hour chimes a tiny little bird coos or a little happy family dances around.

I was soaking in an oversized bath, attempting to put everything into perspective while gathering my thoughts. Some days I felt I was getting better. Each time I would relax my mind casted back to the beginning. The beginning of my life in Switzerland. The first time I met Nicolas. A wall clock, a cuckoo clock, in dark wood hung behind the bar of 'The Snowboat'. It hung behind Claude's head. Not paying any attention to it then, in fact forgetting entirely about it. Anytime I relaxed more details would come to me. I was becoming comfortable in my own skin. Comfortable to remember. Step by step, day by day improvements were occurring. Perhaps I was going to be luckier than Annabelle. Did it have any relevance? Was it important, one of those things which creeps into the mind, the memories at a very crucial time? Or did it mean absolutely nothing, except for the fact I was becoming paranoid and remembering things which weren't there? Was my mind just used to fighting, needing a new fight to keep me occupied? With great difficulty trying to banish the memories and the importance if any, of that stupid adorable cuckoo clock, in vain as it constantly found its way of hijacking my recollections. Now without scepticism believing it was telling me something, indicating a highly important secret I must unravel. This idea believed with utter conviction was now in my blood to resolve. I must return.

PART TWENTY-TWO

SILENT THOUGHTS

CHAPTER NINETY-EIGHT

A Cry for Help

Depression is horrific.
Depression is critic.
Depression can kill.

When a friend can't be found,
When a frown comes across the forehead,
What is one to do when there is no shoulder to cry on?

Depression is unbearable.
More so when it's unspeakable.
Depression is insufferable.
But for the sufferer it must be suffered.

What is one to do when there is no support?
Depression is intolerable,
More so when it's impossible.
But the impossible must be made possible.

What is one to do when there is no help?
Depression is horrid,

More so it is hostile.

But the helpless must be helped somehow someway.

We all need a shoulder to cry on, we all need support.

CHAPTER NINETY-NINE

The Roll of the Dice

In 2001 I took a gamble. Sometimes they pay off, sometimes not. Gambles have been known to be the best in life's changes. Giving one so much back in return of the risk. My gamble with Nicolas was not worthwhile overall in the end. There was too much invested, too much to lose, gaining only my freedom, something I already had before I rolled the dice and claimed my hand. In so many ways I've lost, in other ways I've won. In all ways I've learnt. Time wasted, a million lost. I am now an unbeatable woman. No more does fear dwell in me. I have finally won, I am now free to live. In the very end I survived. Without hesitation I am onto my next endeavour. This time something's have changed. I do not seek a rich man. No I have learnt my lessons with regards what wealth can bring. I have a fortune. Charles's fortune. I will always have his love in my heart and endearing memories to carry with me. It is not essential to have another million or two. The things I want now are the real things which matter. No amount of money can buy them. Full recovery is number one. Eventually I will seek for someone who is nice, someone decent with morals who is tender, regardless of his bank balance. We all need a change from time to time, now it's my turn. Someone who will love me till the end of time. Never to harm me, only to nurse me back to health and show me the way to love. Teaching me how to love in return. I am so damaged, unsure if I can really remember how to love. I knew him many years ago. Reminding me of the play *Snowdrops in the night,* like the play we only had a single encounter. This is my time. Life here I come...

CHAPTER ONE HUNDRED

NOTHING

You have stolen from me
You have stolen so much.
I take nothing from you
Nothing at all.

You have hurt me, hurt me
Attempted to murder me.
I have done nothing to you
Nothing at all.

I wanted to be happy,
I wanted to live life.
You have taken my happiness,
You have taken my life.
Yet I have done nothing to you
Nothing at all.

You have stolen my youth,
Now tarnished it with pain.
Shown me that life is made harder,

By the ruthless who careless.

You have shown me merciless pain
I recoup my life, I hope not in vain.

Leave me alone,
Let me start over again.
I forgive you, forgive you it all.
Yet I still have done nothing to you
Nothing at all.

CHAPTER ONE HUNDRED AND ONE

Truth Disguised

In the end when all is weighed up and considered I planned well. The extensive cleaning of the crime scene, the for sale sign at the end of the driveway. That was as cunning as a thief in broad daylight robbing a house out in the open with a most natural reason for being there. The darkness of the truth disguised. False identification always a must. A new name. Despite dealing with the Beaumonts and the situation well, there was one thing a most important aspect I could not alter, the Albanians. They are involved and they are coming.

CHAPTER ONE HUNDRED AND TWO

Soon

I stood on the hill only stopping for a moment. I just had to return. The yearning and burning in my gut was too much to ignore. The four-hour train ride was worth one glimpse of him. My heart wanted to enter The Snowboat, sit down have a drink and gaze at Claude's beauty until the daylight sky gave way to night when anything can happen. It was the first butterflies I felt in years. Excitement for something I could not right now have. But one day he will be mine and I his. One day. Those wonderful blue eyes, those manly hands. That sexy body. His kind eyes. I wanted to kiss those tender lips. There were so many things I wanted to do, but couldn't. I just needed to see that face one last time before I transform myself fully, before the person he met in 2001 was gone forever... Nicolette. One day I will return to him. I will spend time with Claude. I will make him mine. He will love me. Someday when the time is right he will get to know Grace Van Burge and I he. The good me. The not so fucked up me. We will love each other, marry and have children. We will, we will, we will. Someday. I forgot how wonderful he looked. He was more beautiful than I remembered. Behind the bar his head bowed cleaning. A most special smile captured my face. I felt warmth in my heart. Not wanting to but knowing I had to tear myself away. Tears welled as I half turned to walk away, for one last second I took my final look. Distracted by a blonde woman who walked upstairs to the main open-plan area of the bar. Before seeing if they kissed I hurried away. I couldn't stand another stabbing to my heart. I will remember him as he his. As he stood there. That is the image I will carry with me until it is safe to return. Under my breath reassuring myself as I walked up the hill and away, "I will see you soon."

CHAPTER ONE HUNDRED AND THREE

Switzerland My Forever Friend

I have become withdrawn

To the hardships and heartaches of life, I was not forewarn

I have too young become weatherworn and emotionally overdrawn

At the tender age of twenty, I went to throw myself from the Matterhorn

A suicidal persons trusted friend

Into happiness it will help send

A deadly height to transport one to their ultimate end

On my travels from the train, I noticed the Finsteraarhorn

Heard an attractive ship, on Geneva Lake blow its blaring horn

Awaking me to life, emotionally reborn

For a moment the ships horn sounded like a saxhorn

In my heart Switzerland became a forever treasured gemstone

It saved my life once or twice, it's still not gone

And it helps one who is terribly let down, that the people are very, very nice not once scorn

Always willing to lend a helping hand

I am no more a silly girl, or what one would consider a greenhorn

I plan to live old and long

I am delighted, excited, ecstatic and not at all benighted

And with life's battles I am prepared to fight

Experience has made me aware, I am now sharp-sighted

With happiness united

No more am I withdrawn because to life I am forewarn

Cherishing the beauty found, not the helping hand from the Matterhorn's height

Switzerland is my forever friend

CHAPTER ONE HUNDRED AND FOUR

Austria

Apart from our first Christmas together in 2001, I had never visited Austria. Christmas time was truly the most magical time to be there. It was coming up to Christmas again (2006). I did not have tickets to the Christmas concert this year, but I had every intention on walking by the concert hall, recalling that happy time. I was thinking of ways to get myself excited, as the place I really wanted to be was Switzerland, Zermatt. I will return, not all is lost. I will see Switzerland and the Matterhorn again. They will become my home once more. As the train departed Zermatt train station my heart felt crushed. My mind was racing with every thought known to man, except for the Beaumont's. As the train pulled away from the village, I thought about Charles and how much I need him right now. Closing my eyes taking a deep breath at peace I felt. I finally felt at peace. Smiling to myself as I could smell the spices of Austria. Freedom I am on my way.

CHAPTER ONE HUNDRED AND FIVE

Grace Van Burge

I am Grace Van Burge, I am twenty-six years old tomorrow. The year is now 2006. I am five feet two inches tall. I have dark brown eyes, short dark brown hair with tanned skin. A beauty spot on my left cheek. I have lived a precarious life in my short time on this earth. I have killed four people in my young life. Including a man I truly loved. I am a force to be reckoned with. I possess and flaunt a saintly face but not a saintly nature. People have forever pushed me into situations I did not wish to be in. Forcing me to commit crimes it was not in my nature to commit. Now nothing is beyond me. My body, my face are what helps me through. Getting me far. It is these components which encourage people to overlook my guiltiness. I act well, kill better. The past has now been buried. It must remain at rest. The past will however insist on presenting its ugly face. That's life. That's how my life operates. This I know will happen for that I am prepared. In due course I will take precautions. It is I who determine my destiny, not they, not they. Never them. I am in control of my life. He who dares take me on will see the pit of the earth faster than they reckoned. I am Grace Van Burge. I am a woman of the world. I am one of those unfortunate souls who have been exposed to too much for my tender age. I have no morals, no scruples. Don't take me on. I will kill. I will kill you! All I want from life here on out is peace. Peace and perhaps a little love. So leave me be. Leave me be.

CHAPTER ONE HUNDRED AND SIX

Snowboat

Snowboat, Snowboat
Beautiful boat.
Your beautiful boat of strong,
You're big and robust.

You could withstand a large storm,
An avalanche,
Or glaciers flowing from the mountain tops.

Your location exquisite.
Your boat of strong and snow.

Snowboat, Snowboat
Beautiful boat.
Oh yes you are.